DARK MAGIC IN CAREA

The feast was over, and the hall's oak doors swung open. While King Palamon watched with loving devotion, his four-year-old son, Prince Berethane, walked in to the loud applause of the guests. Beside Palamon, Princess Berengeria murmured, "He's such a lovely child!"

A smile split the boy's chubby face. He broke away from his attendants and dashed toward his royal parents.

But suddenly lightning flashed from outside the windows. Then a ghostly funnel extended itself down *through* the roof, like a tornado in shape, but much smaller. And it was composed of swirling flames. The flaming cloud reached toward the floor, probing this way and that, then shot toward Berethane.

The flames caught him and sucked him into the swirling vortex, and the funnel closed over his shrieking and writhing form.

By Dennis McCarty
Published by Ballantine Books:

FLIGHT TO THLASSA MEY

WARRIORS OF THLASSA MEY

LORDS OF THLASSA MEY

LORDS OF THLASSA MEY

Dennis McCarty

A Del Rey Book

BALLANTINE BOOKS • NEW YORK

A Del Rey Book
Published by Ballantine Books

Copyright © 1989 by Dennis McCarty

Library of Congress Catalog Card Number: 89-90702

ISBN 0-345-33865-0

Printed in Canada

First Edition: July 1989

Cover Art by Romas
Map by Shelly Shapiro

THE AUTHOR WOULD LIKE TO DEDICATE THIS VOLUME TO HIS ELDER DAUGHTER, ERIN FRANCES McCARTY, WHO, AT THE AGE OF FIVE DAYS, CAME HOME FROM THE HOSPITAL, TWINED THREADLIKE FINGERS INTO THE WEAVE OF HIS RED SWEATER, AND GAINED A SLAVE FOR LIFE.

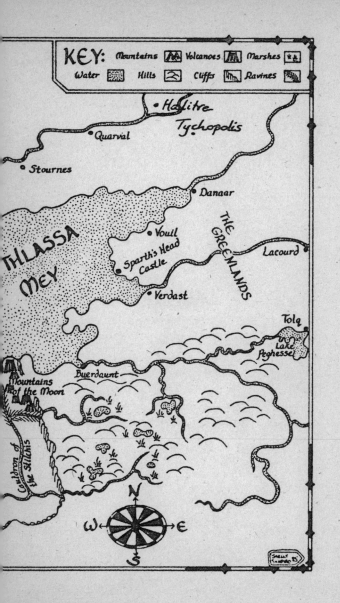

KEY: Mountains · Volcanoes · Marshes
Water · Hills · Cliffs · Ravines

•Halitre
Tychopolis
•Quarval
•Stournes
•Danaar
THLASSA
MEY •Vouil
Sparth's Head
Castle
THE GREENLANDS
Lacourd
•Verdast
Tolq
Lake
Peghesse
Mountains
of the Moon
Buerdaunt
Cauldron of
the Stllchis
N
W E
S

Chapter One:
The Encampment

PRINCE URSID'S TENT was brown. The undyed fabric was the color of a curse; no decoration broke the solid drear of plain canvas—and all men about the Thlassa Mey knew why. Ursid had forsaken all show and all pleasure in his quest for vengeance against Carea and Carea's newly crowned King.

Harbic the courier considered that fact. Buerdaunt had been at war with Carea for five years; during that time, Ursid had become a great leader. He had won many battles. But he had not gained his revenge, for Palamon sat on Carea's throne in place of deceased King Berevald and Carea fought on. Harbic swallowed nervously as he slowed his horse and observed the turmoil in the Buerdic camp. Ursid would not like the news Harbic bore him.

Harbic swung from his saddle and walked into Ursid's tent, to find it occupied only by Diomedes, the young leader's *aide-de-camp*. Diomedes hurried about, preparing food. He hardly even looked up as the messenger approached. "You act official," he said in the midst of his bustle. "I suppose you've come to speak to the Prince."

1

"Indeed, I seek Ursid, high Prince and Constable, and noble Count of Faux."

"You're lucky to find anyone here. He's been in the mines for the last two days; you nearly missed me, too. I just came back to fetch him a bite to eat and a wineskin. You'd have had bad luck finding him if you'd got here any later."

The war had made Ursid a human blaze; his energy as a leader of men inspired many tales. "Then I am glad I found you," Harbic said. "Now we must make haste to reach him, for I bear great news that needs to be delivered."

Diomedes' stubbly face curved into a smile. "Great news, eh? Well, sit yourself down and have a sip of wine while I finish here. Then I'll take you to him." He gestured toward a campaign chair, opened a chest, and lifted out a large wine cup. "What's your great message?"

Harbic watched Diomedes fill the cup. "I am not sure that I should rest before my message is delivered to the Prince's hands."

"Oh, go on. Quench your thirst; rest your legs awhile." Diomedes laughed. "I can tell you it's all the rest you'll get for a long time. Tonight's going to be a busy one. Drink up now, and tell me what words you bring; it can't be such a secret that my Lord Ursid's own body servant can't hear it."

The messenger shrugged and did as he was told. He took the wine cup and drank, then dabbed his lips with a napkin before he spoke. "It is no secret. All across the lands, the populace is dancing wildly; all the common folk have heard the tidings ere the nobles in the field have learned of them. The word I bear is this: the war is done. A treaty has been signed with Carea and peace now reigns across all lands."

To Harbic's surprise, Diomedes received the words as grave news indeed. He glanced out at the stream of soldiers and horses that clattered past the tent's entrance. Then he made a thoughtful sound. "Um."

Harbic's doubts about delivering the message grew. "You don't seem pleased. I would have hoped such news would bring loud cheers and gleeful songs. The order from the King is that this siege shall lift upon the morrow and these troops shall all march back into our homeland. I would think such orders would be welcome; you yourself cannot have seen your home for many weeks."

Diomedes sneered. "I've been away from my woman for a long time but I'll tell you in straight words that there's things to be gained here a man can't get at home. I was a lowly housecarl when war broke out; why, I had less authority than a barnyard cat. But I've made my fortune since. I'm a knight, now, not to mention personal attendant to the most powerful man in the realm, next to the King. My Lord Ursid doesn't just look on me as a servant. He'll lay out a map of the city and he'll say, 'What do you think, old fellow? Shall we put a tower against that wall there or should we build onagers and heave a few rocks in at them, hey?' And if some ambitious man wants a commission from his Lordship, he's going to come to me and slap a few gold pieces into my hand so I'll grease his way for him. That's not to mention the spoils of battle, because his Lordship always leads us to victory. It's a good business, this war; I'll be a long time finding a better one. Therefore, friend, I hate to see the end of it."

He turned and laughed a short laugh. "But be that as it may, all good things have to end. A fellow can make his way in a land that's at peace, I suppose, though he has to bustle harder."

"That's so," Harbic said. "And I must criticize your words. This war is worse than death to those who've suffered at the hands of striving armies. Wives and mothers grieve for sons and husbands who shall ne'er return."

"That's their problem, isn't it?" Diomedes picked up the goatskin and the satchel of food he had gathered for his master. "You know, I don't envy you, having to give your message to the Prince. Peace marks the end of a bonny enterprise for me but it'll be an even nastier dish for him."

Harbic rose and followed the hulking retainer. "I fear that much."

Diomedes paused at the tent's entrance and allowed the messenger to catch up. "Do you know the Prince very well?"

"I've never met his Lordship face-to-face."

Diomedes grunted. "But I see you know his reputation. You know the way he hates Carea and the whole Carean royal family. Why, all the killing he's done isn't a mustard seed to what he'd like to do against them. I really wonder what he's going to do with himself once the fighting stops."

Harbic pondered those words as the two men joined the bustle of the Buerdic camp. The besieged city of Hautre lay at the northern edge of the Greenlands and was a staunch ally of Carea. The army Harbic saw now was the cream of Buerdic chivalry; warlike purpose saturated the camp down to the lowliest knifeman. Clearly, Ursid had devised some stratagem; squires prepared armor, sharpened and polished swords, while grooms threw saddles onto horses. War's noises assaulted the senses from every direction and clouds of dust rose through the last rays of the setting sun.

The Buerdic army had camped amid the hickories and beeches which ringed Hautre at a distance of about a quarter of a league. Now Diomedes led Harbic the courier toward the grove which stood nearest the walls. Harbic noticed great heaps of earth concealed beneath trees; in fact, the place looked more like a construction site than part of an armed camp. Men pushed carts of fresh earth one way while other men hurried the opposite way with bundles of fagots or empty carts.

In the center of the grove stood a huge outdoor kitchen. Three fires blazed; over each hung a cauldron suspended from an iron tripod. Piles of meat, mostly fat cuts of pork, lay heaped beside each fire and cooks bent to throw pieces into the kettles. A line of men waited on the other side of the cauldrons. As they arrived, each pair of men lowered a pole from their shoulders and set down the big pot it carried. Cooks sweated as they ladled into the pot the oil rendered from the pork fat. An occasional curse tore the air as someone caused the smoking liquid to spatter over bare skin.

Harbic watched with awe until Diomedes caught him by the arm and pulled him onward. The trees seemed to shelter an army of madmen. But as the two passed farther into the grove, Harbic understood. They came to a great pit and at the bottom of it yawned a wide tunnel, carefully shored and pointed toward the city's wall. Three ramps led into the pit and they walked down one, passing men who carried pots of smoking oil or bundles of sticks into the tunnel or who pushed earth-filled barrows out of it.

They found themselves in an eerie netherworld. Odors of damp earth and rancid grease quashed the senses and hardly a torch glimmered in the darkness. The tunnel crawled with insects. The rancid smell must have attracted every cockroach, every wasp and centipede within a league of Hautre.

Heavy timbers supported the crumbling ceiling; for all the stink and the bugs, the place was an engineering marvel. They finally came to a branch in the tunnel and found a knot of supervisors directing the workmen with commands and frantic gestures. Chief among them stood a tall, dark-faced young man who moved as one used to being obeyed. His face was fierce, intense, and well-tanned, but three ugly scars contorted the skin. One lay across his forehead while two other scars slanted down from it, twisting with each shift of his expression. Harbic had never met the young man but he knew it was Prince Ursid, Count of Faux and Constable of Buerdaunt, leader of the armies of Lothar the Pale.

Ursid bent to mark something onto a chart, then straightened and smiled at the two newcomers. "Ah, Diomedes, you have brought me stuff to satisfy my needs until we're through." He took the satchel and wineskin from his *aide-de-camp*. "I've neither supped nor slept for thirty hours and still more time must pass before the issue's brought to resolution. But who's the stranger tagging at your heels?"

"The King's messenger," Diomedes answered. "He asked to see you, so I brought him here."

"And well you did; I have no time to entertain him in my tent." Ursid stopped to swallow a draught of wine, then spoke between bites of beef as he addressed Harbic. "So tell me, fellow, wherefrom do you ride?"

"Buerdaunt, my Lord. The King extends his greetings to you."

Ursid smiled and the scars across his face seemed to relax a little. "Ah, indeed. Before this night has run its course, I hope to send back tidings which will please His Majesty. My engineers have excavated cunning mines beneath the walls of yonder city. Even now, our preparations reach their peak; we soon shall set our fires and burn out all the shoring. Close-packed brush and endless pots of lard will blaze white hot, the shoring will collapse, and Hautre's solid tower will fall next. Then you shall see the warlike spirit of my knights as they assault the town."

The plan impressed Harbic. "I've never watched a sapping operation to compare with this one."

"And you've not seen the half. We'll wait till dark so smoke cannot be seen a-billowing from the ground or at the tunnel's mouth. There's been no sign of countermining, so we know the town does not suspect our strategy. Their watch will just be standing down; then we shall strike and overwhelm them all."

Harbic looked uncomfortable. The message he carried could hardly be considered a fitting reward for all this stout labor. He found himself afraid to deliver the King's edict but he had no choice. "My Lord, I still must show you the King's word."

"Can't it wait until we're finished?"

Harbic swallowed. "No. I think it best you read it right away." He reached into his courier's pouch, then handed Ursid a rolled parchment.

"Oh, very well." Ursid took the parchment, broke the seal, and read it hastily. Then he read it again, more slowly, his face growing dark and terrible. His eyes flashed and he glared at the messenger. "Are these the King's own words?"

"Indeed, my Lord."

"What madness can this be? How can he let his agents sign a peace with jackals and foul adders? These accords would lift the spoils from our victorious hands upon our very moment of success." His voice rose as he read aloud. "'You shall immediately lift your siege and take your troops away from any land allied to Carea.'" He hurled the paper to the ground and his cry filled the tunnel. "By all the gods, what treachery is this?"

"I sympathize, my Lord."

Ursid's eyes bored into the messenger. "Oh, do you sympathize? My men are to be robbed of victory and I am forced to quit the only course which makes my life supportable? Look hard, now, fellow; look at me. Observe the jagged scars Carea's wiles have placed upon me. Will I be denied pursuit of justice and revenge?" His fingers curled about the hilt of his longsword and he lifted; the weapon slid from its sheath with a sound like a viper crawling across tiles. "You, dog, shall die. No man may come to me and tell me that I must be robbed of vengeance."

Harbic quailed before the young Prince. "My Lord, I beg your mercy. 'Twas not I who wrote the edict, signed the treaty, or consented to the terms of the accord. Your sword does not lust after my poor blood; I'm only one poor man, who was assigned to pass the news."

Ursid snarled his rage into the terrified messenger's face, then his eye cleared, he managed to calm himself, and he glanced into the stunned faces of his officers. He looked back at the messenger and lowered his sword. "Indeed, your words have truth. 'Twould be unfair to slay you; still I say I am enraged. The Fates once more have blocked my path. For one goal do I live: to see Carea fall. If this war ends now, how long must I wait to vent my rage and anguish on the bloody field?"

Then he smiled a little smile at Harbic and once more pointed his sword at the messenger's belly. "One way and one way only may you save your life."

"What way is that?"

Ursid laughed a low, throaty chuckle. It was as if he enjoyed a joke which only he could appreciate. "You'll have to swear that you are not yet here."

Harbic looked at the young Prince. Had he gone mad? "I do not understand."

"You'll make yourself appreciate my meaning, else you'll die. You've been detained somewhere. I neither know nor care for what excuse you may devise but you'll not bring this message till tomorrow. Long before that time, this wall will have been breached. We will possess the town."

"But that's deceit, my Lord."

"Deceit?" Ursid spat the word. "And what is not deceit? I gave my youth and honor for the love of miserable Carea's fair Princess. For love of her I courted death itself, and still did she revoke her word, rejected all the love I bore for her. She and then her brother, newly crowned King Palamon, told lies to me. Don't tell me of deceit; be still, except to render me a binding oath. If e'er the question's raised about the day you brought me word of peace, you shall reply that you arrived upon the morning after this besieged city fell."

Harbic spoke softly. "I see my life hangs in the balance."

"That is so. If you do not agree, you die."

"It is a hard choice."

"Then I shall philosophize." Ursid issued Harbic a steely smile. "Our land, Buerdaunt, is victimized by plain geography the same way I am victimized by fate. Carea rules the straits far to the west; all ships which sail into the Thlassa Mey pass only at her pleasure. Fortune's hand has therefore placed her in position thus to strangle us, to throttle off our trade. In that same way, Carea's Palamon is given force of prowess over me. He's taller than am I, more firmly built, and though his age has slowed him some, his skill in tournament exceeds my own.

"E'en so, our fair Buerdaunt can take her rightful place among the nations of the world, in spite of disadvantages. And I may overcome tall Palamon and gain my vengeance o'er the royal family of Carea. Will's the key. Our will to gain our destiny must far exceed the will of those Careans. Else, we fail. And now we have our test of will against this piece of paper you would force upon me. I shall not comply. I'll not deny my men the victory; I'll not allow smooth words from diplomats to keep me from my goal, my own revenge, the birthright of my land. So sways the issue. Hautre falls tonight; the very gods could shout to me 'Desist'—and I'd not stop."

"I see your meaning, sir."

"Then you shall live." Ursid put his sword away. "As long as you agree that you have not yet brought your message."

Harbic bowed his head. "As you direct."

Ursid turned from the messenger as if the man had ceased to exist. The Buerdic Prince hurled orders for firing the mines, sent men and materials to each point along the maze of tunnels. Harbic could only watch silently until a sentry arrived from the tunnel's entrance. "The sun has set and night descends."

"That's well," Ursid replied. Officers withdrew and shooed the last workmen from the emptying passage. Only a few men remained, those who would torch the fuel crammed into the tunnels. Ursid gave final orders, the engineers threw torches onto lines of kindling, and the flames roared away, toward the walls of Hautre.

Everyone ran toward open air; Ursid came last. Even so, the heat and smoke pursued them and by the time they reached the sweet air, they were all gasping for breath.

Attendants appeared from all directions. While the smoke billowed out of the tunnel, they strapped armor onto the back of each knight who emerged. In moments, Ursid and the others were decked in battle dress. Then the young Prince leaped onto his courser and led his best knights toward the edge of the trees.

The city stood dark before them. But an eye which knew where to look could see little pinpricks of light between the trees and the city wall; tongues of flame licked out of the tunnel's ventilation shafts. In a few places, tall grasses burst into flame from the heat below. There was no way of knowing the enemy's reaction to such a sight.

It was a disarmingly quiet moment; the specks of light winked, then went out one by one. The earth at the base of the nearest tower subsided, the tower itself trembled, leaned, hesitated, then toppled with a sort of tragic dignity. As it struck the ground and shattered into fragments, the sounds of its collapse reached the watching warriors. The ground leaped with the shock; the rumble was fearsome even at that distance, and Harbic shuddered as he heard faint cries—the screams of the wounded and the dying. A great gap had appeared in the wall, an invitation to the watching army.

"Now onward, Buerdic knights," Ursid cried. "We ride for victory or death." He raised his sword, spurred his courser, and galloped toward the gap with a great company of knights behind him. Entry to the city was his. Treaty or no treaty, Buerdaunt would soon be sovereign over Hautre and all the lands about.

Chapter Two:
The Battle of Hautre

A WAIL ROSE from the stricken city as Ursid and two thousand knights thundered toward it. He had timed his blow perfectly; a quarter of the night watch had been killed by the wall's collapse. The Buerdic warriors plunged through the rubble, then threw themselves against the defenders. Men bellowed war cries, swords ripped into armor and flesh, and fighting spread left and right.

The defenders held back the onslaught no better than a wall of sand might hold back the ocean. Ursid's knights had rehearsed carefully. A few hundred battled their way to the city's gates, slaughtered the defenders there, and threw the portal open. Others surged through the streets and cut down anyone who dared resist. But the main body, over a thousand knights, swept toward the stronghold of Keep Securete, which stood atop a low hill at the center of the town.

The drawbridge began to rise even as the attackers reached the fortress, but Ursid was not to be denied. He spurred his courser, felt great muscles surge beneath him, and his mount cleared the end of the drawbridge and clattered across. He was not alone. Goaded on by his audacity, many of his loyal knights also attempted the jump. Some missed—horses and riders screamed and clanked as they rolled down the embankment and into the moat—but many followed their master.

Over a hundred knights thundered into the gatehouse, past portcullises and between wooden barriers. They fell on the stunned defenders, hacked them down like so much barley, and a few leaped from their horses to release the bar and allow the drawbridge to fall back into place.

Even at that, the forces of Hautre's Baron Ulfin rallied to pin Ursid and his men in the castle's gatehouse and outer ward. In the gatehouse itself, soldiers scrambled to the upper levels to dump oil through murder holes onto the knights that poured in—there had been no time to heat the oil to boiling or the tactic would have been deadly. Even as it was, many horses reared and hurled knights into the dust beneath the deluge.

Ursid cursed and vaulted from his own mount; he and a few of his stoutest men clattered up the stone steps to the chamber above the murder holes. They moved quickly for all the weight of their armor and they fell upon the defenders like a raging plague. Oaths and shrieks of pain echoed through the great pile, and Ursid found himself battling two grim-faced warriors. "It's him, the leader of the Buerdic tribe," one cried. "If we can cut him down, we might so awe his host that their withdrawal could be forced."

"That hope is vain," Ursid cried. "Prepare to meet your deaths." He snarled with battle's special lust as he threw himself against them. A sword bit into his shield and tore it from his grasp, but he returned a blow which sent one swordsman crashing to the stones. The other man turned to flee but Ursid was on him like a toad on a cricket. His blade carved into the back of the man's neck; the fellow threw up his arms and crumpled.

Ursid wrenched his weapon from the carcass and looked about. His men had cleared the chamber; Buerdic knights could pass through the gatehouse below without further danger. Still, the crash of battle from the castle's outer ward told him that the stronghold was far from taken. He turned and hurried back down the steps.

In spite of being caught by surprise, defenders snatched up shields and weapons and poured forth to meet the invaders. The fighting was bitter as Ursid waded into the fray. He struck right and left at every opponent who passed within reach; sweat poured down his face, and he had to struggle so hard for air that he nearly gagged on the stink of his own hot breath. But he forced himself onward, into the thickest part of the mêlée. He paid no heed to strategy or safety; his features locked into a mirthless battle grin, and he mowed down his opponents like a human scythe.

Then, above the din of the fighting, he became aware of a particular shout: "Stop." The voice was clear and loud and it caused even Ursid to pause. He glanced about between sword blows. "Young Count," the voice cried. "It's time we met and spoke together."

The fighting lurched to a halt, and Ursid looked up at one of the towers bordering the castle's outer ward. Heads crowded the tower windows; many men and women had been watching the battle. But from one of the lower apertures, torchlight silhouetted a slender figure in armor. "Come down and we will speak," Ursid cried. "But one false move will prod this battle to its fell conclusion."

His words were followed by a pause. The courtyard which had rung with the clamor of steel against steel now knew silence broken only by the occasional gasp of a dying man. The ironbound warriors of both sides laid their weapons down and strained for breath; some dropped onto one knee or pulled off their helmets and panted. But Ursid stood motionless and waited for the approach of the castle's lord. Sweat rained down his face, and his flesh stuck to his inner clothing, but he displayed no fatigue as he rested his hands on the pommel of his sword and eyed the approaching party.

Torchlight broke from a gate at the base of the wall, and Ursid centered his gaze on the leader, a dignified old man who carried himself with noble bearing. Though the man was encased by armor, he had plainly seen too many summers for battle. He wore neither helmet nor hood of chain mail, and the torchlight bounded off the white straggles of his hair and beard as he gazed sadly about the courtyard. He walked toward Ursid.

For his part, Ursid stood with feet spread wide apart, lifted his sword, and rested it on his shoulder as he addressed the old noble. "Am I to know that you are Baron Ulfin, who is master of this fiefdom?"

"I am he." The old man eyed Ursid's face. "And you must be the Buerdic Constable, the leader of these deadly ravagers. I knew my city lay in danger from the time you camped outside our walls."

"Indeed," Ursid replied. "Your city's fate was sealed when you declared allegiance to Carea, my sworn and mortal foe."

The older man grimaced with resentment but he could only let Ursid's reply pass. "You've done some bloody business," he said. "Your sword is knicked; your shield is gone, and blood adorns you from your crown to sole. Now tell me, did you bathe your armor in the sanguine element before you came? If not, I know that my most gallant men have yielded up their hearts' blood to provide you with your paint. I'm told you are a conqueror most rigorous. But still and all, remove your helmet, please, that I might see the face to which I speak."

Ursid silently handed his sword to Diomedes, pulled off his gauntlets, then lifted his visor. He undid the leather thong which held his basinet, his great helmet, to his camail, the band of chain mail which protected his throat and shoulders, then lifted the helmet free. He was soaked with sweat. He scoured his blood-sticky fingers through his matted hair; when he shook his head, he sent off a spray of collected perspiration. The evening air kissed his dripping face as he handed the helmet to Diomedes. "Now, Baron Ulfin of the town of Hautre," he said. "Am I to know you seek surrender terms?"

The old man's face became even more hostile. "While you have breached my castle's outer wall, the inner sanctuary stands as strong and able to confound your

army's blows as ever. I'll only yield this place to you if
you will swear upon one lone condition: that this fair
town of Hautre be spared the pillage and rapine with
which it's threatened. If you will promise that our citizens and their belongings shall be sacrosanct, then I will
yield my castle up to you."

"The time has passed for you to make conditions. You
did not surrender to me during siege, but after I had
stormed the city's walls and breached them. So it's I who
shall decide the fate of all your populace. All you can do
is hear the terms which I propose and yield to them, for I
have won the day."

Baron Ulfin wrung his hands. "And yet I offer you my
castle keep if you will compromise."

Ursid waved the older man into silence. "I do not
compromise with any man. I've conquered you; I therefore have the right to dictate terms. The citizens of
Hautre shall be reviewed by me and my best knights
tomorrow morn, outside the city's gates. They shall be
bowed and circumspect; then I'll decide their fate. You
held surrender till I split your walls; therefore I have the
right to slay your people, to the last wee babe if I so
choose. My knights shall occupy the town tonight but I'll
allow your criers to pass word of my intentions. After I
have looked upon your citizens, I then shall dictate
terms to you."

"Your words are hard."

"Yes, so they are." Ursid turned from the older man
and ordered Diomedes to issue instructions for the occupation. Then he turned back to the defeated Baron. "If
you will not accept them, tell me now—and we shall
take the fray up once again."

The older man struggled to contain himself. His face
turned red, his mouth worked, but at last he managed a
civil answer. "Where shall I meet you?"

Ursid returned a look that was cold and brittle as a
winter's morning. "Our first encounter's in this very
place, the time is now, and my first terms are thus: you
must allow my knights free entry to each hall and
chamber of this pile, and trust to what small mercies I

may grant out of my own accord. Complete surrender is
my fee, or else all here shall die ere morning's light."

"I must protest. Have you no chivalry?"

"There is no place for chivalry in war. Do you accept
those terms?"

Baron Ulfin of Hautre seethed like a potion but Ursid
had kept the city closed from the outside world for
weeks; there was no way the old man could know of the
peace between Carea and Buerdaunt. "I must accept,"
he said. "My bailiff will arrive in moments to present you
with the keys to every portal, save the private rooms of
my own family."

"Nay. Of every room."

The old man's voice rose in its anguish. "This is inhuman."

"So is every war."

"And I must open up the very rooms in which my wife
and daughter and my sons repose in slumber?"

Ursid nodded.

There was another pause as the old man looked about
the yard. There was no help for him there. Hautre's defenders and the garrison of Keep Securete were beaten,
bloody, and many were dying. He looked up at Ursid, his
wrinkled eyes blazing. "If such a doom is thrust upon us,
then we must comply. But you may rest assured that
none of us shall sleep this night, for fear of you and those
in your command."

"Such is the fate of conquered enemies."

Baron Ulfin turned on his heel and stalked away. And
while Ursid waited for the bailiff of the captured castle to
bring the keys, his men disarmed their foes. He waited
for word from Diomedes, who coordinated with the
knights securing the rest of the city. It would be a long
night before Ursid would see the inside of his tent again,
but the excitement of victory would keep him alert.

He looked on silently as his men set off to render the
city defenseless, then took time to examine each
chamber of the castle while a scribe noted down any
contents worth bearing away to Buerdaunt. It would

prove a profitable victory, he decided as he made his rounds.

Though he and Diomedes finally returned to his pavilion, he was still awake when the sun announced the coming of the new day. He sent Harbic the courier back toward Buerdaunt with the news that Hautre had fallen the very day before word of the truce had arrived, then he and Diomedes put on clean armor and rode toward the city's gates.

The road toward the main gate was lined with people. From the lowest beggars, to shopkeepers, to craftsmen and the guildmasters and tradesmen of the town, the population had turned forth to beg for mercy. They huddled alongside the road by the thousands, keening, lifting clasped hands, turning pale faces toward the Buerdic conquerors. Many wore horse collars or nooses about their necks as symbols of their submission; some of them even threw themselves into the dust before Ursid's horse to plead for mercy.

For his part, Ursid was not moved. He had seen this sort of thing before, each time he had taken an enemy city. The people were always worms who groveled before the conquering army to gain favorable terms of occupation. But he placed no faith in demonstrations; he knew those same people would have jeered and spat at him if they had been the victors. His words to Baron Ulfin had been for effect only; he would take his booty and render Hautre a broken city, worthless as an ally to Carea. Then he would leave. The demonstrations of the populace meant nothing; they did not even figure in his plans. He had decided the terms of occupation on the first day of the siege.

He nodded in approval as he rode through the jagged portal which had once been the city's main gate. The gate itself lay in sections at the side of the road; even the timbers which had formed the frame and lintel had been torn from the stone walls. "You've done superbly," he said to Diomedes. "You could not have carried out my wishes more completely."

Diomedes beamed and looked like a great hound

being petted. "We took care of the smaller gates, too.
They're all in pieces."

"The chains which guard the broadest thoroughfares
—have they been stripped from place as well?"

Diomedes' smile never faded. "They've all been
pulled out, taken back to camp, and dumped. I'd wager
my mother's eyes that you could gallop a horse from one
end of this city to the other without breaking stride. But
look for yourself." He pointed to the streets which
opened off the main avenue. The entrance to each one
was bordered by shattered stones, where the eyebolts
for the chains had been torn from place.

Ursid looked and nodded. The chains had been in-
stalled to keep an invading force from riding quickly
through the city. They were another line of defense destroyed. He clapped Diomedes on the back and smiled.
"You've carried out your orders well, old man. You
please me once again, and with my pleasure comes ad-
vancement."

The Buerdic leaders rode to Keep Securete. They
crossed the drawbridge, then clopped through the castle's bailey and into the inner ward. They dismounted
and their metal-clad feet scuffed across the flagstones as
they strode into Baron Ulfin's great hall. Baron Ulfin, his
bailiff, and the other officers of the city and the castle
itself, stood waiting for them.

Ursid faced the older man and removed his gauntlets.
"The showing of humility I saw this morning pacifies my
heart," he said blandly. "No pillage in the town shall be
allowed and Keep Securete shall be allowed to stand,
although a garrison of my troops shall remain."

Baron Ulfin nodded and looked relieved. "It pleases
me to hear it, sir."

"Think nothing of it. I do not intend to gain my
greater end by ravishing young maidens, setting fires, or
watching while my men slay suckling pigs. But still and
all, your opposition has to bear some sort of price."
Ursid accepted a scroll from Diomedes, glanced at the
parchment, then handed it to the beaten noble. "Herein
are written your surrender terms. Take all the time you

need to understand them, then apply your signature upon this space." He pointed toward a line at the bottom of the document.

Baron Ulfin took the scroll and read it. His face fell. The paper dropped from his fingers and he stared up at his young conqueror. "These terms are hard."

"Indeed they are," Ursid replied. "I hope you do not think me so naive as to besiege your city, conquer it, and risk the lives of all my men without demanding heavy tribute in the bargain."

"But fifty thousand talents. Such a sum will cripple all our trade for many years."

Ursid pointed toward one of the clauses of the document. "This paragraph states clearly how much time you have to pay the tribute—ten long years. If you will husband monies cunningly, it can be paid without an undue hardship."

"It says my daughter must be given up as hostage till the monies are paid over. All those years—I cannot do it. She's my very life." Baron Ulfin looked up at Ursid pleadingly. "I have two sons; take either one of them and I will gladly sign your document. But Alcyone, my daughter, is my pearl, the center of my soul. She'll suffer more because she is unused to hardship or imprisonment. My sons are schooled in knightly duties. Hostageship will leave them straight and strong. The fate you have described will ruin her, for she will waste away without her family's love, despairing, cursing every endless night till she's returned."

"Exactly. That is why she's specified. The use of such a hostage will assure delivery of the monies specified."

The old man cradled his head in his thin hands. "Ah, such a choice. How can I give her up?"

"If you had not allied yourself with those who are my enemies, there'd be no need to make that choice." Ursid's face reddened as he cried out to the assembly. "Let those who make Carea's King their ally listen well —for Palamon's my enemy and those who side with him will earn my fiercest wrath." He turned back to Baron Ulfin. "Do not bewail the news of your hard fate, old man. I know how torment feels, for I have suffered at the hands of those Careans till my soul bled free of all compassion and all chivalry. So do not throw yourself at me; Carean lies have made me such a shell bereft of human feeling that you would as well entreat a stone. If I am harsh, do not blame me, blame them." Ursid glared at his shocked audience, then stalked from the chamber.

Chapter Three:
Berethane, the Heir

KING BEREVALD HAD been dead nearly a year now, and Palamon still hated being the new King. He had wept at the grand old man's funeral rites and not just for Berevald—some of the tears had been for himself. He hated the thought of wearing the crown. He hated diplomats who knew hundreds of words with double meanings, he hated the slimy courtiers who smiled out of all their faces and made even the diplomats look honest and upright, he hated all the attention he received, and he hated the crowds and the constant flattery. Sometimes he felt like a man wading through a swamp.

But Aelia stood at his side and made life good. She knew the court's ways as well as the pilots of Artos knew the shoals and currents of the Thlassa Allas—she knew every convolution of every twisted little mind that tried to suck a favor out of the King's ear. Without her wisdom to help him, Palamon would have gone crazy.

Best of all, the two of them had wandered all love's pathways together; they had bathed themselves in every scented pool, had sipped the nectar from every deep blossom. After a year of marriage, Aelia had presented Palamon with a son, a fine, lusty lad with red toes and

pink fingernails and a face which turned purple whenever he wanted feeding—which was always. So Palamon
could not complain. If he shook his head and ground his
teeth in the presence chamber, he still laughed, kissed
his family, and held his son, once he walked to private
quarters.

For five years, war had raged between Carea and
Buerdaunt; it outlived Berevald and the first months of
Palamon's reign. He counted it his first real accomplish-
ment when he put quill to paper and ended the slaughter.
The Buerdic diplomats' robes rustled as they picked up
the document, blew the ink dry, and handed Palamon an
identical parchment with Lothar the Pale's signature on
it. Hostilities would end the instant of the signing, and
the two monarchs would meet in the city of Danaar to
hammer out the final terms of peace.

Palamon leaned back in his seat, sighed, and caught
hold of Aelia's hand. "It's done," he said. "The carnage
now is set aside and life can spring once more about the
shores of our beloved Thlassa Mey."

"You've done what you set out to do," Aelia said. She
smiled down at him. "And now a celebration must be
held."

"Indeed, a full and lusty one. Come, scribes, proclaim
a holiday. Send heralds all across the war-torn lands; our
revelry will split the heavens with its joyful shout."

That signing had taken place a fortnight ago; now Palamon smiled as he watched the result of his proclama-
tion. Tournaments, carnivals, musicians, and jongleurs,
all the good things filled Upper and Lower Carea. Palamon's stoutest knights and nobles filled Castle Conforth's great hall for the celebration banquet.

Every adult in the royal family was there. King Palamon, Queen Aelia, Princess Berengeria, Princess Bessina and her husband, Flin, all marched into the hall and
seated themselves at the head table, which stood on its
raised dais. The nobles stood and applauded. Then they
went silent and seated themselves once more as Palamon
lifted his arms.

"My friends and staunch supporters," he cried. "You

have heard the reason for our gathering. The day has
come at last, when we may live in peace and brother-
hood across the Thlassa Mey. We've celebrated on the
tilting grounds and in our temples; inside our homes, returning husbands have insured their wives some pleasant, restful nights." The hall broke into good-natured
laughter at this remark and Aelia favored Palamon with a
wry smile.

Palamon went on. "Now let us break our bread together and enjoy ourselves, in hopes this peace shall
reign until the sea absorbs the land and all the mighty
gods conclude man's years on mortal soil."

The great hall erupted with shouts and applause, then
the meal began. Tumblers and acrobats spilled onto the
brightly lit floor. The nails of the great dogs rattled
across the flagstones as they patrolled among the rev-
elers to lick hands and wait for scraps. After the main
courses had been served, a herald announced fitting entertainment; Arcite, a gifted troubadour from a far land,
would sing before the assembly.

Princess Berengeria had dressed herself as she always
did on these occasions—she wore a lace gown with high
collar and full sleeves. From her place on Palamon's left
hand, she spoke to the King. "Who is this man, Arcite?
From this applause that fills your hall upon the mention
of his name, his fame precedes him to our midst. And
yet, I know him not."

Palamon smiled back at her. "But soon, you will," he
said. "He's traveled much; his name is known and loved
by all who've heard a single one of his bright melodies."

"I see." Berengeria eyed the minstrel charily. "He is a
comely man, I judge. It's my suspicion that he has his
choice of serving wenches when his songs are done and
he has left the floor."

Palamon laughed. "Perhaps," he said. "But listen.
We'll judge his voice as cautiously as you have judged
his manly shoulders and his bulging thighs."

Arcite walked to the center of the floor, tall, blond,
and well-formed, as Berengeria had noted. The applause
washed over him like happy waters, then he beamed and

bowed toward the King and all the noble guests. He raised his lute, thanked the gods for allowing him to perform before such a festive audience, and then began to sing.

His lute strings wept sweet melody and his voice followed after, filling all ears with beauty, with radiant sounds that so dazzled the hearing that they were almost painful in their purity. He sang a tender country ballad about summers before wars tore at the Thlassa Mey. Beautiful maidens of verse danced before noble swains, fields of barley and rye tossed beneath a smiling sun, love flourished and blossomed.

"My troth," Palamon heard Berengeria say. "He sings most sweetly."

Arcite sang his ballad through, then launched himself into another song. He lost himself in the depths of his music, as if no longer aware of the hundreds of eyes resting upon him. He was making love, really; Palamon heard Berengeria catch her breath and realized the same thought had struck her. He was making love to the hall, to the pure air, to the Muses themselves. His eyes fluttered shut, his fingers floated dreamily across the strings, and his lips sleepwalked through the lyrics. His melody turned into a precious liquid, into wine; it stirred the soul as tenderly as a maiden's first, winelike kiss. Palamon closed his own eyes and listened happily.

When Arcite finished, silence gripped the hall. No one whispered and every eye fastened itself on him; even the dogs lay quietly, bewitched by the magic of his melodies. Then the minstrel bowed and let his lute drop to his side; the effect was like a roomful of people coming awake all at once. Applause surged through the hall like a storm.

Arcite bowed, smiled, waved, then walked out of the chamber. The dinner went on and other entertainers performed, but the guests paid them little notice after the young troubadour's performance.

After the final course had passed before them, a group of knights at the rear of the hall began to pound their table in unison. Laughter and shouts rose like banners, then a chant of "the Heir, the Heir," grew until it rocked the walls. It did not stop; it increased in volume until the King himself stood with a wry smile.

"Am I to know you men desire to look on Berethane, my son and Heir to this land's throne? I swear, it seems his popularity exceeds my own, e'en though he's but a hairless child."

The men laughed at the King's remark, but the shouting kept on. "The Heir, the Heir."

Palamon almost laughed. How could he not feel pleasure that his subjects loved his son almost as much as he did. "If you would have him come," he shouted, "then let me hear no more of these restrained and flimsy-livered murmurings. I wish to hear you say it. Will you have him brought? Call yea or nay."

"Yea," came the shout from the floor. "Yea, we shall see him." Amid cheering and applause, Palamon laughed, then called a page forward and sent the lad to the nursery with the summons. Prince Berethane, it was proven again, was immensely popular wth the nobles. Though he had enjoyed it, the call from the floor had been the expected thing. He rejoiced and hoped Berethane would be more comfortable wearing the crown than his father, when the time came.

In only moments, the nobles roared their approval all over again as the hall's oak doors swung open. In walked Palamon's four-year-old son. Female attendants moved on each side of the boy and steadied him while cheers made the walls tremble. He was beloved to the point of adulation, was Berethane, if for no more than the way his father doted on him. He was all but worshipped by every man in the army, from the lowest levied peasant to the highest general. For his own part, he laughed and began to dance at all the attention; a smile split his chubby face and he swung his eyes this way and that, while the shout went up again. "The Heir, the Heir."

He wore rich robes of cloth-of-gold, his tiny legs had been bound into miniature leggings, and one of his nurses had sewn him a towel-sized cloak which suited him perfectly. Palamon heard Berengeria laugh and say,

"He is a lovely child." Then the boy broke away from his attendants and dashed toward his royal parents.

But he never reached them. From nowhere, thunder shook the hall; lightning flashed and dazzled from outside the windows. A vicious wind slashed the eaves as if winter had returned to deliver a tempest from nowhere. Peals of foul climate's violence shook the building, platters rattled as if seized by an earthquake, and the little Prince stopped in his tracks, frozen by terror.

No one in the hall could move; each one was paralyzed by the prodigy. Then a ghostly funnel cloud extended itself down *through* the lofty roof. It took a shape like one of the summer tornadoes which tore at the Greenlands, but was much smaller. And—wonder of wonders—it was composed of swirling flames. Winds swept around it and whipped the fire from the torches along the walls, then even sucked the life from the bonfire in the center of the chamber. The flaming cloud reached toward the floor like a grasping tentacle, lowering, lowering.

The cloud's nether end probed this way and that, as if searching for something, then shot toward Berethane. The flames caught him and sucked him into the swirling vortex; the funnel closed over him and danced an evil dance about his writhing form. The stunned guests could see him inside, shrieking, struggling against the walls of the cloud, his eyes bulging with terror. No one could move to help him, not even Palamon.

The apparition vanished as suddenly as if it had never existed, plunging the hall into darkness. Screams and shouts filled the place and attendants rushed to relight torches—but as lights glimmered once more, Palamon cried out. He leaped from the dais and rushed toward his son, who lay on the floor, motionless as a stone.

Palamon's heart heaved itself into his throat. He threw himself toward the little body, slipped, and knocked over a row of chairs in his rush. "Now mighty Pallas," he cried, "I pray no harm's been done to my poor boy." Cold sweat pulsed from his forehead as he broke through the gathering crowd and threw himself to his knees beside the child.

Breathless physicians ran up at the same time and bent over Berethane. They loosened his clothing and probed for a pulse. Their expressions turned grave and they looked at Palamon. "Your Grace," one whispered. "He's turned as cold as any corpse—and yet we feel a pulse, though it is feeble and irregular. There cannot be a doubt; he is the victim of some potion or some charm."

"Magic." The word swept through the hall as Palamon cried out and threw himself across the little body. Magic, powerful magic, had stricken Berethane as a stone would flatten an insect. The color drained from Palamon's face, the sweat popped from his brow, then he lifted his head and laid his scarred hands across the tiny body. He stifled his own tears and began a trembling prayer to his patron, the goddess Pallas.

"O mighty Pallas," he began. "I know not the source of unknown magic which strikes down my child. But pull from him the foul enchantment that's beguiled his tiny limbs. Let life resume its course, for him and all of us. My sword, my horse, my crown, my kingdom, e'en my life, are piled together in the scales for him. O mild and tender Maiden, hear me and endorse this plea and prayer. Let evil not bereave my poor wife and myself. Give us thy hand as thou hast given oft before—reprieve him from this fate. Or else his life, like sand from out the glass must flow. Offer us thy sleeve and sympathy, that my poor child might stand."

The prayer grew in Palamon's throat, his fears overwhelmed him until he clutched his fingers toward the heavens. Then he went slack from the strain of the effort. The great hall had gone silent as a crypt. Moments passed and still the child did not stir. His condition did not change.

Aelia finally ran up and knelt beside Palamon and the others, while Berengeria and those closest to the royal family followed. "Poor Palamon," the Queen said in a trembling whisper. "You've known great anguish over all your years, and yet your face displays your pain to me—a stronger grief than ever you have felt."

He looked at her; she was a pillar of strength even then, though tears glistened at the corners of her eyes. "This tragedy is worse than any other," he whispered back to her.

"And yet you must have done, my love. Our child's the victim of enchantment by some evil faction. All the powers of the Maiden cannot take away a spell."

He stared at her, then at the faces which peered down at them, and something popped inside him. His poor boy had been struck down by some human fiend, had been laid low like a pawn lifted off a chessboard, and with no more feeling. Why did the world have to be so foul a place?

He wrung his hands like a wild man, then stood, clenched his fist, and brought one hammerlike blow down on the banquet table nearest him. The table leaped like a startled deer; platters and wineglasses crashed to the floor and Palamon's voice filled the room. "Vengeance, vengeance, vengeance. By the gods, I shall not rest till I apply hot irons to him who struck this shameful blow. He cannot hide; I'll seek him at the farthest corners of the Thlassa Mey." He whirled about, ordering everyone from the hall, and had Berethane carried back to the nursery, where more physicians already waited.

The child did not die. Hours later, the physicians reported that his pulse never varied. But he hardly lived, either; his body remained as cold and as motionless as the sand from a tidal pool. They used all their knowledge and art to restore him, but arrived at the conclusion that only the fiend who had cast the spell could remove it.

Dawn lay ahead, but everyone in Castle Conforth was still awake. The royal family made their way to the Castle's chapel, where Palamon and Aelia knelt to spend the rest of the dark time in frantic prayer. Berengeria followed them and stood at the rear of the holy chamber; she could not hear their whispers there, but she well knew the nature of their words. After a bit, she also knelt and uttered her own prayer. She begged Hestia, patron goddess of the hearth and of wedded love that the magic might somehow be dispelled. And for her own sake, she asked that she might play some rôle in the great events which would surely follow.

The prayer done, she stood and nervously fingered the high lace collar of her gown. The delicate material had been woven into patterns as intricate as the starry belts of the night sky; it soothed her fingertips but its softness could not ease the horror of everything that had happened. The world was still unclean, she thought. She had watched the evil wizard, Alyubol, die five years ago, yet the phantasm which had burst in on them had thrown even that fact into question. Had Alyubol really died or had he tricked them all? Did his contentious spirit still walk the land, did he still spread grief and discord? She shuddered and wondered if Palamon was thinking the same thing.

Palamon finally sighed and stood. He unfolded himself stiffly, for he had knelt a long while. Aelia straightened beside him, a slender, dark-haired counterpoint to the mass of his body. She was tall for a woman, but she looked tiny as she stood there beside him. Her face seemed doubly thin as she peered up into her husband's eyes and said, "What steps will you now take, my love? I beg that first you send regrets and cancel all the meetings 'twixt yourself and pale King Lothar of Buerdaunt."

Palamon did not seem himself. His look sent chills down Berengeria's spine and his voice was low, resolute, and hard. "Nay, nay," he said. "I'll see him on the date we've set."

"But why? The peace is signed; all details can be filtered out by diplomats. Our son lies stiff and motionless."

The lines on Palamon's face etched themselves even deeper. "Indeed, I know it. We both looked on him." He returned her gaze. "My Lady and my life, I still must beard King Lothar in Danaar. My thoughts are thus: the spell which struck our poor boy down smacks strongly of the work of Alyubol. Though he is five years dead, his foul disciples live, and doubtless follow evil magic as his legacy. 'Twould not surprise me if some fiend among them cast this spell upon our child."

He drew himself to his full height and pulled two keys from a pocket sewn into his doublet. Behind the altar, one of the chapel's low ceiling beams passed just within his reach. A mighty, two-handed sword hung overhead, clamped to the beam with iron bands. Few other men could reach the locks which secured those straps, but Palamon was taller than other men. He put his keys to the locks, swung back the bands, and let the big sword settle onto his fingers. He scowled and held it before him; candleflames gleamed off the polished blade and filled the holy chamber with mystic light.

"But Alyubol and Lothar had a pact," Palamon said. "The pale King ought to know what followers the wizard left, and what their powers are." Passion seized his face as he looked from the great sword to his wife. "My son has been bewitched. Am I to let deceit and little notes from mincing diplomats delay my search for his salvation? Nay, I tell you. I'll meet with Lothar, place my angry face an inch or so from his, and put my questions. I will surely know if he has aught to do with this atrocity. If that should be, then war will follow as the smothering dust comes on the heels of kine.

"This sword has hung here through these five long years. I never carried it to battle, for I could not bring myself to use a holy sword for slaughter in some game of nationhood." His eyes flashed. "Now that has changed."

With a brutal grunt, he thrust the blade downward. The tip pierced the flooring like a bodkin stabbing a roast and the weapon stood vibrating in the candlelight. Then the tall monarch threw himself to his knees before it, clasped his hands, and began a prayer like, yet unlike, the one he had uttered earlier. Berengeria bit her lip to hear him pour out his grief and rage to the goddess Pallas. "O holy Maiden," he cried, his voice trembling. "I have served thee long; I've felt thy fingers laid upon my brow. Forgive me in my grief and loss, for now I beg indulgence in an angry song. My son lies silent. Magic's secret prong has pierced and laid him low. I beg thee now to lead me to the human boar or sow who struck him. To my vengeance they belong. I'll have them by the ears; their throats I'll slash, to bathe in their foul blood. Please grant this boon though others you deny me. Let me thrash all those who laid foul witchery's cocoon about my boy. I'll risk the sharpest lash if I might have my vengeance soon."

Berengeria pressed her fingers to her lips. Berethane's misfortune had changed Palamon in a single night; it was terrible to watch. And she knew Aelia also recognized the change. Berengeria could see the double distress which wracked the Queen. The prayer—Berengeria had never heard anything like it, at least not from her brother. It was so full of hatred and fury that she feared him and feared for his soul even as he uttered it. As he finished, wiped away the perspiration, and rose, she had to speak to him. "Beware of blasphemy, O Palamon."

He glared back at her. He had never looked at her that way before. "How can a man blaspheme when he entreats the goddess for the life of that low beast who struck his son?"

"Your Pallas is a patron of the art of healing. Wisdom, courage, kindness, faith are all her virtues. I find few of them in that last sonnet; all you ask is blood."

"I asked for healing once—to no avail," he shot back.

"The goddess mends all wounds and sicknesses, depending on the faith of him who makes the plea," Berengeria said. "But you must know full better than myself, that laying on of hands has no effect when magic is the cause of the affliction."

Palamon grimaced. "I know it well." His features worked; he looked as if he would strike himself for lack of a better target. Could she even be certain he was still the brother she loved? "But fear you not," he finally went on. "I'll have them both. I'll have poor Berethane restored and have the villain's blood in the bargain."

Berengeria looked away; it was strange, she reflected. Berethane had been Aelia's son, as well as Palamon's. Her grief was great; she had wept over the boy just as Palamon had. But if Palamon's grief was no greater than his wife's it still seemed *larger*. His pain cried out, filled the castle, as if a portion of himself had gone with the child. She thought about it. Palamon had watched the boy grow with the fascination of some country innocent viewing a joyful mystery. Berethane had lent Palamon a new intensity of living that the tall monarch had never displayed before. Now it seemed that all the joy in Palamon was stilled with his son; all that remained were grief and fury.

But that was a subject which could destroy them all. Berengeria turned away from it. "So," she said. "You still shall travel to Danaar. How soon?"

Palamon blinked, then answered. "My vessel was to sail tomorrow. I will not delay it even one short day."

Aelia reached out and took his hand. Her fingers twined with his and she gazed into the depths of his gray eyes. "And what if you should meet your death? We've seen what powers stalk this land, as potent as in days of Alyubol. So what if you should die, my love? Where I knew joy in you and Berethane two days ago, a fortnight could bring word that I have lost you both. That would destroy my world itself; what thing could I do then?"

The fury bled from Palamon's features; his mouth sagged. Berengeria almost wept all over again to watch while the natural tenderness of his nature, his love for his Queen, warred with his rage. He kissed Aelia's hand and returned her loving look. Berengeria felt embarrassed even to witness such a scene. But she did not leave and a guard who happened to approach just then did not seem to matter to Palamon either, so greatly had Aelia's question affected him. "O wife," he said. "Do not entreat me thus. My heart and soul tell me what I must do and I cannot deny them. True it is that I could meet my death—but if there lurks a minion of the evil wizard, Alyubol, then death could just as easily strike here." He forced a smile. "Now do not grieve; that fortnight you have mentioned will expose the secret of our son's affliction. You shall see us both restored to you."

Aelia sighed and stroked her husband's cheek. "There are great risks. You meet the Buerdic King where he can spring some trap to crush the life from you."

"No." He shook his head. "Lothar is no fool. He will not dare to have me slain in any way my death could be traced back to him. He needs this peace e'en more than does Carea, and he knows that harming me will bring the war to a renewed and deadly life."

"And you believe he holds the key to curing Berethane?"

Palamon pulled the *Spada Korrigaine* from the chapel's oak floor. "I'm sure of it, for he knew Alyubol and used the evil wizard's friendship ruthlessly. I now know why my father thought so ill of him. Though I know not yet all there's to know about his subterfuge, I know that he retains a world of spies. He has to know this tale, as surely as we stand here, and I must go before him, gaze deep into his face, and learn myself what secrets he conceals. No embassy or emissary can do that for me."

"Then you must go," Aelia said simply. "But if you come to harm, my waning years will pass like glaciers down a mountainside, all bare and destitute, and slow as death's own passage."

He kissed her. "I'll not be slain." He reached toward Berengeria, and the three of them stood in a little circle. "You two and Berethane have taught me love—a lesson I was not allowed to learn in younger times. I shall return to you, or else my soul shall wander o'er the world in sad bewilderment until the end of all recorded years."

Chapter Four:
Arcite the Balladeer

BERENGERIA HURRIED AFTER Palamon as he strode toward the chapel's door. "O Palamon," she said. "If you must do this thing, then give me leave to travel there with you. I've eaten at your table five long years, and never done a moment's service to the Crown. My uselessness must end; allow me at your side. I'd give you aid and succor in your travels."

He stared at Berengeria until she blushed. She had made her request on impulse; the boredom of court life was driving her to distraction. Could not a Princess perform some useful service? She had been bred and reared in the shadow of the Carean throne, after all—when would she function in one of the offices for which she had been trained?

But she found no sympathy in Palamon's eyes. She read surprise, she read embarrassment, she even saw a flicker of resentment, as if she were upsetting plans he had already made. "My plan had been to summon noble Flin and ask him on the journey," he replied flatly.

"Flin." Berengeria's mouth tightened.

"I know you don't approve of him, or of his wife," Palamon said. "They grate upon your upright, proper nature. Still, he served me well throughout the war."

"Ah, yes," she replied softly, half to herself. "You placed him in command of troops because he is a male and he is married to our niece, Bessina. I've but decorated these vast corridors and been as useful as the lace upon my collar."

"That lace has its purposes," Palamon said. "And so have you. Forbear. I know it is a tender thing with you. But you're a maiden, therefore cannot take a role in national affairs. Have trust in me: it shall not be thus always."

"It galls me," she said. "Yet you want my trust, and I must give it as a token of my reverence for you. O Palamon, I'm sure that you shall reconsider."

He smiled sadly and shook his head. "I'm sorry. Flin shall go with me."

She clenched her teeth. "Why was it Flin, and not myself, was born a man? Why is't? Must gender be a prison to me? Flin—must you choose him, of all the warriors in this court?" She wrung her hands. "One vain and empty sword arm? Has he guile to aid you in discussions with the Buerdic King? And will his vain, fair wife be pattern for the maidens of this realm? My rôle's to serve this land—and yet I sit and wait while others do the tasks that ought to be assigned to me."

"Both you and Aelia, my beloved Queen, will take the reins of our broad monarchy. Is not that rôle enough for you? If not, why should I take you in my own wife's place? If I'm to have a woman at my side through this adventure, why should it not be my Aelia?"

"What right have I before the Queen? Indeed, you trap me with your logic; our fair Queen has preference over me, though still no right because she, too, was born a woman."

"Princess," Aelia said. "I have no lack of functions. I've a spate of duties to fulfill my need to serve. Have trust in your poor brother; time will answer all the questions you have posed."

"Very well," Berengeria said at last. But she could not

erase the hurt she felt; she could not keep the disappointment off her face.

Palamon put his callused hand under her chin and lifted until her eyes met his. His face brimmed with fraternal love; he smiled as he had not smiled since before the banquet. "Believe me when I say I've thought this matter out. My reasoning is sound and totally without a blemish."

Berengeria forced herself to smile. "I'll try to understand," she said.

Then an interruption closed the conversation. The guard who had entered earlier announced a newcomer: "The noble knight, Sir Flin, would enter."

The guards swung the chapel door open and Flin strode in as if Castle Conforth's holiest cloister were nothing more than a garderobe to him. He wore black, burnished armor and looked handsome as sin with his face close-shaven, his hair and black moustache neatly trimmed. Berengeria looked at him coolly. His birth had been in villainy, after all; he had married into royalty by way of Princess Bessina, Berengeria's empty niece.

He walked toward them with beaming face, almost as if gloating at his triumph. Berengeria glared as he kissed the Queen's hand, then bent to take hers. She could not touch him; she lifted her hand out of his and said, "You need not kiss the hand of one who does not love you, gallant general. You've won the high regard of both the King and Queen—you have no need of mine."

He stared at her openmouthed. He was speechless, which in itself was an amazing thing; Palamon actually smiled a little. On a better day, he probably would have laughed out loud. Berengeria lifted the hem of her gown and swept from the room, to walk the endless cubits of bright corridor which led to her own chambers. The layered lace of her high collar chafed against her throat —how she wished for the time she had not been forced to wear such collars—and moisture stood against the deep blue of her eyes. Who was she angry at? Was it Palamon, Flin, or even Bessina? She was not sure. She feared for her brother. She feared for his son. And she felt more helpless to do anything than she had felt even as a hostage in Buerdaunt.

She reached the white oak door to her own chambers and grimaced as one of the sentries held it open for her. "I thank you, sir," she said, because it was the proper thing to say. She was not even allowed to open a door for herself. She had been reared to do great things—and for what?

She hurried through her white marble sitting room, which was empty as a blown egg, and into her bedchamber. There, she found one of her maids-in-waiting. "Where are the others, Daphne?" she asked.

"My Lady, most have sought their beds. Some three or four talk in the garden."

"Oh, Daphne," Berengeria said with a sigh. "I wish I were a man; then would I seek revenge beside my brother. Still, I'm told that waiting is my portion. Call them, then, my pretty maids, and we will wait together. This dreary night has been a horror for us all, and yet I cannot ease myself with sleep."

Daphne walked away. Before long, she came back with four other young women. It did not surprise Berengeria that most of them carried their prayerbooks. "Come, my Lady," Daphne said. "Let us go into the outer chamber, where we'll help you find some cheer. Andromeda will play the harp for you."

Berengeria turned her back so she could rub her eyes. "Indeed," she said in a husky voice. "The harp, an instrument condemned by ancient sages as licentious, full of sinful revelry. Though it has grown respectable in recent times, I'll listen to Andromeda's fine notes and contemplate the ancient attitude." She forced a smile onto her face. "I'm sure we've wept and prayed and fretted quite enough, all six of us. We need some naughtiness."

She went with her attendants into the sitting room. But though she walked among them, she was not of them. They talked of the most recent marriage in the court and the picnic which would take place soon, but her mind was far away from such subjects. Oh, how she

felt for Palamon, and how she would have loved to help
him if he would only let her!

She settled onto a couch and watched as Andromeda
seated herself before the gilded harp in the center of the
chamber. The maiden's arms extended toward the
strings; she plucked them into sensual vibration, and
melody bloomed like a smile from the gods.

Berengeria leaned back and closed her eyes. The harp
made rich and soothing music. She had never bothered
to learn its mysteries; now she wished she had studied
the divine instrument. Whatever Andromeda did or did
not know or care about the inner workings of the Carean
court or the world's intrigues, she knew how to produce
music. At least that was something.

But there came a rapping on the chamber's door. Berengeria looked over her shoulder and grimaced as the
guard outside announced that the Chamberlain wished to
speak to her. But wait; perhaps the Chamberlain brought
good news—perhaps Palamon had relented, changed his
mind, and would allow her to accompany him after all.
She raised her hand to stop Andromeda's playing and
motioned for one of the maidens to open the door.

The Chamberlain entered, a tall, balding man twice
Berengeria's age. He had a hooked nose and a mouth
turned down at the sides in a look of sad resignation. His
expression told Berengeria that he was not happy with
his mission; that meant his news could not be anything
she wished to hear. She looked up at him and her face
went blank.

"Princess," he began. "I hesitate to interrupt your
morning, but the King and Queen command me. I have
brought Arcite, the Balladeer, to sing and play for you in
fervent hopes that he might bring you cheer."

Berengeria's eyes widened, then she looked about
with an incredulous laugh. "What?" she cried. "Palamon
expects to soothe my fears for him and for his child with
singing from Arcite?"

The Chamberlain bowed his sad face. "Forgive me,
Lady. I but bring the message as I was instructed. You
yourself were instrumental in his coming to this court,

and he has asked to pay his homage to you face-to-face. The King and Queen have acquiesced in this."

Berengeria's mouth wrinkled. Was Palamon trying to insult her? Why should she listen to a minstrel while all the castle was still grieving over the fallen Prince? Surely, a man as understanding as Palamon did not mean to imply she was a mere girl, with no capacity for grief and concern. She shook her head, bewildered at what could possibly be on the King's mind; he had, after all, traveled beside her all the way across the Thlassa Mey.

"Very well," she finally said. "I must respect their plea. But warn your troubadour that he invades my realm within this chamber; and upon this day I'm not receptive to intrusion. This refuge's as stricken a location as exists within this castle on this day, and I shall rule it with a sad and tedious hand. Inform him that I doubt his audience will be as warm as that which greeted him last night."

To her surprise, Arcite himself stepped into the chamber. He must have been waiting right outside the door; doubtless, he had heard her words. But the cool reception seemed to bother him not at all. He bowed to her, then glanced about at her maids-in-waiting while he retuned his lute and the Chamberlain beat a hasty retreat. "It seems that I'm to entertain a sullen camp," he said with a twinkle in his eye.

Berengeria looked up at him and tried to be polite; after all, he had had no role in the night's horror. Still, it was too early in the morning and too soon after catastrophe for smiles. "I hope I have not seemed discourteous," she said.

"'Twould be impossible for such a one as you to be discourteous. The blows, scorn, and abuse would heap on me as highest praise, received from your fair person. Just to view this room and all these lovely creatures lodged within is payment for my efforts."

All the women in the chamber simpered at the flattery, all but Berengeria. Pretty gowns, pretty words— that was an empty portion; that was no meat for her table. But Arcite either did not notice her expression or he intentionally let it pass. His instrument was shaped like a melon cut in half, with the neck bent back and strings stretched over the face of it. His fingers worked magic as they moved across it. He began a jolly song, slightly bawdy, calculated to bring forth laughter. The song featured an old cuckold and his silly wife; the music lacked the beauty of Andromeda's playing, but it brought laughter from everyone in the chamber except Berengeria.

> "Up came the old man, buzzing like a bee.
> He looked into the kitchen to see what he could see.
> 'Tell me, O woman, what can all this be—
> What's this coat a'hanging here where my coat ought to be?'
> 'You old fool, you blind fool, why can't you so well see?
> 'Tis nothing but a blanket my mother sent to me.'
> 'Travel for a dozen leagues, mayhap 'twas only three.
> But buttons on a blanket I never more did see.'"

The song went on and on. With each verse, the husband's suspicions became fiercer and the wife's excuses became more impossible. When it was finished, the attendants clapped merrily and Berengeria also put her hands together once or twice. But when she spoke, her tone was unkind. "We have it now, my maids. This is the way we are to be consoled and entertained—with songs and tales of foolish womankind, and how the vain, adulterous wife is thwarted by her husband's honest eyes. And we, like empty hens, applaud and laugh before the man who has insulted us."

For the first time, Arcite's face fell and he looked nonplussed. "Princess, I beg your pardon. I did not desire to give offense. I only hoped to cheer you with a silly song." A look of genuine remorse spread across his face; he knelt and stretched his arms toward her. "If I have troubled you, then it's my wish that my own breast be split by sword or axe, that any thoughtless words be snatched from me before they can offend you yet again. I make apology and hope with all my heart you can forgive."

Berengeria sighed. She did not know the heart of this man, but he had made a pretty apology and it cooled her hasty anger. "Arise," she said. "If I am waspish, do not take it to your heart."

He did rise and his smile returned, but it was more thoughtful than it had been before. "You are an honest and a noble woman," he said. "You would not be waspish or unkind without the goad of disappointment and an evening full of pain. I'd ease your troubles if I could. What type of song would please you most?"

"Before you came, Andromeda caressed my ear with music plied from harpstrings." Berengeria pointed toward the big instrument, where Andromeda still sat. "If you can play a melody with beauty such as that, I'll hear it and be pleased."

Arcite looked at the harp and his easy confidence flooded back into him. "Ah, yes. The harp—the instrument enjoyed by the exalted gods." He looked at Andromeda, who was plainly pleased by the attention. "Young lady, play again, and I will match your melody by playing harmony. And if the spirit does not fail me, I will form a verse or two which, with the Muses' aid, might please your ear."

Andromeda's fingers once more began their lovely work. Berengeria watched with a smile—it was plain that he had charmed the maid-in-waiting, had dazzled her with his manner. He was an experienced showman and knew how to turn every setback and distraction into a further showcase for his talents. The harp's notes swelled through the chamber as they had before; Arcite listened for a moment, enjoying and absorbing the melody.

Then he began to play. His fingers caressed his lute's strings into a counter melody which accented and emphasized the harp's beautiful sounds. That impressed Berengeria. It surprised her that he would subjugate his own playing for the sake of the sound two musicians could produce together. It pleased her to see him place art before ego.

But when he sang, it was the crowning magic of all. He improvised, built rhymes and verses out of thin air and scattered them about like blessings. His song was an adaptation of an old, sad ballad Berengeria had heard before but in his hands it assumed a whole new poignancy and life. The chamber filled with his sweet tones. Berengeria knew what he had done: his playing accented the beauty of the harp, but both melodies only provided a setting for the magic of his voice. The melody which rose from his throat was clear as maidens' tears and sharp enough to pierce a heart; it was nothing like the clipped tones in which he had sung the first song. Again, he had turned everything to his advantage, had made himself the center of his audience's concentration. But the magic of his singing was so overwhelming, it did not matter.

Berengeria lost herself in the sweet sea of his music; it transported her, even while she watched it transport the other women in the room. Her universe became hazy and indefinite and every visible mark pointed to the man who made the divine euphony at the center of it. The simple song became profound and she found herself wiping tears from her cheeks.

Even Andromeda was overwhelmed by the performance; Arcite's artistry lifted and inspired her, drove her to heights in her own playing that she had never before even approached. Berengeria grew jealous of the maiden, jealous that Andromeda could share the song's inner world with Arcite, and sure that there were secrets and delights in that world which a nonmusical Princess was not allowed to taste. But for all that, she found total pleasure, total enjoyment.

At last it ended. When the last note died away in the music-sweetened air, silence reigned. No applause followed and no one spoke; each of the women sat, rendered dumb by the experience. Berengeria struggled to frame words. "Lovely," she whispered at last. "Beautiful."

"I thank you, kind Princess. Am I forgiv'n for thoughtless verses, now?"

Berengeria felt herself blush and that embarrassed her, though no one in the chamber even noticed her reaction. "I made such comments in an angry humor; please do not think overmuch of them."

"Indeed not. You corrected me full justly."

Berengeria eyed him. Was he sincere or was he simply a vassal, speaking the words his patron wanted to hear? In either case, he had answered well. "I like your tunes," she said. "Will you now give us one more song?"

His smile blossomed. "Indeed I will, Princess. 'Tis my regret I had no opportunity to speak with you before the tragedy last night. When first I looked upon your portrait, I advised myself that I would make a song for you when I felt equal to the task and understood the subject well enough. Long have I lain awake, a-pondering that task, and these last moments I have come to know you. Would you hear my song of you?"

"I would gladly do so." Then she paused. "Still, and all, your talents are so great that any man or woman whom you sing of easily could be made to look ridiculous. I have been sharp with you and now regret my words. Will you assure me that revenge dwells not in you and that your song is not some biting satire?"

He shook his head. "No satire could I sing of such a noble lady as yourself. I've seen the stuff of which you are composed, and wager you're as brave as any warrior: resourceful, strong of heart, determined. Truth to tell, I'd heard of you before I ever came into this kingdom, and I had made my mind to meet you. I have heard a host of flattering tales of you, yet they do not begin to total your entirety. I'd like to count you as a friend."

She nodded jerkily. "You may."

"I thank you. Now I shall begin my song." And he filled the chamber with sounds more wonderful than any he had made before. He sang of Berengeria's beauty, of the beauty beneath the outer beauty, of the way she had held her chin up and kept her wits about her during her famous trek across the Thlassa Mey. He made the gentlest and most sympathetic fun of her well-known determination to marry for love alone, and he finished with a verse begging the gods that she might find a noble and gentle husband who could deserve her.

For her part, Berengeria could not resist the song. It thrilled her, elated her, and flattered her beyond words. The kind verses were enough to inflate any ego, but she was even more touched that the beautiful sounds, the melody itself, had been created for her sake. She hardly felt capable of inspiring such a performance and suspected that it came more from the troubadour's talent and devotion to his art than from her own worthiness.

But whether she took the song literally, it was plainly another tour de force. When Arcite had finished, she led the applause. "A lovely work. The very gods above must have assigned your talents to you, sir. Your virtuosity is fit to praise the gods themselves."

He laughed. "I thank you. I have praised the gods with song and hoped my efforts were devout enough—but praising you is greater pleasure. I could do it at such length this chamber would decay and turn to rubble ere my words would be exhausted."

"You are quite the flatterer."

"Nay, nay," he said with a laugh. "I never flatter—I've but said what is in my heart."

Berengeria smiled back at him. "A flattering prankster, that is what you are, but still, you're pleasant company. Now will you grant a few more songs to season all your hyperbolic words?"

To Berengeria's disappointment, he shook his head. "I think not, noble Lady. I have done my duty here and helped restore your spirits. Even more, these faces here . . ." he gestured toward the ladies surrounding him. "These smiling faces tell me I have had success and sung good songs. I learned long years ago the danger of remaining for too long upon the floor. I'll not attempt to stay too long, for that would risk your boredom. After all, my songs are sage and allspice—flavorings. I dare not try to make a meal of them."

The handmaidens in the room showed their disappointment with sighs and Berengeria did the same. Still, she could see that Arcite's performance had tired him, so great had been his effort. So she did not argue. "I will not make you sing against your will. But you must promise to return to us each day and bless us with new songs. Will you do that?"

He flushed with pleasure. "Indeed, I will."

"Now I will give a gift to you." She turned to Daphne. "Please bring my jewelcase."

To Berengeria's surprise, Arcite stopped her. "No, no Princess. I do not need your jewels, nor do I want them. They are not of you; their surfaces are cold and hard."

"But one small ring would bring you wealth and would provide for you for many days."

"I shall receive it if it is your wish. But still, fair Princess, I do not want your wealth."

Berengeria looked into his eyes. He was a young man, but not too young—no more than a year or two from her own age. To learn his art, he must have traveled with other minstrels about the Thlassa Mey since his childhood. But he did not have the look of a minstrel now, nor any kind of subordinate; his face bore the stamp of command. His expression would have been offensive on the face of any other commoner. "Please take the ring," she said. "And if you see a better gift which you find fitting, you may have that, too."

"Indeed, I'd have a finer gift from you." His eyes met hers. "If you'd present that better gift to me, extend your hand."

Berengeria did so. To her surprise, Arcite knelt and took it in his own. "I now will place my lips against this hand in a most humble and subservient kiss. But just the back of it may my lips touch; I do not claim the worthiness to kiss the palm or any other part." He kissed the back of Berengeria's hand tenderly, then clasped it between both of his.

To her surprise, Berengeria heard clapping once

again. She blinked, looked about, and saw all her hand-maidens applauding Arcite's wit and gallantry. When he released her hand, she could not keep herself from applauding also. He was a fascinating man; his every move was a performance, yet there was no real falsehood or undue pride about him.

He stood, vowed he would return the next day, and walked from the chamber. Berengeria watched him go until the door closed behind him, then she rose and went to fetch her Book of Hours. All the while she softly hummed the melody of the last song he had sung. His music had filled her with a new spirit. The grief of Berethane's affliction and her frustration at being left out of Palamon's quest to find the answer to that spell had been driven from her, at least for the moment. Berethane would be cured, she knew it. She would somehow come to serve her land, and Arcite's music had given her the heart to endure until that time.

Chapter Five:
Navron

SEVERAL EVENINGS AFTER the fall of Hautre, the Buerdic army settled into camp on the east bank of the River Fleuve, a third of the way between Hautre and Buerdaunt. The sun sank toward the west and the playful last light danced off a sea of men, stacked arms, horses, baggage wagons, and the lavish tents of the few nobles who had remained with the force.

Most of the lords who had besieged Hautre had already ridden toward Buerdaunt and had left the marching soldiers and the baggage far behind. But Ursid remained. He knew his men, knew they were loyal to him. They were his limbs, his troops, his father, mother, bride; and most of all, his children. The clatter and warmth of the camp would be displaced all too soon by the sly chatter of the court.

Palamon had escaped him, at least for the time. That was the worst; fate had denied him his great object. He had not been allowed to look on the tall monarch's face at some great moment of Carean defeat. Ursid had won victories, he had brought riches back to Buerdaunt, but the war had been an even affair overall. Now any chance for total victory was gone. Peace was a terrible thing.

47

He would make the best of it. Some opportunity had
to await him, years down the path of life; Palamon could
not elude him forever. Ursid consoled himself with that
thought as he sat in his tent, writing dispatches. He
would dispose of his force for the time being; so many
men were to be discharged to their former lives as serfs,
so many knights assigned to his personal entourage, so
many to other nobles. But Lothar the Pale was a child-
less monarch and Ursid was his nearest blood relation.
Once the throne of Buerdaunt passed to him, Carea and
its King would never escape his wrath.

Diomedes entered the tent and interrupted his dark
thoughts. The burly servant ambled toward him with the
air of someone toting up a list of errands. "We've made
our camp for the night in good order, my Lord," Diomedes said. "The Counts of Jolier and Galliardy are in
their own pavilions and the common soldiers are ready
for the night."

"That's well," Ursid replied. "And all our hostages,
how do they fare?"

Diomedes smiled and shrugged. "They fare well
enough. Lady Alcyone, the Baron's daughter, would like
to talk to you."

Ursid sneered. "Then she may wait until we've
reached Buerdaunt. My Diomedes, never place your
faith in female hostages. When they converse with you,
it's so that they can place your manly instincts at their
call. I spoke unto a female hostage once; it was my mon-
umental error. I will let this maiden wait—she'll speak
before our King and in a room that's full of witnesses."

But voices outside the tent interrupted Ursid. Mutter-
ing started up outside, then grew so loud that neither
Ursid nor Diomedes knew what it could mean, coming
from an encamped army.

"What's happening without?" Ursid asked.

"I don't know. It was all quiet when I walked through
camp before."

"Go out and see and bring me back the tale of what
might cause this murmuring. If I am needed to put order

in this camp, then I will rise. But if it is a matter that you can attend yourself, do that for me."

Diomedes bowed and left. He was gone for some moments and when he came back, he bore a perplexed expression. He walked in slowly and rubbed his short beard.

"Well? Tell me what it is."

"I can't rightly tell you that. I think we're being serenaded from across the river, though why that would happen is more than I can guess."

Ursid studied the servant's face, then stood. "This makes no sense to me." He wore neither shirt nor doublet and scars trailed in every direction across his body. They were an enlarged reflection of the ones which marred his face.

He donned a gambeson against the coming chill and the stares of his men, then walked into the evening air. He found his soldiers still sitting at their campfires, each man motionless, each man staring across the river which flowed a half-league downhill from them. He had watched these same men earlier in the day and they had practically collapsed where they had halted their march. Even after they had rested and made camp, they had lain about, talking, napping, making display of their fatigue. But now every one sat up alertly and they all gazed toward the west.

Ursid tried to follow their eyes but the setting sun blinded him; nothing faced his eyes but glare and the empty, black shadows of the far bank. What were his massed Buerdic soldiers looking at?

A cluster of men stood at his approach. "What causes all these mutters?" he asked.

One of the men haltingly replied. "I don't know what it was, my Lord. It was a woman, I think, but it was so far away I couldn't swear what she really was. And she sang to us, though if you asked me directly, I couldn't actually say I heard her singing. It's just that she struck me as being a woman and it seemed right that she should be singing."

"The man who jokes at me shall risk his life."

The fellow sat down quickly but one of the other men protested. "No, sir. We aren't joking. But wait; the sun's setting. After it's gone and the glare's faded, maybe you can look for yourself. There's not much you can see looking into the light that way."

Ursid waited impatiently until the sun passed below the rim of the horizon—but as it disappeared, the shadows on the far bank became even darker than before. Even so, one of the men shouted, "Look. There, she's just a white speck."

Ursid stared until his eyes watered but he could see nothing distinct. Were his men playing a prank? That could not be: the whole camp was staring across the river as if a thousand men had only a single set of eyes. Ursid looked across the mass of them once more, then strode back to his tent. "Fetch clothing," he ordered Diomedes. "I will ride across that stream and find what thing makes soldiers into dreamers."

He threw on clothes for riding, then sent Diomedes to prepare a horse. It would take too long to saddle one of Ursid's own light palfreys; instead, the *aide-de-camp* brought back one of the sentry's horses, still sweating from picket duty. Ursid leaped onto it and set off toward the river at a smart trot.

He covered the distance quickly but when he reached the river's bank, all he could see across the flowing waters were sand, grass, shrubs, and trees. He could see nothing that lived. It was all very perplexing.

A massive curiosity rose up in him. What could have affected his men that way, what could have set his entire camp to buzzing? He looked down at the water as it faded to a pale blue ribbon between two black shores. Fording a river at the onrush of evening was folly—but sometimes folly was the only way a man could attain his goal. He spurred the animal and it splashed into the stream.

It really was foolhardy to explore some unknown river in the face of the wakening night. Then his ears caught a faint sound, a kind of wailing, a singing sweet to the ears but tinted with a melancholy note that set his nerves on edge. He looked across the river; he could see nothing. But he had heard the song his men only thought they had heard. Whatever else, they had not lied to him.

So he rode on and reached the far bank without difficulty. He cantered his horse along the sandy shore and peered into the trees, but could see nothing unusual. He had not even thought to provide himself with a torch—and now darkness had fallen and the camp he had left was nothing more than pinpricks of light in the distance. It would be useless for him to dismount and search for footprints; he could barely make out his horse's ears against the gathering gloom.

He paused. Though his curiosity raged, he debated whether to spend the night sleeping on the riverbank before continuing his search in the morning. But he no longer even considered going back to his own cot.

He rode on, letting his horse pick the way. Brush crunched beneath the animal's hooves and Ursid could make out looming shapes; leafy thickets passed close at hand. He forced the horse onward, the brush closed around him, and the lights of his camp disappeared from view. He had no idea where he was going.

But another light gathered itself behind him. Looking back, he could tell the moon would soon rise and that it would be full when it did. So he would not be lost, at least. He would somehow find his way even if he pressed through this brush and into the night.

Then he broke through the brush and the wall of a city rose up before him like a vision before a pilgrim. The fickle moonlight played off towers and along decayed, crumbling battlements; fantastic buildings loomed beyond the wall. But all stood silent and dead. Not even a cricket spoke; no sentry rattled arms or flashed a lantern, no night bird called against the silence.

He reined in his horse and stared. He had studied his maps carefully; no city stood in this place. That was why he had ordered his army to pitch camp here. But this city stood before him now, a broad swath of structures which contained nothing more alive than pale stones that reflected the moon's weak light.

He shook his head against his shock and consternation. It was only a dead, deserted city and no patrol would appear. Though mysterious and unnerving, the place was as harmless as a hermit's grave. No living form paced the wall, no road led to the gate, and as he moved nearer, he could see that the gate itself had rotted and fallen in. Curiosity drew him on; he guided his horse toward the opening.

But the animal reared and whinnied; Ursid fought to keep his seat as it thrashed its forelegs and surged beneath him. With a litany of curses, he gave up trying to calm the creature, dismounted, and tied its reins to a bit of brush. Once it seemed to realize he would take it no closer to the dead city, it quieted. It stood where he tied it, though its eyes still bulged and tremors of fear shook its flanks.

He drew his sword and crept toward the rotted gate, then peered in at the square visible beyond it. He could tell guards had once stood their watches at the portal: a brace of skeletons lay before the crumbling timbers, their disjointed bones mingled with the decayed shafts of the halberds they had once wielded. But however he listened, no sound entered his ears; not even a mouse crawled among the bones.

The urge to go on tugged at him. He felt a desire to pass the rotting gate and explore the city but he also found, to his amazement, that he had become afraid. One part of his mind was no more anxious to proceed than his horse had been. The sweat beaded on his forehead and he wiped it away, chilly in the moonlight. He was brave; he knew he was brave, but the streets beyond the gate gaped and leered at him as if they waited, as if they harbored some unknown horror, some unspeakable surprise which hid itself to leap out at him.

"A magnificent sight, is it not?"

Ursid's heart somersaulted in his breast as he whirled toward the voice and clawed for his sword. He came face-to-face with a man he knew—Navron, the evil, plotting minion to the insane sorcerer, Alyubol. He blinked with relief that it was nothing more, though Navron himself was a sinister sight.

Ursid thought to challenge the leering face in front of him but the evil mystic spoke before he had the chance. "Your bravery is great, Buerdic Prince. There are only a few who would stand on this ground before Kruptos without seeking safety in flight."

"Then what could keep you here, you useless man? This city must be evil to the stones for you to find an interest therein. Pray tell, what is your purpose here? Why do you lurk in darkness and accost me?"

Navron smiled and the evil which filled him reflected its black nature in his expression. Evil. That was the fellow's trade, after all—the transport and sale of evil. Even though Ursid had once done business with this man's master, the stink of such evil made the young Prince grimace. But the distaste which registered on Ursid's face did not daunt Navron.

Navron gazed past Ursid, up at the towering walls of mystery, and smiled as if in rapture. "Have you not heard of Kruptos, my friend?"

"I've not. What's more, I've never been your friend."

Navron adopted an expression of surprise. "You are saying you never supported my Lord Alyubol? I remember it differently."

"I found myself allied with Alyubol but that was only for a day or two. I did not feel regret at his demise; it rid the world of his great—evil." There was that word again. Ursid put his sword down, though he did not shove it back into its scabbard. He did not trust Navron but neither did he fear the dead-pale face with its thin lips and dark moustache. "The one regret I felt upon the day your master died was not for him. It pained me that the Princess and the Prince of far Carea slipped from my hands. Whatever things I had to do with Alyubol were on account of them, in hopes that he could help me gain her favors."

"You admit, then, that you were his ally?" Navron grinned as he spoke the words, like a barrister producing a confession.

Ursid turned away in disgust. "Faugh. Turn my words whatever way you wish."

But Navron was relentless. "You forget, my dear fellow, the reason behind those two days. You lent your support to my Master for reasons of yours. You are right. He was evil—but evil's a force. Adopt it and you may accomplish all things you desire. Behind evil comes power to gain that revenge you pursue. Now I ask you to join with me; I will make no more pretense. I have followed you here, to this city of Kruptos. I knew its dark mass would appear on this night, for the pale moon is full and the hundred-year-cycle has placed it on this very spot."

"How now," Ursid replied. "You have described this place as if it were a flock of birds or else perchance some constellation of the stars. You act as if it roams and follows cycles, to appear now here, now there, now in some other place."

"So it can."

Ursid's voice deserted him; Navron was even madder than Alyubol had been. Ursid should never have allowed himself to assist the mad wizard five years earlier, even for two days. He certainly would not tolerate the evil wizard's henchman now. Still, he had no reply to Navron's mad words.

"Do you know of the dark deities?" Navron asked.

"I've heard some rumors now and then, of darkling forces which oppose those worshipped by all decent men."

Navron smiled and reached to pat Ursid on the shoulder, but the young Prince stepped back. Again, the gesture of revulsion did not produce any effect. "Very good. You are schooled in a bit of odd lore. I assure you those tales are as firm as the alphabet. Deities unknown to you battled long with the gods many eons ago. But your gods won that war and imprisoned those deities underneath mystical seals for eternity. Now, do you know where those seals may be found?"

"I do not know. And what is more, I do not care."

"But you should, for the seals are in there." Navron

gestured toward the mysterious city's rotted gate, which hung loosely ajar. "At the center of Kruptos stand twelve mighty temples. Therein, all the twelve awful prisons still stand. And my twelve patron gods throb beneath divine locks, only waiting for me and my cult to come worship them."

The idea repelled Ursid. It was horrible, blasphemous. "How could you worship beings such as those which you describe?"

"I am evil. You've said it yourself."

"You're evil and insane. And I should slay you."

But Navron only continued as if Ursid were listening to him raptly. "So this city of Kruptos is prison to deities my cult adores. But seek for those temples, those walls, that wide open gate in the morning, and they will be gone. For this place is divine and accursed; it will fade with the new sun's bright light and will follow its lone, endless course 'round our globe. Once a month it appears, every time in a different location. Every month, at the full of the moon, it is found someplace new. Do you know why you found it?"

"No."

"You've an army encamped on the banks of the river, indeed?"

Ursid nodded.

"And your men heard the singing?"

Ursid stared at the evil man. Yes, his men had heard singing. And Ursid had followed it to this place. "What know you of the singing?"

"It's the lingering spirit of Kruptos; it calls for new souls. If you'd come in the space between the sun's dying rays and the moon's cleansing light, you'd have met that same spirit you sought. And you'd then have been joined with the guards of the city." Navron smiled darkly and gestured once more. This time, his extended finger indicated the two skeletons lying before the rotted gate.

"Those are nought but lifeless bones."

Navron laughed, then he wiped the laugh from his mouth and his gaze stabbed into Ursid like a lance.

"Though you call me a madman and liar, I'm certain you hear with your soul. You believe every word I have uttered. You know this great city remains here before us one night; then day comes and the city fades out of men's view—and those skeletons rise. Those bare bones and the bones of some thousands within walk the long, phantom streets, do the business of this mystic realm while it lingers in hidden dimensions. Go into the city of Kruptos. Remain till the dawn, fail to exit before the sun's rays strike the tallest bell tower, and there you'll remain as a phantom for all of eternity."

The tale was too incredible to be tolerated. Ursid laughed into Navron's face.

"You may laugh at me," Navron said. "Still, solid proof stands before us. Remain through the night; show your courage and linger till dawn. Then we'll see if I've uttered a tale which deserves your derision."

"I welcome such a challenge," Ursid extended his right hand toward Navron as if to shake hands, then he thought better of the gesture and refrained. But he would accept the madman's challenge. "I shall remain upon this place, to see what comes about. When dawn's new sun shines down upon our brows and proves you false, then you shall die—for you shall wait with me. But by the gods, we'll both sit out this night in silence. I will hear no more of your demented words. They make me angry. Make no noise until the dawn, or else my sword shall drink your swinish blood."

Though Ursid's words were deliberately brutal, Navron smiled like a man invited to a banquet. He plainly believed Ursid's threat, for he did not speak again. He pulled his flowing white robe about himself in a contented gesture, turned toward the dark city's gate, and seated himself on the moist ground. For his part, Ursid did not sit. He remained standing, his ears straining to receive every sound, his sword drawn and ready.

The night seemed endless. Silence claimed the forest; no animal stirred except Ursid's horse, which now and again drummed its hooves nervously on the ground. The stars crept across the night sky. Ursid felt sleepy but he refused to yield to the feeling. The white-robed villain opposite him was not to be trusted; Ursid knew his life could end like the flight of a mayfly if he dozed in Navron's company.

After a lifetime of crawling night, the first pink of the new day outlined the trees to the east. Ursid rejoiced that the city remained, though its walls were still dark in shadow. He steeled himself; he had thought long on Navron's wickedness during the night and he intended to carry out the threat he had made. He would have no more compunction about killing the mystic than he would have over cutting the head off a venomous serpent.

The light gained and Navron stood. "Are you prepared to die?" Ursid asked. But Navron did not reply. He only looked at the young Prince, smiled, and pointed toward the dark city's gate.

Ursid followed the gesture. To his amazement, the bones of one of the skeletons lying before the gate stirred like dry leaves. They gathered themselves together as if controlled by strings; joints popped back into place, skeletal fingers wound about the decayed halberd, then the apparition sat. The skull turned and the empty eyeholes stared about. Ursid's blood ran cold; he felt the grip of those eyeless sockets.

The other skeleton gathered itself, stirred, rose. Fleshless bones clicked and clacked and the two ghastly figures paraded before Ursid's disbelieving eyes. And what was worse, he could see many more through the gate; the town had awakened and the streets teemed with unholy life. Then, while Ursid's heart pounded, the two skeleton sentries moved to the crumbling gate, grasped the two sections in lifeless fingers, and drew them to. Rusted hinges creaked a dreary note that thrust ice to the center of Ursid's soul.

A flash of light caused him to look up. The highest tower of the ghastly city glowed from the new day's first sunlight and at that instant the city flickered before him like an image on a pool—and was gone. It had vanished as completely as if it had never existed. In its place stood nothing more than the trees and shrubs of an empty forest.

Ursid's mouth fell open. He had seen it; it could not have happened, yet he had seen it. He tried to convince himself his senses had lied, but Navron's triumphant face assured him that was not so. Kruptos was a magical city indeed, a vile place filled with unknown forces. If Navron had said it was the prison of the dark gods, Ursid could have no reason to doubt him.

"You've seen for yourself that dark Kruptos continues its trek." Navron said. "In a month, on the night that the moon becomes full, it will stand once again, but some leagues from this place. East of Tranje will be the new site."

Ursid looked at Navron sourly. "The very sight of your thin, grinning face insults and goads me, knave. I've neither stomach nor desire to hold a conversation with you. Foulness is your meat—you stand as far from knighthood's honest standards as Buerdaunt from far Carea. I have seen the sight you wished my eyes to see. Now what is that to me?"

"We can help one another."

"How?"

Navron hesitated. When he spoke again, it was with a sly, sidelong look. "Your great enemy, Palamon, holds in his sway a sword."

"The *Spada Korrigaine*," Ursid interrupted. "I saw it given to him as a gift."

Navron nodded. "You're aware of the weapon, I know. Now for years, he has kept it well guarded within his tall castle. Nor battle nor high ceremonies induced him to break the iron bands which secured it."

"If this past war'd continued, he'd have needed it."

"Tush," Navron said. Then he went on. "Alyubol would have imagined a way to regain it—but while he lies dead, all his genius is lost. Still, he left behind potions and charms. Our cult's growing by leaps and by bounds—I've instructed my cohorts to take one such magic and use it 'gainst Palamon. I'm convinced that if I could excite and enrage him enough, he would take down the weapon, would use it. That is just what has passed—so now I and my followers have a good chance to secure it—outside of his castle, he's vulnerable."

"What can that mean to me?"

"We both need one another. You wish for the death of tall Palamon, I need the sword."

"Why?"

Navron hesitated. "There is treasure within the dark city, beneath the same seals I described to you earlier. Only that sword has the power to open each seal, to expose gold and monies beyond a man's dreams."

"What care I for such a foolishness?"

"I did not lie before when I told how the city would vanish." Navron waited. But Ursid had no answer, so the mystic continued. "Tall Palamon's sailed for Danaar and he carries the sword. If we both worked together..."

Ursid interrupted. "Now listen, knave. If I could bring some harm to Palamon, I'd look the foulest forces of this world full in the face and never flinch. But still, I do not trust you. Tell me all; I think you're holding back. Are not these same dark gods you have described imprisoned by the seals you plan to split?"

"Yes, indeed. They are there." Navron's hooded eyes twinkled in the light of the new day. But they did not twinkle the way a young maiden's eyes would twinkle at a ball, or the way a child's eyes would twinkle. Theirs was the twinkle of something sinister, brooding deeply, lurking, waiting to be set free. "Leave the Dark Ones to me. We will humble old Palamon and all of his family. Why, I might even have plans for his sister; does that interest you?" He looked into Ursid's eyes but Ursid only glared back at him, so he continued. "You'll gain wealth far beyond your most covetous dreams. I myself..." He chuckled. "I will have at my call the most powerful forces imaginable. I'll be easily able to stroke all my friends and then punish my enemies." He laughed again. There was the light of madness in his eyes; it glittered like the madness that had lurked behind the eyes of Alyubol.

"Um. Why do you need me?"

"I have stirred up a brew to bring Palamon hence, and his mighty sword with him. He's vulnerable, as I have said—but we must work together to pry him away from the sword. All your interests repose in alliance with me —shall we play for the highest of stakes, for control of the universe?" Navron's breath came hoarsely and his eyes devoured Ursid.

"You answer me with generalities and useless phrases," Ursid shouted. "I have no need to make a pact with you. I'll gain my vengeance in the way I choose."

Navron giggled. "But such ways are now closed to you. Peace has begun its long reign. Our two needs blend together like spices and wine. Think again. There is time to decide, but not much. I will come to you when you have made your return to Buerdaunt. I will ask you again. Think on all of the things you have seen and then answer my plea."

Ursid stared at the man. He was truly evil, loathsome, and mad. "I have no need of such a human maggot as yourself. Make your query when I've reached Buerdaunt, but do so in the knowledge that you'll die when next I see you. You are quite as mad and dangerous as any rabid dog." The young Prince turned away and began to untie the reins which had restrained his horse all night. The animal stamped as Ursid hauled at the leather lines.

Navron followed him and touched his shoulder, but the younger man turned on the older. "Avaunt, you evil spirit. Keep away. Why do you so pursue me? How can you so fearlessly attempt seduction of a stalwart man, protector of Buerdaunt? Did not you hear the threat I laid against you? Can you not believe my words? Away from me, or I'll not wait until the time I next confront you. I'll strike you down this instant. Flee me or prepare to feel the bite of pitiless, cold steel." Then the Prince turned back to his horse. He mounted and headed the animal toward the River Fleuve, his encamped army, and the men he trusted.

Chapter Six:
Danaar

THE CITY OF Danaar loomed over the waves where the River Fleuve flowed into the Thlassa Mey. It was a hive of merchants hidden behind a sooty stone wall. It lacked the ancient grandeur of Buerdaunt or the hillside stateliness of Upper Carea but it was well chosen as a meeting place between the two kings: it had remained loyal to neither side during the war.

The allegiances of Danaar had swung back and forth, levered by whichever land seemed to have the greatest chance of winning the war. Danaar was a city of merchants. Loyalty and military support were commodities there, to be bought and sold the same as any other product with a tempting market price. And while that made Danaar a poor ally, it made her the ideal site for a confrontation between two rulers who did not trust one another.

Sharks swam in the bay. Palamon saw them as his Carean galley labored toward Danaar's stinking waterfront. The River Fleuve emptied the detritus of all the northern Greenlands into the Thlassa Mey, as well as the refuse from the city itself; Palamon was not surprised to see the bloated shape of a dead horse bobbing among the

waves. All about, lesser debris speckled the water and
the stench rose from the bay strongly enough to turn a
man's stomach. The black fins which cut the surface
showed the numbers of the deadly fish; they fed in the
bay like trout enjoying a hatch.

Flin climbed up to the galley's sterncastle and stood
beside Palamon. The younger man looked natty as
always; he had wrapped his legs in dark breeches rather
than tights, his doublet was studded with shining squares
of brass, and he had neatly trimmed and oiled his hair.
Palamon smiled to see him. Like his wife Bessina, Flin
was vain, but his love of himself was somehow charming. It fitted him; it perfectly matched his love for life in
general. No problem ever existed for Flin, and for that
reason, if for no other, Palamon had selected him as
companion on this expedition.

Flin the Brigand he was called and he had earned that
title through years of riding those same Greenlands
which the ship now approached. But he was plainly not
thinking of his past as he stood beside Palamon. "Nasty
fishies," he said, following Palamon's gaze to the backs
of a couple of sharks which knifed toward a swollen carcass of unknown nature. "That's grim sport if ever I saw
it."

"The place itself is grim," Palamon replied. "Well was
this chosen for a meeting 'twixt myself and Lothar; there
are no delights to cause distraction."

Flin laughed. "That hardly recommends it. Remember, some of us have to pass away the hours while
you two have your tug-of-war. But delights lie where you
find them. This is a seaport, after all, so I think I'll find a
distraction or two."

Palamon smiled at the younger man. "I'm sure you're
right."

The beat of the hortator's drum rang through the
ship and Palamon could feel the vessel surge against
the current as six dozen rowers labored to force it
up the constricted river. Quays jutted into the waters
like blades and both men were surprised to see throngs
of people line the waterfront to watch the galley

land. They cheered lustily, children jumped up and down to get better views of the foreign royalty, and maidens even threw flowers toward the approaching ship. Flin caught one bouquet and grinned back at the comely lass who had hurled it; Palamon had to smile all over again. The young rogue's reach included women he had never even met.

Straining sailors shoved the brow—the ship's gangplank—toward the dock and a company of soldiers struggled to keep the enthusiastic mob away from the shoreward end. Danaar had not suffered during the war as had the inland fiefs and the Greenlands; the people of this city did not show the bitterness toward the visiting kings which might have marked some other place. Palamon felt himself flush at all the attention.

They met a delegation from the local ruler, Count Destus. Palamon and Flin mounted the horses which had been brought for them, the knights of their escort mounted, and they rode through streets lined with the cheering and the curious.

The commotion and the crowds made Palamon nervous. Flin, however, loved it. He beamed and waved at the throng as the two men rode toward the center of the city. And the sight of Flin bathing in the crowd's reception made Palamon feel a little better. "From your response to all this civil noise, I swear they'll think you King instead of me."

"Nay, my Lord," Flin replied. "You are legendary, I can vouch for that. But you can be sure I'll take all the adulation I can get. I'll gladly accept any that might roll off you."

"These folk would cheer the Prince of Thieves himself if he should pass along this street today. In fact, were they to cease their shouting, I would wager you could hear the cheers for Lothar from the streets most near the inland gate. If he arrives behind us, you will hear them then, although he would have burned this town and all its people if they'd ever blocked his path."

"Wave back to them anyway," Flin said. "You'll enjoy it."

Palamon laughed at Flin's manner and waved to the crowd. But still, he could not really enjoy himself. A little pleasure lay in such adulation, but not enough to erase from his soul the bruises which lingered there. Berethane lay bewitched, stiff in his bed in Upper Carea. Palamon's hand fell to his side. His face became grim and he spoke quietly to Flin. "You jest with me and I appreciate it. Still, I must remind you, I did not embark and journey to this place for cheers or conference or for the building of the peace. I seek the secret to reverse that same enchantment which has seized my son and threatens his young life. For all the cheers which any throng may hurl at me, I swear you are the only person who can bring an earnest smile onto my lips."

Flin looked at the tall monarch in surprise and a new grin spread across his lips. "Why, thank you."

Palamon again held up his hands to the crowd, but he took no joy from it. "Do not thank me; it is a well-known truth. But do not do it all too often. That could turn upon itself and anger me."

Then Palamon went silent as one face in the crowd seized his attention. For less than a moment, he saw a strikingly familiar woman standing at the back of the crowd. He could not place her features; she appeared only for a few blinks of the eye, mouthed a sequence of words, then disappeared into the milling throng. She had light hair, wide eyes, fair skin, and the garb of a priestess. The phrases which remained in his mind seemed more than she had actually uttered. "The balance teeters at the middle point; diplomacy tells all. His fate awaits you south and east of Tranje, but there's still another route."

"What happened to you?" Flin asked. "You were lecturing me, then you went quiet."

"I thought I saw someone."

Flin looked where Palamon had been staring. "I see a lot of someones."

"No, that is not my meaning." Palamon fell silent again; the face and the words mystified him. "The balance teeters at the middle point; diplomacy tells all. His fate awaits you south and east of Tranje, but there's still another route." Had the woman spoken of his son, Berethane, or did Palamon even understand her meaning? What about Tranje—Arcite the Balladeer hailed from Tranje; could he be the subject of the sentences? "The balance teeters at the middle point." What balance? Would Palamon's confrontation with Lothar the Pale tilt it further to the good or toward the foul? and "There's still another route?" What did that mean?

He had seen some kind of vision, he was sure of that. But each word of it bred a new question and he knew the answers to none of them. For all that, he was both chilled and elated as his party made its way through throngs which he no longer even noticed.

The horses clopped toward the center of the town. Palamon's guard of Carean knights surrounded him and ahead of them rode Count Destus' men. Hidden in a leather case behind his saddle, Palamon carried the *Spada Korrigaine*. Even at that, and for all the crowd, he hardly felt overarmed for a jaunt through these streets. His eyes combed through the mob, searching for the face which had whispered the strange message. But the search yielded washerwomen, laborers, dark faces, and desperate men who appeared capable of any act. The mysterious maiden clearly was not going to reveal herself again.

The meeting with Lothar the Pale would take place at Keep Danaar, Count Destus' stronghold, a dank castle which overlooked the city from atop a low bluff. But first, the Carean nobles were taken to a cluster of houses in the center of the town, a villa almost, which appeared to have been built before the city had grown up around it. In fact, as Count Destus' emissary told Palamon, that was exactly the case. "These buildings were constructed centuries ago, before the time of Parthelon, the Emperor who civilized these wild and sprawling lands. This place has been preserved and is a house for nobles who may visit our fair city."

"And Lothar—where will he be staying?" Palamon asked.

"The Buerdic King arrived just yesterday, in company with his youthful Constable, the Prince Ursid. A force of knights and arms arrived with them, some several hundred men. But since they are so many, they cannot be placed within the walls. They've camped upon the plain outside the town. Each day when meetings are arranged, both you and he will ride to Keep Danaar, and there will have your conference."

That was good. Lothar and Ursid had not been allowed to bring their army inside the city's walls. Still, that army itself was a symptom of the distrust lingering between the two lands. And Ursid—Palamon had not looked on Ursid since Alyubol had died five years earlier. He had never faced Ursid during the war—but he had heard of the young Prince's exploits on the field of battle; Ursid's hatred for Palamon and Carea was popular lore along the Thlassa Mey. But Ursid did not matter. The Buerdic King was the man best able to answer Palamon's questions, most likely to know the story behind Berethane's demise. Palamon frowned and spoke again to Count Destus' Chamberlain. "When does the conference begin?"

"Tonight, Sire."

"I'll not wait. I wish to go to Keep Danaar immediately, there to closet with the Buerdic King."

Count Destus' Chamberlain seemed to swallow several words before he could speak again. "Your Grace, I said that it has been arranged for you to meet tonight. You must have need to bathe and change your clothing ere you meet with him. High Keep Danaar will still be standing when the evening comes."

"I smile dark smiles at your delaying words. The image of my prostrate son is ever in my mind; I am refreshed and bathed enough for now. I'll have a private talk with Lothar and I shall not wait. So get you off to make arrangements."

The troubled man went away and a short time later, fresh horses were brought for Flin, Palamon, and the Carean knights. "I have to hand it to you," Flin said brightly as they mounted. "You've ruined at least one man's day already."

"I never claimed to know diplomacy. But if I trouble all the Buerdic lords as much as I have troubled him, perhaps I might at least claim some small skill in haggling—more than I thought I e'er possessed."

One of Palamon's knights handed up to him the leather sheath housing the *Spada Korrigaine* and the tall monarch unwrapped the great weapon. The sun glinted off the blade and its flash filled the villa's little courtyard. As always, the sword produced many gasps of admiration.

But the weapon caused another stir when the Chamberlain returned to them. He told them with a relieved look that King Lothar had consented to the unscheduled meeting, but his face became bleak once more as his eyes lit on the *Spada Korrigaine*. He looked as if he were on the verge of tears. "Your Grace," he said. "For all your royal titles, I cannot allow you to retain that mighty weapon if you are to stand before the Buerdic King."

"Oh, no?"

The poor fellow's tone was apologetic almost to the point of groveling. "It is the ancient law and custom of our court—no weapon is allowed before the Count or any noble visitor unless it can be kept beneath a cloak. You do not go to battle in our halls—the Buerdic party made that point with emphasis. A longsword might you wear if you must have a blade upon you. But if it pleases you, you should not bear that fearsome weapon. Let it stay behind."

Palamon frowned as he looked at the glittering, deadly length of the *Spada Korrigaine*. "It does not please me, sir, to leave this blade behind me in this foreign city. How am I to know I am secure unless I bear the weapon of my choice?"

"You are secure within these quarters," the Chamberlain protested. "And the high Count's forces guarantee your safety."

"Do they? What if there is treachery?"

The poor man appeared to be almost on the verge of
tears. "Please, Sire. It is a custom long observed within
our halls, and also in your own fair land. You must
comply, if only for the sake of lasting peace."

Palamon sighed. Reluctantly, he handed the sword
back down and instructed a quartet of his guards. They
would take it back to his chambers and maintain a vigi-
lant watch until he returned.

One of his knights handed him a longsword and a
scabbard and he contented himself with that as the pro-
cession started toward Keep Danaar. Palamon remembered these dark streets—he had spent many months in
Danaar during the terrible years after he had left the
Knights of Pallas and before he had learned of his royal
heritage. Even then, with all the tumult his life had seen
up to that time, he could not have dreamed the twisted
course events would take. So now he was back in Danaar, seeking some clue to the strange malady which had
seized his son.

No cheering throngs lined the streets this time, no
flower petals floated down on him from rooftops. His
demand for an immediate meeting had left his hosts unprepared; his party was met only by streetfolk, who
stopped to stare at the strange uniforms of his escort.
Their mouths dropped open as they realized they had
seen the Carean monarch. But the silence did not bother
Palamon—he had never felt himself molded to be a king.
He had no love for cheering throngs or the ceremony
they demanded. He thought more about the face he had
noticed earlier.

It was only past noon when they arrived at the gates
of Keep Danaar. Palamon noted that the honor guard
which greeted him had been hastily assembled; he also
noted the cobbled paving which surrounded the citadel.
That alone bore mute testimony to the age of the fortress; in former ages, he knew, the ridge's summit had
been a grassy common, the same type of green which
surrounded Castle Conforth in Upper Carea. But Danaar
had grown over the centuries and all that surrounded
Keep Danaar now were houses, stables, and paving.

The gate swung open and the castle's walls embraced the Careans like cold arms. Palamon reined in his mount, dismounted, and attendants led the horses away while the party walked toward one of the central towers. As for the tall monarch's escort, those staunch men were taken to the castle's kitchens to receive a fresh meal, since it drew close to time for the afternoon's repast.

The Chamberlain led them below a low archway and along a corridor, the stone walls of which were dark and slick with age. Then the corridor broadened into a well-lit anteroom which contained a quartet of trumpeters. The four men raised their instruments and blew a loud series of notes, then a deep-voiced herald stepped to the oak doors and cried, "The noble Palamon, King of Carea." The doors swung open as if by magic.

When they entered the chamber, Palamon found it round and high-ceilinged, with walls of quarried granite. The dark stone reflected the light of the torches with little sparkles, for it had been highly polished and contained much mica stone. But it reflected little actual light; the impression was of a dark but starry sky. The room was nearly empty and the few men present all fell silent at Palamon's entry.

At the far end of the room stood a towering dais; on the throne atop it sat a white-haired, pale-skinned man, who gazed down at Palamon with a face barren of emotion. But as Palamon approached, the seated man stood and moved slowly, regally, down the steps of the dais. So this was Lothar the Pale's towering throne. Apparently, the Buerdic King had had this replica of his dais in Pomfract Castle quarried and brought to Danaar, so he might be elevated above his courtiers here as he was at home.

The pale monarch made his way silently toward Palamon. He had dressed himself magnificently and the hem of his ermine-lined robe caressed the stone as he moved. His chamber boy followed him; the lad's expression was proud, haughty, even arrogant. Palamon noted the slightness of the Buerdic King's stature, along with the fact that he stopped on the bottom step of the dais to lessen the difference in height between the two of them. Even at that, the pale monarch was so short his eyes barely came to Palamon's throat.

They silently measured one another; and after a moment, Lothar spoke. "We greet you, freshly crowned Carean King. The late war's hard events have not allowed acquaintance 'tween us; now we're pleased you have agreed to see us, though 'twas with small notice."

"My eagerness prevented me from waiting for the proper hour," Palamon said.

Lothar turned his back on Palamon and climbed a step; when he faced the tall monarch again, their eyes were almost even. "So we are informed. We're told a hard event has come on you."

The Buerdic ruler's manner was aloof, almost negligent. Palamon studied the purple cloak which cased the narrow shoulders, the ermine collar which pressed against the neck. He noted the jeweled crown which rested on Lothar the Pale's cornsilk hair. Though the two monarchs were of an age, Lothar was far Palamon's senior in experience. He had ruled for more than a dozen years. Palamon knew the pale ruler enjoyed that fact and looked on Palamon as little more than a rank amateur in affairs of state. Palamon had to smile grimly; it was an accurate assessment.

But accurate or not, the senior monarch's attitude filled Palamon's belly with fire. "Good King," he said. "Be certain that we are not meeting for some diplomatic wrangle, nor discussing any petty county to be ceded to Carea or Buerdaunt, with two additional small pecks of barley added to the royal revenues. I've journeyed to this early meeting to seek the man who struck down my poor son." Palamon glared at the Buerdic monarch and the resentment which filled him put a hard edge on his words. "You speak plain truth: a tragedy has struck my house and I will not attempt to fence with cunning phrases. Many times have you consorted with the evil Alyubol, who knew techniques of foulest magic. Now my son, my tiny, four-year-old son, has been laid low by magic's force. His soulless form lies silent in his bed."

"So have we heard. But Alyubol is dead."

"Then will you swear to me no follower of Alyubol still bears allegiance to you? When I first received my father's throne, I swore the war between our two proud lands would cease. But this I say to you: a war that's ended can still spring to life as quickly as an ill-quenched flame. My son is taken from me. Therefore I tell you that my life will have no meaning till the time a way is found to bring him back to me, and he who did the deed receives his punishment. I greatly hope that you will help me in this quest, and I more fervently bear hopes you had no hand in such a craven deed." Palamon's voice rose until it rang through the chamber. He knew in his heart he would carry out his thinly veiled threats if Lothar the Pale had any part in the catastrophe.

But to Palamon's surprise, a puzzled look came across the Buerdic King's features. "You need not raise your voice toward us, Carean King. We grant we sometimes traded with old Alyubol. But since his death, his followers have scattered. News of your son's fall shocked us as much as anyone about the Thlassa Mey." He leaned forward on the large scepter he carried as a staff and peered into Palamon's face. His bare-chested chamber boy looked out from behind his robes like a naughty child. "How is it that we now are liable for any act of magic which occurs?"

"The spell which took my son displayed the mark of Alyubol's necromancy. All his followers have scattered, that is known. But how may I be sure some one or two have not been scattered into your domain and service?"

"We've never had a thing to do with them." Then, to Palamon's greater surprise, Lothar's expression softened. "Still, bear with us. We do not have an heir; we're not compatible with our fair Queen—thus we may only try to guess the grief your son's affliction causes you. But we can tell you on our honor we will try to help you in your quest to find the man who laid him low." He stepped to the chamber's floor and placed one hand on Palamon's arm. "The time has come when we should go to dinner, for the noble Count has ordered food. It waits for both of us, so let us sit together and discuss what we may do for you. How might we prove no tree within our realm can shelter any man so base that he has cast a spell to grieve your family?"

The mild reply left Palamon speechless. Lothar the Pale's considerate manner was the one reaction the tall monarch would never have expected. Was the Buerdic King sincere or was he hiding something? Palamon had no answer; he only realized that his anger had been turned, that he was losing his grasp on the moment. There could be no doubt that Lothar was as much a master of these word games as Palamon was a rank beginner.

Count Destus appeared then and escorted them from the chamber while a chorus of trumpets cried through the halls. Rows of tables had been laid in the great hall; scores of knights and nobles had already seated themselves. Torchlight glinted off armor, flagons of wine, and eating utensils. The dying notes of the trumpets brought a clatter of armed men standing as the two Kings entered the room. Lothar, Palamon, and Flin followed Count Destus toward the table at the head of the chamber and Palamon saw the Buerdic King speak shortly to one of his nobles. "Where's the Constable?"

The noble replied in a muted voice. "He treats with all the knights who have encamped outside the city's walls. But we have sent a messenger to him and he should soon arrive."

"We'd have him with us during all these sessions."

The noble hurried away and the Count and the two Kings took their places behind the chairs assigned to them. Another clatter followed as the nobles at the tables resumed their own places. For his part, Palamon felt ill-at-ease. If Lothar and Buerdaunt had nothing to do with Berethane's sad state, who did?

So Palamon fretted and stewed while the feast began in barbaric splendor. Servants brought slabs of roast beef and lamb, fish, fowl, and heaping platters of boiled vegetables. Bands of jesters, fools, and jongleurs roamed the hall to tell bawdy stories or perform feats of balance or juggling; clowns capered and carried on. Pantomine, comedy, and singing vied for space with huge hounds that wandered between the banquet tables, licking greasy hands and fighting over bones.

Then the trumpets sounded and a herald's voice filled the chamber. "The noble Constable of fair Buerdaunt has now arrived." Palamon looked up and saw a young man standing at the rear of the hall, tall and richly clothed. It was Ursid, the Buerdic Prince who had once courted Berengeria. And from the look on the young Prince's face, it was plain that he also recognized Palamon. His eyes blazed with hatred's dark flames.

Chapter Seven:
In the Maze

THE SUN SMILED down on the royal gardens of Castle Conforth. Hedges, flowerbeds, and manicured rose-bushes sprawled in the happy light, flushed with the bloom and blossom of the young summer. Greenery filled the gardens from the castle's central towers to the outer curtain wall; that greenery formed a sea of delight which lapped against the massive foundations of the great citadel.

A newcomer to the garden could easily have lost himself among the endless mazes, terraces, and little groves of fruit trees. The place cast the aura of an enchanted haven, a fragrant celebration of summer, a spicery for delightful court picnics in honor of the pleasant season. Couples strolled among the hedges, musicians wandered behind them to fill the air as full of music as it was of fragrance, and children tore about, playing tag on the lawns and in the mazes.

At the center of the largest maze lay a little pond where frogs sang their deep-throated songs at night and ducks and swans plied the quiet waters by day. It was a lovely setting; nobles who wandered the maze for the first time often cried out in delight as they emerged from the green byways into the colorful sanctuary.

On the afternoon of the picnic, the lawn about the pond was graced by young women who promenaded through the greenery like lovely fowl or sat listening to the troubadour who sang at the water's edge. And at the center of those who were seated, Princess Berengeria reclined on a low couch, propped up on one elbow. Her eyes rested on the singer. To anyone who might look, she appeared to gaze at him with rapt attention; only she knew she hardly even saw him as she pondered the subjects which fretted her.

Where was Palamon? What had he found, what had he learned; would he lay hands on the man who could cure little Berethane? She would not know until his galley returned to the great harbor of Lower Carea. But though all she could do was wonder, she did that with a vengeance.

She still sagged at the thought of Palamon leaving her in Carea with her serving-maids while he took Flin along to share the excitement of the quest. But he was her beloved brother and she could never put him far from her heart. She had watched him on the day Berethane had been born; she had observed him while the child had grown, learned to walk, then learned to speak. Now Berethane lay cold and silent in one of the towers which looked down on the garden. Poor Palamon.

She knew Palamon would succeed; he always did. But what price would he pay in the coinage of despair before he achieved that success? She knew he would never tell her the final tally, and likely would not tell Lady Aelia. He did his aching privately. Even those closest to him were not privy to what lay hidden in his heart.

Her train of thought brought a little smile to her lips. Had Palamon not left her behind, had he not felt the chagrin of leaving her out of his quest, he might not have sent Arcite to her chamber. The minstrel was a treasure, the one bright light of the last few days. His songs had become the center of each day; he plied his lute for her in her chambers, in the gardens, at meals. He never sang for long at one time but each melody was like a new gem set into the crown of her soul.

Her smile faded. Arcite, though he might be a musical wonder, was also a commoner. She was a Princess; her duty was to the Crown. She would need to take care; she could not sully her brother's court by keeping the handsome musician about her too much.

Her eyes slipped shut but, oddly enough, that did not keep her from seeing. A wind rose and the clouds raced before it, gathered, blotted out the sun. She felt herself shiver. The waters of the pond became restless and little waves lapped greedily at the shore.

The waves drew her attention, mesmerized her, seemed to wash onto the shore as if pushed by some new and evil hand. She could not look away. Then something scuttled from the water, a crayfish the size of a frog, its shell pale as flesh rotting in a slough. Its pincers clicked and clacked as it made its way across the ground. A second one followed it, and another. The three of them made a revolting little parade.

Other creatures followed the three crustaceans; a militia of bugs and vermin writhed from the water. Worms slithered onto the shore. Clumsy crickets with ribbed shells leaped and sprawled, giant cockroaches, millipedes, spiders, and mantises crawled toward her. All of them were pasty pale, the color of death—of slime. Was this a vision—if so, what caused it? Whatever the case, she could not oppose it, could not make it go away. It all revolted her; she felt her stomach leap with nausea as the repugnant swarm approached.

Then a bird's song caused her to lift her head and she realized with relief that she had dozed off. But even at that, the dream's image lingered in her mind, a repulsive shadow which made her mouth curl in distaste. The sweat stayed moist on her forehead and her skin had gone cold and clammy. It was a dream, a dream, but she would remember it a long time.

She rubbed her eyes. The lawn lay empty beneath the warm sun; all her maids-in-waiting had left her in the company of the swans and the bees. From a distance, across the rows of hedge that formed the maze, she could hear the tinkle of chimes and female laughter.

"Ah, you've awakened. You have only slept a little time. Now are you feeling well?"

Berengeria looked about to see Arcite the Balladeer standing at the border of the hedge behind her. He gazed at her and a smile lay across his fair features. The sight of him drove away the creeping images of her dream but she was still perplexed: why was he allowed in this place when her maids-in-waiting had left? She had to fumble after words. "My women, sir," she said. "Where have they gone?"

"They went to string the maypole."

"And left me here alone with you? I'll have to speak with all of them—to me it seems uncouth to leave one's Princess sleeping and alone before the eyes of any minstrel."

His smile broadened. "Nay, nay. You cannot blame them, for the Queen gave full permission to attend the day's festivities."

"What? Was she here?"

"Indeed. She trusts me, don't you see? She feels no qualm at leaving me with you, to watch and play my lute while you enjoy your rest. Your ladies say that you have not slept well of late."

"No. Matters trouble me." And this conversation troubled Berengeria; earlier doubts returned. Arcite was a comely fellow and he performed divinely on a host of different musical instruments. But he had come to the Carean court less than a fortnight ago, which seemed a short time for him to gain such a measure of Aelia's trust that she would allow him to wait alone with a sleeping Princess. Still, Aelia had been Berengeria's guardian before she had become Palamon's wife. She devoted herself to Berengeria's well-being and her ability to judge a man was without equal. If she believed Arcite trustworthy enough to gaze at a sleeping maiden, then most likely, he did possess that virtue.

At any rate, he was a pleasant fellow; Berengeria could not argue that point. Why should she take offense?

"Then here we are," she said, stretching. "So come and sing to me a cheerful song."

"I will," he said. "But wait a moment." With a twinkle in his eye, he turned from her and reached into the hedge, while he began a strange whistling. It was a liquid sound, like the warbling of a songbird. He whistled and hummed for a time, then he turned back toward Berengeria and she released an astonished laugh. In his hand, he held an oriole—he had somehow coaxed it out of its hiding place in the hedge. That alone was enough to push the last vestiges of Berengeria's unpleasant dream from her mind.

He walked toward her, beaming. "I cannot always do this," he whispered. "It requires a warm and winelike day, the kind of day that makes all creatures drowsy, full of spring's warm pleasures."

Berengeria stared at him. "I've never in my life seen such a thing. And yet the bird still sings—how did you do it?"

"It's just a trick I learned. It's of no use, but still amusing when it works." He arrived at her side and presented his cupped hands to her. Between his palms, still singing, sat the bird. But when Berengeria reached to accept it, it stopped its music, struggled from his grasp, and fluttered away. "I'm sorry," he said. "It was frightened of you."

Berengeria felt a moment's resentment but then she laughed again. "I see it was. Well, if you have so soft a manner that you coax wild birds from hedges, then I do not need to fear you. Come and sit with me and sing a song, for I am not inclined to join the gaggle at the maypole."

So Arcite relaxed his features into a benign expression and plucked at his instrument.

"One fine day I saw a sparrow, sitting in a tree,
And he was singing to his mistress, chirping lustily.
I asked him how he learned to make such lovely melody.

He told me of the insects which he swallowed
   greedily.
Said I, 'My feathered comrade, I would leap about
   with glee,
If I might see the day that I could sing as well as
   thee.
But if I have to swallow bugs; if that must be the
   fee,
Then I resign myself to living life out silently.'"

Berengeria listened to the little ditty and in so jolly a
tone was it sung that she willingly gave more laughter
when it had ended. Then her smile faded and her eyes
became more serious. The man before her was a true
prodigy at his art; she had never heard anyone make
music to match his. And though it flustered her to put
her thought into words, she longed to hear the song he
had sung for her in her chamber a few days earlier. "Sir
Balladeer, I would that you would sing..." then she fell
silent.

"But ask a song, my Lady, and if it should lie within
my power, you will hear its notes before that swan in
yonder pond has swum another fathom."

"Oh, I know it lies within your power, for I heard you
sing it to my maids and me." She paused again. "And yet
I fear you'd think me vain."

"Impossible." His gaze caressed her and his face
broke into the smile she had seen before. For all its
pleasant nature, this smile seemed to possess a knowing
edge. "You wish to hear the song I made for you."

"I own it flattered me beyond the pow'r of words to
say it. I suppose it's vain of me—I know it is—but that
is still my wish."

"Then have no fear. I am so honored at your pleasure
that I have no thoughts at all. But still, I hope my brain
may function well enough to let that song return to me. I
scarce remember all the words and music."

"You tease me, sir, and well I know it. Still, I'll let
that pass. Your talent gains you latitude."

He grinned and plucked at his instrument. "I know."

Berengeria lay back on her couch and listened to the song Arcite had composed in her honor. It really was vain of her and she knew it, in spite of anything either of them might say to the contrary. And yet the song was so lovely and its very existence was such flattery, she could not refuse herself the luxury of hearing it once again. She would never have asked for it before her maids-in-waiting but she did enjoy hearing it one more time, alone with Arcite.

When the song had ended, she sat up and eyed him with a little smile. "The song is lovely. Can there be no gift which might be grand enough for payment?"

He knelt before her and their eyes locked. They stared at one another for what seemed an eternity, then Berengeria extended her hand for Arcite to kiss, as she had before. But she intentionally turned that member until her palm faced up, revealed to him. The brilliance of his blue eyes poured into the depths of her own and he glanced down, took her hand in his, and placed his lips against the palm. It was only a kiss on the hand, yet she enjoyed it as much as she had ever enjoyed any taste of forbidden fruit.

His lips touched her palm once, then again. He held her wrist firmly and placed a kiss there, then against the inside of her elbow, then on the cloth which covered her shoulder. He was being overbold and she knew it—yet for the life of her, she could not mind. A magic had sprung up between them, the attraction of two vessels drawn toward one another by powerful lines.

Before either of them could speak, he twined her in his arms, his mouth covered her own, and she felt herself return the kiss. It was wrong, it was a selfish indulgence. What would Palamon or Aelia say if they found out? Yet the kiss went on. Her hands settled on the broad span of his shoulders, then wrapped about his neck and she re-turned his embrace.

At last the kiss ended. Their lips parted, their faces separated a finger's length, she gazed into his eyes and felt the sweetness of his breath play across her cheek. "Princess," he said in a halting voice. "I fear the payment is too great. A wealth of songs could not deserve such grand rewarding."

She stared at him and her face fell. She felt her mouth twist as she realized what she was doing; it was more than just a selfish flirtation. She stared at him, then glanced away and stood up.

"I'm sorry, now," she said quickly. "It's time for me to go." She pulled away from him and hurried toward the maze's twisted aisles.

Arcite put down his lute, hurried after her, and caught her by the wrist. "I've been too bold," he said. "But please forgive me. I will swear before the watching gods that I was captured by your luster, maid, and had no more control o'er how I moved than any three-day babe."

Berengeria stared back at him. "You are forgiv'n," she said. "But still I cannot stay. Please entertain this picnic's other guests." She gathered the hem of her gown about her ankles and hurried on. She did not stop until she reached an archway which led into one of the castle's towers. She walked past a startled warden who happened to be counting up a roomful of stores, then made her way up a circling flight of stone steps which took her to one of the inner ramparts of the keep. She walked through another archway and found herself atop a wall, looking down past massive stone crenellations, down onto the gardens she had just left.

Below her lingered Arcite. He stood at the maze's entrance and looked about, searched among the laughing maidens who jammed the garden. He was looking for her; she knew that. He had retreated to pick up his instrument, then had hurried after her through the maze, but had gone slowly because he did not know its wanderings as she did. By all the gods, he was a handsome man. He looked up and his gaze fastened on hers. He hurried toward the tower. His lute bounced and his sword beat against his legs as he started to run, then he disappeared behind a bulge in the stonework. Berengeria did not move. If she ran from him, she knew she would only be running from herself. In only a moment, his face appeared beneath the arch. "Princess, please do not flee."

"I never shall," she said. "But still, we must not see each other anymore."

"Ah, should we not? Am I a leper—or are you? Did that one kiss which passed between us carry some disease?"

"It did."

He looked into her eyes and leaned his head to one side. "What, then? I see no rash, no pockmarks, feel no pain. If we are passing some disease with one small kiss, it is a pretty sickness, so I say."

She scowled at him. "You heartless flatterer. Is not the thing I have to tell you difficult enough without your making play of it? Cannot you see?"

"See what? That you are fair, of pleasing eye, and noble both in face and manner? Yes, I grant a kiss did pass 'tween you and me, an instant's dalliance. But no one saw. What harm's in that? The pleasure it did give to me was so immense, I'd hoped it gladdened you one measly tenth as much as it pleased me. Now let it pass, for we are humans, given much to human whims. There's been no scandal; no one saw your sin."

"It does not matter," she said. "It was weakness of the soul in me, an invitation to some future heartache. I can't let you see me, e'er again."

He reached out and took her hand. "Do not say that. That fate would be too hard for me to bear."

"Oh, how much pleasure lies within your touch, Arcite," she said. "But now I have to draw my hand from you, like this, and back away. You are a heartless rogue —you sense the feeling that I have for you and know full well the impropriety of Princesses who tryst with any common man. Please, let me keep my dignity, do not pursue me."

"Princess," he said. "I cannot keep myself from you. I'll use the word that you avoid—love. Is not it so? You love me just as much as I love you."

"Ah, me," she said. "That word describes it. Yet my soul and body are proscribed from you, as you should realize. If love arises between us, then it must be crushed, for love and marriage to a troubadour is not a fate allowed to me."

"And yet," he said, "You've found no nobleman to love. How many have come courting, to be sent away with tails between their legs?"

"Please, do not mock me."

"I do not."

She turned away from him and looked out over the garden once more. "I'd no idea that rude tale was common knowledge."

"You are famous for it. But if love is mutual between us, then let's tempt the Fates and pledge it to the world."

"Oh, no." She shook her head and laughed rudely. "Oh, heavens, no. I tempted fate one time, five years ago. I tried to love a man when we both knew we were denied to one another by the Fates. The grief and guilt which issued from the wound that love produced have formed a boundary I'll never try to cross again. I've learned my lesson." She looked back at him. "Now I must speak unto the Queen. I have to ask that you be given escort from our land."

His face fell but she did not allow him to interrupt. "Please do not think me hard," she went on. "It must be thus. Arcite, when your red lips pressed down upon mine, it opened up a volume which has lain unread within my soul for many months. I'll use the word I fled a moment back—I love you. I have done so from the time you sang to me that first day in my chamber, yet I never realized it till this day."

A smile spread across his face and the harvest of the smile was a laugh. "What kind and marvelous words. I had not dared to hope you'd ever love me. Let me tell you, then, I'll go you one 'love' better. Why, I loved you even 'ere I met you. When I heard your story from a traveler and later saw a portrait of your face, I loved you then. So greatly did I yearn to meet you that I journeyed to this place. Oh, happy day. What treasure am I granted." He whirled away from her, grasped his lute, and strummed a set of happy chords.

"No, no," she cried. "Have you no ears? There cannot be a love between us. Can't you see? You're but a common man, although it gives me pain to say it. I'm a Princess, lacking in the reach of power to award my favors unto you."

"I love you more than melody, and you love me. So let us wed upon some future date—our story will be one the like of which no man has lived in all history."

She glared at him. Did he have no ears at all, to hear what she had just said? "You fool, it cannot be."

"Why not? Have I not earned the right to love you? Then I shall. Propose a quest for me. Name some great artifact which I must win in some far land and I shall gain it. Anything you ask. The threat of death will not deter me, nor the fang of any dragon. I'll away to do your bidding on the morrow."

"No, no," she said. "Please understand, Arcite, to state this one hard fact again pains me as much as you—I cannot wed a commoner. Please do not look upon me in that way, for it is full as much a curse to me as to yourself." In spite of her anger, she had to pity him. He could not help his station in the world, any more than she could help hers. No matter what she felt, she was Berengeria, Carea's Princess, and she was made up of the principles that had been fed to her since her birth. She could not bring herself to do what flighty Bessina had; she could not marry a man unacceptable to the Counts and Barons of Carea and the realm's royal council. She could not do such a thing to Palamon or Aelia, no matter how much she might love Arcite. "Can you forgive me this refusal?"

He paused, a raft of emotions played across his face, then he scratched the fair blondness of his head. To her surprise, he drew his sword and, before she could react, he knelt before her with the weapon's hilt clasped between his outstretched hands. "If it must be, then so it shall. Here is my sword, which I place ever in your service. I direct the tip at my own breast and tell you: place your hands on mine and push the point into my flesh.

More gladly will I feel the steely tip than leave your blessed side."

"No, do not mock me."

"I do not. If you'll not let me bask in your sweet light, you must present me with a quick and easy death."

She grasped him by the arms and tried to lift him, but was not strong enough. "You know I'd never do it."

"Then you must allow me to remain within these walls. Now hear my vow upon the Muses, who direct my life. My love is Berengeria, who swears to marry both for love and to a man of noble blood. So must it be. To that same goal I now direct myself; may heaven's lightning strike me down if I do not, before the year has passed, find her the man who boasts the qualities required to gain her hand."

She laid an anguished gaze across him. "Please, please Arcite, you must not mock me."

"I do not," he repeated. He stood and put his arms around her. "I've pledged upon my sword a solemn oath to serve you. If I cannot be your mate, then still I shall devote myself to you and to your happiness. But still, allow me now to beg one last and lingering kiss from your fair lips."

His mouth descended and their lips met for the second time that day. Berengeria bathed in the pleasure of it, even while she shook her head at herself. What was she doing—how stupid could she be? He had pledged to forfeit his life if he did not find her a nobleman whom she could love, but how could she ever hope to love any other when this lowly minstrel had seized her heart. Could she scandalize the court by giving herself to a commoner? She could not. What would she do?

The kiss ended at last, though Berengeria did not have it in her heart to stop it on her own. Then Arcite smiled at her as if he had made no great commitment, turned, and was gone.

Chapter Eight:
An Encounter

URSID GLARED AT Palamon, then glanced about the chamber before he fixed his eye once more on the tall monarch. "I see you have not changed from bygone years," the young Prince said in a cutting voice. "As you usurped my place before, so have you done within this hall. I am accustomed to the chair upon my monarch's right-hand side. I see that you have taken it." He laughed but there was no mirth to his laughter. "So was it that you took the place I held beside your sister, Berengeria. Full well you know the low usurper's trade."

Palamon felt the blood rush to his face; after all, he had not traveled to Danaar to be insulted by Ursid. It took all his early training as a Knight of Pallas for him to frame his answer in quiet tones. "I sat where I was asked to sit. If you would 'range the seating at your pleasure, you will need to council with our host. But know you, lad—I did not come to argue over trifles."

The livid scars which crossed Ursid's face flashed in the torchlight and his lips formed a caustic smirk as he replied. "Ah, yes, the proud Carean King is reasonable. Once more, Ursid is in the wrong—the monarch's son is taken; peace stands near to hand. This is no time to argue over old lost loves and insignificant betrayals. So it was through the weeks I sought the love of Berengeria. The old King said 'We'll talk another time; for now, observe the way the falcons soar.' or, 'On another day, we'll talk of this. But wait for my return, for now I leave on progress.'" Ursid sneered again. "My wait continues."

Palamon had no quick reply to Ursid's hateful words because there really was a note of truth to them—and Palamon still regretted what had happened. Ursid had labored long and earnestly for Berengeria's hand, and had performed great service for her. But Berengeria had been unable to return his love and who could censure her for that? A maiden could not make herself love a man. It had all been unfortunate—and horrible things had come of it. For all his own grief, Palamon could not begrudge Ursid his bitterness.

But Flin had a quick answer. He looked up from his seat with a lazy smile and addressed the young Constable. "I'm an expert on love and your words strike no chord with me, fellow. If your love for Berengeria were as full and as true as you say it is, the gods would have rewarded it with a successful end."

Ursid glared at Palamon's friend. "Indeed, young jackanapes, that shall there be. When I have slain this Palamon, and no two stones of far Carea lie together, then the end shall be a happy one for me."

Count Destus took on a look of great discomfort. "Be reasonable, young Constable."

"I did not come here to be reasonable."

Palamon's mouth tightened. "I do not fault your anger; still I would remind you that the war is over."

"Not for me. This pause may last a year, a score of years, or end tonight. But fighting shall resume. Why, bless the gods, for they have brought my enemy within my grasp, where I can challenge him and slay him— here, before these men of fair Danaar."

"Then do you challenge me?" Palamon straightened from his seat and he returned the younger man's glare.

"If there were hope you'd answer it, then yes."

"You make me angry."

"Good."

Palamon struck the hilt of his longsword, for Ursid had as much as called him a coward. He had insulted all of Carea and Palamon's family before the entire hall. But the tall monarch paused, sat back down, and took a deep breath. "I'll not allow my passion to usurp my reason," he whispered to Flin. "A man must discipline himself, must throttle down the hatred sown in him by others. After all, I have a greater rage—the rage which brought me early to Danaar." Flin did not reply. Palamon waited until his calm had returned, then he spoke carefully to Ursid. "We have our differences and I will not deny that there are reasons for your angry words. But still, I must pursue my son's salvation. Let me seek the man who laid him low and tend to him before we argue."

Ursid did not reply directly to Palamon. He laughed mightily, turned toward the watching nobles, and extended a hand toward the tall monarch. "Delay, delay, delay, delay, delay. This is the honor of Carean kings." A few among the crowd snickered and Palamon's anger rose once more. And Ursid kept baiting him. "Then I will have it this way, Palamon. I call you by your given name because I cannot find it in my heart to call you King. I challenge you to combat. For your son, I care no jot nor tittle for his fate, for I've no reason to. What care you or your sister for the low indignities I've suffered for your sakes? Should I give heed where you have not? I spit upon your son."

Ursid expelled a mass of spittle which struck the stones beside Palamon's foot. "You spit upon my son?" Palamon cried. "You blatant cur, who dares to laugh upon the striking of a boy of four short years. How dare you say such things? By all the gods, if you still wish a duel, you've got one." He leaped from his seat, threw his hands onto the young Constable's shoulders, and hurled him backward.

Ursid staggered toward the wall, then released a cry and launched himself toward Palamon. "I'll gladly fight you, you decrepit heap of ageing flesh. Let weapons be provided—we will battle to the death." He threw himself against the tall monarch and the two men scuffled like mad wolves, back and forth across the floor.

Lothar and Count Destus shot to their feet, and the Buerdic King glared at the two men fighting before him like schoolboys. He waved to the guards standing along the walls and bellowed an order. "Separate them. We will not allow grown men to act thus in our presence."

The guards rushed to pull the two apart. For his part, Flin also leaped up and helped haul Palamon away from Ursid. "I'll answer your request," Palamon cried at the Buerdic Constable. "Let us do combat, for you'll fare no better than you did the last time that we met in tournament."

"We'll not be fighting in Carea," Ursid shouted back. "And you'll not have your complement of strong Carean knights to back your arms."

"Yes, we are in Danaar." This time it was Count Destus' voice which filled the chamber. "And I hold sway. No tournament or duel transpires within these walls without my full approval. Now, King Lothar, what have you to say to this encounter?"

Lothar cast angry eyes upon each man, then drew himself up to his full height. The Buerdic King was half a cubit shorter than Palamon but he appeared much larger in his own anger. His presence filled the great hall as he took control of the situation.

He turned to his nephew and heir. "Ursid, you must apologize to the Carean King. To challenge any monarch is a sin; to challenge him when he is freshly come for conference is more so."

"I cannot apologize."

"You must." Lothar the Pale's pink pupils flashed and his glare speared Ursid as the angler spears the carp. "It is your duty as Buerdaunt's high Constable to take no action which endangers all well-being of our nation. Thus, apologize or forfeit your position."

Ursid was overcome by the force of the smaller man's personality more than by the threat. Though Lothar had only the physical stature of a twelve year old, his pres-

ence amazed Palamon. Ursid clenched his teeth, bowed
to his King, then turned toward the tall monarch. "If it's
my duty, I apologize," he said, biting his words off as if
he would gag on them. "But still, Carean King, bear
memory that I do not retract my challenge from the love
of you, or from respect for all your titles, or for kindness. You're not worth the strife to my own land which
is the price if I do otherwise."

"Ursid." Lothar the Pale's voice silenced the younger
noble. "Contain yourself."

Ursid glared as if he were about to explode. "I'll
speak no more, my liege."

"A wise precaution," Lothar observed. He looked
from one man to the other, then spoke in a ringing voice.
"The war between our lands is ended. I will not allow
our hatreds to resuscitate it." He turned toward Palamon. "As we both know, old Alyubol is dead, and to be
straight with you, I have eschewed relations with all sorcerers since last I dealt with him. I've found such men to
be inconstant, and their goals do not align with mine. Be
that a lesson to us both, Carean King, that wizards are
unsteady allies."

"Still," Palamon said. "It's natural for me to start my
search by questioning the man who knows them best:
yourself."

"I dealt with one when Berengeria was hostaged," the
Buerdic King replied matter-of-factly. "That ended, as
you know, five years ago. I have not seen your Alyubol,
nor any other since. Therefore, I say, I have no help to
give to you. But too, as I have also said, all sorcerers
within my kingdom shall be brought to me and questioned."

Palamon smiled a dry smile. "It's not a common occupation. I believe it shall not overtax your marshals."

"No, indeed. But what more would you have me do?"

That question did cause Palamon to pause. After all,
what more *could* Lothar do if he were telling the truth?
Had the scene with Ursid and Lothar's quelling of the
hot-blooded Constable all been a performance for Palamon's sake? How could the tall monarch know—and

even if that were the case, what could Palamon do about it? He could not trust Lothar—but if the pale King were lying, Palamon could not find it in his face. The tall monarch sighed; perhaps his journey to Danaar had been a fool's errand after all.

Then, to Palamon's surprise, Ursid spoke civilly for the first time. "Do you remember one who's named Navron?"

"I do. He served as Alyubol's chief henchman."

"Indeed." There was still no friendship in Ursid's eyes but at least he kept his voice to normal levels. "I speak now for Buerdaunt's sake, not for yours, tall Palamon. My King has told me it is in the interests of Buerdaunt I reconcile myself with you. Therefore, I tell you that the man Navron was seen by me not seven days ago. He sought alliance with me."

"You refused?"

Ursid spat once more. "My ruler and my mentor stated perfectly the risks involved in making allies out of sorcerers. They are inconstant friends. But still, I might contrive to find him for you."

Palamon gaped at Ursid's new tack. If the young Constable was willing to go to such lengths simply for his King and country, Lothar's influence over him had to be powerful indeed. In any case, Palamon would accept such a windfall from whatever quarter it came. "If you can do so, and if it should lead to Berethane's recovery, you'll have undying thanks from me, as well as everlasting friendship."

Ursid chuckled; the sound of his mirth was like a pig's cough. "I do not do it for your thanks or friendship. And perhaps I am a fool to think of it at all. I'll send a man this moment to make contact if he can." He turned on his heel and strode from the chamber.

Palamon's head was ready to spin at this turn of events. He looked at Lothar the Pale. "I do not understand your nephew; this new aid he promises does not agree with all the hate which fills him."

Lothar sat down and resumed his interrupted dinner. "He's loyal to his King." He looked up at Palamon. "Our lands can never be fast friends, you know. That should not be a revelation to you; our geography prevents alliances between us. Still, it's in my interest to keep the peace for now. To that end, then, my nephew served my interests and your own."

Palamon did not answer. The Buerdic King was cool in discussing the way of things. That amazed Palamon all over again, that the diminutive monarch could address such a tender subject so calmly. The enmity between the two lands was a tragedy rather than the simple fact of life Lothar made it out to be. How long would this new treaty last? A year? Five years? Palamon looked away. He was completely out of his depth in dealing with the man beside him.

After the feast, the two monarchs went on to the conference which had been planned for that evening. They haggled over many points during the session and talks continued long after their followers had become bleary-eyed. There were trade routes and policies to be decided, ambassadors had not yet been exchanged, and there was the delicate question of borders between the two realms' spheres of influence. For his part, Palamon discussed the matters reluctantly and did his utmost to leave each question undecided. Berethane's future controlled his mind; he could not give his best effort to any other matter. He was also aware that his preoccupation was exactly the reason Lothar was so insistent on settling each question as quickly as possible. The Buerdic King was a tough and shrewd negotiator; whether or not he had had a hand in the magic which had stricken Palamon's son, Buerdaunt had still benefited from it by at least the margin of their discussions.

Palamon's head was buzzing by the time Lothar had finished with him. He sighed with relief as he and Flin left and made their way from the hall. A dozen Carean knights waited in Palamon's escort; he and Flin watched as they lit torches for the trip along Danaar's dark byways.

A spat of rain had scattered across the city while Palamon and Flin had been closeted with Lothar; dampness still hung in the air and the torchlit streets glistened before them. Their hoofbeats sounded off walls and buildings as they passed through the town.

The night was dark. There was no moon and the streets were lit only by an occasional gleam from some window and the torches of the Carean knights. Palamon loosed his longsword in its sheath; he had lived in this city years ago and knew it to be a dangerous place at night. And the streets were so dark he still could not recognize where he was.

All at once, footsteps pounded out of the darkness. A man hurtled toward them from an alleyway; he rushed into the lantern light, even as Palamon looked toward the sound of his footfalls. He was a ragged rough-looking fellow and he hailed the Chamberlain in a gravelly voice. That courtier looked at the man with distaste, though he did lean down to hear the newcomer's words.

They exchanged phrases, then the Chamberlain turned to Palamon. "He says he has been sent with news for the Carean King. Some knights have laid their hands upon a devious sorcerer."

"Where is he then?" Palamon cried. "And what can be his name?"

The ragged man ran to Palamon's horse and shouted up at the tall monarch. "I don't know anything about him. A noble pulled me out of my corner and sent me to find you."

"Then lead on," Palamon cried. Palamon put spurs to his horse and surged after the fellow, who scampered back along his alleyway. In spite of all his rags, the man ran wonderfully well in the confined darkness. The alley was so crooked Palamon had all he could do to keep his horse from losing ground to the nimble runner.

Flin followed Palamon into the cramped space and so did the tall monarch's escort. Their hoofbeats thundered off the crooked walls but they did not all ride the jagged way at the same pace as the King. The light from their torches became irregular as they stretched out along the narrow passage. The torchlight formed ghastly shadows as it bounced off crates, rubbish, and overhanging buildings.

Suddenly the alley opened out to form a small court and the torchlight gleamed off the helmets and breastplates of a large number of mounted men. They held no prisoner and wore no colors; Palamon could not even guess the land of their origin. But there was no mistaking their intent. No sooner had he seen them than they laid spurs to their horses, leveled their weapons, and charged.

The ragged guide must have been their dupe; he was no more ready for this charge than the intended victims. The lurching horses knocked him over like a loose block of wood and he screamed as their hooves carved him into ribbons against the cobblestones. Palamon heard no war cries, no trumpets; this was death in a gutter, grim and bloody. He tried to snatch out his longsword. But the tip had barely cleared his scabbard when the first foe reached him and struck him a stunning blow on the side with a mace.

Pain roared through him like erupting flames. He backed his horse away from the assailant but there was no room; he could feel the animal's flank rub against the rough plaster wall beside him. His mind raced. The assassins had chosen their trap well; was Ursid behind it? Why would the Constable have arranged such a trap without Lothar knowing? Was there some other force acting here?

There was no time to answer such questions; Palamon would die in his saddle if he hesitated a heartbeat. He was unarmored and lightly armed against an unknown number of ironbound killers. He ducked the following blow he knew was coming and allowed himself to slide from his saddle. Only on the ground, amid the forest of horses' legs, would he stand a chance of survival.

As for Flin, Palamon heard the young knight cry out behind him. "We have treachery, do we? That's good, I say. A little steel on steel will make my blood rush hotter than the sight of two well-dressed men haggling in a closet." Palamon smiled even as he landed in a heap.

Though he faced death, Flin was always Flin.

The crash of weapons spread along the narrow way as Palamon leaped to his feet. His right shoulder was numb from the blow he had suffered, so he held his sword in his left hand and struck up at the armored body on the horse above him. His steel tip scraped through armor and brought a scream and blood; the man fell almost on top of him.

Confusion ruled the night. Weapons clanged, men cursed, horses stamped and reared. Palamon's knights had thrown down their torches as they had reached for their weapons; the alleyway plunged into darkness as if the battle were taking place at the bottom of a well. Palamon had no idea what had happened to Flin or to any of the knights of his company. But some were alive and fighting, to judge from the fray's fury.

A harsh voice cried out in the darkness, one Palamon had never heard before. "Dismount, dismount. He's dropped from his horse. Dismount; we can't let him escape. Stratagems will not help you, Carean King. Palamon, you must die."

Chapter Nine:
Dark Night and Sharp Blades

FIGHTING'S FURIOUS DIN crashed along the dark alleyway as Palamon and his knights struggled against the armored assassins. The assassins far outnumbered Palamon's escort, so the battle could only be a short one. Palamon's teeth locked into a furious battle grin and he worked his longsword with all the skill of a master warrior. But his blade grew dull from carving into armor; no longer were his strokes powerful enough to fell their targets. How he longed for his *Spada Korrigaine*.

Palamon nearly stumbled over a dozen different men who lay bleeding on the wet cobblestones and he knew that most were his own knights. If the assassins had their way, his life would not last much longer. The Careans had to find some refuge. "Flin," he called. "Flin, get closer to the place I stand." But there was no answer; Flin must have fallen already. Palamon's heart turned cold within him.

He fought furiously and worked his way along the wall; so complete was the darkness that even this slight movement was enough to confuse his opponents. Men struck members of their own party; screams and curses filled the air. Suddenly, he felt himself slipping into a vacant space; he must have reached an angle in the wall he kept at his back. At the same time, a sword's blade tore the cloth across his left shoulder, bringing blood and agony. His knees buckled and he cried out as he fell backward. "The King has fallen before me," he heard a voice shout. "He's down, and soon shall be reduced to meat."

Palamon rolled to one side to avoid the blow he knew was coming; sure enough, the sword clanged against the paving on the space he had just vacated. And he used all his might to strike the darkness above the space. His blade bit into something, he heard a gargling cry, but then his sword's hilt was twisted from his hand.

Suddenly, he felt a draught of wind behind him and powerful fingers closed about one ankle. Before he could react, he felt himself dragged through a doorway. He tried to struggle to his feet, to defend himself against this new menace, but a familiar voice stilled him. "Hush. If they think they've killed you, let's not disillusion them by scrabbling about. Let me slip this door shut."

It was Flin; the young knight had not fallen after all. Palamon rolled quickly away from the door and allowed Flin to push it to. Then the two men sat with their backs braced against the wood of the portal. "By all the gods," Palamon whispered as he felt the wound to his shoulder. "How came you here?"

"I just happened to find this unlocked door in the darkness. Each time I hear one of our own men bump against it, I open up and pull him in. There's four of us in here now, counting you."

Palamon breathed a sigh of relief. As always, Flin was Flin. He found his wound to be only a minor cut and that was good, but at that same moment, he heard the thump and clatter of more combatants pushing against the door. He leaped to his feet. "How can you tell which warriors are our own?" he asked.

"Our men are fighting for their lives, so they'll have their backs against this wall." Flin jerked the door open in the darkness and Palamon heard him grunt as he hauled another man through. "Sure enough, it's Sir Marl." Then the door shut again.

The fighting subsided outside the chamber. "They're all down," Palamon heard a voice say. His heart sank. Nine good men had fallen, then, for there were only three knights besides himself and Flin in the dusty-smelling room. He listened through the door and heard the sound of ironbound feet scraping across the paving. "Where is he?" the voice came again.

"I can't tell," came another voice.

"Find him. He has to be here somewhere."

Palamon tried to pull the door open but Flin prevented him. "You don't want to go out there." Flin's voice was a harsh whisper. "They'd mow you down like a staked lamb."

"My men lie bleeding on the ground."

The other survivors of Palamon's escort leaped to Flin's aid and restrained the tall monarch. "He's right, your Grace," Sir Marl whispered. "And if Carean knights lie dead outside this door, they've found reward in Paradise. They fell performing sacred duty: preservation of their monarch's life."

Palamon fell to his knees, clenched his teeth and beat his fists against his thighs. "My son is fallen. Nine good men have died. I'll hunt the man responsible for this and wreak a payment from him which will be remembered well about the Thlassa Mey for all eternity."

"But now we have to flee," Sir Marl said.

"Right," Flin agreed. "But first, let's push everything we can find up against this door. They could look in here for us anytime."

It was no sooner said than done. By feeling about in the dark, they found a stack of bags which were heavy with some kind of powder. While two men held the door against quick discovery, the others barricaded it with the sacks. Then, once there was so great a weight against it that it could never be forced from outside, they began to feel their way about, to explore the inside of the building in the darkness.

"Does anyone have a flint and steel?" Flin asked

quietly. "Maybe we could make a torch." But no one had anything, so they had to grope their way. The building was divided into two large chambers; in the first, they found stack on stack of the powder bags, while the other seemed to contain only a few huge washtubs. It was all quite inexplicable, though Palamon felt sure the place would be more easily recognized if they could only get a good look at it.

Then a light appeared above them. They all stared toward it and saw a plump old man in nightshirt and nightcap, standing at the head of a flight of stairs. He stared back at them, his mouth hanging open with his shock. "By the gods, who are you men?"

Flin's laugh filled the chamber before he thought to choke it back. "It's not so strange," he said. "We're in a bakery." In truth, the place that had seemed so foreign in the blackness became mundane in the candle's weak glow. It was, indeed, a bakery; the bags of powder were flour, the tubs were for mixing and kneading, and a row of large ovens lined the far wall, along with stacks of firewood. But there was no time for amusement at this discovery.

Palamon leaped toward the stairs. "You need not fear us, fellow," he said. "I am King of far Carea, and will bring no harm to honest tradesmen."

"But you can help us," Flin added. "The street outside is full of assassins. We have to find another way out of your building."

"But there is no way," the astonished man answered, all the while staring from one bloody face to the next. "There's only one door."

"Then we will make our stand in here," Palamon said quietly, for the forces outside had commenced pounding at the bakery's single door. In moments, they would splinter the wood. If they were able to claw their way past the flour bags, the little group would be cornered.

"No, wait," the baker said. "Come up here with me, for I might be able to help you."

They rushed up the rickety stairs and found themselves in modest living quarters. The baker's wife cowered behind an open door as the men rushed into the couple's bedroom. "My window looks out on the roof-tops," the baker said. "Perhaps you can escape that way."

"We thank you, fellow," Sir Marl said. Then he paused to detach his purse from his belt. "Take this; it may defray the damages."

"But they have to come with us," Flin said.

"Indeed they do," Palamon agreed. "For if the killers learn about their help, their lives will not be worth the price of two dead hens."

"No sooner said than done," Sir Marl replied. Then he turned to the quaking couple. "Throw on some cloth-ing and escape with us."

They all rushed to the window at the far end of the little chamber, while at the same time they heard a crash and a great shout from below. Flin threw open the shut-ters and looked out. "It's perfect. A short drop to the roof peak below, and we're out. Someone had better help the old folks though."

One by one, they climbed through the window and into Danaar's chilly evening air. Palamon climbed through first, followed by his three knights and the baker and his wife. Flin climbed through last, carefully closed the shutters as he emerged, then dropped to the roof behind them. They made their way along the roof peak cautiously in the darkness, reached a joint between that building and a lower one, and followed the edge of that until they came to a low wall which trailed along a broad avenue. They had traveled some hundred cubits and could still hear the assassins ransacking the bakery.

The wall was twice a man's height but Flin did not hesitate. He hung down as far as his arms would allow him, then dropped to the paving. Palamon followed. "Now lower down the lady," Palamon called. "And we will catch her."

Fright plainly petrified the old woman as two knights suspended her by her arms, then dropped her to Palamon and Flin, who caught her and lowered her gently to the pavement. The same procedure was followed with the baker, after which the three knights also descended to the street. "Your Grace," the baker said in a quavering voice. "Is it always thus with you?"

"It seems to be tonight," Palamon answered grimly. "Now we must flee. Have you a place where you might find some shelter for a while?"

"My brother keeps an inn," the baker's wife said. "We'll go there."

"Then take these coins." Palamon handed money from his pouch to the baker, adding to Sir Marl's donation. "I doubt the damage done unto your property will be beyond repair; yet you will lose some goods withal, as well as several days in cleaning out the wreckage. Now farewell, for we must fly. You have the thanks of proud Carea's King."

Palamon, Flin, and the knights dashed down the shadowy street. Perhaps the assassins had lost their trail but they still had to assume the worst. "Which way?" Flin gasped as they ran along.

"We must return unto the villa. There I'll fetch the *Spada Korrigaine* and turn the odds to favor us."

They ran a way, paused to hide in the shadows and look for pursuit, then ran on again. It took them a long time to reach the villa where Palamon and his escort had been quartered. When they arrived, they found a stunning scene; the guards lay in heaps along the halls, and in the rooms, the men had plainly been drugged. Only a few responded to jostling and cheek slapping, and even those acted confused and sluggish. Evil forces had been at work here, even while Palamon had been fighting for his life half a league away. Alarmed, Palamon lost no time; he rushed to his chambers and threw open the wardrobe which contained his mystical blade. But the *Spada Korrigaine* was nowhere to be found.

He frantically pillaged the wardrobe, hurled clothing and haberdashery from the way, but it did not matter. The blade and its case were gone. Then the crash of steel made him lift his head. He rushed to his chamber door, peeked out, and saw the corridor already awash with blood. Flin and the three remaining knights, along with those guards who could stand, were locked in deadly combat with armored men. The assassins had caught up with the Careans. Even as Palamon stared, Sir Marl and another knight fell beneath brutal blades. Most of the sentries were ignored by the attackers because they were still too unsteady on their feet to pose any threat. The odds against the defenders were dozens to one.

"In here with me," Palamon cried. Even as Flin leaped into the chamber with the tall monarch, the last friendly knight fell with a cry. The attackers charged the heavy door but could not reach it before Palamon threw it shut. While they pounded on the stout portal, he rushed through one last search for his precious sword. But he had no time; bloody blades made a terrible din as the assassins hewed at the layer of oak which separated them from their two victims. "It seems that we must lead a fugitive's existence for a while," Palamon said. "The window, quick. And while you pry it open, I will gather gold and find another blade."

They leaped from the chamber scarcely a breath before the maddened killers shattered the door and burst into the room like ravaging hounds. Palamon and Flin dashed across the villa's courtyard, plunged down an alley, and vaulted the stone wall which surrounded the place. They landed safely in the street, but that meant little. Where would they go? If the assassins still pursued them, it would do them no good to try to make their way to Keep Danaar. Besides, they had no way of knowing that Lothar was not in on the plot, though why he would take such a reckless step was more than Palamon could fathom. Nor could the tall monarch understand why they had not simply let him return to the villa, drugged him along with his men, and killed him quietly. But there was no time to ponder such questions.

Wherever Palamon and Flin might flee, they had to hurry. No shouts arose from the grounds they had just fled but Palamon could hear the scraping of armor against stone as the pursuers tried to scale the wall he and Flin had just vaulted. Palamon smiled. If there was no other advantage to being without armor, at least they had been able to clear the wall. Armored knights would have to scrabble about for a long time before they could duplicate the feat, though they could outflank the Careans by running to the nearest exit.

Palamon and Flin tore across the street, into the first alley they came to, and past what appeared to be a cluster of warehouses. Their footfalls and the rasping of their breaths echoed back to them from the dark, damp walls which loomed on both sides. And as if their plight were not grievous enough, the clouds above picked that moment to belch a chilly rain.

At last the two men stopped and turned toward one another, both of them panting like dogs on the hunt. "Do you hear anyone?" Flin asked. "I think we've given them the slip."

"Perhaps," Palamon said. "But their pursuit will not abate. We have to find a place to hide ourselves."

Their eyes scoured the alley's rain-slicked walls until Palamon finally spoke. "There. Look there." A steeply angled wooden chute extended down toward them at a height of four or five cubits. Its upper end pierced the depths of an unknown building and the rain streamed down it; still, it did look wide enough to admit an agile man. "Now quickly," Palamon said. "Help me up."

Flin's fingers locked together to form a step for Palamon. The tall monarch placed his muddy foot into the waiting support and Flin lifted with a grunt, flinging the King toward the chute. Palamon's fingers collided with wet timbers; he was able to catch hold and clambered up. But Flin would not be able to leap up after him unaided. Gritting his teeth, Palamon hoisted himself until only his lower body dangled from the opening. "Now leap and catch my legs," he cried. "Climb up and we shall pass beyond detection."

Flin gave a great leap and his hands wrapped around Palamon's ankle. From there, while the rain rattled off the chute, he climbed along Palamon's body, hoisted himself into the soaked channel, and the two men made their way upward. It was a nasty climb; they had to wage a fierce struggle against rain, slick timbers, and splinters.

The wood of the chute had been rubbed smooth by the legions of goods which had slid along it; still, by bracing their elbows, knees, and toes against the sides, they made steady progress. Once they clambered past the border of the building's wall, the way became easier until they emerged onto a dark wooden platform. "By the gods, we're here," Flin whispered. "But I wonder where 'here' is."

They felt about in the black and Palamon's fingers rubbed across a heap of rough sacks; the same type of sacks they had found in the bakery. "So," he said. "Our route continues to be paved with flour. Some wealthy merchant must possess the title to this building. Yonder chute's the way by which this flour is loaded onto wagons."

From the sound he made, Flin had slumped down onto the flooring. "At any rate, they'll never guess we've climbed up here."

"We cannot know that," Palamon said. "Let us move along." They made their way farther along the platform in the darkness, crawling on hands and knees, feeling before them so they would not stumble through some hole or off some unprotected edge. They found by touch that the building contained more than just flour. They encountered amphorae which likely stood full of wine, racks of rich clothing, and then they crossed a long, empty stretch of planking. They reached the edge of that and located a ladder. Up they climbed, to find themselves on a wooden catwalk above some sort of bin.

"I wish we had some light," Palamon said. "For it appears that we have stumbled to a dead end."

"Maybe not," Flin said. "Lower me by the legs and I'll try to find out what's below us."

Palamon grasped Flin's ankles and supported the younger man while he slipped over the edge of the catwalk. When Palamon's arms reached their full extension, he heard the young knight laugh. "Let go. We've found a bin of hides. They don't smell as nice as a lady's throat but they'll make a bonny place to keep out of sight until morning."

Palamon relaxed his hold and heard the sound of a body landing on something soft. "Make way," he said then. "I'm going to jump."

"Jump and roll and there'll be no harm. These things must be two fathoms deep in here."

Palamon did so and found Flin's words to be true. He landed on hides that were soft, pliable, and full of the musty aroma of their preparation. Even in the darkness, he could tell they were of the highest quality, luxurious examples of the tanner's art. They formed a soft sea which extended away from him and down beyond the range of his touch. "They must be waiting, ready to be shipped," he said. "They'd not be tossed together in this place for periods of storage."

"Who cares?" Flin was rolling about on the soft hides, flinging them up in the air, burrowing into them. "It's as strange a bed as I've ever lain in and I'm an expert on beds. But 'twill make a soft place to sleep and in the morning, we can sort things out."

Palamon looked toward the young knight, though he could not see him. "Perhaps. If it is possible to sort things out. Strange men have drugged my stalwart guards and tried to kill us twice. My holy sword, my *Spada Korrigaine*, is stolen and we cannot even know who did these deeds."

"You worry too much. These sword-swinging devils have the upper hand now but let us get a little rest and then we'll set them by the ears."

Palamon smiled in spite of himself; Flin never lacked confidence. But it was late and Flin was right in a way; the two fugitives had found the perfect place to hide from those who wanted to murder them and there was nothing more they could do until morning. He covered himself with soft hides; but, try as he might, he could not attain slumber's depths. Questions buzzed through his mind and made sleep a hopeless goal.

After a time, Flin's muffled voice came to Palamon from between the hides. "The way you're shifting around, I almost think you're lying in a bed of ants. You can't lose sleep just because someone's trying to kill you."

Palamon smiled a grim smile. "I cannot think of any better cause for losing sleep."

"A beautiful woman's the only acceptable reason for that. If there were one with us now, maybe I'd twitch and toss the way you do. As it is, I'm going back off to dreamland."

Palamon listened as the younger man yawned. There were no visionary maidens in crowds to tell Flin, "The balance teeters at the middle point." And the machinations of wizards and statesmen did not upset the young knight in the least. No mysteries, no terror lay in midnight attacks; when he awoke in the morning, Flin would do what he had to do, then he would eat, make love, and sleep again.

But not Palamon. Palamon pondered Alyubol and the cultists, Lothar, and Ursid. Why was there no peace and love; why did such men inhabit the world? Why did Berethane lie in a coma? Despair filled him and he murmured to himself, "I hate them all."

"Who?" From Flin's sleepy voice, Palamon knew the younger man lay awake after all.

"Those who make this world a playground for their heinous villainies."

Flin yawned. "Don't tar every rogue with the same brush. I'd love to make the world a playground for my own villainies."

"You try to turn my anger with your wit—but still my belly sours to think on those who drove us here. If it were in my power, I would smash all those who stir infection, and I'd do it ere the sun could rise."

"How would you know whom to smash?"

Palamon hesitated; when he replied, his voice was lower. "You deftly blunt the edge of anger, friend. 'Twas wisely done, for undirected passion is no more than foolishness. But still and all, I'll have my vengeance. Mark my words."

Flin's voice grew somber. "I've never seen you this mad."

"Nor have I. I never realized that rage could claim me so. Forgive me; I will rant less in the future."

"I hope we're both able to rant by tomorrow night," Flin said with another yawn. "There seem to be an awful lot of people who want to kill us."

Palamon smiled at last. "Do you really harbor doubts about survival?"

"No. I'm going back to sleep. The smell of these hides makes me drowsy."

"And I, too." But Palamon had trouble doing so. He tossed and turned for what seemed an eternity before sleep claimed him.

At last dawn arrived; Palamon could tell by the points of light which appeared along the warehouse's roof. He could hardly see anything from the hide bin but the light did increase until the odorous sanctuary filled with gray shadows. He could see Flin dimly; the young knight had buried all but one leg in the bin's contents; still, the hides which concealed him rose and fell steadily with his easy breathing.

Palamon reached forth and pulled a hide from Flin's face. "Awake. We must be on the move."

Flin twitched, coughed, blinked, and opened his eyes. "Morning already? Where in blazes are we?"

"It will return to you. But listen." Palamon heard a sound, a scraping sound from below them. That was followed by the unmistakable clatter of wooden wheels and the cursing of a muleteer. Someone was pulling a wagon into the warehouse.

A rough voice echoed from below. "No sun dogs this morning. That means a good start, a few days free of rain. We'd better load fast and be on our merry way." The man's speech was reassuring, nothing more than the business talk of a merchant's hireling. At least he did not sound like one of the men who had tried to kill Palamon and Flin the night before.

"No sooner said than done," came another voice. "Come on, then, guide me so that the wheels are on the marks." This was followed by more curses, the creaking of wooden axles, and the crack of a whip. Whatever they were doing, the men were now working directly below the two fugitives.

Palamon looked about. The inside of the bin was still a mass of shadows but he could see what might be a ladder trailing up the far side of it, some eight or ten cubits away. It was hard to decide whether they should try to slip away or remain hidden where they were.

More noises rose from below. Finally, one of the workmen spoke in a loud voice. "Is she all lined up? Good, then let 'er rip."

Palamon heard a scraping sound, as from a steel bar being dragged across wood. Then came a thud and the world about Palamon and Flin gave way. They began to slide down, down, enveloped in an avalanche of tanned hides while the walls of the bin slipped past Palamon's outstretched fingers. He caught his breath as they hurtled into an unknown void.

Chapter Ten:
Berengeria's Journey

THOUGHTS OF ARCITE plagued Berengeria and her hopes turned to the Temple of Hestia in Lower Carea. She wished she had the wisdom of its priests. She loved the handsome minstrel, yet could not marry him in front of Palamon and Aelia—and he tempted her flesh in a way she was afraid to battle alone. She would consult the High Priest of Hestia, then—if anyone could advise her, he could.

She walked to the Queen's rooms. She would tell Aelia of her decision; the older woman had been a priestess of Hestia during her own maidenhood and would surely understand Berengeria's fears. The sweet air blowing in off the gardens foretold a lovely day and the colonnade which led to the royal chambers stood awash with sunlight. Rain had fallen the night before; steam rose from the paving stones in pleasant clouds and filled the nostrils with a smell that was damp and earthy.

Berengeria found Aelia sitting at a desk, signing dispatches. The older woman looked up and smiled, though Berengeria could also see the sadness which weighted her soul. "I fear from your expression, dearest Queen, that Berethane still lies in magic's grip."

Aelia nodded. "He fares as poorly as he ever has. The blush of childhood lingers on his cheek and yet he is as dead to us as if he'd been cut down by plague or pestilence."

Berengeria cursed herself. Her own troubles were nothing, compared to what Aelia and Palamon were going through. She laid her hand on the Queen's hair. "I'm sure my brother will set all things right again."

Aelia sighed, then brightened and pulled a rope. An attendant hurried from the far side of the room, whispers were exchanged, the attendant hustled away. Then Aelia's eyes found Berengeria once more. "Perhaps he shall, my gallant Palamon. But then, perhaps he may meet some catastrophe, for forces lurk which yearn to see him dead and all the land about the Thlassa Mey laid waste. Ah, me. Fate's whims are strange; 'twas you who were reared up to rule Carea. Palamon was well content to stay in knighthood's gleaming ranks. Yet now he rules while other Fates await my Berengeria." She studied Berengeria's face with a little smile.

The Queen's expression puzzled the Princess; but she did not ponder it. She had come for important words. "There lies a matter which I would discuss with you."

Aelia tilted her head to one side. "How so?"

"I need an escort on the morrow. I would ride down to the lower town to seek the counsel of good Hestia's priests."

Aelia placed her quill back in the ink pot. "Then you have troubles?"

Berengeria hesitated before she replied. "Perhaps not troubles—questions. Matters are confusing me, not least of which was some small incident which took place just yesterday."

Aelia smiled again: the Queen actually appeared to be on the verge of laughter. "Ah, yes, a conversation which took place between yourself and musical Arcite."

"But how did you find out?"

"I hear all tales. You've lived beside me more than twenty years—you know I have the means to eke out information in some subtle ways. Do you think any incident occurs within this castle unbeknownst to me?"

Berengeria bowed her head. "I should have known. But since you know, you have to realize how greatly I require the High Priest's counseling."

"Dear girl, you need not think your holy soul's been rendered past salvation by a minstrel's kiss."

"No, that is just a part of my confusion."

At that moment, an attendant strode in, pounded the floor with his staff, and made an announcement in a loud voice. "Arcite the Balladeer has come to sing, in answer to the Queen's request."

Aelia turned toward the newcomer. "Admit him, then. His coming is quite timely."

The attendant turned away. Arcite walked into the chamber carrying a lute, but stopped in his tracks when he laid eyes on Berengeria. "Princess, I'd no thought that you were here. I'll leave the way I came."

"No, stay," Aelia said quickly. "I understand your singing voice will please this maiden's ear as much as mine."

For her part, Berengeria fumbled for words. The sunny yellow of the minstrel's hair trapped her eyes; she could only stare at him, at the manly breadth of his shoulders, the sweep of his torso, the tapering of his thighs. He was a comely man and she realized all over again that she did love him. What a prank fate had played on her by matching them, and then by bringing him to the Queen's chamber while Berengeria was there. "No, stay," she said after an instant's hesitation. "And I will go."

Aelia looked from Arcite to the Princess and Berengeria was more sure than ever she saw a flicker of amusement cross the Queen's features. "Our dear Princess departs for Lower Carea before another day has passed," she said to the young man.

"Indeed?" Arcite exclaimed, his voice full of enthusiasm. "Then let me join her escort."

Berengeria's jaw dropped. The situation was becoming ever more impossible; Arcite's company was the one thing she most wanted to avoid during her journey to the

Temple. She suddenly wished the Queen had not been present, so she could speak openly with the balladeer. Did the Queen know *all* that had passed between them? No, that was impossible—she might know about a kiss or kisses, but she surely could not know of Berengeria's admitted love for the man. The Queen might not have been so amused by the situation if she had known that. She would have sent Arcite packing, which Berengeria both desired and feared.

In any event, Princess Berengeria could not let Arcite go with her on her pilgrimage. She would be polite—she could not speak ill to the man she loved—but she had to make the journey alone. Even in the cool of the Queen's chamber, she wanted to throw her arms about him, to devour him with her touch, with caresses. Even a saint could not have kept her mind free of earthy notions in such a presence. "No, no, kind sir," she said. "For all the high regard I hold for you, I'll journey by myself."

Aelia looked from one of them to the other. "Now don't be hasty, dear. Why, I would think a joyful song or two along your journey's way might do you good. Arcite, I'll countermand this maiden's order this one time. Prepare yourself to leave tomorrow morning."

Berengeria's breath wheezed from her lungs and her stare recoiled from one face to the other. "By all the gods," she exclaimed. "I am undone. The Fates are persecuting me; I swear it's so."

Now Aelia really did smile. "Why, dear, what can you mean?" she asked. The bright blue of the Queen's gaze pierced Berengeria like an icy gust.

Berengeria tried to stammer a reply but she had no idea what to say. Her outburst had been a mistake; if she continued along that vein, she would reveal the truth of the passion between herself and Arcite. But if she said nothing, she would still be inviting the Queen to guess that truth. At last she threw out her hands in despair and rolled her eyes toward the ceiling. "I swear all meaning is embroiled and lost within the eddies of my mental currents. Great Lady, all my troubles are but nits against the losses you've sustained these last few days. E'en so, my soul is vexed; please bear with me."

Aelia glanced from Berengeria's face to Arcite's then back. Had she guessed? Berengeria could not tell. For his part, Arcite did not even try to conceal his pleasure at this turn of events. "Princess," he said. "Please rest assured that nothing out of place shall pass between us. And besides, some six or eight stout knights will separate myself from your sweet side. What harm can lie in that?"

Berengeria stared at him. She needed all the power of her will to keep from either striking him or throwing her arms about him; she could not decide which. "I do not fear you, sir," she said coldly. "Nor do I think that anything improper e'er would cross your mind. But still, but still . . ." She sighed. "I need to be alone."

"I sense the conflicts raging in your soul," Arcite said. His smile had vanished. His eyes drank in her face and he looked as if he would take her in his arms any moment. Berengeria braced herself to step back; but to her surprise, he sank to his knees before her. "I can repeat my vow of yesterday," he offered, his face as serious as if he were taking holy orders. "I know what frets you, royal maid. Believe me when I tell you my intent is chivalrous. You are as safe with me as if I were your own, your loving husband. Why, you're safer still, I say, for men exist who can neglect their wives—which I would never do to you, my royal patron."

"Do not mock me," Berengeria said.

"Know that I do not. You own my reverence, my good intent, my loyalty, my arm, my song, my wit."

Berengeria glanced at Aelia. This scene being played between the two lovers was too blatant; the canny Queen would recognize the bond between them as surely as if they proclaimed it through the marketplaces of Upper and Lower Carea. Then the matter would be out of Berengeria's hands; poor Arcite would go to prison, banishment, or worse. Most likely, the grief occupying the Queen's brain was the only thing which had kept her from perceiving the truth already. "Please rise," Berengeria said. "And speak of this no more."

"Do you believe my words?"

"Whatever you may wish. But rise."

Arcite rose; his smile returned. "Then let me utter this much more: I shall not speak to you along your journey, save to give response to your own statements, or to give what music you desire. If I should vex you more than some soft breeze might vex the hummingbird, then you may send me back."

"That's finely spoken," Aelia said. "And I plainly say I see no harm in it."

Berengeria stared at Aelia. The older woman must have gone blind. Plainly, Aelia was as much under the young man's charm as anyone else in Carea's court, except Berengeria herself. Wherever she might turn, Berengeria was outflanked by the Fates—Arcite would join her escort to Lower Carea. Difficult, difficult. She thought back to Palamon, to the love she had borne him before they had learned their true relationship. She would never go through that again. She could never again seek the love of a man whose birth forbade their union—she still felt too much pain from the last time. She looked into Arcite's eyes and she knew how Tantalus must have felt.

The next morning, her party set out for Lower Carea, with Arcite sitting astride his own horse, singing a jolly song. His voice was as pure as the crystal of a fine goblet and the sun beamed down on his smooth features. How could any woman keep from wanting him? At last she relented and allowed him to ride alongside her, and the leagues between Upper and Lower Carea passed away as if by magic.

The Temple of Hestia stood at the center of the lower city's broadest square. Towering columns surrounded it on all four sides; they stood as a barricade to the world's materialism. The common people were not allowed past the immense porch, where stood the altar for public ceremonies held beneath the open sky. Only because Berengeria was a member of the royal family was she allowed into the inner shrine, and only because she had been reared in the practice of the temple and the worship of Hestia was she allowed even past the shrine, into the sanctuary. But she was afraid as she approached the dark, scented chamber where she was to meet the High Priest.

A space of time later, she returned from the chamber, talking to herself. The priest's counsel had not begun to satisfy her; she felt bitterly disappointed. He had responded with no greater sympathy or understanding than had Aelia the morning before. But then, he was a man of faith; not an assigner of responsibilities. She had gained nothing by her visit to this place. So she left him, made offerings at a few of the temple's shrines, then walked through the echoing sanctuary to the broad plaza outside, where Arcite and her knightly escort waited for her.

She squinted as she first stepped into the spring sunlight; the plaza was painfully bright compared to the subdued shadows of the temple. She noticed that Arcite was nowhere to be seen, though the six knights of her escort turned toward her as she descended the temple's steps. They had apparently been listening to one of Lower Carea's strolling street singers, for a young, fair-skinned maiden with a lute disappeared across the plaza as Berengeria approached.

The six knights snapped to attention, though a bit sloppily, Berengeria thought. The leader, an experienced knight named Sir Lambeth, saluted her. "We're pleased to note your Ladyship's return. Are we to go to other shrines?"

Berengeria bowed her head and drew her shawl more closely about her shoulders, though the day was warm. "No," she said. "I've no desire to stay here. Bring my horse and we will ride back the way we came. But where's Arcite, the minstrel?"

"His singing tired us; he departed," Sir Lambeth said. That was a strange answer, Berengeria thought. She could not imagine the brilliant troubadour's melodies tiring anyone. He did lack the curved attractions of the female singer who had hurried away across the court-

yard but it also surprised Berengeria that he had not
stayed to hear the maid's performance. Very well, he
would find his own way back to Upper Carea and she
would have the afternoon to think, free of his troubling
presence.

One of the knights led her horse from the temple's
stables. Again, Berengeria was puzzled: none of these
handpicked knights was acting with the keenness she
had come to expect of them. Perhaps her sullen mood
had infected even them.

So she put on a brighter face; after all, a Princess of
Carea was expected to act in a certain manner. Bowing
beneath the weight of her own concerns was not among
the things which were acceptable. She forced a smile
onto her lips and pointed it toward Sir Lambeth. "Indeed, it is a lovely day. Perhaps we shall enjoy the ride
back to the upper town, e'en though Arcite shall not accompany us."

Sir Lambeth grunted an inaudible reply, then turned
to mount his own horse. That offended Berengeria again,
even as two other knights helped her mount her own
palfrey. But her outlook brightened as they passed out of
the city and the road took them past swaying fields and
soft-green olive groves. She was young; there was still
time for some rewarding kind of love to come to her,
though how it would come when her heart was full of
Arcite was something she could not guess.

The seven of them rode silently for a long time. Berengeria had been too lost in her own thoughts to speak
but only after they had left Lower Carea's gates far behind did it occur to her that the knights of her escort had
not been speaking among themselves, either. She looked
at each one of them; each man sat rigidly, eyes fixed on
the road ahead. She smiled and turned to the leader. "Sir
Lambeth, would that you appeared less dour. Is't not a
lovely day? Come, let us have some mirth and conversation as we ride."

But Sir Lambeth still said nothing. As they reached a
path which intersected the main road between Upper
and Lower Carea, the four knights spurred their horses.

They pressed about Berengeria too tightly for her to escape, one of them stripped her reins from her hands, and they led her at a smart trot along the new trail.

She spun about wildly and tried to leap from her mount but one of the men grasped her shoulder with one hand and shoved her roughly back into the saddle. "What is the meaning of this outrage?" she cried, her voice heavy with anger. But still no reply came.

A set, fanatical look seized each man's face. What had turned them from her—these men were six of the most loyal Carean knights. What bribe or threat or persuasion made them haul her along this strange road? Who was behind it?

They traveled west, toward a long, mountainous peninsula which jutted into the ocean. She could not guess why the six warriors had abducted her but such questions did not matter. She had to escape before all civilization fell behind and she was completely at their mercy. She tried again to drop from her saddle but that was useless. She was caught by her arms once more and shoved back into place. Then the knights sped to a gallop, hauled her and her horse at a mad pace up hills, past a peasant village, toward a pass which lay high between two of the northernmost mountain peaks. Was that the plot? Would they take her through the mountains, then toward some secluded ocean beach? Was she to be placed aboard some vessel, kidnapped, perhaps by one of her more ruthless suitors? Or was she being taken for some purpose even more foul?

They hurtled through ever rougher terrain; the trail led toward the towering peaks. Clusters of great boulders had fallen from the craggy heights and dotted the slopes before them. They headed toward an imposing group of the largest monoliths.

Then, from among those great stones, came a sight which made Berengeria's blood run cold. Four mounted figures in white robes rode toward her escort. Their robes ended in hoods of undyed wool; all she could see were gloved hands and shadows where faces should have been. But the whiteness of the fabric was all too familiar to her. It told her a horrible tale: they were the robes worn by the minions of the mad wizard, Alyubol, who had been dead for five years but whose followers still lurked.

So she was captured once again. Whoever these men were, she knew their purposes were evil, and the thought of being at their mercy made her shudder. Then the six knights who surrounded her slowed. One of the hooded figures spoke a single word: "Halt." And when the knights had halted, two of the white-robed men pounced on Berengeria, dragged her from her saddle, and bound her hands. She shrieked and struggled but it was no use; they shoved a gag in her mouth, tightened the ropes about her wrists until they hurt, and carried her toward another horse.

Chapter Eleven:
Following the Princess

ARCITE AWAKENED. THE throbbing in his skull told him that something evil was afoot, even though he could scarcely remember where he was. But his instincts guided him; he scrambled to his feet and ran toward the Temple of Hestia. His mind cleared as he dashed into the great square where the temple stood; he remembered the cause of his fears.

He had tired of sitting with the knights of Berengeria's escort. He had sung them a melody or two and they had received the ditties well enough, but singing lost its pleasure with his beloved Berengeria out of his sight. So he had fallen silent and, since there had been nothing better to do, he had allowed his nose to guide him to a little street bakery where a man was putting bread into an outdoor oven.

That had given him an idea. How surprised the Princess would be, he had thought, when she emerged from the temple to find him waiting for her with fresh butter, milk, and loaves of bread so hot they steamed when cut open. It would be a pleasant snack and the knights of the escort would enjoy it as well. Or so he had thought.

But how painfully he remembered. It had taken some

doing to find milk and butter but he had succeeded. And he had carried those products and a full basket of loaves with him to the temple. But as he passed the temple's stable and drew toward the knights themselves, he had stopped, suspicious. A maiden sang to them, a comely maiden dressed in white robes. And to his trained ear there had been something decidedly nasty about the melody.

He searched his brain. What was it he had not liked about the song? There was something mystical, magical about it—he had heard tales of such singing, which transported men's minds off to strange places. He had even heard snatches of such singing around vagabond campfires and in darkened graveyards. The maiden had been no good. But before he could throw down his goods, stop his ears with torn rags, and dash up to the woman and silence her, everything had gone black. From the throbbing of his skull, he knew what had happened. The maiden had had an accomplice—someone had discerned his purpose, had struck him from behind, and had dragged him into the alley behind the stable. And as he dashed into the square, he saw his worst fears confirmed: the knights were gone and a quick check showed Berengeria gone, too. The strange singer had finished her song and her evil purpose had been achieved.

He dashed into the stable and collared the old monk who kept the place. "Now quickly," he asked, trying to keep his voice as calm as possible. "Tell me how long it's been since those six royal knights departed?"

The monk eyed him in surprise. "Why, it was a good bit ago, master. The Princess came out of the temple and they fetched their horses, then they rode down that street there."

Arcite followed the man's extended finger. The street led in the general direction of Upper Carea. Perhaps that was a good sign. "But just how long?" he repeated.

The monk screwed his grizzled face into a thoughtful expression. "It was awhile. 'Twas the time it takes to say several matin prayers, at least."

Arcite cursed, then stopped himself. He was in the presence of a holy man after all, even though the fellow might be the lowest minion of the temple. Still, no more time could be lost. "Then fetch my horse and hurry. When that's done, it's crucial that you take this ring unto the deacon of this temple." Arcite pulled forth a large, jeweled pendant which had hung about his neck on a golden chain. "Our Princess's life's in danger; no more time can pass before I give pursuit, but be you sure the message is delivered to the Queen. She'll know this pendant, and reward you and your order, too."

The old man's eyes grew wide. "Indeed, indeed," he cried in an unsteady voice. Then he hurried away on bandy legs to fetch Arcite's horse.

As soon as the animal came, Arcite leaped onto its back and turned its head toward the square. "Remember all my words," he cried down to the monk. Then, without waiting to see what the man did, he set spurs to his mount and galloped toward the street where Berengeria had passed; he scattered onlookers this way and that as he hurtled in pursuit.

He had no idea where they might have ridden; he could only follow in the hope they had not turned from the main avenue. At last, however, his misgivings overcame his haste and he dismounted long enough to ask a shopkeeper whether the group had passed by. "Yes," the man said, "they were riding all together, toward the southern gate."

Arcite leaped back onto his palfrey and spurred the beast toward the city's entrance like a man possessed. But once he had reached the road beyond the gate, he had to slow down. He hurried along, eyeing the surface with keen eyes, uttering silent prayers that he had not lost the trail. But there was precious little to be seen. Gradually the stones of the road's surface grew ever farther apart until it was more dirt than paving, but even then the dust had been so churned by hoofprints that he could make nothing of it.

But suddenly he did see something—a trail intersected the road and led toward the right; and he could tell the trail's surface had lately been trodden by several horses. The tracks converged, mixed together, overlapped one another in strange patterns. There was only one possible reason for that; one member of the party must have been struggling against the rest.

He sped up and scanned ahead. The tracks kept on and on; they stretched toward the Altines Mountains, which lay to the west. The band must have been riding at speed from the look of the evidence. But what would the knights do with Berengeria when they reached the craggy peaks? Who was behind the enchantment and the abduction? He shuddered to think.

He rode on into the afternoon and the peaks looked ever higher, ever nearer. He rode into foothills scattered with giant boulders and he could see where the trail led up to a lofty pass between two giant peaks. Then something off to one side caught his eye. It was a palfrey, grazing among the boulders. It was Berengeria's palfrey.

He thrust his knees into the sides of his own frothing mount, leaned, and turned toward the lone horse. When he dismounted and strode toward it, it eyed him mildly, then resumed its grazing. Where was Berengeria? He glanced about, but could find no other sign that men had passed this way in a long time.

Hidden among a thick cluster of the giant boulders which had rolled down from the mountain's peak, stood six more horses. And atop the six horses sat six knights, the knights of Berengeria's escort. They were all snoring, sleeping off their enchantment. The hoofprints all about told him another story; other riders had conferred with the six knights. They had left the knights here but they had plainly taken Berengeria with them.

He made a fist. Perhaps she was still alive. In that case, she had to be on the other side of that pass by now; if he hurried, perhaps he could still save her. He leaped onto his horse and rode in pursuit.

Darkness fell but the moon let him keep on, even though the trail was difficult to follow in the darkness. At last, on the far side of the mountains, he saw the lights of a village and the waves of the Thlassa Allas, stretching away in dark lines in the moonlight. He had reached the end of land, some little trading village on the western edge of the peninsula. An inn and a stable remained open so he stopped to rest, to partake of some supper, and to ask questions. "Have three or four men come into this place, accompanying a woman?" he asked the stableboy.

"No, sir," the boy replied. "There was three men come through tonight but there warn't no woman with them. They was driving a wagon full of long boxes."

Boxes? Wagon? That could have nothing to do with the party Arcite followed. There had been no wagon tracks where Berengeria had been transferred. "Were there no others?"

The lad shrugged. "None that I saw, but there's a ship a-loading out beyond the beach so there might of been someone else."

Arcite smiled. "Is this a seaport, then?"

"We do enough business to live," the boy replied. "See, if a fellow ships to some point on the Thlassa Allas, or any ocean port, he can avoid a duty by shipping from here. I mean, the ship doesn't have to pass through the Narrow Strait, does it? We're not Lower Carea but we get our share of traffic."

"I see." The village was a port for smugglers. That would make it a natural destination for a captured Princess, no matter what the stableboy had or had not seen. Arcite pondered the situation as he walked to the inn and then ate a light supper. All his instincts pointed the same way; if there was a ship in the harbor, Berengeria was aboard it.

He called the innkeeper and put an important question. "When sails that vessel there in yonder bay?"

The fellow stroked his chin. "Soon, I know that. She's lain offshore for two days, though only her officers and some passengers have come ashore. She's taken on goods all day by lighter so she must be about full."

"So she could sail at any moment."

"Probably at dawn, or close to it."

Arcite gulped down his meal, paid the man, and hurried down to the beach. An onshore breeze kissed his face and wafted the stink of the sea to his nostrils; it told him the ship would not sail until the tide turned. That would soon come, though. He had time, but not much time.

He raced along the beach and located the lighter which the innkeeper had mentioned. It was not a lighter, really, but a little barge moored at a small wooden dock. It was plainly built to be rowed by two men and could only carry small loads of cargo. But it was too large for him to operate alone. Arcite considered the shoals the innkeeper had mentioned. Where there were shoals, there were shipwrecks, and where there were ship-wrecks, there was salvage. It was natural that Beren-geria had been spirited through this little port. What better place to ferret her out of the country than a haven for smugglers and wreckers?

He ran along the shoreline, then stumbled across something in the darkness and fell cursing into a washed-up pile of seaweed. He leaped to his feet and thrust away the soft and clinging fabric of the weed, flinging the last bits onto the sand in disgust. But then he felt about and discovered a small rowboat, turned keel up against the elements. He had to stifle a laugh; this was the fishing fleet of this village—a rowboat to ferry scavengers to and from shipwrecks on the shoals. If he searched long enough, he had little doubt he would find others.

But this one would serve his purpose. He turned it over and slid it into the water, then stood in thought for a moment. It would take a long time to row to the ship against the wind; if he waited, she would sail and Beren-geria would be gone with her. If he was wrong and she remained ashore—he could not ponder that. Every in-stinct, every nerve heard the Princess' heart calling to his from the ship which lay just beyond reach.

He set his jaw, pushed the light craft into the breakers until the water was up to his waist, and clambered in, with much grunting and rocking of the boat. He was no sailor. But he grasped the oars and quickly got into the rhythm of his rowing. His progress against the breeze and the waves was steady, though it was slow.

The vessel was a large merchantman; he could tell that much as her dark mass loomed ever greater ahead of him. An eternity of rowing passed and he washed close to the ship; he could hear her rigging creak as she wallowed at anchor. The waves lapped against her side and made noises like throttled birds. He rowed toward the vessel's bow, caught hold of the great hawser which secured the anchor, and made his way hand-over-hand to the forecastle. It was tricky business, especially when he came to the hawser pipe where the anchor line passed into the ship itself. But he was able to climb to the forecastle deck and roll, gasping, into the shelter of a hatch cover.

Then he heard a hollow *clunk*! followed by a sleepy voice. "Who's there?" He cursed. The little boat had collided with the ship's side and had alerted the anchor watch. He ground his teeth and held his breath as he listened to footsteps approaching along the starboard rail. They stopped short of where he lay. He had escaped detection for the moment but where was he to search for Berengeria?

The forecastle deck was as dark as the inside of a mine. Clouds had obscured the moon and the world snuggled beneath a blanket of murk. Again he heard steps, this time from inside the forecastle itself. How many men made up the anchor watch? Surely, not more than two. But that would be enough to trap him if he remained above decks too long.

Yes, there were two. He could hear them talking at the ship's waist. One had been inspecting the cargo, insuring that it was secured against rough weather, while the other had been the man who had called out earlier. Four eyes—Arcite had to elude four eyes. He rolled onto his knees and made his way to the forecastle's aft rail, where he could look down on them.

"Passengers all turned in?" asked the one who had just come on deck.

"Just lately. They was laughing and talking in their cabin until all hours. Mighty strange lot, if you ask me, with all their robes and their foreign gestures."

Arcite's heart leaped as he remembered the white-robed woman he had seen in front of the temple. He was on the right track.

"Ah, well, I suppose it don't matter as long as their gold is good. But a mighty strange cargo, if you ask me. All those boxes—you'd think they was shipping bodies."

Arcite strained to hear more. Boxes? Boxes of bodies. The stableboy had mentioned boxes; the villains must have made another transfer, the signs of which Arcite had missed in the darkness.

The two watchmen changed to a different topic and made their way toward the vessel's stern. He cursed them silently; he had to learn where the boxes were stowed. But there was only one thing he could do—he had to get into the hold somehow and search for Berengeria.

He found the ladder which led down to the main deck, then scuttled down it like a rat down a rope, dodged to the shelter of the ship's boats which were nested before the mast, then saw the opening he sought; the forecastle companionway yawned two fathoms ahead of him. Somewhere within that dark structure would be the ladder which led into the forward hold. He looked about one last time, listened, and darted through.

In the forecastle, he found himself surrounded by snoring. He huddled against a bulkhead and listened, while the sweat popped from his forehead in torrents, for he had found his way into the crew's berthing. He crawled across the deck until his fingers encountered the ladder into the hold, then turned himself and crawled down the steep steps on his hands and knees, silently, hardly daring to breathe. The gathering foetor told him he had found his destination. Poor Berengeria—what fiends had apprehended her, that dared plunge her into such a place!

He had to search the hold with his fingertips, for there was no light. But he did find the boxes. They lay all in a row in the forward hold, lashed to the deck. Hurriedly,

he pried one open with his dagger, reached in, and—
horror of horrors—touched cold flesh.

His breath died within him. Had they killed her? No,
the face was that of an old man, with beard and moustache. He lowered the crate's lid back into place and
moved on to the next. Another body—what fiends these
were, or what ghouls. But at least it was not Berengeria.
The next was the same, and the next, but the last held
the inert form of a maiden. Was it she? Was it his beloved? No, for Berengeria had always worn lace collars
which concealed everything below her throat. This dead
maiden was dressed in a low-cut gown.

He withdrew his fingers, settled the box's cover back
into place, and breathed a silent prayer that he might be
forgiven such a sacrilege against the dead. Then he
slumped into a heap, rested his back against the pile of
cargo, and wiped his forehead. What a strange shipment
it was, for the bodies were not bloated or decomposed.
Though they were cold and lifeless, they remained perfectly preserved.

But where was Berengeria? Had he blundered? Was it
possible that she was not even aboard this vessel, which
would set sail at dawn? He sighed and sagged against the
crates while desperate thoughts raced through his mind.
Berengeria still had to lie somewhere aboard this vessel.
The love they shared, though she might consider it forbidden, still connected them; he could feel her heart
beating only cubits from his. She was on the ship; she
had to be on the ship.

Did the death boxes he had already searched have
false bottoms? Had he held his fingers inches from Berengeria without knowing it? That was possible—but
only barely. They were only shallow boxes; no room lay
in them for hidden bodies.

He felt for the aft bulkhead and rested his head
against it. Since he was now at the widest point of the
hull, the hold had been divided into two sections. Perhaps that was it—perhaps she had been hidden in the aft
hold. But he found no openings in the bulkhead and even
as he searched, he heard dozens of feet thunder across

the deck above him. Dawn must have broken; the ship was getting under way. He sighed and hid himself between the stacks of cargo and the bulkhead. He could only wait for his chance to search further and hope that he had been right—that he had not left his beloved Princess ashore in her moment of desperation.

Chapter Twelve:
Tychopolis

DOWN PLUNGED PALAMON and Flin, two fathoms, three fathoms, until they landed with a whump that jarred the breath from Palamon's body. Even after they stopped falling, the hides beneath them continued to settle while others piled on top of them, pressing them down without mercy. Palamon knew he had to react. He had to find an open space before the rain of hides smothered him.

There was no longer an up or down, a right or a left; he could only inch his way in the direction of least resistance. At last he pried upward on a hide that was dangling before him and saw light. His hand rubbed against a stout pole. When he looked into the opening, he saw he had landed in the wagon; a cubit of hides pressed down on top of him but the layer of hides beneath was well past the height of a man.

The muleteers labored feverishly; they had not even noticed this unusual addition to their cargo. They were large, rough men in their thirties and they hustled about the wagon with quick, precise movements. They threw in hides which had fallen out past the sideboards that formed the wagon's box, they greased axles, and they filled the crate beneath the seat with tools and food for the journey. Then Palamon pulled his head back as the two men climbed the wooden sides of the wagon in order to lash a tarpaulin across the top.

But where was Flin? Palamon launched his hands and feet into delicate probing motions at the thought that the young knight might be smothering some place amid the cascade of hides. But a movement against his legs told the tall monarch otherwise. He struggled against the leathers' weight, reached down, and grasped a hand. Then he pulled until Flin's head was even with his. "What a ride," the younger man breathed. "Where are we?"

"We're in a teamster's wagon. Move a bit and you can peer between the sideboards, just as I have done."

Flin inched his way forward, peered out, then drew back his head and grinned. "This is perfect. I used to see plenty of these big freight wagons during my days riding the Greenlands. All we have to do is sit tight and they'll take us out of this accursed town slick as a gut."

"But I must reach pale Lothar and the Count of Fleuve, to tell to them the wrath which burns inside me at this treachery."

"You're too damned honorable—you haven't any concept of how nasty your enemies can be. You don't even know who they all are yet. As like as not, either Lothar or the Count already knows someone is trying to kill you—because like as not, one of them is behind it. At least. For all we know, they could both be in on it and your friend the Constable with them."

"I can't agree. As we both know, pale Lothar is no fool; his purposes can only suffer harm if I should die within this town. I'm sure he'll help us find and deal with those who perpetrated the atrocities of this night past— most likely Alyubol's old cohorts and no others."

"Maybe," Flin replied. "But don't bet on it. Humor me. Let's wait here, let these fellows take us beyond the city's walls, and then we can decide what to do."

Palamon sighed. Wisdom lay in the younger man's words. "I am the first to grant that politics and wise diplomacy are two hard schools in which I never have done well. Perhaps you're right, though all my instincts say to face Count Destus and the Buerdic monarch in the light."

"That would be the honorable thing to do," Flin agreed. "But honor never got anyone anywhere. Let's ride this wagon and see what happens."

They did so, though it irked the tall monarch to be hauled from Danaar like so much baggage. The two men lay immersed in hides and peeked out from time to time to watch the city's streets creep by. The ride was a slow one. But after what seemed eons, they felt the cobbled paving give way to the softer earth of a country road and peeked out to see Danaar's walls receding behind them.

"Now we must free ourselves," Palamon said. He began to pull at the aromatic hides, to tunnel his way up through them. They did not have far to climb but it was hard work all the same, for the hides were broad and clumsy to move. Both men strained to sit up against the weight, struggling to escape the overlapping folds. All at once, panic blew into Palamon's brain like a miasma; he felt strange and he doubled his struggles to reach the top of the wagon. And by the thrashing at his side, he could tell that Flin was doing the same. But it was of no use; drowsiness curled clammy fingers about his senses. He felt his motions become ever feebler, until he lost himself in blackness.

Time passed. The first thing Palamon comprehended was the aching in his midsection. The second thing was that he was now lying on the ground, and that he could hear gusts of wind and the buzz of men's voices above him. He coughed, gagged, tried to roll over, then blinked his eyes as his world became comprehensible. He and Flin were lying side-by-side next to the freight wagon, which now stood empty. The two angry muleteers, along with two other men, eyed him in a manner that was plainly hostile. "Where are we?" Palamon asked.

"You tried to steal a ride to Tychopolis is what you did, and that's where you are," one of the muleteers answered. "How you got into my wagon I'll never know, but I know what happened then. The potions used to tan our hides put the two of you to sleep like a couple of babes; you're lucky you're not dead. If you'd just lain still, they wouldn't have done much harm, but you must have started wrestling about, which means you breathed in more of the vapors, which means you got knocked out like a drunken sailor. Serves you right, too, a couple of well-dressed men like you getting caught in a prank like that."

"Yes, I have been a prankster all my life," Palamon replied dryly. "And never more than on that night of games and silliness. But you are right, of course: there's been enough of jesting. I apologize." He stood and felt himself; at least the two muleteers had not relieved him of his sword or his gold while he had been unconscious. "I see that you're an honest fellow. I will not reveal my name, or that of my young comrade, save to say that we were both in danger in Danaar and had to find a hiding place."

"Rob someone, did ye?" The second muleteer spat into the dust beside Palamon. "Ye've been doing some mischief, then, if ye were a-hidin' in the hides. But it's all the same to us, for we've asked after the night watch and he'll have a man around in a jiffy. That'll do for you."

The watch. Palamon felt no desire to confront the watch in this strange city. He still did not know who the author of his woes was, or whether all of his troubles issued from the same source. Therefore, any new face could be a fresh and deadly enemy. The two Careans had to get away from these men and find their way back to friendly soil. But Palamon's thoughts were interrupted as Flin sat up and rubbed his hands over his eyes. "I'm hungry," the young knight said. "Where are we?"

"It's no miracle you're hungry, by the gods. You were stowed away in our wagon for three days."

Palamon bent over Flin but the sudden movement made him dizzy and he nearly fell. He braced a hand against the wagon, cleared his head, then helped Flin to his feet. "If it will make you gentlemen feel better, I can

tell you that we are not thieves, nor villains. This was all
an accident. If you desire, we'll gladly pay a fare for all
the distance that we traveled." He had begun to move
away from the man while dragging the still-muddled Flin
after him but he paused long enough to pull a couple of
talents from his pouch. "Here, that should give you sol-
ace for our prank."

The wind blew his hair into his face as he tossed the
coins to the ground before the two muleteers. Their eyes
widened at the value of the pieces and they bent to
snatch them up. Before they could straighten, Palamon
hurried himself and Flin along the street and around the
corner of the building. Flin quickly found his feet; his
walking steadied. But it was plain that his head still had
not completely cleared. "Where are we?" he asked again.
"And why am I so hungry?"

"We're in a city called Tychopolis," Palamon replied.
"And we've not eaten for three days, which should explain your appetite."

Flin blinked at him. "Tychopolis?"

"Tychopolis. What, do you know the place?"

"I know it as well as the lines on my own palm." He
laughed a smug laugh. "It's a holy city."

"A holy city?"

"Oh, yes. They worship Tyche here, in a dozen temples. She's the goddess of good luck and rolling cubes, as
it were. And they're very devout. Worshippers come
from all across the Greenlands to place wagers at her
tables."

"They gamble?"

Flin winked at him. "They worship. The place used to
have some other name but no one knows it anymore.
They built halls full of gaming tables—they're really
temples, mind you—and the wagerers come from miles
about. Yes, my friend, we've found a bonny town to be
hungry in. It's full of places where you can satisfy any
appetite known to mankind."

Palamon felt unsure whether to be pleased or not. It
was good that Flin was familiar with this new terrain;
that would surely come in handy. But Palamon had been

reared as a Knight of Pallas and he preferred not to think of human beings in terms of their appetites. Still, his approval or disapproval of such a place as this would have to be put away for the time being, for he heard the sound of arms clicking in the street behind him. He grasped Flin by the shoulder and hauled him into the nearest dark alleyway.

"What are you doing?" Flin asked.

"I think I heard the watch."

"You mean you're still worried about what those clowns back at the wagon said? You can forget that. No one in this city is going to care what you did in Danaar, as long as you don't start trouble here. As like as not, the fellow didn't even call the watch, but told you he did just to get you to pay."

That information did not help Palamon feel better. Still, it did make sense. He poked his head out of the alley's shadows and saw no one. "So where go we from here?" he asked quietly.

"We go to the center of the city, to the place they call the bazaar. That's where everything happens. We have some dinner and then we relax for a while and decide what you're going to do about your friends back in Danaar."

Palamon nodded and they began to walk in the direction Flin had indicated. Either Tychopolis was not a large city or the freight wagon had unloaded near the center of it, for a short walk brought them to a broad central square ablaze with torchlight. Palamon had to marvel at the place. Towering temples surrounded the square but none was like any temple Palamon had ever seen in his life: across the broad front of each one, a forest of torches burned in brackets. Their flames danced sideways in the windy night; they burned all different colors. Potions and chemicals had been added to the flames to make them glow any number of hues; each building tried to outshine its neighbor. On some, bonfires had even been built along the towering façades. The smell of the fires and the hot smoke choked the senses and leaping windblown flames shot into the darkness like jagged teeth.

The square was alive with the smell of incense. And from the open portals of the temples poured more clouds of smoke and mists, as if each one was full of the sacred blazes of sacrificial fires. Men and women of all castes, all classes, thronged the square, and over all came the babble of voices from the uncountable pilgrims to this strange holy place. "Come along," Flin said as he pulled Palamon's arm. "We can get food in any of the temples; they feed the pilgrims at practically no cost. It's only a small offering."

"This seems a heathen place," Palamon said doubtfully.

"No, no. These men and women are all as devout as anyone you might meet in your own court. I've seen 'em go into this place and come out. Why, back in their homes, most of them are as stodgy a lot as you'd ever care to see. It's just the spirit of Tyche on them that makes them act this way—at least that's what I've been told. It purifies them and cleanses them of earthly avarice." He looked at Palamon and smiled a secret smile. "And it cleanses them of a good part of their wealth, as well."

The two men picked their way across the square and walked into one of the temples. Inside, Palamon found a scene even stranger than the one outside. The ceiling was low enough to touch and supported by great timbers, carved into the likenesses of writhing dragons. Everywhere, at the top of every column, snarling reptilian heads bared fangs and leered out of the clouds of incense smoke.

Below the dragons' heads stood rows of tables, ornately carved and covered with felt. And at those tables the pilgrims gambled in great numbers, all the while invoking the name of the goddess Tyche. Some cast lots, some played the game of the wheel, while others wagered over cards. The babble of voices united into a din which was nearly deafening. All about him, Palamon heard fervent prayer, the cries of those who succeeded in their gambling, or the groans of those who lost, all punctuated by the jingle of loose coins and the rattle of the games. "This is the hall of worship and debasement," Flin said as he guided Palamon by the arm. "Beyond this are the kitchens, where the pilgrims can find all kinds of dishes to eat, baths where they can rest and cleanse themselves, theaters where they can take their leisure, drink wine, and watch dancing maidens or jugglers or clowns. It's not all worship, you see. It's said their bodies couldn't stand the strain if they worshipped every minute."

"This does not resemble any of the rites I am accustomed to."

Flin grinned. "They put their souls into it, though, you have to admit that. You can see it for yourself."

Palamon looked at the younger man. "And have you worshipped here? It seems to me this type of bacchanal would be greatly to your liking."

Flin's grin turned into a laugh. "Yes, I've laid down a few coins before the goddess and I've taken my ease in the baths and the theaters. But between you and me, it was more for the bacchanal than for the cleansing."

Palamon smiled dryly. "It's in my mind the same case holds with all these frenzied folk."

"Hush, hush. Don't let them hear you saying that or they'll toss us both out of here like a couple of dirty rags."

Palamon said no more as they made their way through the noisy hall and into a quieter chamber beyond. Though large, this second chamber was not nearly as large as the first and was set up like a common inn. The two men sat at a table and maidens quickly brought them flagons of wine, steaming slabs of roast beef, and every kind of tasty morsel. Because it was the first food to pass their lips in several days, the two guests ate with great spirit.

Once they had filled their bellies, Flin stretched out on his chair and sighed. "That's better. I'm beginning to feel like a man again."

But Palamon stood and looked about. The very ease

of this place troubled him. "Your words may all be true, but to my mind we've little time to dally in this nest."

"Why not?"

Palamon gazed down at Flin. Though the young knight was a dear friend and marvelous companion, Palamon would never begin to understand him. "We must return to Keep Danaar, or else begin our trek to lands allied with us. Cannot you see? Each moment which escapes before I find the man behind these villainies is one more moment lost, one tick of time removed from my son's life. We must be on our way; I have to find the man who stole my sword. I must believe he'll be the same as he who struck down Berethane."

Flin sat up. "Yes, I'm sorry. It's easy for me to forget things in a place like this. But where will we go?"

"I do not know just yet. There are a host of matters to consider in that choice of questions to be answered. They can be discussed while we seek out a stable. I assume that in this town we'll somewhere find two horses for our purchase."

"Oh, yes," Flin said as he stood up and brushed himself off. "You can buy anything here."

"Then let us hurry on."

They found the innkeeper, or whatever one called the man who kept this eating chamber, and Palamon made an offering by way of payment for the food. He was surprised he needed to pay no more, but a priest told him the kitchens were kept only to feed the worshippers, and not for profit. Yet in the next chamber, those same pilgrims were allowed to wager their last farthing and, Palamon had actually seen when he had entered the place, they were cast into the street if they had no more. Palamon had to shake his head all over again at the strange nature of the temple. But it was not his place to pass judgment on any temple or on the strange sect which worshipped at this one.

But as the two men made their way through the crowded gambling chamber and toward the street, Palamon stopped short. "That man who passes there," he said to Flin. "Did you just see him?"

"I'm not sure. Which one do you mean?"

Palamon nearly bit his tongue in his haste; his temples pounded and a roaring filled his ears. The throng which packed the temple wore every type of clothing, from the silks of the rich to the worn linens of poor merchants. But one man passed among them who wore garb Palamon would have recognized anywhere. "The white-robed man who passes from our view and down another corridor. Do you know where it leads?" Palamon began to run in that direction, then stopped short. He did not want to be noticed, not now of all times.

"I think it leads to the baths."

"We must not lose him, for his robes evoke the cult which followed Alyubol. That man's an evil minion, so I say, and thereby harbors information." Palamon clenched his fist and pounded it into the palm of his other hand. Then he clenched his eyes and spoke again. "O Pallas, thank you for this little clue. This fellow shall be telling us his tale before the night is finished, so I trow."

"That's right," Flin said as he caught up with the tall monarch. "But if you want to 'take him to one side,' as the saying goes, this is a poor place to do it."

"We'll find him," Palamon replied. "Then we shall decide what course to take with him."

He and the young knight followed the figure into a long corridor lined with carvings of pastoral scenes, statues of women in various stages of undress, and paintings of fish and sea birds. The floor tiles were laid out in colored patterns which suggested fanciful sea demons. Palamon knew Flin had been correct, that they were headed toward the baths. But what would they do once they reached the white-robed man's destination? The dampness of the air told him they were already close. They would have no choice but to disrobe and enter the bath chamber itself, like any other customer, and Palamon had no great desire to face one of Alyubol's minions without a weapon close to hand. Besides, how would he even recognize the man without his white robe?

"Wait," he said to Flin. "Do you know whether there

are any other passages which lead into these baths?"

Flin stopped. "I don't know. But if they're the same as most baths, I doubt it."

"I doubt it also. Very well, then. Let us wait for him at greater distance. We will see him leave if we can wait him out. Then we shall follow him; I have no doubt he'll lead us to some foul and pagan sect; then we can find some way to put a noose around them all."

They made their way back to the chamber of the dragons' heads and mingled with the frenzied gamblers there. But all the while they kept by turns an eye on the corridor which led from the baths. Novices crisscrossed the floor, making sure that all in the temple took part in games of chance, so both Palamon and Flin had no choice but to join. They spent their time at the table nearest the baths, one laying down wagers while the other eyed the corridor.

Before long, Palamon touched Flin on the back. "That's him." It was the same man Palamon had seen before, and this time there could be no doubt. His robe was an exact copy of the robes Alyubol and his minions had worn every time Palamon had confronted them. And in the one instant the man's face flashed into view, it showed the mark of fanatical cruelty, the loathsome sneer which was to be expected of any member of that cadre. Palamon allowed Flin to make one last wager, which he won, while the robed figure moved toward the temple's portals. Then, once he had safely shown his back, both men followed him.

It was hard to trace him as he made his way through the milling throngs in the city's torch-dazzled square but Palamon was a tall man. He was able to follow the pointed top of the fellow's hood well enough to trace him to a narrow side street. After that, the trailing was easier. "Be careful," Flin whispered. "He may have friends."

This street was dark, though the buildings which lined it showed affluence enough. If the man was going to his sect's lair, it was plain that they still held the loyalty of some wealthy patron. The houses they passed were tall, with ornate doors and wrought-iron balconies that extended over the street. After a long walk, the fellow stopped and rapped on one of the doors. Instantly, Palamon and Flin ducked into another doorway to watch what might transpire.

The door opened, a robed head appeared, and the two minions of Alyubol whispered together. Then both figures vanished into the building. Flin turned to Palamon with a little smile on his face. "It looks as if you've got your coven. What do we do now?"

"I doubt that we can bring the local Count's authority into the matter," Palamon said. "I doubt that he would act upon the word of some mere citizen, and no one but a fool would e'er believe me if I told them I was King of fair Carea." He looked into Flin's eyes. "It is ironic—I have loathed the throne and all the burdens it has placed on me through every day since I have gained it. Now, when I would find it useful to possess the scepter's weight, I have no proof."

"We carry monies enough," Flin offered. "A well-placed coin or two will buy us all the henchmen we want."

"I think not. Men whose loyalty is purchased for a sum, can prove rebellious. Let us go as far as possible with just the two of us."

Flin grinned and clapped him on the back. "First-rate thinking," he said. "That's just the way I'd do it myself."

Palamon smiled and continued. "Indeed. I thank you. Let us search about this block of buildings and see just how we might gain entry, or at least obtain a view of what transpires within."

They scampered out of the shadows and searched along the street for a ladder or an unlocked door. "Many of these houses are left empty most of the time," Flin said. "Some of the worshippers come here regularly and possess enough wealth to own homes in this city. Most of the time, the places stand empty or stay in the hands of servants. If we can get into one, we might be able to get to the rooftop."

"A good idea," Palamon agreed. But even though they tried several doors, they had no success. Besides,

Palamon had no wish to be apprehended like a thief in the night. They made their way around the buildings until they came to the alley which ran along the back sides of the lavish residences. But the alley was bordered on both sides by high stone walls.

"They don't mean for us to get in," Flin observed.

Palamon had been counting the houses they had passed since entering the alley. "I estimate this space of wall is part of that same house our evil fellow entered. Look you here, a tree extends its limbs across the neighboring wall. That well might be our avenue."

"It's in the right place but that limb's too high," Flin said. "How do you propose to get up there?"

Palamon looked up. The walls presented a blank face so high a man could not hope to leap up and grasp the top, even by climbing on the back of an accomplice. "You say the houses in this sector are as oft unoccupied as not?"

"I've been here enough times that I can assure you of it."

"I saw no lights in either of the houses flanking this which is our goal. That's as I would suspect: the cult of Alyubol would not prefer close neighbors. You have said that anything can easily be bought in this strange city; then go you and purchase us a goodly length of rope."

"That's good enough for me." Flin started down the alley on the run while Palamon cautiously made his way back around the stone building. He watched the place well into the night. The dim lights which could be seen beyond the front windows never changed; no one came or went. And at last Flin returned with rope and a humorous story of the extremes he had been forced to go to obtain it. He had wound up purchasing it from a carter, who had snickered at the tale Flin had told him of open windows and winsome maids waiting to be wooed. And Palamon had to smile as he listened. Such tales came naturally and pleasantly to Flin.

They scurried back to the alley; it was only the work of moments for them to hoist themselves onto the stout branch and haul the rope up after them. Soon, they had settled themselves amid the swaying branches; they shivered because they were more exposed to the wind than they were on the ground.

The tree stood in a court which was narrow and deep and provided room for a considerable garden. But it was an adjacent court which drew Palamon's attention. In that house, he could see two men sitting at table on a high balcony, shielded from the elements by the house beyond them. They argued fiercely; their voices drifted up to him in the night air and caused his hackles to rise.

And he recognized both men. All the circumstances of the last several days, the knights who had tried to assassinate him, the drugging of his own knights, the theft of the *Spada Korrigaine*, were explained by the sight laid out below him on that veranda. For the white-robed man had thrown back his hood; the oily blackness of his hair and moustache contrasted starkly with the paleness of his face in the torchlight. And the other . . . Palamon should have expected as much, though it staggered him to see any member of the chivalry so debase himself as to consort with the evil wizard's men. But it was natural enough, because hatred breeds ignobility. The other man at the table was Ursid, Constable of Buerdaunt.

Chapter Thirteen:
The Storm

ARCITE WAS A sick man even before he remembered where he was. He had fallen asleep in the ship's hold and now the vessel was moving; it made its way through heavy weather, rolled with unseen winds, heaved him about the hold, forced his stomach out his mouth. He grasped a nearby line, for the goods in the hold were all lashed down, and he tried to stand. But nausea doubled him over again. His belly ached as if he had swallowed spikes; he had never been this miserable in all his days.

Seasickness! He had heard the word but had never understood the meaning as he did now. He retched, once and again, until there was no more for him to spew forth. Then he retched again, the pain of his heaving guts all the worse because there was nothing there to expel. At last the spasms eased and he lay back on the pitching deck, sweating, gasping, dizzy in the odor of his own vomit. He would not last long at this rate; he had to do something.

In years, he had never allowed his lute to leave his side. Now it would have to save him from distress. He felt about in the darkness, found it where he had left it stuffed snugly into the space between two crates, then

braced himself into a sitting position and touched the
strings. All about him, the wooden world of the ship's
hold pitched and tossed but at least he felt a little better.

He concentrated on tuning the instrument, on producing soft notes, and his misery finally began to subside.
The nausea came and went by stages but no longer was it
the ravenous horror which had swarmed over him before. His music filled him, comforted him, drove away
the vile world of the ship and its cargo, replaced those
things with peace and beauty. That was what his music
had always been able to do for him.

And as he played, he began to think. How long had
the ship been under way? It occurred to him that the
vessel must have sailed into a considerable storm; she
would not pitch and roll this way in normal weather. It
also occurred to him that the vessel was riding in the
troughs of the waves, which caused her to roll more than
if she had been meeting the seas head-on. How he
wished he could peek above decks long enough to tell
where he now was.

In a storm like this, crewmen would be swarming
across the decks; he was trapped. Besides, he was afraid
to stop plucking his instrument, for fear the sickness
would return again.

But he did stop playing when he saw light flicker at
the top of the forecastle ladder. Someone was coming.
He slid his lute back into hiding and peeked from behind
the stock of boxes. A man—no, several men—were descending the ladder, guided by a lantern swinging in the
first man's grip. With every pitch of the ship, they
gripped the wooden railing and hung on for dear life, as if
they feared the storm would hurl them from their perch;
clearly, they were no more experienced seamen than was
Arcite himself.

They wore white woolen robes. The man in the lead
reached the ladder's foot, steadied himself, and motioned the second man to follow him. Then he shouted
toward the top of the ladder. "There is room in this hold,
Gondarkhan. Bring her down."

The voice which replied from above was deep, melodious, and sinister. "We will all come. Prepare yourself, Mellan."

"I will." This voice came from the second figure on the ladder and it was only then that Arcite realized she was female. In fact, she was the woman who had sung to the knights in front of the temple moments before he had been struck down. He slipped farther behind the crates, softly drew his dagger, and cut two small squares of fabric from his cape. He chewed each square vigorously and quickly and used them to stop his ears—if this was the singer he had seen before, he had no desire to listen to her melodies.

But he would need to do more than stop his ears. He put the dagger away, strapped his lute to his back, then drew his sword and peeked out again. More figures made their way down into the hold, fighting to keep upright as the vessel reeled and shook beneath them. And—he could hardly believe his eyes—one of them was Berengeria. But she was free of fetters; she was not restrained in any way. Someone had thrown one of the cult's white woolen robes onto her, over her lace gown—Arcite could see the hem of the gown protruding below the robe—and they ushered her about as if she were some sort of new initiate. She plainly did not know what to do next. She moved as if in a trance. Her eyes were fixed straight ahead and she occasionally scratched at herself or waved her fingers as if to drive away flies or some noxious insects which were hovering about her. One of the men, the one called Gondarkhan, was whispering into her ear continually, telling her how she should move.

There were several of them; they filled the far end of the hold. And the woman who had led the party was going to sing once more. But then one of the cultists bent to examine the boxes which held the bodies and Arcite's course was decided for him. "The cases are opened," the man cried. "For what reason, I wonder?"

"A sly interloper," Gondarkhan shouted. "Spread out; search the hold, call the captain."

There was no course for Arcite but to fight. He staggered against the ship's motions as he heaved himself up, but managed to leap toward the nearest opponent. "Your lives are ended, you unholy scum," he cried in the loudest voice he could muster, hoping to stampede his opponents with a wild charge. And it worked. Two of the villains scrambled up the ladder with loud shouting, though the others faced him and drew their swords.

For her part, Berengeria moved as if lost, beset by some sort of vermin. Her motions became erratic: she rubbed her arms and face with increasing fervor, staggered against the ship's rolling, then lost her balance and fell into a heap. And the evil maiden did not join the battle at all; she braced herself against the vessel's heaving timbers and began to sing. The bits of rag in Arcite's ears helped but they could not block her music out altogether. In desperation he began a song of his own, loud, lusty, and irreverent, to counteract the effect of her melody.

The first man lunged at Arcite and the minstrel cut him down with a single thrust. These fellows were clearly no swordsmen; the villain lacked any of Arcite's extensive training in weaponry. But the second man knew more of the deadly craft and he dueled Arcite while the last, Gondarkhan, yanked Berengeria to her feet and dashed toward the forecastle ladder. With a cry, Arcite rushed at his second opponent, beat down his guard, and sent the man's severed hand flying to the deck. Then, while the fellow screamed and clutched his truncated arm, Arcite rushed after the others.

The situation was desperate; Arcite ignored his heaving innards as he cleared the top of the ladder, bolted out of the forecastle, and found Gondarkhan still clutching Berengeria's wrist while he harangued the shipmaster. "You've let stowaways enter your vessel to desecrate our sacred rite. You low scoundrel, for what have we paid you? They all must be killed."

The only bright side of the situation was that the villain plainly thought more than one man had attacked his party. But there was nothing else to cheer Arcite: the vessel was rolling in the troughs of tremendous seas.

Spray filled the air; waves crashed onto the decks and forced everyone on the vessel to cling to something for support. He could see some shore line precariously close on the starboard side; the gale was blowing too furiously for the ship to bring her head out of the trough and she was in danger of being blown aground. Even as he reached the deck, Arcite saw a great, green wave crash down from the port side, tear the ship's boats from their lashings, and wash them into the sea, along with a section of rail.

There was no time to think; before any of the staggering party could react, Arcite timed the vessel's roll, dashed toward Gondarkhan and Berengeria, and snatched her away from the villain. He yanked her out the forecastle companionway and onto the deck. All about him rose screams of anger and dismay; fists and weapons clubbed at him; he did not allow himself to stop. But the hardest blow of all was Berengeria's expression as he dragged her after him. She was plainly entranced and she brushed at him as if he were only one more of the invisible vermin assaulting her. She plainly did not understand he was saving her; her look was one of shock, surprise, and sheer hatred.

But he could not change his course now, even if he had wanted to. As soon as he dragged the Princess onto the weather deck and into the teeth of the tempest, no man alive could have kept them from what happened next. The vessel rolled again, another wave crashed over the windward rail, and a wall of water hurled them the same way the ship's boats had gone.

Arcite felt the deck fly from beneath his feet; then he was in a world of raging waters which threatened to tear him from the body to which he resolutely clung. And Berengeria screamed. Her cries began to rend the air the instant the wave struck her and she kept on until her last shriek was cut short by the foaming billows. Arcite struggled to keep both himself and the panic-stricken woman from being lost in the raging seas.

He felt his free hand collide with something solid. It was one of the ship's boats wallowing in the raging sea, its side caved in by the force of the wave which had torn it from the ship's deck. Its gunwales would no longer hold out the water; it was little more than flotsam. But at least it stayed on the surface—it might even save their lives.

"They're gone, they're gone. By all the gods most merciful, they're gone. But now where are we?" Berengeria's cry caused him to redouble his efforts. He grasped her about the waist and held onto the staved-in boat for dear life. And as the force of the tempest twirled them about, he saw the merchantman limp away, its sails thrashed to tatters by the wind, its men struggling against the storm. He and Berengeria would have nothing to fear from that quarter and now he felt closer to her than ever he had before. "My love," he cried. "It is my guess that you were mesmerized by wizardry. I thank the gods your will has been restored. But have they harmed you?"

"I don't know, for I remember nothing save the crawling of those horrid insects." Her words were choked off by the heaving waters. Berengeria's arms closed about Arcite in an embrace that was full of relief, of an awakening from a nightmare—and of love. Then she regained possession of herself; she released him and clung to the boat's broken timbers. "If we should kick together," she cried, "I believe we might influence the direction of our drifting."

"What a woman I have found," he said in admiration. "That tactic's brilliant, especially because I hear the thunder of the breakers not too far away." Indeed the crashing sea swept them down onto the beach. He and Berengeria had to kick and keep their wooden float between them and the shore; if they did not, they could be caught by one of the towering breakers and their shattered boat would likely be hurled down on top of them, to crush them like insects.

They had just managed to turn themselves the right way when they felt the sea lift them like a giant hand. They made a breathless descent and Arcite struck something firm and grainy, which knocked the breath from him, made him dizzy and groggy until he was unable to resist as a second wave crashed down on top of him and hurled him farther up the beach. He lost sight of Berengeria just as he lost consciousness.

He fought against the blackness which engulfed him for a long time; then it withdrew and he opened his eyes. He had been hurled far up the beach by the force of the seas and Berengeria was struggling toward him, her clothing soaked and tattered, her amber-colored hair drenched and hanging about her shoulders like heavenly moss. He found the strength to clamber to his feet, caught her by the wrist, and they ran together into a thicket which overlooked the beach. There, they dropped to the ground and lay together, panting and exhausted, while the angry sky pelted them with raindrops.

They lay for a long time beneath the weeping skies, too weak to move. Arcite could only listen to the pounding of the waves on the beach and its image in the harsh breathing of the maiden who lay beside him. At last, gathering his senses a bit, he rolled himself onto one elbow and looked down at her. In spite of wind and rain, Berengeria now slept as soundly as a babe in a cradle. She was curled up like a wet kitten, and the heavy robe the cultists had put over her gown lay across her, wet and clinging, covering everything. But on her cheek and through a tear in one long sleeve, he could see the gooseflesh the cold air formed. He looked about but could see no better shelter, so he sat up and removed his cape. Granted, it was soaked through, but it was no more soaked than she was. He lifted her, wrapped it about her shoulders, and laid her back on the wet ground. Lastly, he placed a soft kiss on her cheek. She never even stirred.

He still had his sword and, by some miracle, his lute still hung from his shoulders on its leather strap. But it had taken a fearful beating: he looked at it sadly and concluded that it would never be the same, even once it had dried out. He poured the seawater from it and almost wept; it would warp, the joints would split open, its melody would never delight another maiden. If he took great care in letting it dry, perhaps it would still be playable, though barely so at best. He loosened the strings, removed them from the instrument, and tucked them inside his jerkin. Perhaps he could preserve them as well, if only for emergency use.

The afternoon passed and the storm raged on but it did blow itself out as darkness spread her cape across the land. The rain stopped, the wind softened and changed direction. Arcite welcomed that. A breeze began to blow from the land, an easy breeze which carried warmth and fragrance with it instead of the vile, slashing wind which had chilled them earlier. And the stars came out to form a field before which he could see the last, tattered clouds race after their departed brothers. As the evening deepened, the only remnants of the storm were the two castaways' soaked clothing and the great waves which still crashed onto the beach below. At last, in spite of the dampness and the lack of shelter, Arcite joined Berengeria in sleep.

When he awoke, daylight had come. Birds sang in the trees nearby, the sky was a deep blue, the sun smiled down, and the glowing warmth of the morning belied the raging tempest which had clutched them the day before. He extended his arms to stretch, but he found his cape wrapped about his shoulders.

A pleasant laugh caused him to turn his head. Berengeria sat cross-legged on the ground a few paces from him and watched him with a smile which brightened the morning even more than the sun. "I woke an hour or two ago," she said. "I saw you shivering in your sleep, and so I thought you needed your broad cape e'en more than I."

He returned her smile and sat up. She had removed the woolen robe placed on her by the cultists and she was a vision of beauty in her torn gown, even though it had been ruined by the sea and her ordeal. "O maiden," he said. "What a pleasant sight you are. From what I saw of you upon that storm-tossed ship, I could not know your state. I feared you'd smiled your last and I might ne'er again survey your lovely features at my leisure."

"You flatter me."

"No, I do not. I speak unvarnished truth."

Her smile never wavered. He could tell she was pleased by his words, whether she took them seriously or not. But he could not keep from reaching out and touching her hand. "But truth to tell, fair maid, my heart was full of fear for your sweet life—and soul as well. If you had seen yourself within the grasp of those foul chanters, I am sure that you would not have recognized your face."

Berengeria's smile faded and she looked away. "I do not doubt it. They were of the cult once led by horrid Alyubol." She shuddered as she spoke the name and that made him wince; then she turned back toward him. "I thought him dead; I thought his evil legacy was lost five years ago when he encountered flaming death. But now I find his cult to be as strong and bent on evil as it was when he still breathed. Poor Palamon was right: it was Navron who sent the spell to strike poor Berethane, and monstrous evil stalks all those who live about the Thlassa Mey."

"You must have gone through Hades yesterday."

"I cannot e'en remember. All I know is what I saw before they sang to me; great evil is afoot." She came to him and they wrapped their arms about one another. "They sang to me and my poor intellect was torn away from me like some tot's nourishment, wrenched from its helpless fingers. What a horror. By the gods, I hope I never see such days again."

Her mouth twisted with the anguish of her ordeal. Tears brewed at the corners of her eyes. "My world filled up with bugs, with vermin. I knew nothing, was aware of nothing but a hateful, crawling horde. I tell you, something's coming, though I know not what it is. Those crawlers have a meaning—they portend some evil I cannot begin to name." She shook her head and took a deep breath. "I'd want to die before I'd see and feel such vileness one more instant, even in my dreams."

She trembled violently, then put her arms around Arcite and clung to him the way a drowning man would cling to a reed. He returned the embrace with all his heart but for all the love and sympathy he felt for her, he could not deny the thrill her touch pumped into him.

"We'll deal with them," he said. "Your brother will succeed, this cult will be destroyed, and their foul stamp eradicated from the Thlassa Mey."

She buried her cheek against his chest; her shaking stopped and she was plainly not about to let herself display any further signs of weakness. But again, it thrilled him that she drew comfort from his embrace. "I hope your words are true," she replied. Then she sat back and smiled once more, driving her ordeal from the conversation like a brave shepherd lad driving a lion from a hillside. "But it is breakfast-time," she said. "And I am sure you have a stomach."

"A meal would please me, love," he replied. "Your beauty is as magical as any talisman but I can only wish its magic were the sort that conjures inns and dinners, rather than such strong enchantments over wandering minstrels."

"You'd be surprised what magic can be found upon this shore line." Berengeria reached behind her and brought forth Arcite's lute, newly dried and not terribly warped. Berengeria had filled it full of raspberries. "It made a useful basket," she said. "The day was warm and there was nothing else for me to do but gather from the bushes of this unfamiliar land."

He smiled up at her. "But what of dangers which you might have found?"

"You nervous man. I've danced with danger oft enough throughout my years. A hillside is a refuge when compared to some dark city street. Fear not for me."

Arcite ate some of the raspberries; they were tender and sweet, the first berries of spring. She had chosen them carefully, he could tell. "You fill me up with wonder," he said as he ate. "You have no right to so enchant a man and still maintain you dare not love him."

Her expression changed; he saw her eyes cloud. "That love has trapped us both," she said softly. "It is no salve, to be applied at will. And it confounds me full as much as it does you."

Then they moved toward one another as naturally as two lodestones. Berengeria dropped the lute, the raspberries scattered across the ground, and the young man and the young woman lay in one another's arms. Their lips clung together, their breaths mingled, Berengeria's mouth turned soft beneath Arcite's. He could not keep from gorging himself on the full delight of her kiss.

The moment ignited a flame inside him. He knelt beside her, cradled her head in his arms, and kissed her again. She was a delicate meal laid before him; he plied his lips against her forehead, her cheeks. And she did not forbid him; he marveled at the freedom he had been allowed. Had she forgiven him the fact that he had not come to her in noble garb? Did she return his love to the point that such things no longer mattered?

He would not ask. Her sleeves and collar were high and full, laced down the tops of both arms. The lacy covering concealed her throat, her shoulders, bosom, and arms; it was attractive and strangely fitted to her personality, yet more an old woman's garment than the gown of a Princess. He bit his lower lip and fumbled to unlace one sleeve.

"No," she said, but he did not listen. She had not meant the word; it had been a weak barrier, for decorum's sake only. He undid the laces, loosened the fabric from her wrist to the angle of her jaw, and let it slip downward.

"No," she repeated, more firmly. "You must not see me."

"I hear your words," he said. "And yet I'll not believe them. One white shoulder's touch, no more, no less, will I demand—no more than what is fitting for a man who loves you more than life itself."

Arcite saw her eyes flash—was she really serious? "No," she said one last time. "Ah, by the gods, can I be weak as this in my refusals? Am I so puny-hearted, I who have left suitors in my wake like clods turned up behind the plow? Deep in my heart I fear you, sir."

"You need not fear me."

"I do. I fear your touch, your hot embrace, and all the passions which it stirs in me. I cannot—will not—let you look upon my naked flesh." She tried to turn out of his arms, but he was too fast for her. The fabric dropped from her shoulder and his eyes found the reason for her modesty, the blemish her high collar and long sleeves had concealed.

Jagged scars traced their way from the nape of her neck, along her arm, to a point below her elbow; white, flashing weals, some torturer's sacrilege on the lustrous beauty of her flesh.

"Yes, ugly, ugly," she shouted. "You have labored hard enough to see my shame. Now does it please you to survey your passion's prize, to look upon the merest portion of my great disfigurement?" She stopped her struggles and glared at him, dared him to gawk at her scars.

Arcite could hardly find words. "Who could have done this thing?"

"Foul Alyubol, when he possessed control of Usmu, a demonic spirit. I am scarred and ugly underneath my gowns, like some poor insect, shriveled up beneath a lustrous shell. So what of your love now? Or of the flame, the heated torrent which has forced you on until you moved my gown's protecting folds? Is it now quite extinguished?"

She sighed and lay back without even bothering to cover herself. For his part, Arcite knew shame, more shame than she did. Had it been any wonder that her modesty had warred with her passion. He fumbled for words. "Princess, love, I feel as does a man who violates the hospitality of some kind host, who hunts on closed-up fields. My passion's turned to dark remorse; I beg forgiveness."

"Then I grant it. But such words will not erase the images my scars have burned into your brain. How can you ever look on me the way you did a moment past? You should have left things as they were."

He lifted her and held her to him. "Nay, maiden, for these scars lie but across the skin. It is what lies beneath my shallow vision's boundary I love. Do you think I could love you less because some evil being marred your surface? Then I pledge my love again, within the full sight of these blemishes." He turned her in his embrace and kissed the length of her scarred arm. She did not resist him but he could tell by her breathing that she was impatient, that it still troubled her to have him look upon her marred flesh.

His lips anointed her shoulder and the loosened gown fell away to reveal still more of the weals left by Alybol's tortures. Her back was covered; the jagged tracks crisscrossed across her ribs and spine as if someone had tried to weave the flesh itself. Tears leaped to Arcite's eyes. "My darling, it's beyond belief that even fiends could so abuse you." He clenched his fist. "O gods, if such lay in my power, I would lift these marks and have them laid on me. And ten times more—why, I would gladly make that sacrifice if only one could thereby be removed."

She held one arm across the bodice of her gown and rested her head in her hand as he kissed the length and breadth of her back. Finally, she turned and hugged him. "Arcite," she said. "You are indeed my love, though it is fate's foul prank that this is so. Your love gives comfort to me now; the pains of my past tortures have expired except the shame of knowing that my flesh will never please a gallant's eye."

"It pleases mine," he countered.

But she went on as if he had not spoken. "My grief and shame depart when you bestow on me the balm of your sweet kiss. Then let our dalliance reach an end, for we are separated by the Fates."

He gave her another impassioned caress. "Do not invoke the Fates," he said when he had kissed her a last time. "For you cannot be sure you fully comprehend their will."

She stood and laced her gown back together. "I wish that it were so," she said. "I worship you, Arcite. I must admit my heart soars, just to hear you utter words of love. But what is not to be, is not to be. We must go on and speak of it no more."

He did not argue, though he did not for an instant agree with her. He had seen her blemish and he knew it had made no difference to either of them. Their love for one another was as full, as true, and as blessed before the gods as any love which ever had existed since first the waves rolled across the Thlassa Mey. And he knew he would win that love, that he would enjoy its full rewards, or he would die in the attempt.

"I'll not debate you, maid," he said with a smile. "But still, I say, our place is not to choose what is to be. I've looked upon your blemish and it does not change my love for you one wee iota. If you find my birth to be my blemish, then it can no more than correspond to yours. If I hold love enough to disregard your specks, can you not do the same for mine?"

Berengeria's face danced until Arcite regretted his words. "I do," she cried. "I do, I do; you have no blemish in my eyes. Your birth means nothing to me, for 'tis you I love and not your parents. But my homeland, my Carea, must decide your right to marry me—and I well know the policies of all my noble kin."

"Your brother, Palamon, would not deny us."

She looked at him. "That is true—most likely. Still, he has a nation full of Counts and Barons who may sway his judgment. He's a King, you see. He must act in his land's best interest, as must I myself."

Arcite reached out and held her to him once more. "And yet, if I were noble in my birth, instead of just a wandering troubadour, you say you'd marry me?"

"I would. Indeed I would, and gladly would I look upon the day."

He beamed into her eyes. "Then maid, believe me, for I speak unto the Muses, which are cousins to the gods. Our love is pure; as full, as true, as blessed, as any which has throbbed since first the Thlassa Mey rolled to its shores. If you would have me be a nobleman before we wed and consummate our love, then so, by all the gods, it shall in time be so. Then be you certain in my promise—I have earned your love and now shall win your hand. Were I to need a monarch's purple mantle, still I'd win it for your sake."

Chapter Fourteen:
Diomedes Serves His Master

PALAMON IGNORED THE wind. He stared down at the two men on the balcony and the slavering tongue of rage licked his bowels with a fiery caress. He saw Ursid. Ursid had sided with the cultists, had turned against chivalry, and even against his own King. Of course Palamon should have known, he should have suspected. All the pieces fitted together as neatly as the little stones in a mosaic. But even as he watched the two villains with their heads together, Palamon could hardly force himself to believe the sight. For all Ursid's faults, all his rashness, he had been a knight, a member of an honorable order. For all the hatred which had grown from his misplaced love for Berengeria, he had been an honorable man in his own way. He must have abandoned all that in his pursuit of vengeance; Palamon clenched his fists until his nails dug into his palms.

"Now I can hate," he said quietly. "Ursid had told me of his hates, of lust for vengeance. Now I tell you I have learned to deal in that same passion quite as much as he. I shall destroy Navron, Ursid, and all their cohorts, even if that victory should come with my last breath." He glared about wildly. "I'll see them suffer; I will see their flesh peeled from their milky bones. All men shall quail before the tortures which I shall inflict upon these sinners."

Flin looked up at Palamon but did not answer. So the tall monarch added more. "E'en now I clench my eyes and relish that exquisite image. I shall see each one of them scream many times for every moment little Berethane must spend within their evil magic's grip."

Flin still said nothing; from the look of him, he was so shocked by Palamon's whisper that he could not produce a reply. Palamon suddenly felt humiliated, ashamed of himself. He hesitated, his breathing slowed, then he turned and gazed down once more at the balcony. Ursid and Navron had begun to argue, and the wind carried the words to the two men who watched. The scars across Ursid's features flashed like lightning on a dark horizon while Navron's features reflected his own anger. "You are young and impetuous, friend, and you broke our agreement," the mystic said. "Had you gained your success—were he dead—I would grant you the laurel of victory. But he escaped. I am told there were forty armed men, all seeking his blood, and they could not contain him. All your efforts to have your men follow him into his villa had no more success. But I gained the main prize and, if not for your foolishness, he would have perished as well. If he'd come to his refuge all unwarned, if my magic had time for its course to be run, he'd have died then and there. As it is, he may be seeking us this very moment."

"You are a coward," Ursid replied with a sneer. "I've kept my part of our agreement; I gave bribes and I applied the pressure to remove him from his holy sword. But we had no agreement that I'd not attempt to slay him in my private way. He still may live; so what? I see no cause to quail as you are doing. Let him seek us out; that very hope throws joy into my soul. I do not care for you nor for your schemes. The death of Palamon is all I crave."

"And yet, you're a part of my scheming now, like it or not. And you made the choice willingly." Navron smiled.

"Therefore you'd find it far wiser to follow my counsels."

"Nay, evil man," Ursid replied in a superior tone. "I but pursue the goal I've set myself as singlemindedly as would my mentor, Lothar, my most able King. There is no right or wrong in all the world, but only goals. He strives for his Buerdaunt, I for my own fierce vengeance. But he taught me this great truth: all future scribes will not remember whether some great King was evil or was not. They shall remember only that he reached his goals. Thus, so it is with Lothar and with me."

Navron laughed. His response plainly angered Ursid; the younger man leaped to his feet and drew his sword but Navron only gazed up at his face and laughed all the harder. When he was done, he hardly had enough breath left for speech. "Ah, yes, you have followed the steps of the great politician, your Lothar the Pale. How it all makes me smile. I am evil, you see; I embrace my foul state, I enjoy it, I've made myself one with the world's greatest force. I say evil's a force, like the wind or the sun in the skies or the magma which flows from some great, smoking, fire-spewing cone.

"How I laugh at you all, you Ursids and you Lothars and such, who will use evil's powerful force to reach goals you proclaim for yourselves, while you fear to embrace the great essence. Who *is* evil, I wonder? Myself, who feels love for the holy putridity; I, who am given unto the pure force of the ethic of grand opposition? Or you little men, who use evil to purchase your minuscule goals but proclaim yourselves free of the reek of such ones as myself?" He snickered again. "I'll admit that I have many faults, but at least I'm no hypocrite."

Ursid stared at Navron. Then his sword fell from his dangling fingers, he raised his hands, and he clawed at his own features with a soul-wrenching cry. "Ah, curse you, it is true. I've bartered out my soul to you, a soulless devil in a human form. I knew it from the first; I knew it when I ordered up the death of Palamon—it all grows easier with passing days. How I detest you. What a fool I was to make a pact with you."

Palamon watched the spectacle, watched Ursid grovel and tear at himself. The tall monarch's rage and hatred turned into nausea; he felt sick at watching the young noble. Ursid had become a drunkard for vengeance; the same as a drunkard would debase himself to satisfy his lust for his brew, so Ursid had given up himself. To watch a human being cast away his soul was awful, sickening.

Ursid fell to his knees and his shrieks tore into the fabric of the night. At last he grew quiet, pulled himself together, then stood to his full height. He strode to Navron's side and grasped the mystic by the throat, forcing the older man's eyes to meet his own. "But still, the die is cast; now if my soul is made the forfeit and the price for my revenge, so be it, just as long as I succeed." The young noble turned away from the older man and struck at the nearest plaster wall in a horrible mixture of anguish and rage. "I've sold my soul indeed; I have insured damnation to myself and to my name. And I—an honorable, worthy knight before I met Careans and their wiles."

He snatched a wineglass from the table and flung it against the building's inner wall; it struck with a brittle crash and he turned back toward Navron with a smile that dripped irony. "Know you I considered taking up the cassock and the tonsure at one time? I almost was a clergyman, you see, because my faith was great. But still and all, there was no glory in it, so I took the sword and shield. What battles have I won, and yet the greatest battle was a dream, a sure defeat because I did not know the rules by which I waged it. I could not have won the hand of Berengeria in any case, although she never let me know until I'd risked my life in her behalf." He spread his hands. "And so it is, you taker of my soul, you bargainer from Hades' darkest depths. I'm given now to you. So be it. I have helped you gain the prize you sought within the villa, though the prize I sought was lost. My prize, of course, the life of Palamon. If you are angry, it's not my concern—you have your reasons for the treaty we have made and I have mine. I tell you now and to your face, I would not hesitate again to risk your prize if it should mean that I gain mine."

Once again, Palamon raged silently. The prize Navron spoke of, what could that be but the *Spada Korrigaine* itself? To leap among them and lay to the right and the left with his sword would have been fatal folly, yet Palamon felt thankful for Flin's restraining hand on his shoulder.

"It's too far down and there are too many of them, even for us," Flin whispered, as if he could read Palamon's thoughts. "We could break our legs in the fall, or one of them could put a sword in us from behind. That would be serious."

"I know, I know." But Palamon had all he could do to hold himself back as the schemers continued their conversation.

"Berengeria is your desire?" Navron's expression grew thoughtful, then cunning, and he smirked up into the young Prince's face. "Perhaps I'll arrange that you meet her."

"How?" Ursid's face filled up with new scorn.

"If my cohorts have reached their appointment with her, then perhaps she is hurrying toward our rendezvous."

"Mere words," Ursid replied. "I do not know your plotting's subtleties but I'll not place an ounce of faith in you until the thing you offer comes to pass."

"Ah. You lust for her still but your hopes have been dashed many times. I will see that you meet her."

"If only I could trust you," Ursid mused. He was silent for a moment; when he spoke again, it was on a new subject. "And you have gained the *Spada Korrigaine*. Poor Palamon is lame without his weapon. Bring it here and show it unto me."

Palamon tensed himself. If they made the mistake of bringing the great sword out onto the veranda, he would invoke its magic in spite of all risks. He would call it to him like a finely trained warhorse and he would stand against the lot of them. But the thrill of decision left him quickly. No, he had to do the prudent thing, the right thing. Only by surviving and capturing Navron alive could he bring Berethane back from the clutches of death. Vengeance could wait for that.

Besides, Navron only chuckled at the suggestion. "Ah, impetuous boy, I am sorry. It cannot be done, for the blade's in a wagon. At this very moment it travels, well guarded by some of my best, most fanatical men. We will follow it. Soon, I depart from this place. But I'll still show you something." He smiled, snapped his fingers, and one of his followers hurried from the balcony.

The man returned with a burlap bag, which he cast unceremoniously onto the table. Palamon marveled at that; these villains respected nothing. It would not matter whether the bag contained some sacred relic or chicken scats, for the way they would act toward it.

But he was surprised at what Navron casually removed from the bag. It was a huge pair of black leather gauntlets, set with jewels and studs of polished metal. "You may know that tall Palamon's sword is selective in who it allows to possess it," Navron said, donning the gauntlets. "I myself have been seared by its flames. My old leader, dead Alyubol, knew how to change that. But I don't possess his great genius. Instead, I resort to a less subtle method. Now slash at my hands with your sword."

Ursid stared at him. "You must be mad."

But Navron only smiled. "Not at all. You have said how you hate me; could seeing my blood flow displease you? Come, strike at my hands."

With a lightning motion, Ursid snatched his blade from the floor and brought it down on Navron's extended fingers with all his strength. But to his amazement, it only clanged off the gauntlets as if he had tried to cleave an anvil in two. Navron chuckled with pleasure at the young Prince's consternation. "These gauntlets are gloves of protection. They'll guard my soft flesh from the furies of Palamon's sword. Thus, I'm able to wield it for whatever ends I may choose."

Ursid gazed at the white-robed man with undisguised

loathing. "I do not like your magic. I would hear no more of it. What time, then, do you leave?"

"Immediately."

"That's good. Will you require an escort of my men?"

Navron laughed as if Ursid's loathing only amused him the more. "I will travel the rest of the way with my fellows. If you wish to accompany us, you have no need of an escort. I'll not have them look on the city of Kruptos. They'd have to be fools to desire it, in fact. I have doubts you yourself will bear up to the sight which my chants will produce."

"You cannot breed a sight to frighten me."

"We shall see. Will you go with me then, while your comrades remain at their posts?"

Ursid hesitated; it was plain even from Palamon's perch that the young noble did not trust Navron. "Will Berengeria indeed be there?"

Navron only laughed at that query. He glanced at Ursid as a man would look at a small child who had asked a stupid question, and he laughed until he was out of breath. "You who broke our agreement to follow your own private vengeance on Palamon, you have no right to ask questions of me." He chuckled again. "But perhaps, if I will it, I'll send a request she attend."

Ursid glared at such insulting humor. "My men surround this house. If I grow angry and command your death, it shall take place. It's my desire to see what may transpire at your evil coven. But I will have some four of my own men accompany me. That is my own decision, which I shall back up with arms, if necessary."

"You're impertinent, youth," the mystic said. "Could four men give you shelter amid all my fellows and magic?"

"Four men," Ursid repeated, glowering.

Navron eyed him for a moment, then shrugged and smiled. "It's only a trivial matter. As you may desire. I shall welcome your presence; in fact, I am sure it will prove very useful."

Ursid accepted the little victory brusquely and stepped toward the doorway. "Then I shall choose four horsemen and we all will go together." As he passed from the chamber, he issued orders to his *aide-de-camp*, "Diomedes, place a guard upon this house and all the streets about. And send a messenger back to Danaar, to all my allies there. Carea's King is to be slain wherever found and word brought on to me."

Palamon did not hear a reply, but he knew the command would be carried out, if possible. He would do his utmost to see that it remained impossible. He turned to Flin and his harsh whisper cut the air. "They play into our hands. If young Ursid should leave his guardsmen in this city, then the way to him and to Navron is clear."

"But we have to hurry," Flin replied. "If we play a good game, we'll follow them right to your sword."

"Indeed." Palamon touched his hand to the rope which he had dragged up after him. "We must avoid the henchmen of Ursid. Crawl out and look into the alleyway, then tell me if the way is clear."

Flin made his way to the other side of the tree with lithe movements; he caused hardly a vibration as he slipped away from Palamon in the darkness. But in a few moments he had returned. "It looks risky. It was hard to tell but I thought I spied two men standing where the alley turns into the street."

"Then let us make our way down to the ground within this court. Perhaps a route will lie between this house and others on the block." Palamon secured one end of the rope, then he and Flin climbed down it and slipped through the garden and toward the deserted house. But when they reached the oak door which led to the rear rooms, they found it locked. "Perhaps we'll need to break a window," Palamon said.

Flin grinned at the tall monarch; his teeth showed white and even in the darkness. "Oh, I doubt that. I know a quieter way." He pulled a slim dagger from his belt and pried at the door's complex latch for a time. Suddenly, to Palamon's surprise, the portal popped quietly open. "You see?" he said to Palamon. "It's a skill I learned while in the ripest part of my youth—I don't like to do it in an open street but it does come in handy when you're wooing a maiden who has a protective father."

Palamon did not comment on the explanation. Flin's ways were hardly those he would normally expect of a knight. But then Ursid's ways had been more conventional than Flin's, at least until the last few years, and Palamon knew whom he would choose between the two men.

The inside of the house smelled musty and was as dark as the inside of a cave. They had to feel their way and it was a poor escape route. Palamon wondered how many of these buildings were watched, but that was another hard question to answer. They would seek until they found a way to escape; then they would pursue the two villains.

Flin paused at Palamon's side, then nudged him. "I've found a door that has to lead to the house they were in," he whispered. "Let's look on the other side—maybe these places are connected."

"It seems unlikely. Still, let's try." They felt through each room of the building. But as Palamon had expected, no portals were to be found. It would have been foolish for every building in the row to be joined, though it might have been possible to join the odd pair, by way of creating enlarged quarters.

Flin leaned against the wall, then slid into a sitting position. "We could wait until they've left over there," he said.

"It's not my wish," Palamon replied. "Each moment lost makes more difficult the way to find the trail."

But a crashing at the front door interrupted them; someone was breaking into the building. "Hit it again, both of you," came a voice, the same voice Palamon had heard leading the assassins in Danaar. "I want that door open right now."

"We're caught," Palamon said. "Then quickly, to the garden wall." They ran through the house, knocked over furniture, stumbled, fell, then burst into the garden just in time to see a lamp's glow and the sight of a ladder's

top being leaned against the wall. They were surrounded.

Palamon grasped Flin by the arm, turned him, and
ducked back into the building just as a head appeared at
the top of the ladder. "Then we're surrounded. We have
only one small chance—to slip into the house they just
vacated."

He heard Flin chortle in the darkness. "A stroke of
genius. They'll never look for us in there." The two of
them fumbled their way to the door which connected the
buildings and Palamon heard the tip of the younger
man's dagger scrape against the lock. A splintering crash
told them the street door had been forced open as Palamon heard a popping sound and felt a draft. "Let's
hurry," Flin said.

They slipped through and Palamon pulled the door
shut behind them. From the shouts of consternation he
heard in the apartment they had just left, he knew the
gambit had succeeded, at least for the moment. "Now, to
the street," he whispered. "Before they can recover."

At least there were candles lit in this house; the glow
allowed them to leap through the rooms with the speed
of deer escaping wolves. There was no one in the building; clearly, all the guardsmen had surrounded the house
next door. They reached the street door and Flin stole a
peek in both directions. "The way's clear," he said with a
smile. "Maybe we'll get clear of them after all."

They stampeded along the murky street and toward
the end of the row of houses. But as they turned into the
adjoining street, they saw more armed men quickpace
into their path, cutting them off. They both turned but as
Palamon saw another company issue from the house
they had just left, he knew the game was up. He halted
and settled his hands on his hips even as a spear point
prodded him in the back. There would be no escape tonight. And from the sight of Flin's hangdog expression,
Palamon knew the younger man also realized that fact.

"Look who we have here," one stocky warrior said.
Palamon recognized the voice; it was the same voice he
had heard in the narrow alley in Danaar. And he recog-

nized the owner, now that he could put face and voice
together; it was Diomedes, Ursid's crafty *aide-de-camp*.
The scraggle-bearded vassal grinned up into the tall
monarch's face as he issued his orders. "You thought
you were very wise, looking in on the Constable's meeting, didn't you? Well we're not all fools, though you may
think we are. I've got spies all up and down this street; I
knew you were here before you even climbed that tree."

Flin asked a disgusted question. "Then why didn't
you take us at once, you strange fellow?"

Diomedes chuckled. "I'm not strange—I only know
what works for my purposes. If we catch you while the
Constable is here, it's his doing and he feels very good
about it. But if we get you a day or so after he's left, then
it's my doing and he remembers it when a better position
opens up. You see how it is?" He motioned for his men
to tie the captives. "Now come along. I'm sure we can
find a room cozy enough to hold you for a day or so.
Then, for all your royal blood, I'm afraid we'll have to
do you in."

The soldiers bound the captives' hands and inserted
poles into the crooks of their elbows. They hustled the
two men along the street and shoved them through the
same door they had left only a few moments earlier.

"All right," Diomedes said in his gravelly voice.
"Take them up to the balcony. If they give you any trouble, just pitch them over the side. We'll tell the Constable they fell while trying to escape."

"What if they survive the fall?" one man asked.

Diomedes laughed an unpleasant laugh. "Then we'll
just haul them back up there and pitch them off again.
They'll get the message sooner or later."

"Ursid and foul Navron—where are they taking my
enchanted sword?" Palamon demanded as they hauled
him toward a staircase.

"It'll do you no good to know, so I might as well tell
you," Diomedes said. "I'm not supposed to know, either,
but a fellow can find things out if he puts himself in the
right places. They're headed northwest; they're going to
meet again outside the city of Tranje."

Tranje? Palamon looked at Flin with surprise as guards prodded the two of them up the steps. Why would Ursid and Navron want to meet again at Tranje? But that was not the immediate question. Unless the two Careans could escape, they would be lucky to see another sunset, let alone Tranje.

Flin started to say something but one guard silenced him with the back of a hand. "No talking," the fellow said. "We don't need you two foxes plotting anything. If you even made it this far, you're too dangerous for us to give you any leeway."

Flin screwed up his face. "I wasn't even going to talk to the King. But my bladder is going to burst if I have to hold it much longer."

"That's your problem," the guard said. At that moment they reached the head of the stairs and walked into the room Flin and Palamon had looked down on earlier. The balcony extended past the rear wall of the house and there was a low barrier at the far end, to keep a careless person from walking over the edge. The space was sparsely furnished. A table stood beside the barrier, along with a few chairs, and a couple of couches extended along the rear wall where the stairs went down.

Flin's voice became urgent. "It's going to be your problem if I wet my pants."

"No it won't."

"Yes it will. You don't know what I've been drinking —I'll stink like a breeding hog if that happens."

The guard glared at Flin. "Do you really have to go?"

"Never worse in my life. A fellow doesn't tell lies about a thing like that."

"Maybe we should just kill him right now," one of the other guards offered.

The guard in command shook his head. "No, we'd better not. The Commander doesn't want them dead yet, so we'd better take care of him. Take him over to the edge and let him piss into the garden. Nobody's down there."

The other two guards grabbed Flin by the arms and hauled him toward the end of the balcony, while their

leader stood beside Palamon with his sword drawn. But
Flin was still apparently not satisfied. "You're going to
have to undo my hands, you know."

"You're a lot more trouble than you're worth," one
guard observed, laying a hand on the hilt of his sword.

Flin shrugged. "Do you want to get your fingers wet
by helping me? I don't think so."

"All right," the leader said. "Untie him. But if he
makes one false move, put a blade into his guts."

"Thank you," Flin said. Then he raised his arms to
shake some of the numbness out of his wrists. "That will
make things easier. All right; stand back a little. I'm
pretty shy about this sort of thing. You don't need to
watch."

"We're going to watch every move you make," another guard said. "If you don't think we're going to keep
a mighty close eye on you, then you've got another think
coming. So you can forget any prissy thoughts about privacy; you've seen the last of that. Hey! What do you
think you're doing? You fool, you're getting us all wet,
you're getting it all over us."

Flin's laughter echoed through the chamber as the
two guards leaped away from him and drew their
swords. At the same time, the Commander of the guards
ran toward that end of the balcony. Palamon knew he
had to help, so he put his head down and charged the
man. Though his wrists were tied, he was able to catch
the distracted officer between the shoulderblades with
the crown of his head just as both of them reached the
end of the balcony. The man toppled over the low barrier
with a scream and landed with a clatter of arms.

As for Flin, he snatched up a chair and danced away
from the two guards facing him. When one of them
turned toward Palamon, Flin charged the other one with
the chair, pushed him over the edge after the first, then
brought the piece of furniture down atop the man who
was advancing toward the tall monarch. The whole affair
took only a moment.

"'Twas finished perfectly," Palamon said. "Now cut
my bonds and let us be from here."

"No sooner said than done," Flin answered with a grin. He snatched up a sword and slashed the cords which secured Palamon's wrists. The crash of enraged soldiers surged through the house's lower levels even as he worked. "But we're going to have to find a way out of here or we'll have to start all over again."

As soon as Flin had freed him, Palamon ran to the edge of the balcony where it jutted from the building. "If I have strength to lift you, then you might attain the roof. That is the only route still open to us."

They used the maneuver which had saved them before. Palamon hoisted Flin until he could grasp the lowest edge of the building's roof. Then the younger man pulled himself up, pulled Palamon after, and the two of them were soon dancing along the gables, running through the night a dozen cubits above the street. Shouting filled the alleys below them. They had only one sword between them but they would be able to procure weapons soon enough, if only they could outdistance their pursuit and escape the city of Tychopolis.

Chapter Fifteen:
Night Creatures

ARCITE AND PRINCESS Berengeria were not totally lost. They both knew they had been swept ashore somewhere north of the Narrow Strait and somewhere south of the city of Tranje, a large port city allied with neither Carea nor Buerdaunt. They had only to decide which way they should travel. "I favor Tranje," the minstrel said as they walked along. "For I was born within her sunny walls and know the land's environs."

"And yet Carea is the home I left," Berengeria replied. "The Queen and court will all be anxious at my disappearance."

The gentle morning's breeze rustled Arcite's blond locks while he spoke. "Your wish is my command; we shall walk toward the south."

While Arcite spoke, Berengeria bent to rip away the hem of her gown, which was dragging in the dust and had become frayed and filthy. "Favor me," she said after tugging at the fabric to no avail. "Lend your dagger to me, that I might trim away this excess cloth."

Arcite smiled and gave the weapon to her. "It could not wish for a more pleasant use."

Berengeria laughed at him as she finished her task.

She made a couple of cuts, then tore away the fabric and exposed her lower legs to the warm air. Arcite stopped in his tracks, eyed her up and down, then set his hands on his hips in an exaggerated manner. "My eyes are blinded," he said as he returned her laugh. "I'm dazzled by the sight of your fair ankles, and I gladly would obey your most outrageous order."

Berengeria eyed him. "If I squeezed you now, I'd shudder to behold what might come out. Your flattery is kind; still it encroaches on burlesque, you rogue. Here, take your dagger back."

He danced away from her with another laugh and a shake of the head. "The ivory of your underpinnings dazzles me so much it clears my memory of evil men and shipwrecks. You may keep my dagger and I'll have a gift from you for payment."

"What gift might you desire?" Berengeria asked, her eyes dancing. When he drew her toward him and placed his lips against hers, she almost struggled against his embrace. Almost.

"It was a welcome gift, the kiss you gave me," he said after a moment. "I shall hold it in my heart and prize it more than any ring or piece of jewelry."

"You are a flatterer; your wit and dalliance please me," she said. "But let us hurry on." They released one another and continued along their way.

As morning passed, they came across a trail which wound through the forested hills. "Once more, which way, Princess?" Arcite asked her. "Should we go north or south? One way lies your ancestral home, the other Tranje. I will journey either way."

"Then south, toward Carea," she replied. "I'd love to visit Tranje at some future time but do not wish to risk another confrontation with the men who held me for that horrid night."

"Yes," he said, almost absently. "I cannot help but wonder why they carried you away. And to what purpose did they bear those boxes which were stored down in that dank and musty hold?"

"No man can know, except to say that there is evil at
the bottom of it."

Arcite stood silently for a time, as if in deep thought.
Then they turned south, toward the Narrow Strait and
Carea. They walked briskly through the rest of the morning but they found no sign of civilization. Their bellies
ached with hunger and thirst and their feet ached with
their travel; at last they found a pleasant place in the
shade of a spreading tree and stopped for a while. Berengeria sat in silent thought while Arcite drew several
packages of gut from his doublet and proceeded to re-
string his lute.

Berengeria leaned against a root and watched the
young man at his task. Salt water had ruined the lute;
even she could see that. The neck had warped to one
side and the wood about the sound hole had rippled from
its soaking; the instrument could never hope to produce
notes of the purity she had once heard. But it was all the
instrument Arcite had. She could see the determination,
the concentration in his face as he labored to restore it.

He adjusted each string with the care of an alchemist
producing a potion. He seemed to forget her completely
as he tightened, plucked a couple of notes, then tightened again, while the instrument creaked and popped. It
seemed to Berengeria that it would come flying to pieces
from the strain he was placing on it. But it never did; and
after a long time, he was able to coax a satisfactory melody from its depths.

Only when he had completed his repairs did Arcite
look at her and smile again. He broke into a happy little
song for a moment, then they both rose. They looked
about for roots or edible berries but could find none, so
they went on their way. The sun dipped toward the western horizon and it began to look as if they would be
forced to spend the night out-of-doors. "What is your
wish, my Princess?" Arcite asked as the skies grew dark
and a cold moon peeked through the lowest branches of
the trees which surrounded them. "We can attempt to
find a sleeping place, or we can journey on."

"Let us continue," she answered. So they traveled

into the night, ever alert, eyes open against the speck of light or the mounded shapes of huts which would tell them they had reached some kind of civilization. But they saw nothing; the only human beings in this forest were themselves.

Then Arcite stopped short. "Methinks I saw a thing that moved," he said as he drew his sword. "Keep you behind me."

"I must resent that, sir, for I can help defend if there is need. I'll lift your dagger and an enemy will find that it's no toy."

Arcite did not answer; he held himself as motionless as a statue and stared into the brush ahead of them. Then Berengeria saw what he had seen; a pair of gleaming, yellow eyes which glowed at them out of the darkness. The eyes began to move, not toward them but across their field of vision. A shape walked into the middle of the trail and stopped there, menacing them in the moonlight. "A wolf," Arcite whispered.

He reached behind him with his free hand and caught Berengeria's arm. Then the two of them edged slowly away from the beast, toward a tree which stood behind them. But Berengeria heard a sound, sensed some slight movement, and she looked about. The tree would have been their refuge, but another great wolf stood beneath it, even larger than the first. A growl rattled from the animal's throat. The broad tongue slathered across jagged fangs which gleamed in the moonlight.

The underbrush on both sides seemed to move. Wolves appeared all about and moved into the moonlight to glare at them, as if assured that the two humans were trapped. Berengeria felt her flesh crawl; all about her, yellow eyes flashed, teeth champed, and tongues lolled out of snarling mouths.

Arcite still held her wrist with his free hand. Instinctively, she faced him and placed her other hand on his shoulder. But if she and Arcite had to die without the Fates ever granting them the privilege of consummating their love, at least they would die together. And she knew in her heart that her young man would face death as resolutely as any person could—as she would.

But to her surprise, he pulled her around in front of him and pressed the hilt of his sword into her hand. "Hold this," he whispered. "We cannot draw three breaths before these creatures pounce on us and rend our flesh." He fumbled with his lute, then slid it around on its strap until he could pluck the strings.

Was this how it would be to die beside a minstrel? Berengeria's heart leaped; she loved Arcite all the more for this final gesture. He would die with a song on his lips, at least. He began a lilting lullaby which she had never heard him sing before and the fearsome animals closed in. But she had Arcite's sword; at least one of the wolves would die on its blade before the human prey fell.

But the wolves hesitated as Arcite's melodies caressed the cold air. Hatred and hunger lay in their animal eyes; even so, Arcite's tones had an undeniable effect. In spite of the damage to his instrument, Arcite's playing grew ever more sweet, ever more charming; Berengeria felt sure it would have enticed bugs out of bark.

One of the predators made a sound—the squeaking start to a whine. Then it dropped its eyes and turned away. Another turned away and lay down, then another. Arcite's music was a drug to all the pack; they lost their deadly intent and grew restful.

A gasp sprang to Berengeria's lips; she had never seen a more amazing sight in her life. The notes of Arcite's singing sweetened the air, drew the ferocity from the great, gray canines as a poultice draws the poison from a wound. She stood transfixed; she did not even dare hug him for this, his greatest performance.

Arcite sang on. One of the wolves fell asleep; it was even dreaming by the little twitches it made now and then. Finally the last of the carnivores lay down and closed its eyes. "We must go on from here," Arcite sang, weaving his words into the lyrics of the mystical song. "I do not know how long this strange effect may last."

He kept singing and Berengeria laid one hand on his shoulder as they tiptoed from the trap. They had to step across the first sleeping wolf to make their way but the animal never stirred, even though Berengeria grazed it with her toe. He and she crept along the trail in the darkness until they had passed out of the wolves' hearing. Then they ran.

They ran like frightened children along the moonlit trail as it wound between trees, over hills, and through hollows. They stumbled across roots and ruts concealed in the darkness, scrambled to their feet, and ran on again. They had no time or breath for speech until their fatigue forced them to drop at the edge of a clearing more than a league away from the place where Arcite had performed his prodigy.

"My faith," Berengeria gasped. "I've never seen so marvelous a feat in all my days. Your singing is more powerful than any knight's keen sword. Where did you learn such melodies?"

"I do not know," Arcite gasped back at her. "I only hope those deadly animals do not awake and follow us, for I'm too out of breath to sing another note."

Then he laughed and pressed her to him as they lay in the grass. "Ah, love, the sound of music is indeed supreme among the magic mysteries of this fair world—once one has searched and found the secrets of its inmost depths. I prize the gift the gods have given me, more now than I have done before. The gods allow me to display my skills to you, whom I would give the world to please."

But as Berengeria smiled at him, she jerked back. Something moved and shone in the moonlight. A scaly shape brushed against her ankle, then she screamed as the long, sinuous form raised itself above her leg.

It was a poisonous serpent; somehow they had disturbed it in throwing themselves down in this rough place. Berengeria tried to scramble away from the thing, but she was too slow. Its head lashed toward her, dark scales and white fangs both glinted through the moonlight. But as quick as the creature was, Arcite was even quicker. He thrust out his forearm to stop the animal and caught it in midstrike. To her horror, she heard him gasp and felt his body stiffen against her as the fangs buried themselves in his flesh.

He rose, staggered from her side, and extended his arm, from which the writhing snake still dangled. It was three-quarters the length of his body and was thick and ugly. The sight of it made Berengeria gag even before Arcite took his sword and whisked it in two. "A deadly serpent," he said between clenched teeth as the two sections dropped into the grass. "I'm familiar with the type." He turned toward petrified Berengeria and took an uncertain step toward her. "Ah, lovely maiden, how I would have liked to stay with you. I would have liked to earn your love and taste the sweet, spiced wine of your hot favors. Now, I fear, I'll not be long with you to joy in any temporal delights."

A strange sound, a sort of half sob, half scream, escaped Berengeria's lips. She threw her arms about the young man. "This cannot be," she cried. "The blow cannot be fatal, for 'twas meant for me."

"I've traveled through these lands enough to know the weapons of each animal," Arcite replied. "I know well those effects of venom from such serpents and I feel the deadly syrup coursing through my veins already. Even now, I feel myself grow giddy. I will weaken, then begin to rant and rave, and by the dawn I fear that I no longer shall accompany you." The sweat poured from his face, but he managed to smile through it. "I'd have one final kiss while still I might enjoy it."

He bent to place his lips against hers; already Berengeria shuddered at how cold his skin had become. And even as they kissed, his knees buckled and he collapsed so suddenly that Berengeria fell with him. "Arcite," she shrieked as she scrambled to her knees and plucked at his tunic.

He rolled his head to one side and smiled up at her. "Princess, no regrets. It's worth death's price to hear you speak my name in such a way. We two would have been lovers, that I know; our story would have graced the lips of balladeers and minstrels through the ages. Ah, 'tis not to be. No comets for myself or you, my love, no starry flames a-whizzing through the night. But now my head grows lively. Birds may sing, and people, too. The air was made for song. Tra-la, tra-la." He waved his hands before him, and his voice grew giddy as he sank into the depths of delirium.

Berengeria closed her eyes and ground her fists into her cheeks. What was she to do? His arm had kept the serpent's fangs from her own flesh and now he was dying for his gallant deed. "Is there no way to save you from the sad effects of this foul serpent's poison?" she cried.

"From poison," he answered gaily. "From the poison of the snake, the bat, the scorpion, the spider too. What poison is there in the parsley's leaf, yet it attends upon our dying slowly, slowly. How the stars do glitter. Fetch my lute, for I would sing awhile."

It was the delirium, Berengeria knew. Still, she scrambled in the grass until she found Arcite's lute, lying where he had dropped it. She laid it across him, but he had become too weak to play. He clasped it haphazardly against his chest and continued to sing, more to himself than to her.

It could not be. He could not die this way. Berengeria looked about wildly. It could not be allowed to happen this way; Arcite could not die in a world ruled by just gods. She began a prayer to Hestia but stopped halfway through. Was Hestia the proper deity to receive prayers for this man? Would she answer? Sometimes the gods were put off by the most trivial technicalities—besides, was there not something she could do which would be more positive than praying?

A thought hit her. Akos leaves. She had once watched Palamon use akos leaves, plucked in the depths of a forest not unlike this one. And she had heard great tales of their potency for curing. But could she find akos leaves in the dark?

She ran to the nearest tree and tore through the shrubbery which clustered on the south side of it. Akos leaves had a distinctive feel, she remembered—pliable, yet stiff, hard, and slick, like something magical. She felt what might have been a small herb of the right sort but she could not be sure. She had only known the leaves of the fully grown plant. Panting from exertion and haste, she ran to another tree in the darkness, then another.

At last her heart leaped as she found leaves which had exactly the right feel. She plucked several of them and dashed back toward Arcite, stumbling and biting off pieces as she ran.

She fell on her knees at his side and plunged one of the pieces into his mouth. "Eat this," she ordered. She had no idea of the proper use of such leaves against poison, or whether it would have any power at all. She could only try.

But Arcite did not respond; he only sang and babbled on, spitting out any piece she tried to put down his throat. She chewed another section of leaf, as she had once watched Palamon do. The chewed up mass in her mouth tasted awful, sour and pungent, but she knew that only signified its healing powers.

Arcite fought back as she lifted his wounded arm but he had no strength. She could not see the fang marks in the darkness, but she had no trouble finding the spot the snake had struck. On one forearm lay a great swollen area, as if someone had inserted a ripe fruit beneath the poor man's skin. She was nearly afraid to prod it, for fear it would burst.

But she had to work it. She had to take the chewed paste from the section of leaf and spread it across the swelling. She needed more than one mouthful to do that, so she chewed until her jaws ached. Then, as an afterthought, she bound Arcite's forearm with strips of cloth torn from her own gown. Last, she remembered that sap could be squeezed from the leaves, so she steadied his lolling head between her knees and squeezed a few drops of liquid into his mouth as it hung open beneath her hands.

She had done everything she could think of; she could do no more. Tears rose to her eyes and her breath nearly failed her as she watched Arcite struggle against the poison in the moonlight. Though his breaths were only shallow, he did still breathe and she could feel a pulse. But even the babble of delirium no longer danced on his lips; he had become too weak to form words.

Berengeria looked about at the shadowy trees on one side of her and the silent grasses of the clearing on the other. She did not even know where she was. And what of the wolves Arcite had put to sleep with his song? Were they even now awakening and resuming their hunt?

She would never leave Arcite's side; she vowed it to herself as she caressed him over and again with her eyes. She would not leave him to die, to rot alone in this place, come wolves, serpents, wizards, or worse. But she understood the desperation of it all.

She buried her head in her hands and she wept. But she could not weep all night. Time went by, the moon paraded across the night sky in all her grandeur, and Berengeria kept a desperate vigil. Then she gathered herself together, for she knew what she had to do.

She no longer harbored doubts over which deity to address or as to the efficacy of prayer. She knelt beside Arcite, clenched her fingers, summoned all the faith and hope contained in her being, and prayed to Hestia, deity of hearth and home, with the urgency of her desperation.

Chapter Sixteen:
Peristeras

TEARS SPATTERED BERENGERIA'S face and she prayed as she had never prayed before. She summoned up all her devotion, all her faith, all the strength and power which lay within her soul. She flooded the air with phrases of entreaty until exhaustion crushed her. At last her arms dropped; she dissolved into a heap and fell into a sleep full of desperate dreams.

By the time she awoke, morning had come. She rubbed her eyes and looked up to see blue sky. Leafy branches rustled above her, and a couple of inquisitive sparrows returned her gaze. Arcite still lay motionless. She choked back a sob as she examined him and placed a hand on his throat to find a weak pulse. She also noted that the swelling on his right forearm had gone down greatly. The poultice of akos leaves had turned black and much of it had fallen off but when she touched the skin, she found that it was no longer as feverish as it had been before.

When she stood, she saw something which had escaped her notice the night before. Arcite had fallen at the edge of a large clearing; wild grasses tossed their heads for the space of a hundred cubits before another stand of trees marked the other side. On the far side of the clearing stood a little stone house, with a low wall surrounding it. Berengeria was dumbstruck; how had she and Arcite missed seeing the place the night before? There must have been no lights burning; that was the only reason she could conceive.

The place looked deserted, though the building and the wall about it did appear in good condition. In any case, she would visit it. But did she dare leave Arcite's side? The wolves had not followed them, that was true. But the sight of the dead viper lying in the grass was enough to make her decide. She would carry Arcite, or at least drag him as far as she could.

Though he was slender of build, he was also tall; his body made a heavy burden. Try as she might, she could not lift him even far enough to struggle a few cubits; at last she seized him by the ankles and dragged him toward the stone shelter. But even that was too difficult; the dragging caused his tunic to ride up and the grass stubble and rocks abused his flesh with every step she took.

She gave him one last, longing glance and dashed toward the house. Her breath came in gasps as she rounded the corner of the stone wall, noticed a gate, and burst through it—to fly straight into the arms of a stocky, bald-headed man.

She had been running so hard that both of them staggered with the impact; she gasped and the man looked at her in total surprise. "You have to help me," she cried without thinking. "On the other side of this green clearing, my fiancé lies dying from a serpent's lethal bite." She had not thought out her words before speaking them. "Fiancé" was an improper term by which to describe Arcite, of course. He was her newfound love, a brave and chivalrous companion, but their blood would keep them apart forever. Still, it was the term she had used.

As for the man, his response to her plea was to take her by the wrist and pull her toward the house. Panic filled her as she struggled against his iron grip. Had she placed herself into the hands of some soulless villain? She fought and kicked at him but he hauled her toward the house as inexorably as a mantis draws its prey toward its jaws. A few steps, and the fellow was pulling her across the threshold; and all the while, he remained as silent and expressionless as a moving stone.

She reached into the folds of her clothing and produced Arcite's dagger, the sight of which caused the man to release his grip at last. But even as she raised the weapon to defend herself, she heard a voice from her left. "You'd better put that down, young lady. What ill chance brings you to this isolated place?"

Berengeria gasped and turned to see a little boy standing in a doorway. He looked to be about five years old, though the nature of his gaze and the expression on his lips made him look older than that, almost as if some ancient, worldly, and skeptical soul had been placed into the body of a child.

Berengeria's attention was distracted just enough for the man in front of her to knock her dagger away. Berengeria leaped after the weapon but the lad spoke again. "You need no weapons here. My servant moved for my protection only."

Berengeria glared at the child, then at the older man. "And so he drags me into this abode. Is that for your protection also, or am I intended for some other use?"

The child moved his hands carelessly. "You've misconstrued our actions, and with all good reason. Thus, I must apologize." He turned toward the burly man and executed a series of hand signals. The man nodded, crossed to the other side of the chamber, and stood facing both of them. "My servant, Omo, neither hears nor speaks," the boy said. "And thus he did not understand your words and was uncouth in dragging you inside to speak to me."

Berengeria breathed a sigh of relief. "Then quickly, will you help me?" she pleaded. "My fiancé lies poisoned on the trail, the victim of a serpent's deadly fang."

Fiancé. She had used that word again; her passion for Arcite had selected it for her. But there was no time to think about that as the child turned toward Omo and once more spoke with his hands. The silent man picked up his little master; then the three of them hurried out the door and across the clearing.

"My name is Peristeras," the boy said. "What is yours?"

"My name is Berengeria. But you—I've heard your name before. Bessina, whom I call my niece, told tales of a prophetic, ancient man named Peristeras."

The boy smiled and spread his hands. "I am he."

She shook her head. "No, you're a child. He was, so I was told, an old and dying man."

"And yet we are the same. The difference between the oldest man, the green-eyed youth, and any puking babe is time—and time means nought to me."

"I do not understand completely."

"You are young. Perhaps the understanding will present itself to you when you are more experienced in all the mysteries of this broad world. But tell what brought you to this place."

Berengeria shook her head again. The child sounded like some mystic or philosopher who had spent his life nibbling weeds and insects in the wilderness. She would not question his ideas, though; there was no time. She hurried to explain how she had been torn from Carea's shores, but she was not even a third finished when they reached Arcite. She knelt beside him and felt for a pulse once more. He was still alive, though barely. As for little Peristeras, he looked very grave. He studied Arcite, then the dead serpent. "A funes-viper," he said. "It's miraculous this fellow even lives. Not one man in hundreds will survive the evil potion which its fangs spew forth." He touched Arcite's flesh here and there, then looked up at Berengeria with an expression of new respect. "I see you know some art; I spy a poultice made of akos leaves."

"I learned that from my brother. But Arcite—is there a way to tell if he will live?"

It still felt odd to address a child in such a way. But it seemed the most natural thing in the world at the moment, and the lad replied with all the knowledge and

carefully chosen words of a priest. "Your poultice is the
reason he has lived this long. He'd have expired within
the hour, if you had not applied it. Even so, the potion in
the leaves is not enough to save him. He will die before
the sun sets if we do not take swift action."

Berengeria looked from the boy to her minstrel love.
"The fact that I've prolonged his life is nothing—you
must save him. Can you do that?"

"Yes, I can. We'll take him to my study, where I hold
the reins of mystic forces. We will save the poor man's
life as surely as the sun will drive his flaming chariot into
the sea at end of day." He turned to Omo and made
another complex series of hand signals. The mute nodded, bent, and picked up Arcite as if the balladeer had
been no heavier than a bag of grain, then threw him
across one shoulder. The three of them strode back
across the clearing.

They took Arcite into the cottage, into a chamber toward the rear of the building. The nature of the room
surprised Berengeria because it was, of all things, a library. And it was a very comprehensive library, from the
look of it. Vellum-bound volumes covered one entire
wall, scrolls and scroll cases crowded another set of
shelves, and a table in the center of the room bore tro-
phies, odd mementoes, and flasks containing fingers, bits
of flesh, bone, or wood. It appeared to be a fine collec-
tion of religious artifacts. Yet such items as books were
rare and expensive; only the most wealthy or the most
learned people on the shores of the Thlassa Mey could
afford or understand them. This beardless boy, this hermit who dwelt in the center of the wilderness with his
mute servant, hardly fitted that rôle.

But there was no time to ponder that. Berengeria
watched Omo deposit Arcite on the soft hide rug which
lay before the crackling fireplace, then she stared into
the eyes of the little boy who called himself Peristeras.
He did not even notice her; he studied Arcite with incredible intensity. His eyes blazed with a strange fire, a
brilliant twinkle which captured her gaze and belied the
plainness of his other features. "Good sir," Berengeria

said to the child. "What manner person are you? You possess the face of one who has not even entered manhood, yet I fear you are no tender boy at all."

"My name is Peristeras, maid," he said, repeating the name he had given her earlier. "As you suspect, my body's age is meaningless. But it is not my place to answer questions; not for now, at least. We still must save your lover's life; that opportunity will fade if we should fail to act." He dismissed Omo from the room and gathered into his arms a cluster of the artifacts from the table. He placed them about Arcite, each one with care, as if proper arrangement was of vital importance. Berengeria noticed that all the bits of bone went near Arcite's head. Anything of wood went between his prostrate body and the fire, while the bits of preserved flesh or metal were placed here and there about the floor.

She watched anxiously while the boy made another trip to the table. "Is there aught that I can do?" she asked.

The boy glanced at her as if he resented the interruption. "Yes. Pray for him with all the faith and great devotion which you showed in prayer last night. But do it silently, for I must concentrate, to will the powers of the gods into this room and drive the poison from him. Such a task requires your silence."

Berengeria closed her eyes, clenched her fingers, and prayed for Arcite. And while she did, the boy finished arranging the flasks, took off his tunic so that he was clad only in a little loincloth, and stood over the fallen balladeer. "Ye mighty gods," he cried all at once, startling Berengeria. "Now hear my plea: I ask the aid of forces stored within these flasks to suck the evil poisons from the blood of this poor, fallen man. The powers now are focused and await the wills of all their master deities." Then he turned and repeated his words.

Berengeria paused in her prayer as the fire in the fireplace blazed up, roared, crackled, and sent bursting embers flying through the room. Some of them lit on the fur rug and lay smoldering, but the lad ignored them. He stood to his full height, which was not much, and raised his arms as if he would make himself into a human beacon on some metaphysical sea. The fire sounded over and again, the flasks all rocked and chattered as if scoured by some unseen hand, and Berengeria cringed in spite of herself. At the next instant, everything was as it had been before. The flasks stopped moving, the fire died down, and Peristeras knelt to gaze into Arcite's face. He touched the fallen man's cheek and a dry smile curled his features; again, it was not an expression one would have expected on such a child's face. "Very satisfactory," he said at last.

Berengeria placed her fingers to her lips and watched, then her heart leaped as Arcite sat up and looked about. His eyes grew wide and he stared at her. He tried to rise but stopped, winced, and put his long fingers to his temples. "My head feels just as if it has been filled with buzzing bees and little men with mallets," he announced.

"The pain is good," Peristeras replied. "It is a stimulant that will restore you from the poison's damage."

Arcite looked up at him, then back at Berengeria. "A two-faced boon it is, then. Death might be as sweet a prospect as this ringing, smarting, throbbing I endure."

Berengeria helped him lie back on the rug. "Do not speak so, my love," she said. "This lad, this Peristeras, has just saved your life. Now lie you here and build your strength." She paused, then smiled a crooked smile. "For I do love to look at you."

"Ah, yes," Arcite said. "And I will look on you as well. That is a balm as powerful as any that could be administered."

"Not so," Peristeras said in his high-pitched voice. "This woman saved your life before she came to me, for she applied a mighty poultice."

"You did?" Arcite's eyes danced and he gazed up at Berengeria again. "You shine out more with each new facet you display to me."

"But marvels and the Fates do mill about you both," the lad mused, interrupting Arcite's flattery. "Your auras and your faces show it." He drew a knife from the tabletop and advanced toward them. Only then did Berengeria notice the sweat which covered his nearly naked body. For all the apparent ease with which he had performed it, his act of saving Arcite had plainly required great exertion. But the knife he carried made Berengeria eye him with concern.

He saw the look on her face and smirked; his eyes glittered as if they were windows into another plane. "Do not fear me," he said. "I am not violent. But I have striven for you and I now require my payment." He knelt beside Arcite and deftly sliced off a square of fabric from the young man's jerkin. "And you," he said to Berengeria as he turned and cut some of the lace from her sleeve. "And both of you together." He lifted Arcite's right arm and removed a strip of the cloth by which Berengeria had bound the poultice to the swollen bite. Bits of the dried-up paste of akos leaves crumbled away from the cloth as he laid it with the other two pieces he had gathered.

He gazed at the three bits of cloth, then glanced up at the two adults with an icy smile. "Now I will go from you," he said. "So wait you here, take strength from one another while I seek the secrets which embroil you. I shall return within the hour." he laid the materials on the table, retrieved and donned his tunic, then picked up the bits of cloth and walked from the chamber.

Arcite and Berengeria gazed at one another as the boy departed. Then Arcite reached toward her and she felt one of his hands press against the back of her head to force her lips toward his. Whether this passion was proper or not, his display at least proved he would not die. She silently thanked the gods and allowed him his kiss.

He laughed and brushed some strands of her hair from his face. "The pain which surges through me weakens with such ministrations," he noted.

"Then I suppose I ought to kiss you all the more for that." She sat up, rearranged her draggled clothing, and smiled at him. "But still you are recovering from your ordeal. I shall not drain the strength from you by showering you with thirsty kisses, love."

"Nay." The old twinkle came back to his eye. "Weaken me, O maiden. Weaken me."

"Nay, nay. Rest there, as Peristeras bade you. We'll await his coming."

They talked for a while and then the child walked back into the chamber, carrying a small clay pot. "I've learned of you, the two of you," he said in an enthusiastic voice. "The Fates have wound you up together. Some of that is at the wish of you, sir." Here he looked into Arcite's face. "But some of it is by the order of the Fates themselves. You have a rôle to play, the two of you. Your rôles are mutual, yet separate. Now tell me of yourselves. How did you reach my cottage, and to what place do you now intend to go?"

Arcite began to speak but Berengeria waved him into silence. He was recovering from his ordeal, after all, and did not need to exert himself with storytelling. She told the young conjuror how she had been spirited onto the ship and how Arcite had saved her, had brought her safely to the coast. She told how her minstrel had quelled the wolves with his music and how he had received the blow the serpent had intended for her. But of the passion they possessed for one another and of her doubts concerning it, she said little. After all, it was plain that this strange child knew enough about them already. However much she might love Arcite, she could not escape the fact that she would some day be forced to give him up. It would do no good to tempt the Fates any more than need be by telling the brilliant stranger about the depth of that love.

Arcite never interrupted her or commented, other than to laugh a couple of times. As for Peristeras, he listened in silence until she had completed her story. "The powers of the Fates unite you two," he repeated. "At least for now." He lifted the lid from the little pot he carried with him and moved toward the fire, which was burning low by this time. When she looked over his shoulder, Berengeria could see only that the pot was filled with ashes. Was that what had become of the strips of cloth he had taken from the two of them?

Peristeras lifted the pot, turned it over, and allowed the ashes to cascade in a fluttering shower into the fire. He watched them as they fell, as if he had somehow mesmerized himself. And when the last speck had fluttered into the combustion and disappeared in a little snap of flame, he looked up at her. "What might become of all the love you bear each other is a thing I dare not say." Then he smiled up at her with a child's implike smile. "You thought I did not know? Come now, you have concealed that love haphazardly since first you came into my house."

Arcite smiled at that. Berengeria fumbled for words but Peristeras ignored her and continued. "My interest now centers on the way the two of you are caught up in a vortex, in the evil enterprise by which foul men attempt to devastate this world."

"What?" Berengeria stared into the boy's face. "Will the evil minions hound my steps e'en still?"

He nodded gravely. "Indeed, your royal body will be sought by evil men. They want your blood; your fate is tied with theirs. And for that reason, logic dictates your best course should be to stay away from them. And yet this man, this troubadour, holds sway o'er the powers which must soon be brought to bear upon these same foul men. He must attack their evil with his song; he must pursue the same men that you flee."

He turned from the two lovers, crossed the floor, and threw himself onto a luxurious couch which stood against one oak-paneled wall. Berengeria could not help marveling at the house's rich appointments, considering it was nothing but a cottage in the wilderness, or at the fact that its owner was a child a quarter her age, who lived a mystery and spoke the words of some ancient and learned priest.

But it all seemed to please the boy to no end. The same smile she had seen before crept across his features and his brilliant eyes danced. "Amusing, is it not?" he asked as he looked up at them. "The wisest counsel urges you to seek the southern lands, fair Princess. Yet the need of all that's good within our world demands your lover travel to the north. The fates have chained the two of you together. Tell me, then, what is the sacrifice? Shall you do what is wise, or what is good?" He chuckled at his own paradox, then sat and observed them.

Berengeria had no words; she had no real idea what he was talking about. And from Arcite's silence, it was plain that he did not know any more than she. But at length their young host stood, set his little clay pot on the table which held the artifacts, and eyed his guests. "But you have been through much today. How are your appetites?"

"We have not eaten," Berengeria replied. Then she glanced at Arcite. Though she did not mention it, she had not even thought of food since the viper had struck the night before.

Peristeras also looked down at Arcite. "You should be better, sir. Can you now stand and come to dinner?"

"I think I can," Arcite replied. "The pain has almost gone away."

"You are a strong young man and all the Fates are with you in your great adventure. Then come with me, for I believe my Omo has produced a meal for us. I've worked up quite a hunger, as I'm sure you have yourselves."

Arcite grunted as he clambered to his feet. Then he and Berengeria followed Peristeras into a different chamber. Omo had indeed prepared a meal. A platter of roast beef stood before them, along with a flagon of dark wine, bread, and a bowl of glistening fruit. It was a copious meal, in keeping with the way all the house's other contents contrasted with its rural setting. And even stranger than that, Berengeria noted as she passed a window that night had fallen. By her own accounting, it should not even have been noon, yet it was plainly dark outside. And her fatigue and the aching of her stomach plainly told her more time had passed than she had imagined.

As her host pulled back a chair and she seated herself, she could not keep from marveling at him once again. What sort of creature was he and what prodigy had he

performed in that library chamber while she had watched
and prayed? The healing had not taken moments, as it
had seemed, but rather, most of the day. How had he
performed such a miracle on Arcite? What sort of creature was this child, and toward what adventure would he
lead them? She could not suppress a shudder as he pat-
ted her on the arm and moved on to his own place.

But for all her misgivings, the meal was a pleasant
one. Their young host's conversation was witty and en-
lightened far beyond his apparent years and Berengeria
even learned a few of the hand signals by which he communicated with his manservant. As for the food, it was
simple, yet tasty and extremely nourishing. She finished
the meal, wiped her lips with her napkin, and rose from
the table satisfied.

"And now to bed," their young host said. "I must give
my regrets there are but two bedchambers in this house.
The first I occupy, the other quarters go to Omo. Still, I
think we can accommodate you if you don't object to
sleeping on fresh straw."

Arcite laughed. "Straw could cause no hardship. We
have slept upon the ground the last two nights."

"Ah, so I thought. Then come with me, my friends."
The boy took a lantern from Omo and led the two adults
to the building's entry chamber. There the manservant
produced a short pole, with which he tripped a catch in
the ceiling and revealed a large trapdoor. He pulled the
trapdoor open and released another catch, which
brought a ladder clattering from the darkness above.

"Our loft is comfortable enough," the boy said. "I'll
climb the ladder and my light will guide you." He scurried up the ladder and his lantern's bright light cast ac-
tive shadows in the space overhead. Arcite followed him
and so did Berengeria, gathering her skirts about her
ankles with one hand because Omo still stood in the
lower chamber.

When she reached the loft, she found it to be a long,
low room with a plank floor. The lantern's light revealed
the lower surface of the thatching just above her head; in
fact, Arcite had to stoop to keep from hitting his head on

the beams which slanted away in both directions. But that was not what caught her eye the most. In the center of the loft stood a broad, wooden bed with a mattress of straw. Comforters had been spread across it and it was plainly a warm nest, though there were no bolsters. And it was the only furniture in the loft.

Arcite also looked at it, nonplussed. "There's but one bed," he observed.

"Your eye is good," Peristeras replied with a smile. "And yet I'm sure you see that it is broad enough to sleep some three or four grown bodies. It will hold the two of you with ease."

"Indeed it will," Arcite replied. "Yet this Princess is a chaste and noble maid. It is not well for me to share a bed with her, though it be half a league across."

"How odd. When you were sleeping on the ground, were you not quite as close to one another as you shall be upon this bed?"

Berengeria had no reply for the youth. Arcite only fumbled for words, plainly as perplexed as she. "You may be right," he said at last. "And yet this bed is not the same as earth. I have as much respect for her good reputation and her chastity as I may bear for anything beneath the gods themselves. And yet we both are human."

"As you've been for all the days you traveled through this forest."

Arcite's predicament almost made Berengeria laugh. He had played with their passion, had made endless jokes about it, and had juggled her kisses for days. Now he was the one who was caught up short by the sleeping arrangement.

Still, she had to straighten her face as she reflected that it really was a serious matter. "What about appearances?" Berengeria asked. "E'en if our actions are all proper, the appearances shall be of quite the lowest sort."

Peristeras looked at both of them and his expression became firm, as if they were the children and he the adult. "The gods will know your lust or your restraint, no matter where you might find sleep. For me, it is a matter of no worth. And as for Omo, he has lost the gift of speech and shall not whisper tales." He peered into Berengeria's face. "Besides, did you not call this man your fiancé?"

Berengeria glanced from Arcite to Peristeras. Arcite eyed her as brightly as a new star but she looked away from him. "I did, though it was but a figure of my speech."

"I see." Peristeras shrugged. "It matters not to me. This is the only place I have where you may pass this night. You both need rest and I can recommend this bed to you as comfortable and wide. But if it is your wish to sleep upon the floor, so be it. I am not your chaperone." With that, he turned, climbed back down the ladder, and Omo shot the device back into place. Then the trapdoor closed and plunged the two reluctant bedfellows into darkness.

"I know not what to say," Arcite's voice came to Berengeria, riding softly on the darkness. "But if you trust me and will take my hand, perhaps we shall find rest."

"This may be risky," Berengeria said. She reached forth and her hand touched his. Then they stepped together toward the space where they knew the bed to be.

Arcite's voice came to her out of the darkness, husky, but full of its old playfulness. "It is a lovely bed," he said. "All freshly made, and clean as any bird's wing. And our clothes are filthy. It would be improper to repose in it without undressing first."

"Indeed." She could not think of a better answer. Surely they could pass the night and not touch one another in the luxurious expanse which would separate them. Could they not? She stood back from herself and watched the foolish woman who reached back to unlace her gown.

Chapter Seventeen:
A New Quest

PRINCESS BERENGERIA OF Carea climbed into the broad bed, then lay back and felt the straw beneath her. It was rough, yet soft beneath the coarse cloth of the mattress. Her naked skin reveled in the coolness of the comforters which pressed down on her and she listened to Arcite's even breath in the darkness. How different was her love for him from any earlier love. This was no innocent rapture, this was passion of the mind, the heart —and most of all, the body. She could not keep herself from reaching toward him, from finding his hand with her fingers. Security lay in his touch and she allowed her fingers to twine with his. "I love you," he said. She repeated that phrase, marveling at the nuance and the feel of it. "I love you."

She traced the heavy tendons of his arm until she came to the place where he had been bitten by the viper. His forearm was still swollen, though it was much smaller than it had been that morning. She probed the area; there were still a few pieces of akos leaf clinging to the flesh. She rolled onto her side and reached out with her other hand so she could massage them away.

To her surprise, he seized her in a mighty hug and

forced his lips against hers. But his grip relaxed and he sighed, then rolled away to the far side of the bed. Perplexed, she lifted herself on one elbow and laid a hand on the rippling expanse of his chest. "Is something wrong?"

He laughed part of a laugh. He cupped the back of her head with his palm and brought her near, until his lips touched her forehead. Then he released her. "Ah, maid," he whispered. "We'd yield ourselves up to our passions, if I had my way. And I'm aware you'd let me take my way with you if I demanded it. But I can sense you as you wage the inner war. Your higher instincts make you clench your teeth and stiffen from the rapture which is beckoning. You're not a willing sinner, Princess, love, for all the lusty blood which courses in your veins."

She kissed him for his perception. But while every higher part of her being rejoiced at his restraint, the animal part of her trembled with disappointment. "But if your body yearns for mine as mine for you, I could not be so cruel of heart as to deny you."

"Ah, temptress. But do you desire my passion with each fiber of your soul?"

Now it was Berengeria's turn to sigh. "Indeed, indeed, a part of me rebels. Oh, would that we were other people, love. I'd gladly open up my gates to you, as if I were the city of your birth and you, returning legions of my gallant warriors and husbands of my maids—if only our great love could be recorded onto paper. I am a Princess to my bones. My body writhes against the yoke of royalty—yet from my soul, my heritage o'errides my lust."

Then Berengeria cried out. "By all the gods, why must it be this way?" She made a fist and pounded it into the straw. Arcite was correct; they were poor sinners. Even in the heat of her passion she could not quite throw off the yoke of her royalty, nor he the chivalrous nature which was part of his calling. She thirsted for his touch and that thirst could be quenched only a little by the knowledge that she would be proud of them both in the morning. She sighed, then laid her head against his arm; he was an oasis of warmth in a cold, dark desert. And she prayed that she would be able to find sleep on this night.

She did sleep. When she awoke it was dawn; the new sun's golden light streamed through the louvers at one end of the loft and filled the space with slanting shadows. She found herself curled in Arcite's embrace. But as she remembered where she was, she felt shocked to see herself and this man together in their nakedness. The sweetness of the night was little more than a dream, a soul-stirring vision. She gently slid the man's arm from about her shoulders, rolled to her side of the bed, and dressed herself.

She was again the prim and proper Princess—and that puzzled her. Was she bothered by the thought of having Arcite see her nakedness, the pink of her flesh and the jagged scars of her back? Why should that matter? He had seen the scars before. Why should the introduction of the sun's brightness make a difference? Nonetheless, it did. Love, passion, and shame were all strange entities. Whatever she had felt last night, and however much she loved this wandering singer, she felt relief that they had not actually slipped over the rim of passion's precipice. She also felt relief as she laced her gown back into place.

She heard a sound and turned to see Arcite looking at her. "I had such pleasant dreams," he said. "Perhaps some future time we might again sleep thus. It is a gift e'en more divine than some unearthly vision."

Berengeria looked at him. Comforters were pulled about his hips and thighs but she did note that the hair which cascaded down his chest and belly was as blond as the locks hanging across his forehead. He was attractive in daylight, as well as darkness. She felt the blood rush to her face as she spoke to him softly. "We must get dressed. Our host could come at any time."

"Indeed," he said. He looked into her eyes for an instant, then turned away and picked his tattered clothes up off the floor. But there had been something special in that glance; it had told Berengeria that he understood her need, her feelings, that he felt them too, at least in his own way. She felt closer to him than she had since waking.

She turned her back on him once more to let him dress. Then the trapdoor opened, the ladder slid down, and their host appeared. They had not been a moment too quick to maintain propriety—either that, or they were being observed. In any case, young Peristeras poked his head above the level of the floor and gazed at the two of them with his glittering eyes. "Did you sleep well?"

"Like babies," Arcite said, smoothing the fabric of his tunic.

"That pleases me. I have a gift for you."

They both looked at the child. "A gift?"

He reached down. Omo must have been standing below him because when he raised his hand again, he lifted with great effort a large leather case. And from the ringing sound it made when he set it on the loft's floor, Berengeria guessed it contained some sort of musical instrument. That did not surprise her—the strange child had shown his interest in Arcite's musical talents the night before.

From the way Arcite's face lit up, he plainly suspected the same. He moved toward Peristeras and eyed the case. "And might I look on it?" he asked.

"Indeed, I brought it for that very purpose."

Arcite took the case and laid it on the bed. Then, while Berengeria and Peristeras looked on, he undid the laces which held it shut, lifted the lid, and exposed a mandolin of glorious workmanship. The instrument gleamed with its perfect coat of lacquer and the glowing wood was everywhere inlaid with lengths of gold and silver wire, finely chiseled bits of ivory, and tiny crafted tiles. Arcite whistled. His face lit up like the face of a child on its birthday and he took the wondrous object from the case, cradled it, and tested the strings. "It's beautiful," he murmured. "I've never seen it's like, or even close. And it is perfectly in tune."

"It never shall be otherwise," Peristeras said matter-of-factly. "It is the gift that I was destined by the Fates to pass into your hands. For that lone reason have I lived in this stone cottage since my birth."

The two lovers looked at him, nonplussed. "Your birth?" Berengeria asked. "How long ago was that and what folk were your parents? What became of them?"

But the boy waved away her questions with a laugh. "You have no need of answers. I am here and I have waited; that is all you need to know. The point is this—when you both told to me the history of how you came unto this forest and this cabin, I recall you mentioned that the merchant vessel in your tale bore boxes. Am I quite correct?"

"Six long and wooden boxes," Arcite replied. "I studied them at length while I awaited Berengeria."

"Did they hold bodies?"

Arcite hesitated, then answered. "It is possible."

"You hesitated to answer—but I know they did. My friends, great evil lurks within this world and waits to be released. A loathsome sect will try to send it after us, and soon. To that same end, six corpses are exhumed and stolen from their resting places. This foul cult of which I speak will bear them unto Kruptos. Have you heard of such a place?"

Berengeria had never heard such a name before but Arcite scratched his chin. "It is an evil city, legends say. But more of it, or where it can be found, I've no idea."

Peristeras nodded, his expression betraying more than ever the pink youth of his features. "You'll never find it in the selfsame place two nights a-running. It is only seen in darkness, and no other time but when the moon is full. Each time, it stands upon a different site. A few nights from this moment, it will rest two leagues southeast of Tranje."

"By all the gods," Arcite exclaimed.

But Peristeras went on. "It holds an evil I cannot describe, except to say that if it gains escape, the world we know will face its finish. These six corpses which I have described are being brought to Kruptos to be resurrected by this sect. Six evil ones they are; their like has not been known upon this world for many years. But still they play a rôle; the cultists do not dare release the city's evil without them to help contain it."

A horrible thought came to Berengeria. "Can they be even worse than Alyubol?"

"The wizard Alyubol might very well be one of them."

"That cannot be. I saw his body burned."

Peristeras shook his head. "That does not matter. If they so desire, these men can use another body as facsimile. The ceremony will restore the evil, undead spirits to some human forms selected for the purpose. It will be of no account to whom the bodies once belonged."

Berengeria shivered. "Foul, foul men," she whispered.

But Arcite looked nonplussed. "What have these facts to do with us?"

"Can you not guess? Can you not guess the origin of this fine mandolin? The Fates have given you your art, my friend, and they demand their recompense. Is there a good place not too far from Tranje where oft smugglers come to land their contraband?"

"Indeed," Arcite said. "The Gulf of Ruid is a place like that. It is deserted, save the times when hunters land there in pursuit of seals. And smugglers have been known to use its sheltered waters."

"Ah. Then in the Gulf of Ruid will you find your true destiny, the reason why the Fates present you with this instrument. If you gaze at the back, you'll find some words and music there engraved."

Arcite turned the mandolin over and his eyebrows lifted. "I see it there."

"That is the song which you must memorize and play when you have found the boxes. It will take away the evil in them. We are far too near the time of Kruptos' next appearance for their owners to replace them. You must do this thing."

"Must I?" Arcite looked doubtful. "But I suppose I must," he said after another moment. "For you have saved my life."

Berengeria placed a hand on his arm. "Besides, my

love, if what he says is true, our world can never be subjected to the evil of foul Alyubol again, much less five more just like him. I have seen his acts; I know the horrors he would bring."

Arcite issued her a loving look. "I know. I know your story. I will do it."

"Such a deed will take great courage," Peristeras said. "Therefore, it will not be asked without a suitable reward." He reached to his belt and produced something Berengeria had not noticed before. It was one of the flasks she had seen in his study; this one contained what appeared to be a human finger. Berengeria grimaced as the boy handed it to her. But she took it from him all the same and marveled at its lifelike appearance. "What is this?" she asked.

"You have a brother, Palamon?"

"I do."

"He has some troubles of his own, as I have heard."

"He does. His son was stricken down by magic's art and lies in deepest sleep within the palace. Even now my poor, betroubled brother seeks the man who worked the spell, to see that it's reversed."

"He does so at his peril," Peristeras said grimly. "For some evil men performed the deed to drive your brother to that very act. Now in his quest, he has supplied the instrument required to loose the evil of foul Kruptos' temples. You must bring this artifact to him. It can restore his son."

"A finger?"

"It is given by the gods, as token of their blessing on your house. I'll say no more of it, except to tell you that, if you could know its origin, you'd fall and worship it."

"But wait," Arcite said. "I thought my singing was to cast away the evil of the city and the boxes."

"This is a complex evil, friend. The rôle you'll play will only rid the world of one small part of it. There still is more and these next weeks shall be full troublesome. The sect we speak of also captured you, fair Princess. They did want your body's blood, to help them work their complex, world-destroying evil. As I told you once, your safest hiding place would be in your Carea. But Arcite goes to the Gulf of Ruid, and your place is also at his side. This forms a conflict I cannot resolve. That answer lies in your hands."

"By the gods," Arcite said softly. "Then I'll accompany the Princess back to her own native kingdom. I could not be part of any danger unto her."

"No, I will go with you," Berengeria countered. "Should you face death, I'll face it at your side."

But Arcite shook his head. "You cannot do that, love. How could I be knave enough to have you subject to the dangers of those awful men again."

"You are a gallant man, my love Arcite—but gallantry can sometimes be insulting. Why, you seem to vision me as no more than a useless bag of skin and fluff, to be shut up within some quiet place for admiration only." Her eyes flamed and she added more than she should have. "I must resent your patronizing attitude. I am of royal blood and you, a commoner. Eternal order thus demands that you obey my will."

Arcite's eyes flashed at the insult. "What words," he said, wrenching Berengeria's bowels with his tone and expression. "Now here we are, the lovers who held hands and wept because of passion unfulfilled a half night ago. 'Tis said that lovers quarrel, but I would to heaven it were otherwise, for I find this to be..." His voice trailed off as he glanced over Berengeria's shoulder and out the cottage door. "By all the gods, what creatures are attacking us?"

Berengeria followed his glance and what she saw caused all angry thoughts to drain from her. The foul creatures which had horrified her twice before, the crawling horde which had accosted her in Castle Conforth's maze and while she had been in the cultists' trance, was advancing toward them. And this time, it was real.

The writhing masses she had seen before had been no more than a vision in a dream; she knew that from her discussions with Arcite. But these crawlers boiled up out of holes in the ground, blew into the meadow on breeze-borne wings, and devoured everything they touched. The meadow's grasses fell before them like straw before the flames. Great pale crickets and cockroaches gobbled every twig, every shrub and sprout as the chittering blanket gnawed its way toward the watching humans.

Peristeras also gazed through the doorway and became grave, indeed. These were the kind of vermin known only in nightmares: huge waxy grasshoppers with high crests across their backs and great, engulfing jaws; blind worms; and obscenely swollen spiders. Mantises the length of a man's hand strode across the ground, their pincing mouths groping for prey. Fat-bodied termites heaved their oversize heads along and tried to shove their way to the front of the crawling mass. It was an army no two or three human beings could hope to overcome. Arcite stared, then slammed the door against the oncoming horde.

But Peristeras tried to push him away from the barrier. "Nay, nay," the lad cried. "These are the first, the smallest evil skirmishers which come for you. We must oppose them, if we do fail, no force will stop them as they gain their strength."

"How can they be opposed?" Berengeria cried.

Though Peristeras was only a child, he gestured to Omo and the beefy servant managed to shove Arcite from the door. The boy opened the portal again, to show the slithering army even closer than before, about to swarm over the cottage. Peristeras did not seem in the least afraid; he looked alight with a strange, nervous kind of energy. "These creatures are but symbols of the force of evil which is breeding in this world. They're petty vermin; they are but the crust which forms across the canker you must cleanse. And so it is that they are dealt with in an instant."

The child snatched the artifact—the finger in the bottle—from Berengeria, held it aloft, and released a cry. A wind rushed into the building, eddied about them like air expelled from a bellows, and whooshed back out the door. Berengeria was knocked to her knees by the force of it. Her clothes writhed about her, the wind caught her hair and streamed it out the doorway. She felt too giddy to rise, as if the breath were being swept from her lungs.

The effect on the vermin outside was even more dramatic; the gusts caught them, lifted them, dragged them from the ground and from the tussocks and twigs to which they clung. They rolled back across one another, bounded before the wind's force, helpless as butterflies. The wind swept them back across the meadow like a new tide scouring the flotsam from a beach; in a moment they were swept from view. The stretch of meadow, stripped of foliage as if a fire had swept across it, was the only proof the creatures had ever existed.

Berengeria rose; she and Arcite both stood speechless. With every hour, this strange child who had been their host manifested his powers in some new and daunting way.

But Peristeras did not give them time to become too awed. He handed the artifact back to Berengeria, then continued the conversation as if there had not even been an interruption. "If your Princess still desires to go with you," he told Arcite, "do not deny her. Thus, the issue is resolved. The main point is that you must hurry; what we saw here demonstrates the way the evil grows. Those bugs were symbols of the evil that resides in Kruptos; you will find them in the phantom city, too, but more appalling than you could imagine."

Arcite stared at the lad and Berengeria could guess his thoughts. Hers were the same, after all. Into what mammoth vortex had the Fates sucked them? What had they done to become pawns in some eternal struggle between good and evil? But then a bell rang somewhere in the house and their host changed the subject again. "Good Omo has prepared our breakfast. Come. You need to eat and I will give you food enough to start you on your journey." He stepped to the cottage's little dining room.

Their morning meal consisted of porridge and honey, along with another bowl of fruit. Then their host allowed them time and privacy to bathe themselves and wash their ragged clothes, for they would not soon have another such opportunity. His manner with them was hur-

ried and perfunctory—neither of the lovers could doubt
that he wanted them to begin their journey north as
quickly as possible. And while Berengeria suspected that
Arcite still felt doubts about her accompanying him, she
wished to start quickly for that same reason, in spite of
the mystery they were entering. Once they were well on
their way, her minstrel lover would be unable to protest
her decision.

It was heaven to be clean again. Soap was a wonderful invention, Berengeria decided. She pitied those too
poor or backward to use it. Even though her gown was
still ripped, tattered, and stained beyond cleansing, the
washing had made it soft against her skin and she could
face her journey with a lighter heart for that.

A bright, blue-and-yellow morning had burst upon the
world. The breeze was fragrant with the aromas of the
forest and the grasses and the trail smiled at the travelers
as if to deny that there could ever be a brooding evil
which needed to be destroyed. She smiled up at Arcite
and he at last returned the smile. Then they clasped
hands and strolled north together, leaving behind the
cottage in its now-barren clearing. They looked like no
more than two lovers going for a walk in a garden.

Chapter Eighteen: The Inn

PALAMON'S AND FLIN'S new horses had been expensive and the cost had drained off much of their wealth—even though Palamon was a monarch, his purse was not bottomless. But the animals had still been worth it. They were sleek, fleet-footed, and many leagues lay between Tychopolis and Tranje. Transportation was important; each day's delay brought poor Berethane that much closer to oblivion.

Were they even following the right trail? Did each stride of the horses bring the two warriors closer to a cure for Palamon's son, or farther onto some useless tangent? Palamon could not guess. His mind flew back to the phrases mouthed by the mystic maiden he had glimpsed in Danaar: "The balance teeters at the middle point; diplomacy tells all. His fate awaits you south and east of Tranje, but there's still another route."

There was no way for him to understand the message, either in its whole or in its parts. "Diplomacy tells all." Did that refer to Palamon's skill at wrangling with Lothar the Pale? If it did, Berethane was in gravest danger. Or, "there's still another route." He had no idea what that could mean.

It was all terribly frustrating. He set his jaw at the thought of the evil magic which had trapped his boy. How could any human destroy a child? Ursid hated him —he knew that, since the young Prince had never made any bones about it—but how could any man ally himself with men evil enough to strike down a child? Palamon's mind flew back to the balcony in Tychopolis and Ursid's wrathful words. The tall monarch's heart slipped toward the icy grip of that same emotion which possessed Ursid. Palamon had learned how to hate; he was even becoming proficient at the emotion.

"I've never seen a man squeeze his reins in two but by the gods, you're making a fine attempt at it." Flin's voice broke into Palamon's concentration and his hate. Palamon looked down to see that his right hand had gone white-knuckled, so tightly had he been gripping the leather straps.

He relaxed his aching fingers, held up his hand, flexed the stiffness out of it. "I thank you, Flin. My thoughts were of Ursid; I did not know my tension was reflected in my grip."

"For men who've traveled the world together, you and Ursid don't seem to be friends."

"Ursid has hated me since that hot day I bested him in tournament and kept him from his goal, the hand of Berengeria. For years, I felt remorse at what occurred—but now I realize that I must seek his death the way he has sought mine."

Flin smiled in spite of Palamon's hard words. "I don't believe a word of that last part. You don't have the heart of a man who could kill somebody in the dark—or even in daylight without the heat of battle being on you."

"I can learn."

"I doubt it, really. Besides, how much can Ursid's hatred surprise you? You stole his woman. He deserved it, of course—he's a sadly poor lover. If he'd known what he was doing, he'd have had her wrapped around his finger before ever letting her meet the likes of you. But for all that, I can see how it would cause him to resent you a little."

Palamon winced. His own hatred for Ursid suddenly made him sick. He did not even want to think about affairs between the two of them anymore. "That subject is a tender one, withal."

Flin shrugged. "Then let's talk about it all the more. After all, it might help, even while it hurts, like splashing saltwater on a cut. Then it won't be tender."

"Ah, yes. I could entreat our friend Arcite to sing a ballad on it, just in case there are some few who yet have not received that tale. No, thanks. Arcite of Tranje has enough of songs and wealth, and I have heard too much of my affairs."

"Suit yourself. But if the two of you—three of you, counting Ursid—had had me to advise you, you'd all still be friends now." Flin was teasing, Palamon knew. But it was still a tender topic, one which made him want to discuss something else—anything else.

"Where will we sleep tonight, I wonder," he said offhandedly. They had traveled northwest for days; they had left Tychopolis and Quarval behind and would arrive at Tranje in only a few days more. But though this was a well-traveled road, they had passed no towns lately.

Flin looked at the tall monarch with a twinkle in his dark eyes. "Perhaps we'll sleep beneath a tree. There are crueler fates, you know. Your friend from Hautre proved that much to us."

That was true. They had met a traveler from the city of Hautre and his tale had given Palamon another reason to hate Ursid. The city had fallen to the Buerdic cavalry two days before the feast of the god Nodens, so the traveler had told them. The peace treaty between Buerdaunt and Carea had been signed half a fortnight before that, yet Ursid had seen to it that the terms of the city's surrender had been ruthlessly enforced. The wall had been breached in several places, Baron Ulfin's castle had been slighted, and the reparations levied had been unbearable. All citizens of wealth had fled, including the man who had told them the bitter story. He had been bound with all his goods to Gesvon, there to begin his life anew. Indeed, Ursid had developed some unpleasant tendencies during the five years the war had lasted.

But Palamon would not dwell on it; at least he would try not to. There was only one task before him; that was to apprehend Navron and force him to restore Berethane's health. Only then would Palamon concern himself with vengeance over Ursid. But for all it might sicken him, he knew he would likely still hate the young Prince while he waited to confront him.

They rode on through the afternoon, across grassy, rising plains, and toward the range of hills which separated them from the coastal savannas, the city of Tranje, and the ocean. It was a long day; the sun beat down, they stopped at every stream to water their horses, and they rode as long as there was light enough to see. Only when it became pitch dark did Palamon even consider stopping.

"Wait," Flin said all at once, standing up in his stirrups. "Do I see lights yonder?"

Palamon peered in the direction the younger man had indicated. "It's possible. In fact, I think you do."

"What do you think? Is it a village, an inn, or a castle?"

"It could not be a castle, for I know of none along this stretch of road. And whether it could be a village or an inn, I cannot say. But let us ride until we see it better. By my troth, we'll cut the leagues before us by that much."

So they continued on. As they approached, they could tell the light came from leaping flames; someone had built a bonfire. The firelight flashed off the dark shapes of wagons and a great, barnlike building.

They rode into the shelter of the building and Palamon could tell that it was a large inn, with a stable built onto the rear of it. The wagons were colorfully painted and pulled into a circle on the other side of the road. The bonfire's flames bounded off dancers half concealed by the vehicles, and Palamon could hear music rising from many plucked strings. "Jiptians," he murmured.

"They are," Flin agreed. "They're here to extract a little money from the patrons of this inn if I don't miss my guess. Well, then. We have a place to sleep out the night and entertainment as well. Whether we want to be entertained or not," he added.

"We'll ask for rooms far at the building's back."

Flin glanced at the tall monarch and a look of disappointment hung itself on his features as the two men dismounted and gave their horses into the hands of the stableboy. "You've always been a man of purpose," he observed. "Too bad for you."

Palamon smiled. "I do it just to disappoint you." He gave a coin to the stableboy as he spoke. "Take your blanket and your weapons, by the way."

"Ah. You still fear your white-robed friends might have left someone to greet us?"

"Perhaps. Or maybe old acquaintances pursue us still. Friend Diomedes might not be well pleased to find we've slipped between his fingers. Though this is too far north for Buerdic soldiery to be received with friendship, still I could not be surprised to see a few of them." Palamon looked at Flin. "In any case, I want my longsword to be near at hand."

They walked through the inn's gates and found themselves in a roofed court. Their noses told them which door would lead them to their dinners, and they could ask about rooms there, so they entered and found themselves in a chamber that was nearly deserted. The only occupant muttered softly to himself as he polished the top of the oak counter which lined one wall.

"Good evening," Palamon said. It was to his advantage that, although he now ruled a country, he had lived the life of a commoner long enough to communicate easily with almost anyone. "I'm surprised to see your tables empty. Have you not a crumb of food for us?"

"Yes and no." The innkeeper was a big man with a drooping moustache and he looked at his two guests with a sour expression. "I've ale, bread, and cold mutton. It didn't make sense to cook anything tonight, because those traveling thieves across the road have lured all my guests over there."

"Their entertainments do not interest us," Palamon replied. "You have two guests, at least."

"Glad to hear it," the man said. "I wish I had something better for you. I could skewer a small roast if you want to wait."

"Nay, nay," Palamon replied. "Cold fare is satisfactory. We have no time for lingering, I'm sad to say."

"It makes me sad, too," Flin said as the host poured them two bowls of ale. "Jiptians can put on a first-class entertainment—with good food. Did I ever tell about the time I rode with a tribe of them? I was just a lad then."

"I'd not be admitting that in here," the innkeeper grumbled. "They've got a nasty reputation all among the hostel trade. Damn bad for business—they're worse for us than a plague of locusts." He looked at his two guests. "Just among the three of us, if I could afford a few armed retainers like you rich nobles, I'd send them packing."

"It would take more than a few," Flin observed. "They can be fierce if they have to."

"And being driven away from an inn full of patrons like a vulture being driven off a corpse would trouble them, I suppose. Yes, I won't argue with you. If I made them leave here before they'd weaseled every coin off every last guest, I'm sure they would be offended enough to fight."

At that moment, as if to lend emphasis to the innkeeper's words, a gaily dressed figure appeared in the doorway. "Come one, come all," he cried. "Courtay's tribe has dancing women, music, and secret potions. If you stay away tonight and your manhood fails you in the morning, it will be your own fault."

"Get out of here, you vermin." The innkeeper whirled like a cat and flung his pitcher at the intruder. But the fellow scampered out of sight and the clay vessel shattered against the lintel, spattering it with powerful brew. "I'm about ready to murder one of them," he said, shaking his head in despair.

"You need not commit crime on our account," Palamon said carelessly. "We have no time for such festivities."

"I'm glad of that, at least." The innkeeper walked to

the doorway and gazed angrily at the mess he had made. "At least two dozen travelers have passed here in the last two days and you are the first paying guests I've had in that time."

"Then we'll pay for our rooms right now," Flin said as he slipped the man another coin. "Will someone be around to show us to them when we've finished eating?"

The host knuckled his forehead in appreciation, then spread his hands. "Take any rooms you want. It won't matter, for they're all empty."

As the fellow bent to pick up the wreckage of the pitcher, Palamon gazed at Flin with a puzzled smile. "How generous of you. Now what might cause this new largesse on your part."

Flin smiled back and bit off a piece of mutton. "Because I didn't want him to get too angry when we go out and join the Jiptians, too. I know this Courtay—he's one of the ones I ran with when I was young. If he can't show us better food and a better time than this sad face with his cold meat, I'm going to wake up in the morning with all my hair fallen out."

Palamon shook his head and put on a stern expression. "We have no time for revelry. We must remember what we came for. My poor son is more important to me and, I hope, to you, than some young Jiptian dancing girl's soft thighs."

Any other courtier in Carea would have been turned and intimidated by the tall monarch's stern words. It was a mark of Flin's personality and their long companionship that his smile did not diminish by a degree. "You haven't seen these thighs—they're as good as that Jiptian in the doorway said they are. And what harm can it do? We're not going any place till dawn, anyway. I guarantee you that a bowl of spicy Jiptian stew will go down a lot better than this stuff. Faugh." He discarded his cold mutton with a grimace. "This is tough, even for sheep meat. I think the sheep it was cut from had leaves and roots on it and grew up out of the ground."

Palamon sighed and made a wry expression. Would it

do a great deal of harm for him to indulge Flin, at least a little? "Then very well," he said. "But take this warning —I will not delay my quest for even one short instant. We will eat a quiet meal, will watch the dancers if you care for that, and then we will retire. Do you agree?"

"Of course I do. You're the King—I'd never argue with you." Flin's eyes twinkled and he reached forward to clap Palamon on one broad shoulder. "You'll never regret it. Come on."

Palamon followed the younger man out the door and through the court to the outside of the structure. The innkeeper watched them pass with a look of resignation. At least these two had paid for rooms before they had deserted him.

At Palamon's insistence, the two men kept their long-swords strapped to their sides. "We know not whom we'll meet," he said. "In these parts, on this quest, we could run foul of any number of our enemies. If your suggestion should require that we discard our weapons to gain entry to the Jiptian camp, then I forbid the whole experiment."

"Don't worry, don't worry," Flin said. "They won't like our weapons but I knew Courtay when he was just a lad. He'll let us join him whether we wear armor or bare skin."

They walked across the road. The fire was still blazing and they could hear music, shouting, and laughter on the far side of the wagons. The Jiptians had set up their camp in a grove of trees above a little stream. Palamon suspected he would have found their horses tethered at the water's edge, had he cared to look. And as the two men passed between the lowered tongue of one wagon and the locked-door rear end of another, a colorful sight burst upon them.

Laughter and sounds of revelry echoed all about the fire and the yellow light glared off grinning, wine-besotted faces. Three men in red, white, and green shirts scraped away on lutes and a violin while a fourth pounded a tambor; four women leaped and danced beside them. Ten or a dozen men in travelers' garb watched them, cheered, and made lewd remarks. Another body of the Jiptians sang and clapped their hands in time to the music. Palamon noted the free-flowing spirits, but he was relieved to see that one old woman stood by a smaller, separate fire, and the stew she was stirring in her cauldron did smell delicious.

It was a closely calculated cross between a celebration, an orgy, and a performance. As Palamon and Flin approached the fire, they were interdicted by a brawny fellow wearing the same colorful garb as the rest of the Jiptians. "Are you our friends?" the man said with a smile. "If you are friends, you will not need swords here."

"So you can cut our throats all the easier?" Flin asked with a laugh. "Deltor, you rascal. Don't you recognize me? I hauled you out of the river once when you were too drunk to swim and too stupid to stay on the bank."

The fellow looked offended for a moment, then his eyes lit up and he threw his arms about the newcomer's shoulders. "Flin. Flin the Brigand. May all the gods be blessed, I haven't seen you since before I had hair on my butt. What are you doing this far north?"

"I heard you were here and I came to join in the fun. Where's Courtay?"

While they bantered, Palamon observed the Jiptian. He was a swarthy, powerfully built man, a picture of roguish health and good humor. Oddly enough, however, there was something odd, something not quite right, with his eyes. The moment he recognized Flin, he turned and the fire's light accented a strange whiteness, a milkiness, which almost covered both pupils. Perhaps it was only a trick of the light; whatever it was, the affliction did not seem to hinder the fellow as he wrapped his arm about Flin and the two of them walked toward the trees with Palamon following. "The boss is in his wagon," Deltor said. "He hasn't been too well the last couple of days."

"Then let's go in and see him."

Deltor laughed. "No, no. He'll come out for a look at

the likes of you. Besides, the fresh air and a little stew
will do him good." They reached the largest of the gaily
painted wagons and Deltor mounted the bottom step to
pound on the door. "Boss. You have to get out here.
You'll never guess who's come."

There was a moment's silence, then a hoarse voice
responded. "Flin the Brigand?"

Flin grinned at Deltor, then stared up at the closed
door and cried, "How did you know?"

"I know everything." There was the sound of a body
moving about in the wagon; the wooden frame creaked
eerily. "I'll come out. I want to look at your face."

"Sure. Come out and we'll have a drink together."

The door popped open and a round, heavily bearded
face poked out, followed by a ponderous body. "No
drink for me. I'm in no shape for it today—but I'll have
a table set up and I'll sit out here with you." Then he
looked into Palamon's face. "Who's this?"

"A good friend, an honorable man," Flin said, placing
an arm on Palamon's shoulder. "He's a king in his own
country, no less, and the same as a brother to me."

Courtay looked Palamon up and down. The tall monarch could see by the firelight that his eyes suffered the
same affliction as Deltor's. Perhaps that was part of the
sickness troubling him, which both Jiptians had mentioned. But it did not show any effect on his hospitality.
"I'm a king in my land, too, so royalty doesn't impress
me. But a brother of Flin's is a brother of mine; welcome
to my camp." He clasped Palamon's hand in a half-
hearted grip, then turned to Deltor. "Tell the women to
set up a table here."

Deltor hurried away and returned with a bevy of
women, young and old, who carried sawhorses, boards,
benches, and all the necessaries for setting up a table and
spreading a feast. But when the females laid eyes on
Flin, many of them dropped their burdens and clustered
around him, pinching, caressing his cheeks, allowing him
to steal kisses, and simpering at his every joke or double-
entendre. Palamon had to marvel at the performance.

Had it been his desire, it was likely that Flin could have possessed a harem which would have included half the female population of the lands about the Thlassa Mey. Perhaps he did anyway.

But Flin accepted the feminine attention as no more than his due; he laughed, fondled, squeezed, and pinched in return. Then, after the women had made a bantering departure and the two newcomers had seated themselves across from Courtay, the old woman served her stew. And Deltor leaned over Flin's shoulder. "There's someone else who might like to see you."

Flin coughed and put down his cup of Jiptian wine. "Ellal?"

"That's right." He pointed toward the bonfire. The dance there had ended and one of the four lovely dancing women made a beeline toward their table. Palamon looked on and smiled, for Flin seemed to be less than delighted about the situation, to judge from his expression.

"But she got married," the former brigand said in a harsh whisper. "I heard about it while I was riding on the Greenlands."

Deltor only laughed. "But she always loved you best. You know that, you rascal." He laughed again as the forementioned Ellal settled herself on Flin's lap, pressed her body against his, and moved her fingers through his hair. "You tell him, Ellal."

"My husband isn't here," she said in a low voice. "He got himself into a gaol in Stournes, so I'm alone these days. Or I was until now, at any rate. Remember those nights along the Fleuve, my Flin? The summer nights so warm, as warm as blood, and the cool waters of the river lapping against our shoulders. I will never forget them."

This Ellal was a lovely girl; Palamon could not keep from admiring her beauty himself. She was raven-haired, with skin as pale and pure as doves' wings and lips as succulent as cherries. But he could not keep from noticing that she, too, was troubled by the same affliction as the others, the casting over of the eyes. In fact, it seemed to affect her more than most; she was the least bit lethargic, her voice was almost dreamy. But there was nothing dreamy in the way she bowed her neck to bestow a passionate kiss upon her former lover.

To Palamon's surprise, the kiss seemed to catch Flin unprepared. When it ended, he stared at her for an instant, a puzzled expression gripped his features, then he laughed heartily. "Then everything's just as it was, isn't it? What a celebration."

"Drink up, my men." Courtay cried. "There's more of the spirit when you're done."

"Nay, nay," Flin cried. "If the wine of love's to be had, then Jiptian wine, tempting as it might be, pales in comparison."

Palamon did not feel like drinking, either. In fact he found his instincts rebelling at the general air of celebration and debauchery which surrounded him. "Remember, Flin, you left a wife at home," he whispered.

Flin smiled up at him. "I did. That is where I left her." Then he hugged Ellal all the more tightly. "So you have a husband in prison and I have a wife in Carea. Does that trouble you?"

"They are gone and we are here."

Flin looked back toward Palamon, amid the laughter of the Jiptians. "So you see?"

"I see, indeed," Palamon said as he rose from the table. "But I have eaten of delicious stew and I am satisfied. I now shall find a bed in which to sleep." He looked down at Flin before he turned back toward the inn. "Alone. When you have sated all your appetites, my Flin, return and join me in the hostelry. And we will speak together."

Flin looked the least fraction taken aback but his voice was drowned out by the voices of their Jiptian hosts. "No, stay, stay. We have spirits, we have food."

Palamon smiled politely and shook his head. "I tell you I cannot. For I am on a quest and I must keep my body pure, unsatisfied, and quick. Perhaps another time." He turned from them and walked toward the far side of the circle of wagons. When Deltor tried to block his way, he brushed the man aside more roughly than he had intended to. Flin's laxness troubled him but he had learned over the years that not all people shared his views on the disposition of their bodies. He would try not to hold this night against the younger man.

So he walked from the Jiptian camp and toward the stables. He would look to the welfare of the horses first, would see that they were properly brushed, drenched, and fed, and only then would he seek his own bed. It would be a short night with a long day to follow.

Chapter Nineteen:
The Jiptians

GRAVEL CRACKLED BENEATH Palamon's feet as he crossed the road and walked toward the stables. Behind him, revelry went on unabated in the Jiptian camp. He smiled to himself. He would ever be a poor carouser; the party would go in a more satisfactory fashion without him. But Flin still disappointed him. He knew the young knight worshipped his wife, Bessina. But that worship seemed less binding at long distances than it was when the two were together.

The inn was shadowy in the darkness; Palamon looked up at its mass as he walked by. He could tell that the height was due partly to the fact that a high storage loft had been built atop the part of the building used to quarter guests. It was an interesting design; the open doors at the end of a gable, the beam which jutted out, and the rope which still dangled to the ground were what gave the building its barnlike appearance. Apparently, the inn's workers had lately been loading goods from some transport wagon; that was why the doors had not been closed and the rope had not been put away. Both those workers and the teamsters who had delivered the goods were likely part of the celebration in the Jiptian camp at that very moment.

He walked past the towering building and through the gate to the stables. But that place, too, was empty. And he found the two horses standing practically as he and Flin had left them. The saddles had been removed but the horses were still rank with sweat and Palamon doubted they had been fed or watered. It was all quite disgusting. He frowned and searched about for the barrel which held the inn's supply of oats. If he was going to have to feed his own animals, he was going to see to it they ate well.

It took him a long time to finish taking care of the horses, unfamiliar as he was with the stable and business of a stableboy. But at last he had fed them, had brushed them down, had drenched them, and then had led each one to a stall and had left it with a good word and a pat on the rump. When it was all done, he wiped his forehead and turned toward the stables' entrance. But something was not quite right: the stable doors stood open at a new angle and the animals in their stalls began to stamp anxiously. Something was just wrong enough to prod him toward caution. His pace slowed; then he saw the glimmer of light through the crack between the stable door and the heavy jamb which supported it. Someone was waiting for him.

He smiled to himself. So that was the way of things. Flin, ever lucky, ever joyous Flin, was going to party the night out at the Jiptian camp while Palamon was about to fight for his life against robbers or worse. Virtue was not always followed by a reward. Still, that was not quite fair; Flin was likely to face the same problem in the middle of the night as Palamon was facing right now. And he would likely be in poorer shape to deal with it.

Palamon turned away from the building's entrance but as he did so, a half-dozen men stepped out of the shadows below the hayloft. Each wore the unmistakable garb of the Jiptians. So that was it. Had he offended them enough with his refusal of their hospitality that they wanted to do him harm?

Another figure stepped into the light; it was not a man Palamon knew, but he did recognize the clothing. This antagonist wore the white woolen robes of Navron's loathsome sect. So the tall monarch smiled, brought his longsword hissing from its sheath, and spoke to his foes in a low whisper. "So we must fight. Then be aware, you hound of Alyubol, that you shall be the first foe I shall slay."

To his amazement, the sinister figure threw back the white hood and revealed herself to be a young woman. "You'll never even reach me, fool," she said with an evil smile. "These men are my slaves just as surely as if I had purchased them. Thus, they will die long before you could attack."

Palamon stopped short. So that was it—the whiteness of the Jiptians eyes, their lethargic movements. That was the reason. This foul woman, this servant of evil, this member of the sect that had no name, had woven a spell over them. Then Flin was in ever greater danger than he.

He did not need to look behind him; he knew more enemies would be approaching stealthily from that angle. With a cry, he wheeled and attacked them first, flashed his sword in a deadly arc that laid two of them low, then broke through their line and ran toward the wagons and the bonfire.

The Jiptians overcame their shock and tried to run after him, though he knew he could outdistance them. But there was another threat in front of him he could not outdistance; a wave of figures flooded out of the crowded wagons. His escape must have been communicated to the others; now he faced thirty enraged pursuers, both men and women. They might or might not be armed, but there were certainly enough of them to drag him down, if the evil woman had as much influence over them as she said she did.

His eye caught the inn's storage loft and the rope dangling down. A hope of escape lay in that. He veered toward it, vaulted, and caught at the rope as high up as one hand would reach. Then, jamming his sword back in its scabbard with a lightning motion, he made his way up

the rope, using arms, elbows, and knees, the way a
schoolboy would have done. He had left his youth behind him, but he still made good progress. He had
climbed well beyond the grasp of the closest Jiptians. A
moment's shouting followed, then a female voice cried,
"After him."

Someone—probably more than one person—followed him up the rope; he could feel the vibrations without even having to look down. But the bodies below him
only steadied the heavy strand and enabled him to climb
it more rapidly. If their weight did not snap it and bring
them all hurtling to the ground, he would easily reach the
beam above before they could hope to catch him.

He panted, climbed, and breathed a silent sigh of relief that apparently none of his pursuers had a longbow
handy. Such a weapon would have made his life a short
and hectic business. But what of the female wizard
below him? If she had powers anything like those of
Alyubol or Navron, he was still in a great deal of trouble.
He could only comfort himself that the level of her magic
could not be very great, even though she had somehow
mesmerized the Jiptians. After all, had she been Alyubol, lightning would have blasted him from the rope long
before now.

He could hear her. She cursed, shrieked, and tried to
make her way through the crowd. Then he heard an in-
cantation in a deep voice and he strained to cross the last
cubit of rope between himself and the extended beam.
The rope dangled from a heavy pulley; the other end of it
was lost in the dark recesses in the loft. But just as his
grasping hand caught at the supporting wood, a seething
ball of fire flashed from across the road, zoomed past his
face, seared his whiskers, and the rope to which he clung
burst into flame. So there were at least two cultists after
him.

With a cry, he caught at the beam with his other hand.
And it was not a moment too soon; the rope parted, the
smoking end whizzed past his nose, and he heard the
scream and thud of people hitting the ground below him.
But he had no time to look down; he hauled himself onto

the beam and scuttled into the dark shelter beyond.

He hardly knew where he was and he certainly had no idea where to go from here. Worse, a flicker caught his eye—the fireball heaved by the male cultist had flung sparks into a corner of the loft and a few strands of straw had begun to burn; their flames spread even as he looked at them.

Straw had been heaped here and there along the walls and about the floor; the place would burn like a torch if Palamon did not stop the burgeoning blaze. So he rushed into the corner and stamped madly. But he was too late. The flames spread beyond the scope of his broad feet, raced along the base of a wall, and outflanked him. Unless he could find his way off the loft floor, the spreading conflagration would quickly surround him, would reach the thatch roof, and he would die.

He heard shouting below. Voices sounded through the lower part of the building, then he heard one bellow over all the rest. It was the innkeeper, the big man who had so resented the wandering tribesmen stealing away all the inn's customers. He opposed the invading crowd, told them they could not enter, swore at them bitterly. Then Palamon heard a shout, followed by the scream only a dying man could make, and his blood ran cold. The tribesmen had killed the innkeeper. The spreading flames drowned out the other sounds but Palamon knew he was in a desperate fix; he was trapped in the building as surely as a bear brought to bay by hounds, and even the trap was burning down around him.

He could not go down the ladder now, even if he could reach it through the flames. Above the crackle and whine of burning wood, he thought he could hear the thundering of feet as his pursuit poured through the building. He had to elude both men and flames somehow, so he rushed toward the rear of the structure, bumped into things, tripped and scraped his knuckles, and elbowed his way frantically through the flash and billowing smoke. If he could find some way to clamber onto the stables' roof, perhaps he could elude capture or incineration a few moments longer.

But he reached the end of the loft and found no window, no door, only rough boards secured to the heavy studding. And even those boards had started to burn; he really was trapped. He turned and looked the way he had come but no hope lay there. Flames licked beams and wooden supports; smoke filled the place like a pestilence, invaded his nostrils, and threatened to choke him then and there.

Desperate circumstances required desperate measures. He stepped away from the burning wall, gritted his teeth, lowered his shoulder, and sent himself crashing against the timbers. Smoke blinded him, blazing splinters seared his neck, and the weakened wall shattered like kindling as his body hurtled into space. He was leaping either to injury, to death—or, if the gods favored him, to salvation.

He landed on a hard, slanted surface with a thud that drove the wind from his body. Before he even knew where he was, he had rolled and tumbled a dozen cubits, then hurtled once more into space. He braced his forearms over his head and landed in what seemed an endless sea of hay, through which he plunged until he thought the flesh was being scratched from his body. The dry fodder had broken his fall but he had to get away from it, had to escape before the sparks he carried with him turned it into an even greater conflagration than the one he had just escaped. He rolled from the pile, clambered to his feet, and shook the dizziness from his head. He then realized what had happened: he had fallen to the roof of the stables, then had rolled from there onto a haystack.

Two horses thundered around the corner of the building and came sliding to a halt in front of him; he drew his longsword to defend himself once more. The rider was a dark shape against the sky but urgency swelled his voice. "Get onto the other horse. And hurry; they're going to know what's happened in half a moment and they'll be after you, hot as those flames you broke through." There was no mistaking the voice; it belonged to Flin.

Palamon sheathed his longsword, leaped onto the ani-

mal Flin had indicated, and in an instant they were both
tearing past the front of the burning inn and northwest
through the darkness. They could hear the tumult fade
behind them as they rode away.

But they could not gallop for long. The road was a
dim white stripe in the darkness. To keep on, even on the
brightest night, was folly. An unseen irregularity, a hidden hole catching an extended hoof, and they would be
easy prey for the pursuit which was sure to follow. Once
they slowed down, Palamon spoke. "The fate of those
within that hostelry is grim to contemplate. It tore at me
to hear the host cry out."

"That may be," Flin answered. "But if we went back
there, we'd soon be crying out as well. Those two white-
robed freaks are going to be mad as hornets in an
uprooted tree."

"I did not know how many threatened us. I saw the
one and heard the other chant. But you are right; our
flight will anger them."

"You don't know the half of it. They'll be hot enough
to bite rocks when they see what's happened."

"Oh? Then what has happened?"

Flin sputtered into a cackling laugh. "These are their
horses."

Palamon had to laugh as well, for all the seriousness
of matters. Flin, as always, was Flin. "And tell me how
it passed that you could work this strategy. When I last
saw you, you were in the arms of that loose Jiptian
wench."

Flin began his story but Palamon cut him short. "But
ere you tell your tale, I must declare your wenching to
be quite improper. You have saved my life again; perhaps I should not criticize. But you've a wife who loves
you more than life itself; I cannot let it pass without my
comment."

Flin laughed once more. "I hardly know where to
begin after all that. Of course Bessina loves me; how
could she do anything else?"

"A telling question."

"But she loves me for what I am, isn't that true? And

I'm a lover. If I were to stop thinking of myself as a lover and start thinking of myself as a husband, I wouldn't be a lover anymore. Then where would I be?"

Palamon shook his head. "I have no answer. I am stupefied."

"I love Bessina more than I love breathing, more than food, more than drink. Whatever I might do when I'm half a world away won't make me love her any less. I could swear an oath to that if you like."

"No. There's no need. But tell me this: would you love her the same if you knew she were flinging her fair form at some man in your absence?"

Flin laughed again. "She'd never do that. She'd never find anyone else who could thrill her the way I do. But don't ask about love, Palamon. You're not a lover so you can never understand the way it works; I've noticed that before. To be perfectly honest, I've lain awake nights feeling sorry for you. As for Ellal, she's not a wench and I had no intention of laying a finger on her, so you're condemning the wrong man on that account."

"I'd not have known it from the way the two of you exchanged your fevered kisses."

Flin rubbed his chin thoughtfully in the darkness. "I didn't kiss her, I only returned the kisses she gave me. But I did find it strange, myself. We had some mighty good times years ago, before I met Bessina. But she's married now and her old man may be in gaol or he may not, but it was mighty puzzling, the way she was acting. You see, Jiptian women never touch anyone besides their husbands once they're married. Besides, the other men of the tribe wouldn't stand for it—and here she was, falling all over me with everyone watching and no one saying a word. I knew something had to be fishy. Besides, I could tell something was wrong when she kissed me. I could tell she didn't mean it."

"She didn't mean it? I would have been fooled."

"True, but I've never seen a woman who had much trouble fooling you." He looked at Palamon and his face was a mask of hopeless sympathy. "You're not a lover, as I said. A lover knows when he's hit pay dirt or when someone's just playing him along, no matter how hard she's trying to fool him. Besides, I couldn't tell whether she was really doing either one. Something was all wrong, as if she were only half there."

"Ah. Did you see her eyes?"

"I did. So I say to myself, 'Let's stay around and see what this is all about.' Then you got mad and left and the next thing I know, Ellal and I are walking along the streambank and she's hanging on me like old laundry. And I can hear someone following us. So what happens but she draws a knife and friend Deltor comes running at me, besides. I got the knife away from her and pounded Deltor over the head with a rock, and then I left them there, tied in their own garters. And I say to myself, 'I'd better do some sneaking and find out what in Hades this is all about.'"

"A wise decision," Palamon murmured.

"Of course. So I go crawling back to Courtay's wagon. And what do I see but Courtay, still sitting there slumped down with his nose in the soup. And I hear talking from inside the parlor. It's not Jiptian speech at all, mind you, but our own language—though a strange accent. Of course I had to listen for a while and it turns out we have a pair of old friends from Tychopolis staying here as a sort of rear guard. Well, one old friend, actually. The woman just got here from Carea. The man called her dreamsinger Mellan, and it seems she's been stirring up trouble for you back home. She's the one who put the white eyes on Courtay and his bunch."

Palamon clenched his reins. "Then could she be the one I seek? I'd deal with her tonight, although she be a female."

"Two points to consider," Flin advised. "First, I don't think she had anything to do with Berethane from the conversation. She only specializes in the one kind of spell. Second, I don't think you need to have any of your chivalrous notions about her. She sounded as nasty as any man I've ever listened to."

Palamon hesitated and thought. "The numbers of this horrid cult grow day by day, its seems."

"Right. But let me finish my story. They both know where you've gone, see, and they're a little nervous about me. So the woman takes a bunch of the men and goes to the stables to get you. Sorry I didn't head her off, but I'd have had to let them know where I was to do that. I was sure you could take care of yourself. So I just waited. And sure enough, just as the other one's rounding up all the rest of my former friends to look for me, I hear all kinds of shouting and I know you've gotten past them. But of course the bunch I'm watching starts running to catch up with you."

Flin smiled at Palamon, though the white of his grin was mostly lost in the darkness. "I was proud of you, how you went up that loading rope the way a squirrel goes up a tree. And when the chanters burned it in half, it must have flattened the two who were climbing up after you pretty bad; they were still lying on the ground, along with another one they'd landed on, when the rest ran into the building to catch you. Must have been about three dozen of them by that time."

Palamon nodded. As always, Flin had taken care to be in the best position to trouble his enemies. "Ah, yes," the tall monarch said. "Their horses still were saddled, so you leaped on one and brought them to my rescue."

Flin chuckled. "It was difficult to know where to go, specially when the place started to burn. But if there's a way out of a building, I was sure you'd find it." The younger knight laughed with delight. "But what a surprise you gave me. There wasn't an exit after all, so you made your own—hoo, hoo! I heard this tremendous big crash and I look up and here's the King of Carea, hurtling through the moonlight with burning boards flying off in every direction. I was proud to know you; couldn't have done it better. I saw you hit the stables' roof and roll off the far side, so the rest was easy."

Palamon had to laugh with Flin at the image the younger man constructed. But then he became more serious. "But not from here."

"How's that?"

"We must be off this road as soon as daylight comes,

and well concealed in all our travels. For they plainly know they're followed and they mean to kill us ere we track them back to Tranje."

So the two men picked their way off the road and across the dark plain. It would be a slow, tedious ride but their adventure on this night had taught them the peril of traveling within sight of major thoroughfares. The rest of their journey to Tranje would have to be across open ground.

Chapter Twenty:
The Beach at Ruid

ARCITE AND BERENGERIA were two days from Peristeras' door. They had journeyed through thick forests
and up bulging hills; now they made their way down a
beetling promontory which stood over the Gulf of Ruid.
Arcite paused, wiped the sweat from his face, then sat
on a boulder beside the trail.

"If we're to take the Fates' part, then we should continue," Berengeria protested. But Arcite only smiled and
hauled her down beside him.

"Should we exhaust ourselves beyond the point of action?" he asked, lifting his eyebrows. "Ah, relax a moment, maid. You may not need the rest, but I do." He
gestured out toward the broad waters of the Gulf of
Ruid, the lines of breakers which assaulted the sands far
below, and the sea birds calling to one another above.
"From images like these do I derive my strength and all
the powers of my art. Thus do I feed on beauty, both of
sight and sound." He turned his gaze from the sea and
his eyes poured into Berengeria's. "Your beauty feeds
me too, as much as all these others put together."

Berengeria gazed back at him. "How you've become
my dear beloved. You are like no other man I've ever

met. My brother, Palamon, enfolds a portion of my heart
but in another way. You fill me with love's living, breathing passion." A thought struck her; she shook her head
and looked away. "Ah, a pity is it that I am forbidden to
you."

"Only in your mind."

Berengeria remained silent for a long time. Then, by
way of changing the subject, she pulled from her bosom
the artifact Peristeras had presented to them. "This
finger in its flask," she said softly. "It has the power to
break the magic's hold on Berethane."

"Or so we're told," Arcite replied.

"We saw its power for ourselves," she said. "When it
brought forth the wind and blew away the noxious horde
of insects in the meadow."

"Aye, 'tis so."

She turned toward Arcite. "By all the gods, I pray
that we find Palamon and give this holy relic to him ere
his son expires." She held the flask tightly.

Arcite touched her cheek with a finger; his expression
became tender as he spoke. "You plainly love your
brother, tender maid." He smiled. "But for my part, I
share your hope. I saw his noble face that night when
evil's flaming cyclone pierced the roof of Castle Conforth's hall. I watched it claim his son. Poor Palamon, he
wore the stricken look of one whose fingernails had all
been torn away beneath the torture. Tender love for all
his family has made him vulnerable."

Berengeria's eyes grew soft with reflection. "When
Berethane was born, I saw a sight which showed his
depth of feeling. Palamon awaited all on tenterhooks
while Aelia suffered through her labors. Every cry she
uttered pierced him like a sword, and when the child
arrived and all rejoiced, his first reaction was to rush
unto her side. He only sought the babe as second
thought. And when he was assured that she was well and
Berethane was thrust into his hands all newly swaddled,
he betook the look of one who tries to knead a bubble.
He was frightened of that wee, small babe."

"Indeed?" Though Arcite smiled, he bore the look of

a man who himself would have little idea how to hold a newborn.

"Indeed," she said, resigning herself to that fact, and to the fact that they would never have newborns of their own in any event. "Poor Palamon grew long about the face and gave the child back to the nurse's hands. She laughed and said she'd seen his selfsame look upon the face of many a new father. He would grow to love the child in all good time. Then Lady Aelia took the babe and held him to her breast, for she desired to feed him, just one time before he should be given to the wetnurse. Palamon knelt down beside the bed and watched in awe." The memory almost made Berengeria laugh, but at the same time she was close to blinking back tears. "In curiosity, he used one rough and callused finger, lifting up the baby's hand while it was nursing. Ah, how small that wee hand was, how delicate and like a little flower. Still, the baby wrapped all five pink fingers 'round his father's digit. And I thought a flame was lit behind the face of Palamon. His forehead wrinkled up and though he struggled to withhold them, I well know the tears were raging for release from his two manly eyes. And then the nurses laughed and teased at him and said that it was true—that he would love the child in all good time." She pierced Arcite with a desperate look. "Oh love, my love, we have to save them both."

"We shall. We must." Arcite pressed her to his bosom. "You're right—we must move on. We shall perform the duty given us by Peristeras, then we shall return unto your land and save your nephew for most gentle Palamon." He fingered the mandolin case he carried.

"I hope we are in time," Berengeria said.

"We'll do this errand on our way to Tranje," he replied. "And then a ship can bear us to your homeland." He stood and looked down toward the rolling waters below them. "And yet we cannot know the hiding place of those six bodies. Or whether they were even landed here."

"It is a mystery to me, indeed," Berengeria said in

agreement. "But Peristeras told us to explore this precinct cautiously. He must know something."

They descended along the slope of the cliff and made their way through the trees which grew practically down to the water's edge. There seemed to be little for them to find; the tracks of any smugglers who might have passed had been obliterated by the rains and the passing of animals.

There seemed no reason for them even to be there. They searched for most of the day and found nothing until Arcite happened to spy a small structure peeking out from amid a stand of prosperously growing beech trees. He pointed at it and Berengeria's heart leaped into her throat; the area instantly became a dangerous place. They kept careful lookout as they advanced on the hut but they saw no human, no animal, no sign of life.

The hut was just that, a little shack built of driftwood, branches, bits of bark, and planks apparently torn from some vessel. Had it been the vessel they had escaped? Who could say? At any rate, the hovel was ramshackle, poorly built, and appeared never to have been intended as anything more than shelter for a night. Berengeria could see through the chinks in the wall, though the roof looked more solid. No one occupied the place.

"Should we go in, I wonder?" She looked up at Arcite.

"I see no reason not to," he replied. "Perhaps there might be some odd hiding place inside."

Berengeria smiled dryly. "It doesn't look to me as if there might be any kind of 'place' at all within; I think you'd find more shelter sleeping under bushes."

"I must agree." But they stepped in anyway and spent a few moments looking about. It was a tiny place; if they had clasped hands and stood as far apart as their reaches would allow, they would have been able to rub the opposing walls with their shoulders. The sea breeze crooned eerily through the gaps in the walls and the place creaked and sagged a little more with each draught. "There's plainly nothing here," Berengeria said. She did not like the look of it. There was no reason to be here and she wanted to leave.

"Indeed. It's empty as a tax-collector's heart," Arcite observed. Then he laid his head to one side thoughtfully. "It's strange, you know. The breeze's little song is not unlike the music written on the back of my new instrument."

Berengeria listened. There was, indeed, a faint melody to the whispering of the elements about the place. It was eerie, unsettling. Then, from beneath the sand, a pallid millipede writhed to the surface and scuttled toward her. She gasped and kicked at it, scattered sand about, and tried to pull Arcite toward the door. "I have to leave," she panted.

"Ignore it," he replied strongly. "I have to look at something." He knelt and opened his mandolin's leather case, then lifted the instrument out and turned it over. While Berengeria blanched at the thought of the crawling thing she had buried, she watched over his shoulder and for the first time, was able to get a clear look at the words and notes written on the gleaming wood. The music was not engraved into the wood; it had been printed in enamel with a fine brush, then glossed over with clear lacquer. As she looked over his shoulder, Arcite shook his head. "It's not the same," he said. "It's in the same odd key, as if it might be an opposing counterpoint to what I have; but it is not the same."

Berengeria felt the gooseflesh rise along her neck and arms. With each moment the wind's melody grew louder, more insistent, more frightening. Would more vile creatures appear? The whistling conjured images in her mind, unpleasant images of all the things she had encountered before. The crawling hordes of her dreams and Peristeras' meadow flooded into her mind and she caught her breath. The putrid millipede was only a harbinger. Evil dwelt here, the same evil which had snatched at her three times before. "Enchantment, crawling horrors," she whispered. "We must escape this place."

"No, we cannot," Arcite said sharply. "Why would

our enemies employ their powers of mystical enchantment just to drive all strangers from an empty cottage? I cannot imagine. I'll pick out some jaunty notes to overcome our horror at this place before we both must flee."

He snatched up his mandolin and played a sequence of happy notes, which did relieve the disgust and fear, the crawling images which accosted Berengeria. It was a melody she knew, a little child's ditty which had long sounded in nurseries across the Thlassa Mey. "Sing," he commanded. "If you remember any words."

She hummed along with him, sang a few snatches recalled from her own childhood, and was amazed at the way her spirits lifted, as if an ugly shadow had lost its hold on her mind. Arcite even danced a few steps across the sandy floor of the hovel. Then, as suddenly as he had begun, he stopped. Berengeria's spirit plummeted as she once more heard the wind's music, louder than ever. "Something is not right," he said. "This floor does not feel like an earthen floor at all."

He knelt down, brushed sand and dirt away with both hands, and revealed two long planks. He straightened and stared at her. "We've found them," he cried. "Snatch up a board or two from these decaying walls and we will dig with them."

Moving in spite of the chill which iced her veins, Berengeria leaped to one wall and pulled loose a piece of board. The building creaked and groaned and for an instant she was afraid it would all come down on top of them. But it did not. Arcite was already digging frantically with his sword and she leaped to join him.

They dug and scraped and scraped and dug. They revealed long boxes, laid out side by side in a square pit which had been dug into the soil and filled with sand. Beside one of the boxes lay a crumpled piece of parchment which Arcite picked up and examined. It had been rolled into a ball about the size of a ball of yarn, but when he opened and smoothed it, no writing lay on either side. He crumpled it back and rolled it out the door —and the sound of the breeze's crooning diminished.

But that crooning increased again as Arcite took his sword and used it to pry the tops of the boxes. Berengeria steeled herself to help in the grisly task; as the end of each board rose far enough for her to slip her fingers under it, she strained to lift it, pry it away from the box, and lean it back. It was feverish work; in spite of the breeze and her shivering, she sweated heavily.

Each box contained a body, as Peristeras had warned. Berengeria recognized none of them. All were old men in greater or lesser states of decay, except for the last, which was a lovely woman in the spring of her maidenhood. Berengeria gasped at her; the maiden looked as if she had been dead no more than a day. "By all the gods," Arcite whispered. "Was that the fate they had reserved for you?"

"I do not know," she replied. "But hurry. It is time for you to work the wonder of your singing. If we linger one more moment, I will have to flee."

Arcite's face had become drawn; he looked as if he had aged years. "And such an audience," he whispered. "Six disinterred and grisly corpses. May the gods forgive me if I am unsteady in my voice and slow in playing."

"Do not speak so. You are the only man who's capable of overturning this foul magic."

Arcite drew a deep breath, picked up his mandolin, and once more studied the melody and lyric inscribed on the back. Then he settled the instrument against his thighs. "Stand at the doorway," he commanded her. "If aught should come that threatens life or limb, then you must flee. Do not remain, my love, no matter what foul acts might pass within this chamber."

She looked at him. "My love, I am a Princess, so I'll stay or flee as I desire. Now sing and we will face the danger, both together."

"You are a doughty maid."

"I am a maid in love."

He touched his fingertips against the strings and an entrancing melody floated forth, lovely, sweet, like nectar from the lotus blossom. And the crooning which had been there before wailed above them. When he began to sing strange words in an unknown tongue, the wailing rose to a scream; it was the cry of tortured souls, of unimaginable fear, of hatred, every negative emotion. A contest joined between the enchantment and Arcite's performance—but Arcite was far more powerful. The evil music died away in a last plaintive gasp; Arcite's notes commanded the air; and as Berengeria looked down, she saw the bodies below her begin to swell, to expand like rotting fish, bloating in a slough.

She feared they would explode but they did not. They grew until the rotten flesh was molded square within the confines of the bare pine containers, then they subsided, fell in upon themselves, and one by one dissolved into sprawling mounds of dust.

Except for the body of the maiden. That body showed no alteration whatsoever. Berengeria looked at it with concern; was it too powerful for Arcite or had this poor maid never been subject to the same mystical powers as the other bodies? Or had the others been preserved supernaturally? She could not know the answer but she could look at Arcite as he redoubled his efforts to reduce that body to the same condition as the others.

Then something made her look up. A thicket several fathoms away began to thrash; then a face appeared, livid with rage. It was the face of one of the men who had kidnapped her that fateful day in Carea and its owner was plainly filled with hatred, rage, and fear. "Rise now," she cried. "We must defend ourselves."

But Arcite did not even acknowledge her presence. He sang as if he were alone in the world; the only change in his attitude was a minute shake of the head as if a fly might have landed for an instant on the tip of one ear and disturbed him by that much. But Berengeria knew why there was no answer; he had to complete the melody. He had to sing it through to the last note. As untrained in the mystic arts as she was, she knew what disaster they would be courting if they left the spell incomplete.

The evil minions rushed them before he could finish.

Berengeria steeled herself to live or die at Arcite's side; she snatched up his sword and as the first of the cultists burst into the hovel, she laid the keen edge sideways into his belly. He screamed, doubled over, then pitched head-first atop the boxes of dust, his teeth bared, blood gushing from his fatal wound.

Chapter Twenty-one:
Berengeria's Recapture

THE INSTANT THE white-robed intruder received Berengeria's sword blade, Arcite completed the last note of the song. Even as another foeman confronted Berengeria, the minstrel shot to his feet, seized a plank from one of the boxes, and smashed it into the fellow's skull. That man also fell with a cry. "There still are six or seven who oppose our two," Berengeria cried. "But we are sheltered here. The doorway's narrow; we can hold our little fortress from their wrath as long as we should need to."

But she had not taken into account the flimsiness of the building. Even as she parried the attack of another man through the doorway, some three or four of them must have crashed against the side of the ramshackle building. The timbers creaked, groaned, shuddered, then yielded to the assault. One side groaned toward the two defenders, boards and pieces of bark rained from the roof, twine and rope snapped, and the building collapsed. The last thing Berengeria remembered thinking as the weight of the roof drove her to the ground was that she should try to drop without impaling herself on Arcite's sword.

A falling support struck her across the forehead, but she must have been unconscious for only a moment. When she came to, it was to find herself half-buried, all but smothered beneath the rubble of the building. Then a rough pair of hands stripped back some of the debris, caught her by the wrist, and yanked her to her feet. She found herself facing Gondarkhan, one of the same men who had captured her before. His eyes blazed and he held his sword's point against her belly. "You fiend made of woman's soft flesh," he cried. "The work of a lifetime's destroyed in a moment or two. The whole plan is upset and our schedule delayed by a full generation."

He looked as if he would run her through. And, in fact, Berengeria stood firm against the thrust of his blade; after all, death would be better than recapture by such horrid men. Had it not been a sin, she would have been tempted to run onto the blade herself.

But one of the others must have understood her expression. He caught her by the waist and hurled her away from the first man, knocking her down atop the remains of the building she and Arcite had been defending only a moment earlier. "She's still valuable," the second one cried. "Though we have lost one great treasure, rejoice that her body's returned to us. She is the one who was specified when all is done."

"Wait. What of the other? Where's he?" This voice belonged to yet a third man.

A horrible thought crushed Berengeria: what had happened to Arcite? She glanced about and saw a hand extend itself up from the wreckage. It trembled, then dropped and lay motionless. "Arcite, my love," she cried, and lunged toward it. But rough hands restrained her.

"Foolish woman." Gondarkhan sneered. "When a man has done such harm as he has, do you think we'd allow him to live?" He turned to another cultist who had also drawn his sword. "Go ahead. Finish him."

Berengeria cried out and leaped against the restraining arms. Several men grappled with her as she screamed, kicked, bit, and fought. But it was all for nothing; the cultist's sword stabbed into the debris of the hut, produced a muffled gasp from below, and withdrew a blade covered with blood. Her strength failed her at that sight; she struggled on but she had lost all heart for fighting.

"I felt it strike home," the murderer gloated. He advanced toward Berengeria while he bathed his finger in the blood from his sword. "And we have this fair woman again in our grasp." In spite of the way she cringed away from him, he reached out and smeared the blood across her cheek.

She screamed like a madwoman then, wrenched one hand free, and tried to reach his face with her outstretched nails. But he only laughed at her. "Accept your dead love's last caress." He sneered. "Why, you should appreciate that."

While Gondarkhan restrained her, the man used his bloody fingers to lift a few strands of her hair while he addressed his fellows. "She is lovely. You know, we should claim the reward of her body before we return to Kruptos."

"I'd kill myself," Berengeria cried, spitting at him. He only smiled and moved as if to apply an insulting caress, but Gondarkhan restrained him with a word.

"She's attractive, that's true," Gondarkhan said. "But we cannot defile her. Navron would go crazy with rage. Please remember, Malaat, the old formulae specify that the fresh blood of a virgin's required for anointing the seals. Only that precious substance will soften them, even enough to be pierced by the weapon he'll hold. If the spell fails to work, I would not care to be in your shoes for the words you have spoken. Ah, here come the horses. Good, Anar, I'm glad you have brought them. Throw her up on the saddle of this one and lash her in place."

For all Berengeria's struggles, she could not keep them from lashing her to the saddle. And the words Gondarkhan spoke made her flesh crawl. He had spoken, as had Peristeras a couple of days ago, of her virgin blood—was she intended as a sacrifice for some nameless purpose? She struggled against her bonds and her captors all over again, but to no avail.

She sat astride the horse and the tears rained down her face as she watched the half dozen evil cultists tear through the hut's remains until they had exposed the six boxes. She cringed with each bit of rubble thrown aside because she noted that each one was tossed on top of Arcite's body. Stabbed, crushed beneath debris, what an end for a gallant gentleman!

She shook her head to clear the tears from her face. "O, brave Arcite," she whispered to herself. "On all these nights we took repose together on the ground, and in the bed of Peristeras, why did we not just one time give in to lust and take our pleasure? Now what use was our restraint? The lone result was to preserve my chastity for sacrifice unto some foul and unknown god. Oh, that I were dead and with you now."

As for the white-robed men, they gazed down into the boxes and shook their heads in frustration. "They are ruined, as if they had never existed. We'll leave them."

Even from where she sat, Berengeria could see the corpse of the young woman staring glassily into space. The five male cadavers had collapsed into dust but the female one remained. Even so, the leader of the group expressed no more interest in it than in any of the others.

"We could bring other bodies," Malaat suggested.

The answer was impatient. "There's no time for that now. Many months are required to prepare a new corpse to receive an old spirit. Were it otherwise, we could at least bring the one. Curse the gods, there's no time. And besides, we do not know the damage he's done to their frail, ancient spirits." Hatred for Arcite's act dripped from the leader's lips with every word. Then he turned toward Berengeria. "But we still have got you. Your blond friend has delivered a great loss to us. But your body might help to repay it." He turned toward the rest of the group. "Now mount up. Let's be gone."

Tears rolled down Berengeria's face like drops down a windowpane on a dewy morning. But she restrained her sobbing; she would not allow these creatures to watch her weep. She did not know where they were going. Peristeras had mentioned Kruptos and Arcite had acted as if he also was familiar with a city by that name. She had never heard of it, but she prayed she might somehow die before that destination could be reached.

But her captors talked their evil business with the air of so many merchants discussing the difficulties of pricing a cow. And the drift of their conversation caused her skin to crawl all over again. Kruptos would appear within a half day's journey; that was why they had to hurry. They had to deliver her to Alyubol's evil successor, Navron, before nightfall. And the sun was already passing the midday point.

Berengeria was, indeed, a sacrifice; she would be drained of her blood and that liquid would be smeared across the altars in temples at the center of Kruptos. Her living blood ran cold to hear of it, and not just because of her fear for herself. These evil men were only part of a horrid cult, a cult which had once been led by Alyubol, but was far larger than it had been under the mad wizard's rule. It seemed that Navron possessed one talent Alyubol had not: he was a superior organizer. Dozens of new members had flocked to Navron since Alyubol's death.

The cult's present intent was to release into the world a dozen horrible entities, which would challenge the very gods themselves for control over creation. Berengeria stared at her captors. Were they of real flesh and blood? Were they human? They plotted the demise of humanity itself; her own life was nothing beside the horrors they planned to release on an unsuspecting world. How could they even contemplate such folly?

But she listened to them and watched the scenery pass as they rode through the lush hills, turned north, crossed a river, and turned again. She racked her brain for some escape plan, but no idea would come to her. She worked against her bonds until her arms and legs chafed; she squirmed and wriggled until one of the cultists rode up next to her and slapped her with the ends of his long reins until she stopped.

They rode across a low ridge and looked down into a treeless valley. The sun sank toward the horizon as they arrived before a large tent. And to Berengeria's increased dismay, a flap at the front of the tent moved and who should appear but Navron, the new ruler of this evil empire? He looked up at her, his jaw dropped, and he whispered an order to her captors. "Remove her. I want her away from here."

"My Lord," Gondarkhan said. "She is payment by the Fates for the great loss I have to explain."

"What loss?" Navron's voice grew suspicious.

The other man hesitated, then confessed softly. "This wench and her lover destroyed the cadavers."

"Impossible."

"No, not for them. He used magical singing to drive your enchantments away."

"By the dozen dark powers," Navron shrieked. "I will see them both burned in a pit, burned alive; and their hides shall be stripped from their quivering flesh. All my years of travail have been squandered—for what are we gathered here, now? How can old souls assist us in managing all of the Dark Ones as they are released from their prisons?"

No answer came; Navron's fury had plainly cowed Gondarkhan. The cult leader rushed the underling and threw his fingers about the fellow's neck. The two of them fell to the ground and scuffled about, Navron trying to throttle his victim, Gondarkhan trying to escape. But at last Navron relented, leaped from the man, and kicked at him as he tried vainly to cover his head with his arms. "Are you all stupid idiots, all of you?" Navron cried in his rage. "How could you have let this thing happen? I never should have chosen you fools for the task. Were I dead, I'd be happier, free of the shame of acquaintance with you." Then he buried his face in his hands and began to sob—but his tears lasted only an instant. He wiped his face, threw his head back, and began to rave all over again, until he nearly choked on his own fury.

At last he exhausted himself and stood staring at the shocked faces all about him. His breast heaved, he darted wild glances here and there, then suddenly began to smile. His throat produced a low chuckle which quickly grew into laughter, then into hysterical mirth, until the white-robed leader once more had to pause for breath. He was mad, quite mad; his flights of emotion told Berengeria that much. He was at least as mad as Alyubol had been. She grimaced at the thought; every member of the evil cult had to be demented for it even to exist.

Then Navron began to speak again, though he had to pause more than once to chortle to himself. "We will still hold the ceremony. Nothing has changed in the least."

"Nothing changed?" Gondarkhan cried, his eyes wide in amazement. "Our control's been destroyed. The twelve powers will terrorize us."

"Ah, perhaps. But just one will I free, then I shall bargain ere freeing the rest."

"We will all be destroyed."

"Perhaps not," Navron replied with a careless smile. "But suppose you are right; just suppose we are slain by the nameless divinity. We will have served our great purpose, even so. Will our lives matter, then?" He chuckled, then paused and smirked into the other man's face. "Well?" he finally said. "You surely agree."

Gondarkhan coughed. "Yes, indeed," he finally said. But no conviction lay in his voice.

"But do not tell the others," Navron cautioned. "'Tis best that they not suspect how we've altered the strategy."

Berengeria almost gagged. Even by the standards of his own cult, Navron was mad. And from all that was being said, the sane world was in greater danger than ever. But Navron had managed to calm himself; his new tone was businesslike. "So there's use for the prisoner once more. But for now, for the moment, I want her away from here, ere the young Prince finds her out. Take her off in the trees, feed her something, and I'll send a messenger when he's departed." His lips twisted into an evil smirk. "He has gone his own way, smashed agreements, and caused far Carea's tall monarch to flee my tight trap. He has been far more trouble than all of his services warrant. That's well; I will make him the butt of a joke he will always remember—for all of his life, though his life shall be ended tonight."

Berengeria's captors shook their heads at Navron's words. But they mounted up, put spurs to their horses, and took her back over the crest of the hill. There they dragged her off her horse and threw some food down to her. It did not look inviting; it was meat dried so hard that the largest of the men could hardly break pieces off the main slab with his teeth. The wine they offered her smelled better than the meat looked, but she refused that as well.

She found herself too distraught to eat, anyway. Her head swam with the horror of it all, these men were going to release forces which even they themselves feared, and which they doubted they could control. What madness lurked in the world?

But Gondarkhan only laughed at her. "You had just as well eat. You've no hope of escape and you'll not starve yourself in the time before you shall be sacrificed. Ten or twelve hours, at the most, lie between you and your death."

Berengeria scowled at him. "We'll see."

"Indeed, we shall see." The fellow took a piece of the meat, pulled a dagger from his belt, and shaved off slivers which he popped into his mouth, like an old man paring his nails before an evening's fire. After a moment, he looked at her again. "Have you ever offended Navron?"

Berengeria did not understand the question but she answered it anyway. "Whenever I have had the chance."

The man laughed at her again, though his companions did not. "He did not want you seen at the campsite. How odd."

Berengeria thought about the campsite. "Did that one tent conceal the total of your followers?"

"Not a tenth of them. But they all are nearby. They will trickle down into this valley beginning at dusk; there'll be hundreds before the night's through."

That was interesting information, if disturbing. A day earlier, she had been without any idea there were so many members of this cult. This was to be their great night, when they would usher in the powers of evil. She shuddered again. Then she heard a horse approach and she and her six captors looked up.

"Put her into this sack," came a commanding voice. It belonged to Navron, who had apparently slipped away from the tent. "Cover her from her head to her toes; not a nail's breadth of her may be seen. And this gag—place it hard in her mouth."

The men grabbed Berengeria before she could even begin to struggle, trussed her limbs more tightly than ever, stuffed the gag into her mouth, and double wrapped it with strips of linen. She was helpless, as helpless as a babe in swaddling clothes. Then she was laid on the ground, to listen helplessly while the evil minions discussed the fate of the six cadavers Arcite had destroyed with his song, and the great night of evil which lay ahead of them.

She should never have accompanied Arcite on his mission; why had Peristeras not warned her more fully? Had he been in league with these fiends? Had he been a child, after all, and failed to comprehend fully the dangers himself? She had no idea. But she did realize, as she listened, that her value was more as the keystone in some horrid practical joke Navron was playing than as an irreplaceable source of chaste blood. Any maiden would suffice to anoint the seals, she learned. But Navron desired her for reasons all his own.

Navron's minions had read the ancient spell which had sent the fiery cloud to snuff out poor Berethane. And he had sent his minions to kidnap her for his sacrifice; he cackled and laughed at the joke her sacrifice would be. But on whom? He did not bother to say; his cohorts seemed to understand it already and she was hardly in a position to inquire. Then the evil henchmen snatched her from the ground, stuffed her struggling form into a great sack, and strapped her onto the back of a mule. However much Navron had desired to obtain her particular body, it seemed that desire was not going to be translated into comfort in her last moments.

She felt the mule start up; the bouncing made for a ride that was a form of torture. Once she began to slide off the mule's back; her feet went down, her head went up, and she landed on the ground. But many hands grasped her, replaced her in spite of her struggles, and tied her down more tightly than ever. Then they went on again.

The next time the mule halted, Berengeria could hear the unmistakable sounds of more horses, as well as sounds which indicated to her that she was surrounded by people. And she heard Navron's voice. "The time is approaching, O Prince. Ere this night becomes dawn, you will witness the fall of your enemies."

"What have you there?" came a hostile-sounding reply, and Berengeria's heart froze as she recognized the voice. It could be none other than Ursid. Ursid, who had loved her and had saved her life five years earlier, was now plotting to end her life.

"It's a maiden for sacrifice," Navron said in his smoothest tones. "It's unfortunate but she must die to achieve our great aim."

"I don't like that," Ursid replied. "You never told me there would be a human sacrifice for this. The sword of Palamon was all you needed, so you said." Ursid's voice rose with his revulsion. For her part, Berengeria struggled harder than ever and writhed until she was exhausted, but she could produce neither a sound nor a meaningful movement. So that was the nature of the joke over which Navron and his cronies had guffawed earlier. Ursid did not know it was Berengeria who was to provide the blood for the ceremony.

And Navron was plainly enjoying himself. "We are not children here," he said. "Your revenge over Palamon must require blood."

"Your glee disgusts me."

"And are you still so noble? You've lied; you've conspired. You have joined with me, body and soul. When you sought your revenge over Palamon, you should have known that, to achieve such an end, you would have to join forces with me. That day's come, and you're a part of my evil; the path you have trod did lead to me without curve. Did you not know it had to?" Navron's pause implied that he was waiting for an answer but Berengeria could hear nothing from Ursid.

Then she caught her breath and felt the tears come. She would have cried out, would have screamed his name, if only she could have chewed away the gag which throttled her. For all the unkind words which had passed between them, her heart could not completely expel the image of Ursid fighting to save her life years ago. He was a straw of haven in this foul place, he was a knight and the Prince of Buerdaunt. He could not be fully a part of this evil.

And Ursid did not know the woman for whom he had fought a war was close enough for him to touch. From the lilt to Navron's voice, the young Prince should have been able to tell he was being made the butt of a joke. Berengeria groaned and someone struck her. Ursid did not even suspect what was happening.

Then the conversation between the two men died away. All around her, Berengeria could hear the murmur of voices; something dramatic was taking place. And whispered exclamations told her what that something was. Kruptos! Even encased in cloth as she was, she could tell the sun had set. Now the evil city of Kruptos had appeared. And over the quiet babble of awed voices came a strange, mysterious crooning which would have frozen her blood, even if she had not been a helpless captive about to be sacrificed. What produced the crooning, she did not know. But she had no desire to find out.

And horror of horrors, something was with her in the sack. Her eyes bulged with disgust and she worked her gag until her jaws ached; tiny feet tickled along one calf. A huge insect was crawling across her leg. She tried to keep herself from gagging; she could hardly comprehend the words being spoken outside.

"I know that spirit," Ursid was shouting.

"Well you should," Navron replied. "She will guard Kruptos' gates and will slay the first soul who approaches."

"Then how shall you prevent her from attacking us?"

"By this blade. See my hands? I am wearing the gauntlets, and now I shall lift the great sword. As you see, though it flashes and protests, they keep it from harming me. But the spirit respects its great power. While I face her down, you and I and a few of my company all have the time to pass into the city. Inside, we'll be safe."

The mule which carried Berengeria started up again and the way she hung on its back told her she was descending into the valley. The howling built into a deafening wail and the hackles on the back of her neck rose but she could see nothing, feel nothing more than the hateful crawling across her flesh. If the wailing spirit might kill her, at least that would upset Navron's plans and free her from the horror of those crawling companions. Three or four, at least, now dealt her their unwanted caresses. She could not tell the number and shuddered even to think of them.

But Navron must have been correct, for the wailing soon began to recede. She felt a great clamminess crush down on her, as if she had been cast into a damp donjon. They must have passed into the evil city itself.

They went on and on, with the mule's hooves clopping over paving stones. There was no speaking. Finally, the mule stopped. "Now you all must wait quietly," Navron's voice said. "We will end all of these rites by ourselves."

"And this is why you asked for my assistance?" she heard Ursid ask. "So that I could be a part of this foul ceremony?"

"Yes, for reasons you'll know soon enough," Navron replied. "But you merit the honor." Berengeria could detect a hidden laugh in his voice. "And now we must carry the sacrifice into the temple."

Ursid made a sound that was both hostile and indecisive. But he must have relented, for Berengeria felt hands moving against the ropes that held her bound to the animal's back; then she felt herself being lifted free. Hateful creatures smashed against her flesh and she only wished she could faint—but she could not. A long series of steps must have led into the temple, for she felt her bearer's motions as he climbed them. Ursid must have been performing that task; Navron was surely bearing the sword he had bragged of. She tried to struggle, to alert Ursid to her identity, but she was weary from disgust and despair. Her every move caused her to mush against the crushed bodies which shared her cloth prison.

So she relaxed in hopelessness and allowed the foolish Prince to bear her where he would. Then she felt herself being roughly set down on some cold stone slab. So this was how her life was to end. She set her jaw and resolved herself toward the blow she knew would soon fall.

Chapter Twenty-two:
Kruptos

THE SUN RODE its chariot down the western sky as Palamon and Flin galloped along a gentle slope. Unless they rode far into the coming darkness, they would not reach Tranje that day; the city still lay some two or three leagues to the northwest. But if they did not reach Tranje that night, they would arrive early the next morning.

The sun settled into its house in the west before they topped the hill; the sky shaded to gray as they moved out of the trees and looked down into a broad, shallow valley. The sight laid out before them made them both rein in their horses.

A dark city of devious contours filled the floor of the valley with checkered shadow. At the bottom of the slope, serpentine walls extended for hundreds of cubits, from a wrecked gate as far as the eye could make out in the gathering gloom. A tent city stood a half-league away and dozens of white-robed figures formed a ghastly processional toward the gate. Over all rose the spine-chilling wails of a spectral female figure which hovered before the entrance.

They could barely see her; she was no more than a pale shape formed of tatters. Palamon could not make

253

out her face in the distance, or even be sure she had one.
Even so, he knew as certainly as he knew his name that
she was a supernatural being—and one that was filled
with evil. The apparition's ragged robes trembled above
the darkening grass and he could swear she had no legs
or feet.

One white-robed figure confronted the crooning spirit
with a great sword upraised and even at that distance,
Palamon recognized the sword, as well as the man who
wielded it. The sword was his own *Spada Korrigaine*
and the figure had therefore to be Navron. Palamon filled
his lungs and poised himself to scream the weapon's
name, but did not.

Flin put his hand on the tall monarch's arm. "If you
yell for that sword, you'd better get it. If they know
we're here and can keep it from flying to you, we're
going to be in a world of trouble, not even allowing for
what that ghostie there might do."

Palamon nodded silently and the two men eased their
mounts back into the shadowy trees. "I fear we've happened on some center of the evil cult."

"What's a city doing here?" Flin said in a harsh whisper. "It's not on any of the maps. And that camp—it's
big enough for a small army. I hope we don't have to go
up against a whole army of those troublemakers. Some
two or three dozen would just be good sport, but a
hundred or so could be strenuous."

"I do not know," Palamon answered. "But I can feel
the city's nature in my very bones; it's mystical and evil
to the core." Even as he spoke, a dozen or so of the
sinister pilgrims vanished through the gate, followed by
Navron. The others returned to their camp, while the
crooning spirit hung over the city and sang its frustration
into the gathering darkness. "But this has got to be the
place, the destination mentioned by Navron and young
Ursid when they conferred back in Tychopolis."

"But they said they were going to Tranje."

"Perhaps. But this is still the destination they were
speaking of; I know it in my soul. We're near to Tranje
here, remember. This is where we'll meet Navron and

Prince Ursid, and I shall gain the answer for my son."

Flin gestured down the slope. "I'll believe all that, but it still doesn't explain what we're going to do about all your white-robed friends and your ghost."

Palamon smiled grimly. "I do not know. We might approach the gate and pray for Pallas to protect us."

"Remember, I don't enjoy the boundless faith you do," Flin said. "I've never seen Pallas or any other god. But I see what we're up against here—I know all this is real."

Just then, they heard the jingle of a horse's harness and a voice off to one side shouted, "Who goes there? If you have some business with . . ." then there was a pause and a cry of surprise. "It's the Carean King. Pursue him."

Four men rode down on Flin and Palamon. In spite of the trees and shadows, the tall monarch recognized the Buerdic cavalry uniforms. So. Ursid was in the grim camp—or gone into the spectral city. Why the Prince would have left his escort out on these slopes was more than Palamon had time to ponder. He and Flin yanked their longswords from their scabbards and rode away from the attackers at an angle. That forced the Buerdic horsemen to change the direction of their charge and caused them to spread out along the hillside.

Flin and Palamon turned and gave battle to the two in the lead. The maneuver gave the two Careans the purchase of an instant when they could fight on even terms, and they made the most of it. Flin carved his opponent from the saddle with a single neat stroke while Palamon cut the sword from one foeman's hands soon after. The wounded man wheeled his horse and galloped away.

"Ride to the Constable," one of the others shouted to the injured man. "He'll want to know that Palamon's arrived, for that news will usurp all other plans."

The wounded man wheeled back toward the city. "He must not reach that destination," Palamon shouted to Flin. "Let's after him." They cut and carved in deadly battle with the last two Buerdic soldiers, finally struck them from their saddles, then galloped in pursuit. But for

all the skill Palamon and Flin possessed in battle, they
had taken too long; they would never catch the last
Buerdic rider. He pulled away from them easily.

At the same time, a shout rose from the distant camp
and a wave of bodies surged out of the tents. They
howled like barbarians as they charged toward the dark
city, to cut Palamon and Flin off. If the two Careans
tarried, they would be caught between the unknown
walls and the shrieking mob. "Hurry," Palamon shouted.
"We must catch up with him before he can attain that
city's gate."

But Ursid's man did not get far. In the heat of the
fighting, Palamon had forgotten the sinister spirit which
lurked ahead of them. With a scream of inhuman delight,
that shape suddenly rose up, streaked through the air in
a terrifying parabola, and plunged into the earth in front
of the Buerdic horseman. Then it shot from the ground
beneath the lone rider's mount like a whale breaching
from the sea. The terrified animal was thrown into the air
along with its rider, whom the spirit caught in outstretched talons.

Palamon stared at the ghastly sight. The apparition
was more than rags and tatters; claws grappled with the
falling man and a shadowy face lurked back in the recesses of the cloth hood. The face should have been a
woman's, to judge by the fine features and the long hair,
but it exuded such a look of incarnate evil that it could
not be given so human a term as male or female. Palamon nearly dropped his sword in shock as he stared into
those cavernous eyes, filled with their bottomless malig-
nancy. Then the thing swept past.

It was evil; deeply evil, sublimely evil, full of an unearthly malevolence which made the evil of Navron or
Alyubol appear no more than child's play by comparison. A look of spectral glee lit the features and the creature plunged its claws into its victim. The poor man
writhed in agony; the blood squirted from the ten
wounds and his screams tore the air, drowning out even
the assailant's horrid song. The poor fellow was as
doomed as a fish caught between the jaws of a crocodile.

He writhed, screamed, then died. And the spirit swirled above the two Careans, laughed, stank, exuded its evil for all to see. The white-robed brigade seemed in no more danger than the two, but they quailed before the horror of it all. Their jaws dropped and they fell back before an evil that was even greater than their own.

That gave Palamon and Flin time to spur their horses all the harder and guide the frothing animals past the tumbledown gate, into whatever safety lay inside the city's dark walls.

Then the specter vanished. They could not know whether it had left for good, or waited for them somewhere in the city. Palamon and Flin glanced into one another's shadowed faces, and Palamon reached up to flick the cold sweat from his brow. "My friend," he said. "We've been through many scrapes together. Now I fear we are about to face the greatest danger either one of us has ever known. If you would like to make withdrawal, then I could not blame you."

But Flin only laughed. "You know me better than that, I hope. This place is old and moldy, I'll grant. But we're here now and your friends are surely going to wait outside until we come out. By Tyche's dice, we're no worse off in here than we would be out there. Besides, any man who won't risk his life now and then had just as well lie down and die on the spot. So lead the way, and I'll be happy to follow—and the gods help any of them who stand against us."

Palamon smiled dryly. "That point is in our favor— the almighty gods are not inclined to aid these evil foemen, but to aid us in our conquest of them." He paused. There was a strange feeling to the place; he felt drawn toward the center of the dark city, toward some unknown goal. The very heart in his body felt as if fingers, soft and invisible fingers, were plucking at it, trying to pull him onward. What could cause such a sensation? Was the *Spada Korrigaine* crying out for him, as he had often cried out when he had needed it? Did some other voice beckon him on? Or was he simply drawn toward a trap baited by Navron and Ursid. "O mighty

Pallas, please be with us now," he murmured. Then they rode on.

It was a great and ancient city, but naked of life. Skeletons lay along the streets and in the vacant doorways; over all lay the dust of ages. Palamon could see a broad path tracked through the dust, so plain that he could follow it even in the moonlight. It was not hard to tell which way Navron and his henchmen had passed; they had gone the same way Palamon's heart led him. Was that fair or foul? No matter, he had to go on and trust in the Fates.

An air of fright and oppression floated out of the very buildings, so powerful the two men could feel it press them down into their saddles. Their horses seemed more afraid than they were themselves. Nothing seemed right; little zephyrs of wind whirled out of blank corners and twirled at their hair, and they heard sounds, as if vermin feet were scuttling out of their path. But nothing moved. And the geometry of the place was somehow unearthly; there was not a square corner in the city. No angle was what it seemed to be. The ground did not lie straight below their eyes as they rode, and side alleys appeared in places that seemed to have been blank wall instants earlier. For all the drive to press onward, Palamon could also feel his hackles rise. This place was not a part of the mortal world; he knew that as surely as he knew his own name. The place was a portion of some unknown, some evil part of existence.

They rode past sloping, slanted streets, past buildings whose doors and windows glared out at them like dead faces. It was worse than crawling into an unshored tunnel. And always the path through the dust led them on, along with Palamon's sure knowledge that he was desperately sought, desperately needed by some spirit at the other end of that path.

Then they reached the end of the avenue and saw moonbeams dancing through a large square. A dozen pale-robed swordsmen rushed from a building, barred their way, and screamed at them to surrender.

Palamon and Flin drew their weapons, spurred their

tired mounts, and rode down on the white-robed defenders. Shouts and curses flew at them, but the evil
ones gave way. Palamon led Flin; his charge scattered
bodies like tenpins. He felt his animal stumble and nearly
go down as it passed over a fallen cultist. A scream assaulted his ears but he did not slow until he burst into the
square.

It was a huge, open area; even Upper Carea or Buerdaunt had nothing to rival it. At the center stood a series
of towering temples, massive edifices surrounded by col-
onnades and strange statues, all standing at crazy angles,
as if assembled by demented hands. But they had no
time to mark that; the white-robed men ran after them
and several more issued from another street to cut them
off.

"By all the gods," Flin cried. "Let's have at them.
There aren't that many."

"Enough to lay us low, or keep us from our destination," Palamon cried back.

"I didn't know we had a destination in this place."

"Indeed, we do. My heart and soul insist we have to
reach that nearest temple."

"Are you crazy? That's probably their headquarters."

"That may be true. Still, I am sure it is the destination
which we must achieve. We've penetrated to the laby-
rinth's foul core, my friend, and here we serve the gods
or meet our deaths."

"Oh, fine," Flin shouted back as they galloped their
horses toward the closest temple. "Only now do you
show me what a fatalist you are." But he stayed even
with the tall monarch as they outdistanced their pursuit
and raced toward the temple's steps.

A score of the white-robed fanatics chased them, but
Palamon noticed that they all slowed as they approached
the temple; they feared something about it. He knew
what they feared, too; this place had to be a center of all
foulness. With each pace his horse took, the stench of
evil assailed his senses more strongly.

But it was an evil which had to be confronted.

"Ride up the steps," he shouted to Flin. "And through

the columns, down the corridors. We gain some time on them thereby."

Flin grinned back at him. For all the danger which pursued them, he plainly had not lost his zeal for adventure, even in this awful place. "Palamon, you have a sacrilegious streak I never would have expected. You're a better man than I ever gave you credit for."

"It is no sacrilege to ride a steed through any temple foul as this one." Palamon's horse jolted the words out of him as it lurched up the steps. Then their hoofbeats echoed off columns, a towering doorway, and bulging stone walls. Once they passed out of the moonlight, Palamon expected the interior of this temple to be impossibly dark, black as the inside of a mine. But the stone itself glowed; their zigzag path threaded through an eerie, green world.

Palamon saw something ahead. He reined his horse to a halt, then leaped from the saddle, followed by Flin. There was no sound behind them now; either they had left their pursuit behind or their enemies feared the place too much to follow this far. Even so, they heard chanted words that echoed along the corridors which stretched before them; the voice belonged to Navron.

With swords drawn, they crept toward the paler light and the voice. As they reached the chamber, Palamon stared in wonder at the sight before him. The design of this temple was nothing like the design of any temple Palamon had ever seen before, not even the Library of the Polonians atop its sun-baked cliff. He had expected to see an inner chamber unlike any he had ever visited; even so, this one was a complete surprise.

Spread below him was a huge, sunken area which appeared larger than the temple itself had seemed from the outside. At the center of the great space stood a blasphemous statue, a horrible piece, a being Palamon could have pictured only in his worst nightmares. It was some kind of ghastly fish creature with tentacles about its mouth, bat's wings spreading from the neck and a lizard-looking, grinning, fang-toothed human face at the top.

The statue glowed, along with the rest of the great

chamber; the whole place pulsed with that chilling green light, as if some subterranean heart pumped the radiance through veins in the stone itself.

At a low altar before the statue stood Navron and Ursid. The young Prince bore a look of complete disgust but Navron ignored him. The minion of evil stood with his eyes clamped shut; he wore his huge, sparkling gauntlets and held a dagger over something laid across the stone before him. Palamon's heart pumped in rage; though the form was shrouded and bound from head to foot, he saw that it was a struggling female figure.

But his shock fought his rage. In that instant of seeing Ursid and Navron together, he realized he could not hate the young Prince. He could not find it in his soul to hate Ursid, even though he would have proclaimed that emotion to the world an instant earlier. He could only feel disgust and pity for any man so eaten up by a thirst for vengeance that he could become any part of such horror. Palamon grimaced at the knowledge of what Ursid had given up—and what he himself had risked becoming. The young noble's rage had cost him more than even he knew.

Palamon's breath heaved itself into his throat and he could not stop it. "Ursid," he cried. "How could you be so witless as to let your hate entrap you in this prison for lost souls?" His words echoed through the chamber, the young face snapped about; Palamon and Ursid stared at one another. Palamon shouted again. "Though I be lower than some scorpion, you are the victim when you let your vengeful lust make you more evil than the very thing you most despise."

Palamon's voice echoed away and silence coiled about the eerie room. Navron stopped chanting. The foul mystic glared at the intruders. The look of evil and fear on his face were even greater than the look of hatred which stamped Ursid's features. "You've come here too late, foolish man," Navron cried. "For the plunge of this dagger of sacrifice opens these stones and frees such a force that you could never conceive its full power." Even as the mad mystic spoke, the light throbbing within the temple grew brighter, more sinister, and Palamon glimpsed some dark shape crouched beneath the altar stone's surface, as if it waited eagerly for release. Something horrible lurked there, something greedy and evil, which could change the shape of the world. The weird geometry of the place challenged Palamon's senses, the walls bowed inward, then back out, as if breathing. The whole building assumed the air of a beast which would digest reality, if only it could get free.

He could not even seek the fragile refuge of a doubt; here was an evil so great, so complete, that the mind could not even comprehend it all at once. Hulking shoulders pressed against the lower surface of the altar stone and supported an unearthly head, slathering jaws, eyes greedy for sacrifice. It was an entity he could never have conceived, had he not seen it for himself.

"Then hurry, get it done," Ursid cried at Navron. "Release the blood and use the mystic sword to carve the seal away, for I would see this business at an end. Then I will meet yon Palamon and duel him to the death."

"For Pallas' sake, Ursid," Palamon cried. "Cannot you see that when his work is done, we'll neither one of us be left alive to duel. The beast he would release will wipe us from existence, you and I together. Then what shall become of your revenge?"

"Speak not to me, you lying serpent," Ursid shouted back.

Navron's dagger began its descent. But the delay had purchased time for the victim: the poor woman managed to wriggle her way to the edge of the stone. Even as the knife plunged toward her, she writhed from the altar's top and landed on the floor. She tried to roll away, but she had no hope of that. Ursid pounced on her, caught at her shrouding, and heaved her back into place. But to his surprise and the amazement of the two Careans, the shrouding tore away.

The motion caused the crushed bodies of huge insects to fly from the cloth as it parted in Ursid's hands and he was left with the maiden herself. She fell to the floor again; for his part, he staggered backward, as if he had seen a specter even more potent than the one which had guarded the entrance to the city. Palamon stared in shock as great as Ursid's. There lay Berengeria, Ursid's former love and Palamon's sister. It was Berengeria, whom he had left safe and sound behind the walls of Castle Conforth.

Chapter Twenty-three:
The Crawling Horde

PALAMON'S MOUTH FELL open; now he knew what force had tugged at him—the kinship, the intense love between him and his sister. Even more was at stake than Berethane's life. The threat was doubly deadly. As for Ursid, he nearly fell with his own shock; then he turned on Navron. "You foul and loathsome scoundrel. How in any world could you have brought her to this place? Is what I hear correct? Have I but let you play upon my baser nature? How I hate both you and my own weakness all the more with every moment. Berengeria's to be your sacrifice, you loathsome dog."

Navron glared back at the young Prince with a look full of fear, cunning, and evil. Palamon saw in the man a fit successor to Alyubol; while he did not possess the dead wizard's genius, he did possess a mind quite as unsound as Alyubol's and a nature fully as devious and malignant.

Palamon did not dare to move. But he cried out, "Redeem your soul, Ursid; free Berengeria from his foul clutches."

Ursid's young face writhed into a hopeless mask of

hatred and confusion. "Stay out of this, for I still seek your death."

"Do you still love poor Berengeria?"

Ursid leaped at Navron and knocked the dagger from the evil minion's fist. "In you I thought I had an ally, fiend. But now I find that you are one more enemy to hate. How glad I am that I am now released from my allegiance with such scum as you; I'll kill you first, then I will find a way to kill this Palamon."

"You're a fool, then," the evil mystic cried. "Do you not remember the host I've settled outside this dark city?" He smiled slowly. "With each moment that passes, my power grows greater. You soon shall expire, lad. Along with you perish the monarch you hate and the maiden you love. I selected the spell which laid Palamon's son by the wayside; now he and his sister shall die; his whole family's line shall be ended this night. Ancient Alyubol's wish is complete; 'tis a great consummation. Be happy, Ursid: do you not find your vengeance in that?"

Palamon's blood ran cold. Alyubol's sickness still enveloped the world, even though the mad wizard was long dead. More to the point, Palamon heard the clamor of Navron's henchmen as they broke into the temple at last. They echoed down the corridors; men would soon burst through the door behind him.

At the same time, Berengeria managed to free her hands. She rolled to her knees and pushed Ursid over; then she tried to drag herself away, humping herself along the floor like some frantic worm.

Navron sprang after her. He snatched up the *Spada Korrigaine* and raised it to take her life; it flamed and crackled in his grip, seethed against his evil, and Palamon wondered if the magic gauntlets would actually be strong enough to give the evil mystic control of the sword.

The blade flashed; lightning played up and down the weapon's length and Palamon screamed the weapon's name, once, twice, again. It exploded into greater action than before, swerved, and caused Navron to miss his helpless target.

Palamon screamed yet again: *"Spada Korrigaine, Spada Korrigaine."* The sword struggled in Navron's grip like a great fish. It thrashed back and forth; a corner of the stone altar clattered to the floor where the invincible blade struck it. But Navron's will was more than human. He refused to let go.

It was the power of the gods opposed against the magic of Navron's gauntlets. The blade turned red, then white with frustrated power, and the gauntlets burst into flame with a loud snap. Navron screeched; the gauntlets burned, and Navron's arms burned with them. The flame spread and devoured his entire body. Palamon stared as the man who would have sacrificed the world became a living flame which leaped and gyrated, but could not keep the sword from finishing what he had begun. Palamon did not call for it again; what would the result be, after all, if it flew to his grasp in its white-hot condition?

It was an awful sight, yet fitting, as Navron met the end he had planned for others. Screams shot from his lips, then he fell to the stones, a black and blazing corpse. Palamon, Flin, Ursid, and Berengeria, all four stared in dumb amazement.

A great evil had been quenched, but Navron was also the man who held the secret to Berethane's salvation. All meaning dribbled out of Palamon's mind as the enormity of Navron's death struck him. His knees buckled, he nearly sagged to the floor, and the temple echoed with his cry as he screamed out his grief.

From the great stone slab came an answering bellow, a scream of rage and frustration, rather than pain or grief. The being Navron had sought to release struggled to get out through the hole chipped by the *Spada Korrigaine*. But Berengeria's blood had not softened the seal; the altar was still too firm to be chipped by a random blow, even from the great sword. The temple shook with bellows as two monstrous fingers extended themselves through the opening, writhed, then withdrew in defeat.

As they moved out of the way, a nightmare shape

surged up from the opening; a slimy, slug-shaped thing oozed out like mud squeezing between clenched fingers, and flopped onto the floor. It lay there, green and glistening, then writhed toward the humans.

"By all the gods, this loathsome creature shall not threaten me," Ursid shouted as he drew his sword. He aimed a blow, sliced off the front end, and stopped the thing.

The seal had been damaged enough to let some awful creature into the world, even though the thing was nowhere near as terrible as what Navron would have set loose. Thick green gas belched from the stone like smoke pouring from an uncorked urn. The gas glowed with an evil light, eddied about, and crawled across the floor like an unearthly miasma. Ursid leaped away from it and—to Palamon's hope and surprise, for perhaps it showed that a spark of humanity was left in him—hauled Berengeria with him.

Through the vapors came more of the evil-looking slug creatures. They squeezed through the hole and wriggled across the floor as had the first. Though Flin, and then Palamon, each killed one with a single stroke, they unnerved the two men. They kept coming. They writhed from the stone in a steady stream. They hardly had a shape; they were not much more than blobs, yet they flopped toward the humans with a plain air of menace about them.

"We must escape this place," Palamon cried. "Navron's released some force unknown to us. Who knows what follows?"

"It is foulness, surely," Berengeria replied in a choked voice.

Ursid only sneered back at Palamon; the young noble's mouth worked, but no words came. Hatred still gripped his features. Could there really be hope? Palamon wondered. Would it be better to fight the young Prince to the death then and there? They had no time for that. Palamon knew he could not defeat hatred by laying hatred and anger against it; he could only hope Ursid's hatred warred with knowledge of the horrors hatred could spawn.

More slimy things squeezed from the altar, dozens of them, and the earlier ones all began to swell. They writhed more than ever, twitching and jerking across the floor. Palamon stared at them. Then one gave a last, final heave, and its skin split along the back. The leathery husk fell away and a creature far more fearsome raised its three-cornered head.

It was a pasty, pale mantis the size of a pony. Its insect jaws worked like twin scythes and it lifted its huge forelegs as if they were fearsome weapons, covered by bony ridges which looked like rows of daggers. It peered about the temple, then came at the humans. And all across the chamber, other creatures just as deadly rose from their shells—scorpions, beetles, and cockroaches longer than a man.

Berengeria screamed and shook her head. "Alas, alas, they come at me again, these bugs of evil—each time larger and more putrid than the last."

Ursid stared as if in shock. "They are the very soul of Kruptos," he breathed. "And of all the evil I have courted."

Berengeria reached toward Palamon, but he was too far away, so she looked up at the Buerdic Prince. "Please, Ursid, relent. I must confess I love another man—and though he may be slain, my soul is still secured to his as surely as if we were wed. No other one can have the love I gave to him; I cannot take you for my husband. Still, you have to save your soul and join with us to fight a way from this pernicious place."

"Always, always, there's another one." Ursid clawed at his own face, as he had done at Tychopolis.

Berengeria clambered to her knees and reached for his hand. "Might we be friends? If we cannot share love, might we still share the friendship of our foreheads?"

Ursid's real struggle had to be against himself; he pushed her away. "No, there can be no friendship for us two. It's love or naught. I am what I must be—if I cannot gain you, then I must stand alone."

At that instant, Navron's followers burst into the chamber. "Defend yourselves," Palamon cried. "We are attacked." Then he cried out for the *Spada Korrigaine* and the blade sizzled through the smoky shadows and into his grasp.

He barely had time to face the attackers, who outnumbered the defenders by three to one. With the others, he formed a human square to oppose the fanatics. What apologies and entreaties could not accomplish, fighting did—Ursid stood with them against the evil minions. They surged across the floor in deadly combat, coughing on the evil steam and dodging the creatures which scuttled about, snapping at them.

With the *Spada Korrigaine*, Palamon laid into his foemen. The great blade sliced off arms and severed necks as easily as a housewife's cleaver carving a chicken. The attackers fell back before the tall monarch's furious onslaught.

Half the evil minions fell; the others dropped their weapons and fled, clawing at one another and stumbling as they scrambled toward the darkness outside the temple. But there was no time for relaxing. "We'd better get out of here," Flin yelled. "These bugs are going to kill us, even if Navron's friends don't." He hardly got the words out as he sidestepped a huge scorpion and sliced off one of its pincers.

Some of the crawling horrors dragged off the bodies of the slain, but they were only the first of an army of the things. All across the chamber, slimy green pupae split and ghastly crawlers wriggled free. Dozens of the things formed and still more slugs writhed from the altar stone.

The growing army of creatures stared about the temple with their glassy eyes. Pincers clacked and huge, saw-blade jaws worked with hideous scraping sounds. Another giant mantis lashed out at Palamon as if filled with the lust to kill—to kill as many humans as it could.

The last of Navron's followers hurtled from sight, slipping and sliding as they fled. The creatures did not follow them; they all turned on Palamon and his companions. The four humans took to their heels and raced after the white-robed cultists. Palamon panted as they ran into the corridor. He looked for the horses but they were gone, driven away by the evil ones.

They ran on. They clattered along dark corridors and up ramps, but they arrived at the temple's towering bronze doors, only to find them barred from without. Even as Palamon and Ursid pounded the heavy panels, they could hear the babble of voices on the other side. The evil minions were holding the doors shut, imprisoning the intruders, consigning them to the mercies of the hungry horrors which lumbered after them.

Palamon stared back along the corridor. He listened to the ungodly chatter and saw the bounding heads, legs, and glowing eyes of the chitinous army. "Stand back," he cried. "I'll try to break the door."

It was a desperate measure and he knew it; everything in this evil city was mystical. To strike at the temple doors with his *Spada Korrigaine* was to risk the worst sort of catastrophe. But he stepped back, set his jaw, and swung his great blade at the hinges of one panel.

The blow produced a horrible screech, a sort of long, drawn-out explosion, and the door burst into flame. The sword grew so hot in Palamon's hands that he nearly had to release it, but he was able to hold on. The door glowed, the flame spread, and the entire panel turned dull red. Screams and curses rose from outside and it swung open a few degrees.

Risking burns, the fugitives shouldered the panel the rest of the way open, toppled it, and pushed through with the bugs of Kruptos hard on their heels. Palamon saw the two horses he and Flin had ridden. A couple of cultists had seized the reins and hauled the beasts along, but as the fugitives bore down on them, they released the animals. Even at that, there was no time to clamber into the saddles. The pursuing monsters nipped too close to their heels; Palamon looked back, threw down his reins, grasped his sister's wrist, and ran on. Flin and Ursid did the same.

Before the confused horses could flee, the great insects were upon them. Massive pincers tore away hunks of equine flesh and blood spurted. Stingers plunged into flanks and did their deadly work. The horses screamed in panic, reared, and tried to flee, but they had no chance. In an instant, they had disappeared beneath a mound of writhing horrors.

The massacre of the horses distracted the crawling horde and gave the humans time to flee. "Run down this street with me," Palamon cried. "We'll have to find a place to make a stand."

"Nay, nay," Ursid shouted back. "Navron's foul minions flee ahead and I suspect their strategy. They mean to bar the city's gates to us and trap us here with all these crawling things. Then, even if we should defeat this wriggling army, we'll receive a horrid end when dawn comes. Then will all of Kruptos fade and take us with it."

"What?" Flin said.

"If we remain within the boundaries of Kruptos' walls come dawn, our fate is sealed. With sunrise, it will vanish like the breeze and he who stays entrapped becomes another of its denizens, to suffer through eternity, as if this were a little Purgatory. Even worse than Purgatory, for there is no end, nor any hope of any. Even if we do get out, the white-robed followers of Alyubol will still be waiting."

"We first must overtake these men within the city and escape from this foul place," Palamon shouted. "Then we may worry over what may lie outside."

So they ran. They hurtled toward Kruptos' gates; and though they showed a clean set of heels to the great insects which had paused to devour the horses, the sound of pursuit soon clicked along the streets behind them. What hour of the night was it? Palamon could not guess; there had been no way for him to judge time during the interval he and Flin had spent inside the temple. But the moon had journeyed far across the sky. Much of the night had plainly slipped by, and dawn could burst upon them any instant. He grasped Berengeria's hand as they ran and he tried to pull her along, for she was plainly the weariest of the four.

Then some of their white-robed antagonists leaped from a dark doorway and blocked them. Palamon's chest heaved as he swung the *Spada Korrigaine*. One of the men fell. The others danced away before the weapon's flashing blade, then stopped again to fight. The strategy was plain. These fanatics were willing to offer themselves as sacrifices to slow the fugitives' advance while some cultists ran ahead and warned the army outside to repair and close the city's gate. Palamon grimaced; it could be a deadly strategy. Even as he squared off against the new rear guard, he heard the scrabbling of insect claws ever closer behind him.

"We'd better finish this now," Flin cried. "There's no time to lose." He and Ursid joined Palamon in flying against their foemen with renewed ferocity and this time the white-robed warriors were too slow in breaking off the combat and leaping away. Palamon cut down a couple, while Flin and Ursid each sent another to the paving; that left only one, who turned and fled in earnest. Then Berengeria gave a little gasp and collapsed.

Palamon's heart fell with her but he grabbed her beneath the arms and lifted. His fingers closed on something soft and awful; it burst and a great, red stain spread across the ragged lace of her gown.

Palamon stared in horror, then Flin leaped to her side and tore the material to reveal a huge leech, which had been gorging on Berengeria's blood. Even though smashed, it was the size of a cucumber, and it was plain to see that the poor Princess' vital juice was all that colored its sickeningly pale tissues. Had it been sucking on her even while she had struggled against her bonds or had it been among the horde of creatures which had writhed from the chipped seal? It did not matter, it had done its work and Berengeria was too weak to flee the oncoming pursuit.

Palamon also tried to help, but she pushed all three of them away. "No, leave me," she cried in a weak voice. "The one I love has died at any rate; my life would have no purpose if I lived. Do not delay your flight by aiding me."

"Nay, nay, my sister," Palamon said. "if e'er the time should come when any one of us could strand a gallant maid like you, then there would be no hope for us, e'en if we did escape."

"A love may die but there may be another love to take its place someday," Ursid cried. He lifted Berengeria in his arms; the scars on his lean face gleamed white in the moonlight as they fled onward.

It was a nip-and-tuck race at the best; the leaping horde behind them came very near. But they turned one last corner and found themselves at the gate; it swung shut even as they drew near it.

The legion of bugs leaped at them and they had to fight. The creatures seemed to possess no mystical quality other than unbridled ferocity; still, that looked to be all they would need to destroy the quartet. They leaped against the blades of the defenders without fear or mercy. Palamon, Ursid, Flin, and a sagging Berengeria stood trapped between an unyielding gate and a long column of unworldly antagonists.

Chapter Twenty-four:
The Count of Tranje

PALAMON'S ARMS SOON ached from plying his *Spada Korrigaine* against the crawling horde's assault. The creatures were as large as ponies, large enough to chop a man into dog's meat or pump him full of deadly poison —and there were dozens of them. Even if the foursome killed them all, they still would have to face the gate and the minions of evil who held it shut.

The four defenders whacked off segmented legs, antennae, and stingers, until insect bodies lay in heaps and spewed their ichor onto the cobblestones. New creatures pounced on the wounded ones, dragged them away to eat, and fought over pieces as they devoured their own fallen. Even so, there were plenty to replace the wounded and distracted ones. Palamon's weapon slew three times as many of the creatures as the others together but he could not hold out forever. All four of them were soon bathed in their own blood from countless scrapes and cuts, and the sticky sap of the creature legion covered everything.

Berengeria tried gallantly to stand and fight with the others, but she could not sustain the effort. Her knees buckled and she slumped to the pavement, though she still tried to use the longsword Palamon had given her. Her life was in such danger that Palamon and Flin stepped across her and sheltered her with their legs.

Palamon's face broke into a grim smile as he severed an insect's champing head with his blade, to kick the creature back to the windrows he had already killed. It was funny in a dreadful way that he might consider Berengeria's life to be in danger; they were all four of them in mortal danger. One slip, one missed parry with a sagging arm, and any one of them would fall, never to rise again, to be eaten alive by the implacable horde.

He lost himself in the fury of his fighting, hacking at horrid animals until they lay about him in a pile that was higher than his head. Roaring filled his ears; he heard screams and pounding, but kept on until he could fight no longer.

He had to stop; his arms grew so heavy he could no longer even lift the *Spada Korrigaine*. He finally let it drop and rested the point on the ground; only then did he notice Ursid and Flin staring at him. "That's very good," Flin said with a smile. "I wondered how long you'd go on fighting dead bugs."

Palamon gasped for breath as he looked about. No more multilegged horrors crawled at them over the top of the pile; the battle had ended. The fury of his fighting had so seized him that he had gone on hacking and slashing dead monsters, even after no live ones were left to him. "We've won," he exclaimed in wonder. "We did it. Now we have to strike this gate and knock if off its hinges, then confront the many foemen still arrayed against us."

He rubbed his weary arms. Then he heard a trumpet call, and suddenly the gate swung open by itself. All four of them sagged with relief as they looked out. Bodies, mostly white-robed ones, lay scattered about the valley while infantrymen rounded up those evil cultists who still stood.

More trumpets sounded, commanders screamed orders, and a pack of footmen ran up to lift Berengeria and to help the three men out the gate. A column of

mounted knights waited close by; one of them directed
that part of the operation.

Palamon staggered to the man, then reached up to
shake his hand. But he thought better of the gesture; it
was not enough. He let the *Spada Korrigaine* slide from
his fingers while the knight climbed from his horse, then
the sweat flew from his arms as he clasped the fellow in a
thankful embrace. "I know not where you came from,
sir, but I have never felt so glad to see a force of armored
men in all my life. We thought we'd perish ere we slew
the monstrous force arrayed against us; I had no desire
to face Navron's foul henchmen in the bargain."

"I wish we had arrived some moments sooner, O most
noble King," the knight replied. "We could have aided
you against your otherworldly foes." He looked at the
stack of oozing bodies which lay inside the gate and his
mouth twisted in disgust. "But you destroyed them all,
and I'll not rue the fact we cannot face such nightmare
beasts ourselves."

Palamon heaved a great breath, picked up his
weapon, and enjoyed the fresh air outside the gate. Flin
and Ursid did the same, while several housecarls helped
Berengeria stagger alongside them. She reached for Palamon and hung on his shoulder just to keep her balance;
Palamon saw Ursid's features darken all over again, but
he was too tired to worry about it.

They made their way through the soldiers and met
another knight, a towering man who doffed his helmet to
greet them. "And you must be the monarch, Palamon,"
he said as he wrung Palamon's hand. "And this is Berengeria, the proud Princess of whom I've heard so much.
But who be you, you gallant warriors?" His eyes held
questions as he addressed Flin and Ursid.

"I am Ursid, the Constable of far Buerdaunt," the
young Prince said.

"And my name's Flin." Flin shook hands with the
man but Ursid walked on by himself. "And who are
you?" Flin asked. "How in blazes did you know to come
to this forsaken place?"

The knight laughed. "It's not surprising that you'd

wish to hear my name and title. Very well; I'm Altonrod; I serve as seneschal unto the Count of Tranje. He was the man who ordered all his knights to take the field against the forces of foul darkness which inhabited this city. All the white-robed cultists who are known to us as 'evil minions,' have been apprehended. They will face their punishments directly."

"Aha, the Count," Palamon said. "Does he still live?"

"Indeed he does, though he is wounded and not well enough to join the fray himself. He waits for you inside his litter. Would you go to him?"

"We would," Palamon said. "We owe him many thanks—we'd fought alone as long as we had any wish to."

Sir Altonrod looked at Berengeria and his face showed his concern. "Would you like a litter for the lady?"

"No, I can manage," Berengeria replied. "I shall place a portion of my weight upon my brother, for I'll not be carried anymore. The last time I received support in traveling came when I was enshrouded, bound, and set upon an altar as a sacrifice. I'd not relive that moment for a hundred pounds of jewels." She smiled weakly. "So I'll walk."

Palamon smiled back at her. That sounded like Berengeria. He wrapped an arm about her waist and let her put her weight on his shoulder as they walked toward several covered litters and wagons which stood on the valley's gentle slope. As they walked, he heard more trumpets sound and he saw another company of knights approach around the city's wall. Apparently, they had scoured the valley for any evil cultists who had escaped, or creatures which might have slipped out of Kruptos by another way.

Then a lean, blond-haired man poked his head out of one of the litters and a handsome face beamed at them. Even in the gray of the coming dawn, the face was pale and drawn—but the joy which gripped the features made it striking nontheless. Berengeria looked up and saw that face, then she released a scream of amazement and delight which bordered on hysteria. "Arcite. My dear Arcite, my love, my life. You live; they did not kill you after all." She dropped Palamon's arm, ran to the litter, and nearly collapsed as she tore back the curtain. "Ah, let me look upon you. Love, my love, 'twas you who warned the Count of Tranje that this foul city rested in this place. But how could you have done it? When they took me from your side, you were all buried in debris and stabbed into the bargain. How could you have told them where to send this army?

"The sword thrust spilled my blood," he replied. "But still it did not kill me. After they had taken you away, I climbed from under that poor hovel's wreckage. By good luck or else the gods' good will, I came upon a force of knights soon afterward. They rode to Tranje and then brought the army which you see."

"But how could you have found us here?"

"Ah. Peristeras told us of this place, of evil Kruptos, as you may recall. Where else would they have taken you? Our scouts encountered it without much difficulty."

Berengeria's trembling fingers touched his face, tarrying here and there as if to confirm what her vision told her. Her eyes ran over, and streams of happy tears tracked her cheeks. "And so you rallied this brave Count of Tranje and his knights to save our lives. How can I ever thank you? Name the prize you'd have for this great service."

Arcite laughed and struggled from the litter, even though he was plainly weak from his wounds. He wrapped his arms about Berengeria's shoulders. "There's just one prize I will accept, dear heart—your hand in marriage. Will you give me that?"

Berengeria looked up at him, then at Palamon. "Full freely would I give it, were it mine alone. But still I am my country's property." Then she issued a pleading look at her brother and her King. "Ah, Palamon, would you release me from my obligation? I would marry this Arcite if it would please you."

Palamon gazed back at her and a smiled curved his lips, in spite of every attempt he made to keep a straight face. It was all he could do to keep from laughing; he would give Berengeria the world if she asked for it.

Just then, Altonrod interrupted them to bow low before Arcite. "My Lord, your knights have finished their assignments. Not one baneful creature has been found outside the city, and each man allied to foul Navron accounted for. Some two or three brave men of ours are slain, but victory's complete."

"Ah," Arcite replied. "Then have the evil minions bound and hobbled. Don't abuse them, but be sure not one escapes."

"Indeed, my Lord. To Tranje shall they be taken in the wagons, there to face an honest trial and punishment as justice shall mete out."

Arcite nodded and smiled but Berengeria stared at him as if he had suddenly turned to an insect. Her jaw dropped, and she could barely stutter her words. "Then you are he? You are the Count of Tranje?"

Altonrod smiled as if surprised by her question. "He is, my Lady."

She stared from one man to another, from Arcite to Altonrod, to Palamon. "But he came into our court. We knew him as a lowly balladeer. His talents were unique and wonderful, but still he was Arcite, the Balladeer, to us."

"Arcite the Balladeer he is, fair Princess," Altonrod replied. "Why, from the hour of birth, he has amazed all those who've known him by his love of music. He has studied with all bards who ply their art across the Thlassa Mey. His genius overshadows all of them, but still and all, he is the Count of Tranje by the right of his inheritance."

Berengeria put her hands to her head; her lips worked, she looked from face to face, but she plainly had no idea how to deal with this revelation. "But he came into our court," she repeated to Palamon.

"To woo you," Palamon finished. No longer was he inclined to smile or laugh at his sister. She had the look of a woman freed from a prison, a prison she had built in her own mind. "No man who courted you could gain your love, no matter what his pedigree. You'd turned your back upon a dozen gallants, at the least."

Arcite took her by the hands and smiled into her face. "And when I heard of you and saw your portrait, listened to the tales about your spirit, your refusal to be wed for anything but honest love, I knew you were for me. I loved you from before the moment I first saw you." He folded her quietly in his arms.

"And so he wrote to Berevald, our father," Palamon went on. "And pleaded for your hand. The two of us both knew him to be good and decent, so when I assumed the throne I gave consent for him to court you."

Arcite spoke again. "But I well knew the fate of all those gallants who rode to your court in rich attire, with pomp of knights and drums. They strutted for you like so many fowl displaying feathers. So I made resolve to come to you as no more than a man, a common man, to let you look upon my faults and strengths. And if the gods allowed, then you would grow to love me for myself and I could plead for your beloved hand. And so it has transpired."

Berengeria looked at him in wonder, then threw her arms about him and nearly dragged him to the ground with her affectionate weight. "It was a prank," she cried. "But such a wonder. You would have my hand? You'll have it, sir, and all the rest of me besides."

It was a pretty scene. All the knights and nobles who watched, save Ursid, applauded as the lovers united their breaths in a long kiss. Ursid observed with dead features, but Palamon hardly noticed him, and the others did not mark the young Prince at all.

Then, to Palamon's surprise, Berengeria turned toward him and brought a little flask of crystal from beneath her robe. He looked at it as she extended her hand. "What's this?" he asked.

She looked at the flask, then up at him with gleaming eyes. "It is the artifact presented me by Peristeras, whom I shall explain to you. It is a gift the gods have given you to free your son from magic's bondage."

"My son." Palamon's soul ached at the very mention

of Berethane as thought lit a lamp within him. He accepted the object from her. The maiden he had spied in the streets of Danaar—had this been her meaning? "The balance teeters at the middle point; diplomacy tells all. His fate awaits you south and east of Tranje, but there's still another route." It all seemed clear, except the middle part, "Diplomacy tells all," was unclear. But though he did not completely understand, his fingers trembled as he turned the vial over and over again.

"Could it be true?" he asked softly. "I thought him lost when foul Navron lay burned to pieces in the evil temple. I imprisoned both my heart and soul then, and secured them both from the hope upon that instant." He looked at the vial once more. "Could it be?" he asked a second time.

Arcite spoke softly. "The instrument which Peristeras gave me proved to be exactly what he said it was. Therefore, I see no reason to mistrust his words. That flask contains a portion of a god."

"Indeed, that's true," Berengeria said.

Palamon looked from her to her husband-to-be, then back to the flask. Inside, he could see a finger, still pink with life as it floated in some solution—the finger of an immortal god, presented to him for his son's sake. "I thank the gods," he breathed. "It is a night for prodigies."

"A night for prodigies, indeed," Ursid broke in, with sneering tones. "And, too, it is a night for my humiliation. I am pleased for all of you." He glared into the faces of Arcite and Berengeria. "What pleasure it must be to share your love, to throw it in my face. I marvel at the joy which it must give you."

Berengeria looked at him and her face fell. "Ursid. Yes, you're correct; it was unkind for us to revel in the love we share while you still seek my hand. Will it spread balm across your hurts if I apologize?"

Ursid spat and showed his teeth. "Ah, that should do it. That should close all wounds. And if it fails to do so, how much can it matter, anyway? I have no choice. I can accept apologies and go through all my years as half a man, without the love for whom I staked my life. Or then again, I can refuse apologies and go through life as half a man, without that selfsame love. You play with me again." He grimaced as if he had received a death wound. "Ye gods, why do you not destroy me here? How long must I endure indignities from these cruel folk?"

But Ursid's display did more than he could have intended—it revived all the harsh feelings between himself and Berengeria. Palamon looked away, rather than watch the anger flood into her face. "'Twas never my decision," she cried. "You heaped your love, your cold, unwanted love, upon my head as if you'd bury me beneath it. Have I not a choice? Cannot I wed a man who's capable of speaking to my heart?"

Ursid grew dark with rage; in the light of the coming dawn, his features turned into a black storm against which his scars flashed like approaching lightning. "And I'm refused again. I am to stay as helpless as a babe while you embrace and wed this man—while you dance for his pleasure? But enough. If laughter is my portion, if it pleases you and all the gods to ridicule me, then I'll pay what price I must to silence all your mirth forever."

Flin plainly suspected something; as Ursid finished his angry speech, the former rogue leaped toward Palamon. But Flin stood too far away and Ursid was too quick. The young Prince reached out, snatched the flask from Palamon's hand, and sprinted away, through the valley's long grass. "Catch him," Flin cried. "He's running for the city."

Indeed, Ursid sped toward the evil city of Kruptos. Flin and Palamon raced after Ursid, while Arcite cried for mounted knights to intercept his flight. But Ursid had caught them by surprise. He was a fast man and he was eighteen years Palamon's junior. He showed them all a clean pair of heels; the wet grass whipped against his legs, and, by the time some of the knights had leaped onto their steeds, he had reached the shattered gate. He scrambled up the heap of insect bodies at the entrance, then staggered to a halt at the apex.

He turned only long enough to shout a challenge to the tall monarch himself. "I am one of history's poor fools, but still I'll make my mark, tall Palamon. You say you'd have your son restored to you? Then follow me. If you can catch me in this city, then with all your strength and skill, the flask and all its powers shall be yours. Come, follow me and risk the new day's dawn." Mounted men arrived at the gate, but Ursid flashed down one of the city's dark alleyways and was gone.

With a cry, Palamon leaped toward the opening, but Flin caught his arm and pulled him to the ground. "You can't go in there. The place is going to disappear at any time now. You'll go with it."

"My son is worth the risk."

"Don't be a fool. That's just what Ursid wants."

Palamon brought his fist against Flin's jaw and the young man's grip relaxed. The tall monarch struggled to rise, but a dozen other knights leaped onto him and dragged him down all over again. He could move toward the gate no more than a bear weighed down by attacking dogs. "O Berethane, my son, my lovely son," he cried in anguish. "What will become of you?"

The only reply was a cruel laugh which echoed from someplace on the other side of the rotting gate. While Palamon struggled to rise, the new sun's advancing light struck the highest tower of Kruptos. Palamon heard Ursid scream; then, before a thousand eyes, the city flickered, its image swirled, and it vanished. Palamon blinked in amazement. Where the great metropolis of evil had once stood, not even a blade of grass was now flattened.

The hot tears spewed from his eyes and he covered his face with his hands. His son had been saved and lost all over again, all in a matter of instants. All was gone; Berethane was gone, Kruptos was gone, Ursid was gone. The young Prince, so full of hate, so misguided, had vanished as completely as the city. And as the light

of the new day flooded into the valley, all that was left of
the troubled Buerdic Prince was a hateful memory and
the last echo of the cry he released as the city disappeared. The cry seemed to hover, filled with agony, grief,
and fury. It lingered over the valley a fantastic period of
time, like a bad odor which would not go away.

Chapter Twenty-five:
A Gift to Pallas

NO CAREAN CITIZEN ever questioned Ursid's fate. He had been swept away with the forbidden city; the evil which he had allowed to rule his life had at last overpowered and destroyed him. But he had exacted a great price. The artifact which could have cured Berethane disappeared with him. Though Palamon inquired with the greatest physicians on the banks of the Thlassa Mey, none had the least idea of how to save the child. Palamon pondered sometimes, whether Ursid was quite dead. Or had the evil city preserved him in some terrible way? Would he reappear within these lands in a few generations, when Kruptos returned? If that happened, would he still possess the artifact? It would make no difference—both Palamon and Berethane would be long dead by then.

But on a more pleasant note, Carea would be able to enjoy a lovely wedding; no person who had seen the designs laid out by the royal seamstress and the *charge d'affairs* could doubt that. The gown being prepared for Princess Berengeria had the look of woven smoke; when she tried it on, it hung from her shoulders as lightly as if it had been made of angels' wings. And though the Princess remained herself, Palamon noted a new richness working its way from within; there was little doubt that when the day of the wedding arrived, she would have the radiant look of any new bride.

Palamon awaited the wedding with mixed emotion. Arcite arrived in Carea a few days before the event and he charmed the court as always. But he was an instinctive performer and a consummate gentleman—and he possessed the good sense to know he was not the one the guests came to see. To the disappointment of many, his bride most of all, he refused to sing at the wedding. Palamon had to smile at that; Arcite refused to overshadow Berengeria on the special day and he would not revel too greatly on a day when the royal couple, Palamon and Aelia, were still dealing with their own grief.

For though the child lingered on, all hope of saving his life had to be released, finger by finger. Palamon and Aelia would play their rôles at the wedding ceremony, they would receive their guests, and they would never mention Berethane's name in the presence of the bride or groom. But as day faded into the last evening before the nuptials, they had to admit to themselves that they would hurt.

They would suffer the pain of the child's loss, no matter how joyful and successful the wedding turned out to be. When the two of them completed the last of their court business on the night before the wedding, they joined hands and walked the endless corridors of Castle Conforth to the nursery.

Palamon and Aelia entered the chamber together, as they had entered it every night. His throat tightened as he studied the sunken cheeks, the eyelids closed over great blue circles. He grieved and curled up inside; he would never get over this. Neither would Aelia, though she rarely showed the thoughts swirling behind her face.

On this evening, he reached down and stroked the matted hair. The child's forehead was cold but a finger laid against the little throat still revealed a weak pulse. He sighed and curled his arm about Aelia's shoulder. She gazed down at the little face but she did not touch it; her features were as gray as a cold dawn. "A strange world this," she murmured.

"What's that?"

"A strange world," she repeated. "Unpredictable. Who might have known when I first met you, that we'd find you heir to proud Carea's throne, that our dear Princess would be given out in marriage by your hand, and that our child, which we would love so deeply, would be overcome by some curse left behind by Alyubol and reinforced by overproud Ursid."

Palamon did not reply. Instead, he turned to the physician. "How fares he? As you say each night, I'll wager, he declines the same."

"The same—but now more serious," the physician replied. "Unless he somehow turns the spell away, by morning he shall die."

Palamon groaned. It had been coming for a long while but this was the first time the physician had actually set the limit to the child's suffering. If death had to come, it was all the worse that it should come on this night. He tightened his grip on Aelia's shoulder and used his other hand to cradle her head against his chest. "O cruel world," he said at last. "It is enough to make a man lose faith."

"Nay," Aelia said. "Love, you know those words are false. We shall go on, with faith as our great crutch."

"Perhaps," he said. He hoped she was right; he knew she was. Whatever passed, he would keep his trust in divine things. And then a thought came to him, a momentous thought of the prophesy he had received at Danaar. He had failed to understand it in time: "Diplomacy tells all." Failure to take Ursid's unstable emotions into account had cost them the artifact which would have saved Berethane's life. He had cursed his own denseness ever since that moment.

But there was another phrase, one he had until now thought he understood: "There's still another course." That phrase had nothing to do with the artifact Ursid had taken, and his head swam as he realized the full meaning. It was all a question of faith—the faith he would never surrender.

On the night the flaming cyclone had laid Berethane
low, Palamon had prayed without result to have him restored. But laying on of hands did not dispel magic; that
prayer had not been answered. But had it gone un-
heeded? Tears leaped to Palamon's eyes and he fought
them back as he remembered the finger which had
floated in the flask. His act of faith had, indeed, produced a result, though it had gone awry. "There's still
another course." Despair was not the answer. The answer lay in greater faith than ever, in a demonstration of
that faith.

His heart pounded as he left both Aelia and the physician standing and rushed to the nursery door. Two iron-
faced guards stood their post there and they stared at
him as he burst from the room. "Go down and rouse the
stablemen," he ordered. "I want two palfreys; one is for
myself, the other for the Queen. And soon, before this
night can darken one more hour."

The men looked startled but one of them nodded and
saluted. "Do you want men to ride with you, your
Grace?"

Palamon hesitated. It was a desperate scheme, the
plan which had burst upon him. If he was wrong this
time there would be no further chances. Berethane
would shiver and die and would be lost to his grieving
parents forever. But it was a question of faith, was it
not? And when the moment of truth came, he wanted to
be alone with his wife, their stricken child, and the gods
themselves.

Evil forces could still be afoot, so he had to take pre-
cautions. On a dark, moonless night, he would not be
able to see his hand before his face once they left the
city. "A score of men with torches," he said. "Able men,
who know to follow orders and to hold their tongues."

The guard departed and Palamon returned to the
chamber. He placed his hands on Aelia's shoulders and
tenderly faced her. "My wife and love," he said. "We
must change garb and travel to the coast tonight."

Aelia looked up into his face and the least smile

teased her features. "Do we go to the place and for the purpose I suspect?"

"Perhaps. But let us go and change." They turned from the astonished physician and rushed to their own rooms, where they donned sturdy clothing and cloaks against the night's chill. Then Palamon hurried back to the nursery.

He rushed in and pulled the child from its bed. Poor Berethane—he had shrunken down to no more than a little, shapeless atom, a dried remnant of what had once been childhood's bursting life. Even though Palamon had watched the child waste away day by day, he was amazed at how light the little boy was.

The physician looked worried. "What ails you, Sire?" he asked. "Why do you take the child at night this way, remove him from his blankets, and depart?"

"I have my reasons," Palamon replied. "If there is naught that can be done for him, then I can do no harm by desperate actions." He wrapped the little body with blankets.

"But this is quite unprecedented."

"As is his affliction." Palamon turned for one last look at the man and at the nurses who clustered about him. "But be of ease. At times like these, when all our potent arts avail us nothing, we must act on faith. Now bear you that in mind and pray for me—for all of us." With that, he turned and carried the child out the door.

He clattered down the steps which led from the tower chamber to Castle Conforth's inner ward. There, as he knew she would be, Aelia waited for him at the head of twenty armored knights. They were all stern-faced men, though each face betrayed puzzlement at the hour of the night and the strange mission. "You have him, then," Aelia observed. "But did you not demand a litter for him or a wagon, or some other form of transport?"

"I did not," Palamon replied as he climbed into his saddle. He had spent so much time on horseback over the years that he did not even have to release his grip on the little body to perform that task. "Before this night has ended, he may die," he said by way of explanation.

"I wish to hold him, feel his weight upon my arms, and sense his heartbeat for a while."

Their horses were close together, close enough for Aelia to reach forth and caress Palamon's cheek. He could see a tremor to her lower lip as she spoke. "You are a tender man."

He returned the caress, then wound the reins about his hands. He gave an order and the company clattered across the inner ward, through a gate to the outer bailey, and past sleepy guards and sentries. The portcullis in Castle Conforth's towering gatehouse raised before them and they began their ride in earnest.

As they passed out of the castle, several of the knights lit torches. The brands lined the road like a forest of burning trees, some borne ahead of the royal couple, some following them.

They rode toward the coast. Where Carea met the Thlassa Mey, a high cliff rose from the water and a legion of boulders opposed the relentless waves. The highest point of these cliffs was Palamon's destination. It was a slow journey at night, even with torches, and the sky in the east was growing pale by the time Palamon's nose could detect the salt smell of the sea hundreds of fathoms below.

"Now halt," Palamon commanded. The clapping of hooves on the hard road slowed, then died away altogether. Harnesses jingled, and horses snorted their steamy breaths into the chill. Palamon's knights gazed curiously at him and Aelia.

Aelia smiled. "I thought that this would be our destination," she said. "I've known your meaning for some time, my love."

"You are a wonder, then. Do you approve?"

She gazed at him, her eyes probing him like fingers, as they always did. "Your faith is great, my Palamon. All those physicians we have called upon have met defeat. So let this boundless faith accomplish what it may."

He passed her the child and climbed down from his horse. "Not just my faith but yours as well," he said as he walked to her, took the little body back, and motioned for a pair of knights to help her from her own saddle.

"Indeed," she said. "We go together."

Palamon looked back at his loyal men. "But alone," he added. "We go to do a private business, now. I thank you all for coming, but we pass alone unto the end of land. Retire you now, go back some half a league and wait until the sun should show itself. And take our horses with you, for we shall not need them."

The commander of the company looked worried. "Your grace, there could be danger waiting here within this lonely place. There still are those who plot against your life."

"Nay, nay," Palamon said. "This is a holy place. Here shall we pray. No danger shall await us here."

The man gazed at the royal couple, then he and his fellows saluted, grasped the reins of the two royal mounts, and started back the way they had come. Soon, Palamon and Aelia stood alone with their dying son.

They walked slowly toward the cliff and the sea winds which whipped up along its margin. Ahead of them, a square silhouette against the coming dawn, a slab of granite had been erected at the very edge of the precipice. It was polished smooth and featureless; at its center was carved an inscription:

UPON THIS SPOT DID PALAMON,
THE SON OF BEREVALD, PERCEIVE A VISION

In this place divine Pallas had spoken to Palamon in the midst of his distress years ago. Now, in this place, he and Aelia would entreat her again. The top of the slab was the height of a man's chest and long and broad enough to be used as an altar. On it he placed his son and carefully unfolded the child's blanket until the little body lay exposed to the elements. The child did not even twitch. Palamon took his hauberk of holy chain mail, the hauberk Pallas had presented to him on this very spot, and placed it at the child's feet. And he took his *Spada Korrigaine*, the blade which would cleave any substance, and placed it at the child's head.

"What are you doing?" Aelia asked.

Palamon hesitated, then spoke in a low voice. "These gifts which I've received are nothing to our baby's life. With joy shall I return them to the revered gods if only they will spare him."

"Ah. I see. Then I have something also." She reached into the purse at her waist and produced a plain ring of solid gold, tied to a leather thong. She took the thong and placed it around the motionless child's neck.

"What's that?" Palamon asked.

"It is the Ring of Parthelon, another mighty gift. Our niece, Bessina, gave it to me years ago. I pray the gods accept it with these other objects."

Palamon studied the ring, which glinted dully, then he laid his hand on his son's breast. "This is a treasury of artifacts, indeed."

Aelia nodded but did not reply. Her face looked haggard in the gathering light and Palamon doubted that he looked any better. "Now let us pray," he whispered. So the two of them knelt before their son and the three holy relics. He lifted his prayer to the goddess Pallas, who had been his patron since before he could remember. "O glorious Pallas, in this very place did you give counsel five long years ago, to one who wallowed deep in his own woe. Now look upon a younger, tiny face, made blank and empty. Reach down and erase malignant magic's stamp. Let our child throw away the yoke of his enchantment. Grow within him; let affliction leave no trace."

As he prayed, Palamon felt himself grow desperate. The child had to live; Berethane had to be well again. The holy armor was nothing. The ring and the *Spada Korrigaine* were nothing against the life of his child. Even Palamon's own life was nothing, for it was more than half over. He became desperate in his prayer. "If one of us must die, 'tis I who'll yield my body for my boy's, for he is young. If death's hard blow must fall, I'll be his shield—thus, let me suffer it. Let not his tongue be stilled forever, goddess. I am steeled against my fate, should judgment's bell be rung."

Exhaustion foundered him. He had prayed thus before, to restore life, to save life. Even when he had been in the peak of his manhood, he had not been able to sustain the passion of communication with the goddess for long. But she had heard his prayer. From the very weariness which turned his legs to powder, he knew she had heard his prayer. He clutched the edge of the monument, dragged himself to his feet, and laid his cheek against Berethane's bosom. Pallas, who was above all a righteous goddess, would answer this prayer.

Aelia stood also. She placed an arm about his shoulders and then, to the ears of both of them, came a note of musical laughter, a figment whipped along on the wind like the faint sound of holy chimes. He had heard such a note only once before in his life. He straightened and looked about but there was nothing more to be heard or seen. Then the wind carried ghostly whispering, sounds insinuated into his consciousness like dew forming on a flower. "Twenty years," he heard. "He serves me twenty years, twenty years, twenty years." And though he listened with all his being, the sounds faded away and the wind's music became no more than the music of the wind.

A gasp from Aelia caused him to look down and they both staggered back in amazement. Berethane's body made a subtle change before them, as if some sort of mystic torch flickered above it. The wan face altered, grew somehow transparent, and then vanished completely. The child's nightclothes fell slack and the wind blew them from the top of the slab. Palamon's hauberk and the *Spada Korrigaine* remained unchanged but the child and the ring were gone.

Aelia burst into tears and threw herself into Palamon's arms; for his part, he hardly knew what to do. "By all the gods," he cried, "I offered her my armor, weapon, or myself." He staggered, nearly lost his footing. "But what went wrong?"

Aelia shook her head; her hair moved against his throat. "Cannot you see? Our son himself is her reward. I heard the whisper: 'Twenty years,' she said."

" 'There's still another route'—that's what it meant. It is the only answer. Still it is a brutal price to pay."

Aelia was silent. But even in her silence, Palamon could feel her strength flooding up into him. Of course, that had been the message the goddess had passed the other time, too. Life would burden him with its losses and disappointments. The gods' greatest gift was the power to withstand them. And Berethane would live; he would someday return. "Twenty years," the voice had said. Was that the price? Would Berethane serve the gods twenty years and then return? As Palamon had noted, it was a stiff price—but not much of a price, given the alternative.

They stood for a long time with their arms about one another, drawing strength, each from the other. Their child would return to them and he would be whole and healthy. It made an interesting question for the pondering, after all: where would he spend the interval? What sights would he witness? What heroic deeds would he perform? Palamon and Aelia did not need to speak; their tears blended where their cheeks touched, and they shared thoughts without words through no more than the warm contact of their bodies.

But time passed, the sun approached, and hoofbeats sounded as the company of knights drew near. Palamon and Aelia picked up the items he had placed atop the granite slab, then turned to meet their escort. They stood together, arm in arm, while dawn broke across the Thlassa Mey.

ABOUT THE AUTHOR

DENNIS MCCARTY was born on June 17, 1950, in Grand Junction, a small town in western Colorado. His family traveled a great deal because of his father's work. By the time he had graduated from high school, Dennis had attended eight different public schools, most of them before he was twelve.

He graduated in English from the University of Utah and served four years in the United States Coast Guard. Over the years, his hobbies have included fishing, hunting, photography, and automobile racing.

His greatest love has always been reading and writing fiction, however. He made his first attempt at a novel of science fiction when he was seven. He began writing seriously at the age of twenty; *Flight to Thlassa Mey* was his first published novel.

DAVE DUNCAN

Fantasy Novels:

The Seventh Sword